"YOU LOOK LIKE A CAT FULL OF CREAM."

There was a potency, a vibrancy in Bensen's words that sent a delicious shiver down Jessamine's spine.

"Perhaps that's because I feel like one." She paused; then she just had to know. "Bensen... doesn't Dorothy mind your going out for dinner with other women?"

"Why should she? It's none of her concern."

"But aren't you engaged?"

A smile curved his mouth as he took her hand and turned the palm upward. With a warm, teasing insistency his thumb slowly moved over the sensitive skin, his dark eyes intently watching her.

Jessamine struggled hard against the feelings he was arousing. Things were progressing with such speed...in such a dangerous direction.... Yet somewhere out there, she thought helplessly, there was a woman called Dorothy who could shatter their present private world....

CHRISTINE HELLA COTT

**is also the author of
SUPERROMANCE #22**

MIDNIGHT MAGIC

For terrifying hours after the wreck, Tara had
been clutching a frail rubber raft on the
storm-swept ocean. She lost consciousness
as a final wave washed her body onto a
rocky beach.

A man found her there, a tall silent man who
lived alone on the barren island. He carried
her to his hut, where he dressed her wounds
and nursed her carefully back to health.

Tara was mesmerized by his eyes. Midnight
eyes, she thought of them, wanting to drown
in their sea-black depths. And his touch
was one she would always remember....

CHRISTINE HELLA COTT

A TENDER WILDERNESS

A SUPERROMANCE FROM
WORLDWIDE
TORONTO · NEW YORK · LOS ANGELES · LONDON

Published September 1982

First printing July 1982

ISBN 0-373-70030-X

CHAPTER ONE

JESSE COULDN'T SEE Clifftop from where she stood on the floating pier, for it was perched high on the craggy rock and was visible only from farther out to sea. Cut into the monolithic gray cliff, rough-hewn stairs sprang up from the end of the pier, beginning the ascent to the mansion. The path disappeared behind the rock face about twenty or thirty feet above Jesse's head.

Jessamine Smith-Jones turned back to the water and the small speedboat that had brought her. The boat bobbed on the choppy turquoise waves as the Indian boy steadied it against the log pier, careful of his boat's crisp new paint.

"Do you want a hand with your stuff?" he queried, eyeing her critically, not exactly unfriendly but not friendly, either.

"No, I can manage." Jesse smiled to hide her sudden attack of nervousness. "Thanks for the ride. I enjoyed it."

The boy shrugged. "You paid for it." He fingered the controls, and the engine roared to life. "When will you be leaving?" he shouted at her.

Jesse stammered back, "Well, I—I don't know."

The dark eyes regarded her now with a superior expression that indicated he thought her a "few bricks short a load." Considering, Jesse admitted he might be right. Now that she was here, the whole idea seemed rather daft. A wild-goose chase.

"There's a shortwave radio at the store in Bliss Landing," the boy informed her. "You can call me from there when you're ready to go. Just remember the name of my boat, that's all." Deftly he swung the prow of the speedboat into the wide stretch of glittering blue water that linked the Strait of Georgia to Desolation Sound. The prow lifted high as the boat was gunned to full power. Then, leaving a frothing wake, the *Shaman* veered and plunged south.

The pier rocked beneath Jesse's feet. She shaded her eyes against the hot June sun to follow the boat's progress through the cluster of small islands that were, in actuality, rugged mountain tops thrusting out of the sea. A few seconds later the *Shaman* was lost to sight.

Jesse sighed as she scanned the horizon. Due west, over the water, she could barely see the blue-tinged peaks of Vancouver Island. North, the more substantial islands of Desolation Sound slumbered in the afternoon sun behind another scattering of small islands, some mere slabs of sea-washed rock with one or two stunted pines growing in the crevices. Slowly Jesse turned full circle to face the sheer wall of granite. She craned her neck to take in the height. Somewhere up there was Clifftop, the Everhart mansion. It had been imposing from far out to sea, but what would it actually be like?

She picked up her valise firmly in one hand and her typewriter case in the other, taking one last long look in the direction the *Shaman* had gone. She sighed again as she walked to the end of the undulating pier to begin the sharp climb. The stairs led her behind the rock face into a natural fissure that formed a stairwell. It was wonderfully cool in the stairwell, the deep green shade refreshing. Here the stone steps were worn smoothly hollow, while on the rough walls lichen grew and moldered in patches of olive, green and dusty orange. And winding through the rock, the stairs continued ever upward.

Several minutes later Jesse emerged into brilliant light, slightly breathless. Her eyes smarted from the glare, but she couldn't resist absorbing the fantastic panorama spread before her.

She could see for miles and miles; island after island shimmered in the heat haze, turning to royal blue, purple and smoky violet in the far distance. The sea, glistening a vibrant turquoise, surrounded the islands like some vast living jewel. Jesse was stunned by the magnificent wild splendor, potent in its June serenity and its everlasting solitude. For the first time she understood why the Everhart home had been built in such a remote spot.

She turned now to view the mansion, its thick old walls rooted into the mountain rock. A granite bastion built near the lip of the cliff, it seemed decidedly Victorian in its elegant dignity, though it didn't conform entirely to that style. Instead of tall narrow slits in the walls, the small-paned windows were wide and spacious. Almost all of the bottom floor seemed to be window. And instead of the traditional portal, three wide heavy French doors stood open at the top of a shallow flight of stairs that led onto a wide stone terrace. Vines and creepers softened some of the old-fashioned austerity. At a second-story window one flower box splashed vivid color against the aged gray stone.

The house itself stood in a pool of emerald lawn; clematis and wisteria spilled over rocky outcroppings; hardy geraniums glowed with red fire against the cool green backdrop, and where the lawn meandered away into the forest proper, huge ferns provided an informal and broken border. Thick forest hemmed in the home on three sides—towering Douglas firs, red cedars with boles twelve feet around, spruce, hemlock, alpine larch...a virgin rain forest, dark and deep and undoubtedly wild. The forest seemed to stretch endlessly north and southward along the shoreline, and to the east it gradually swept up and away into the lower precipitous slopes of the mountains. Vancouver, British Columbia, seventy-odd miles south and Jesse's home, seemed light-years away to her, almost as if it existed on a different plane. In this environ she felt completely a stranger.

Passionately she wished someone would come out of the mansion and warmly say, "Hello, we've been expecting you. Please, come in!" But no one did. There wasn't a sign of life.

Now Jesse began to worry whether Mrs. Cecilia Anne Everhart had somehow forgotten the invitation she'd extended. The woman was, after all, ninety-four years old, and the proposed visit might have slipped her mind.

Jesse recalled the meeting with her, now more than a month past, as she made her way to the house. It had been in Vancouver, at the Four Seasons Hotel, where apparently the Everhart family maintained a suite of rooms. Mrs. Everhart had been in town to donate a piece of her property to the city for parkland. Jesse had seen the resulting public ceremony on TV, and it was that short news clip that had sent her running to the telephone to beg a meeting. Mrs. Everhart had happily granted one for the following day.

Jesse decided now that it was unlikely that Mrs. Everhart really had forgotten. She had already realized the woman could be sharp and shrewd when it suited her; when it didn't, she was fragile and gracious, yet superbly haughty. Cecilia Everhart was of the old landed aristocracy, one of British Columbia's pioneers, and this fact was like a second backbone that somehow belied her age; it was also the reason Jesse had been so eager to meet with the old woman. But with no welcome in sight, it looked as though her trip was wasted. Still, it had been worth it just to come and see. . . .

"Well, so you've finally come!" The harsh male voice startled Jesse so that she almost dropped her typewriter case. "I suppose you think two o'clock in the afternoon is a fine time to start!"

Jesse stared at the man in bewilderment as he went on furiously, "What are you waiting for? A formal invitation?"

Black hair fell over his forehead; thick well-defined brows and black eyes were set in a coldly austere face that now, because of his anger, gave him almost a wild appearance. Irritation showed in the tensely held animal shoulders. Jesse opened her mouth to say she would leave *immediately*, but the man didn't give her time.

In an instant he was beside her, brusquely snatching away her precious typewriter and propelling her up the stairs toward the French doors.

Jesse did not want to go.

"Miss Smith," came the clipped voice from behind her, "you came here to do a job, and you've already wasted more than enough time. I suggest you begin cooperating right away!" Suddenly Jesse found herself moving through the doors, the grip above her elbow unrelenting.

"But I'm not—"

"I don't have time to listen to excuses." Jesse was being thrust along so quickly that she didn't have time to look either right or left.

"But you don't—"

"Will you spare me the grisly details? You're hours late as it is!" He urged her into a large room, where sunlight spilled from a multitude of windows. The walls were lined with glassed-in bookcases, and in the center of the room stood a large ornate table surrounded by Gothic-style parlor chairs. A typewriter sat in readiness on the table, with a great many papers neatly stacked beside it.

"But you see—"

"Start!" he thundered at her, pointing toward the table.

"But—"

"Now!" He slammed her typewriter down on the table so carelessly that Jesse winced. Before she could so much as raise her hand to stop him, he'd disappeared through a small side door, slamming it shut behind him.

Jesse expelled a long-held breath, crumpling into the chair near the waiting typewriter. She dropped her valise beside her and forced her breathing to a more even rate. Her heart was pounding high in her chest. What should she do? All her instincts told her to run. But to where? To Bliss Landing? Where was that? And where was Mrs. Everhart? As her guest, Jesse couldn't very well go tearing through Clifftop in search of the woman, though finding her would clear up this misunderstanding perfectly. For a misunderstanding it had to be. That...that man obviously had been expecting someone else.

In case he should suddenly reappear to demand why she wasn't already hard at work, Jesse fitted paper into the typewriter carriage and mechanically began typing from the sheaf of handwritten notes. Logging contracts, shipment dates and lumber footage were neatly transformed under her nimble fingers. She hoped Cecilia Everhart would appear soon to rescue her from this ridiculous predicament. Then she'd be able to get on with her real work.

Cecilia Anne was one of the few who could provide the visual firsthand experience of British Columbia at the turn of the century that Jesse needed. There weren't many such pioneers left to talk to, and of those, most were not well enough to recount their experiences.

There wasn't a sound from the closed door where the man had disappeared, so relaxing slightly, Jesse stopped typing for a moment to study the library. A sculptured jade fireplace with three ormolu clocks on its mantel faced the windows. The floor was of beautiful patterned hardwood, as befitted the floor of a lumber baron's home. Persian rugs glowed in the splashes of sunlight. On one wall was a massive inlaid gold cedar cabinet, and through its partially open doors Jesse could see a TV screen, a video recorder and a stereo.

She typed out another page and wondered what the man would say once he found out she wasn't who she was supposed to be. She could just imagine the tempest that news would provoke! Involuntarily a smile touched her wide rosy mouth. Should she go and tell him now—now that his temper had had time to cool? Or should she wait until he returned—if Mrs. Everhart didn't come first? Better to wait, she finally decided. She couldn't be sure Cecilia Everhart really was here, and she couldn't take the risk of a peremptory dismissal.

Having made a decision, Jesse relaxed a little more. She typed two more pages, then quit again. Something was wrong. She needed music to type. Jesse eyed the inlaid cabinet, chewing on her lip, considering whether she should or shouldn't, and in the end decided she should. *May as well be hanged for a sheep as for a lamb,* she thought blithely. And if she was going to be put to work for an indefinite period of time, at least she would make herself comfortable. The library seemed to take on a different character with music richly filling the air. Jesse settled down to type, and page after page rapidly joined the completed stack.

Her hands poised above the keys, suddenly Jesse stopped. She could *feel* the weight of eyes on her back, eyes that were angry. Her hands fluttered down and quickly typed out half a page, and still the eyes were boring holes into her cotton shirt. She spun around, sending her long straight chestnut tresses flying over the typewriter keys.

The man, tall and wide-shouldered, stood in the doorway, glaring at her from under thunderous brows. Jesse licked her lips. Her glance flew to the stereo in the cabinet and then defiantly back to him. Raven hair almost hid his high fine forehead and at the back brushed the collar of his fitted shirt. Under the thin material Jesse could almost see the powerful muscles and, for an instant, felt a burst of fear. He was probably quite civilized, she reassured herself, despite his uncivilized appearance. She raised an eyebrow and waited. He said nothing, as if meaning to intimidate her by the sheer force of his silence.

Jesse's wide sherry-amber eyes ran down his sinewy length almost unconsciously. He stood lightly but firmly with his feet apart. His long legs were straight and taut, the hips narrow, the bare chest under the partially open shirt mahogany brown. No, Jesse thought, from a purely feminine standpoint, he really wasn't handsome at all. His nose was thin, almost hawkish. And the beautifully drawn lips, set in a tight line of exasperation, were oddly disturbing. The whole room seemed to vibrate with his ill temper. She wondered what could possibly have put him in such a state. Or was he always this way? Ugly thought! Especially if she was going to stay for a few days.

With a semishrug Jesse turned her back to him and resumed typing. When she turned around again, he was gone, and the door to his den, or office, was shut. She hammered through six pages. Then, aware that her shoulders were beginning to feel cramped, she pushed her chair aside and stood up. She moved her body a little with the music to loosen taut muscles. Another look at the door showed it was still shut. Decisively, she darted across to the cabinet and turned up the stereo volume. Now she was almost dancing as she typed standing up, her fingers flowing over the keys with easy speed.

Jesse was almost ready to sit down again when she sensed rather than saw the door open once more. With a strength of will she refused to turn around. She kept right on dancing and typing, even though she knew it must look very odd. The skin on her spine crawled as she felt him approach with a cat's-paw tread. She waited until he was at the table and within her direct line of vision before she suddenly looked up, as though she'd just realized he was there. She stopped typing, and dancing, and straightened up. He was staring at her from under lowered brows with a kind of annoyed amazement, and she felt the dark flicker of his shrewd glance as it traveled down and up her slim curvaceous length, measuring and assessing.

"The report on lumber shipments to Japan is finished," she declared, paper-clipping a sheaf of papers and handing them over. Surprise flashed across the man's dark craggy face, but Jesse willed her own expression to remain blank. He flipped rapidly through the report, yet Jesse knew those quick ebony eyes saw everything.

"Did you proofread it?" Cold and clipped. The eyes regarded her closely, pinning her gaze.

"Yes." Pause. "And I've finished all the letters, too. I thought you'd want them done first." She pushed the letters and their addressed envelopes across the table toward him. "I put my initials on the bottom in place of your usual secretary's." God help the poor woman! Jesse had been a secretary herself years ago, and it gave her a grim satisfaction now to know she hadn't lost her touch.

"How fast can you type?" he demanded.

Jesse looked at him warily. Should she tell him? What would happen if she did? "Ninety words a minute," she finally answered. With malicious enjoyment she added, "Under *ideal* conditions, a hundred."

"Do you need a job?"

"Certainly not!" If she ever did work as a secretary again, it would never be for him.

His eyebrows had shot up at her vehemence. If his mouth had been used to smiling, he might have smiled then, Jesse thought. He stared down at her arrogantly for a second or two, then announced, "I need a good secretary. The job's yours. I'll pay you more than you're probably earning now.''

Here was a man used to getting what he wanted, Jesse realized wryly. But who was he? He was too young to be Mrs. Everhart's son, she decided. Her grandson? Probably.

"Even you, Mr. Everhart, wouldn't pay a secretary the money I make," Jesse answered coolly.

His frown grew deeper. Fire seemed to spark from his black eyes as he stared her down, and Jesse experienced an eerie feeling of being stalked. She took a long steadying breath.

"Indeed? May I ask what other services you offer that you should be so highly paid?" he asked.

"No, you may not!"

That stopped him. She guessed people didn't often say no to him. She felt a smile tugging at the corners of her mouth but put a damper on it and stared right back at him, right into his eyes. They were so dark the irises blended into the pupils, and this made them appear depthless. Jesse shivered slightly.

"I see." His response held a certain potency of meaning that the mere words themselves did not contain. Without even another glance in her direction he scooped up the completed letters and disappeared into his den. The door shut behind him.

Jesse released an explosive breath, then delved into the papers yet to be typed. Time slid by unnoticed as she worked. She refused to leave without seeing Cecilia Everhart, and she hadn't got where she was today—and at only twenty-eight—without a certain single-mindedness of purpose. As the sun dipped toward the far western horizon, it shone straight into the room, rich and golden.

"Miss Smith!"

Jesse started and turned to see a short heavyset woman of indistinct middle age. Her features were set in dour folds, and around her waist she wore a dirty white apron.

At Jesse's questioning look she grudgingly offered, "I'm the housekeeper, Martha Potkins. You call me Martha. Mr. Everhart said you'd be staying the night." Displeasure showed in the fixed downcurve of her thin mouth. "I've spruced up a bedroom, and I'm supposed to show you to it. Dinner's on the table in half an hour, in the dining room. Follow me."

Without waiting, she turned and marched from the room. Jesse grabbed her typewriter case and valise and made haste to follow. She stayed behind Martha Potkins all the way up the grand sweeping staircase, admiring the polished oak that gleamed in the light of the hall chandelier. When they'd reached the landing, Jesse asked of Martha's ample back, "Where's Mrs. Everhart? Cecilia Everhart, I mean. May I see her?"

Martha looked over her shoulder. "Mrs. Everhart?" she asked blankly. "And what would you be wanting with her?"

"I—I'd like to see her," Jesse explained, flushing. She felt so uncomfortable, so unwelcome. Now she seriously wondered whether keeping that sour-tempered man in the dark about her identity had been wise.

"You'll see her at dinner," Martha replied, closing the matter.

"I have business with her," Jesse said firmly. "And I'd like to see her now!"

"What's going on out there?" The sharp querulous tone Jesse instantly recognized, and she quickly located the room from where it originated. Before Martha could stop her, she knocked on the closed door.

"Mrs. Everhart?" she called softly, easing the door open a fraction.

"Ahhh! So it's you, is it? Come in, Miss Smith-Jones; do come in! How lovely that you've come!" She added sharply, "What do you want, Martha?"

Martha, hovering at the threshold, stepped back slightly. "Dinner is in half an hour. And Miss... Miss Smith-Jones's room is the last door on the right, this side." Her mouth drooped lower.

"Fine, fine. Go now!"

Huffily Martha retreated. Jesse, feeling ill at ease, put down her typewriter case and valise. She walked forward, nervously holding out her hand. She was relieved to see Mrs. Everhart's frown blossom into a welcoming smile as the older woman grasped her hand.

"I'm glad you didn't back out on our agreement."

"I hope I didn't come at an inconvenient time," Jesse gasped, thinking something must have gone wrong, for everyone to be so short-tempered.

"Not at all. Did you have a pleasant journey? You're not tired, are you?" She gave Jesse no time to answer. "Have you met the rest of the family yet?"

"I—I believe I've met your grandson, but—"

"Oh, Bensen." Mrs. Everhart interrupted. "Never

mind him." Annoyance shadowed her regal features. Bright brown eyes snapped out of white parchment-like skin, and for a second her lips trembled. She waved an imperious hand, signaling Jesse to sit down.

"I'm afraid he thinks I'm a secretary sent to do his typing."

"He does, does he? Well, he's in for a surprise. Don't pay any attention to him *or* his bearishness. He's not at all like his father—more's the pity."

"Look, Mrs. Everhart, I don't want to stay if it's going to cause trouble."

"What trouble could you possibly cause? Nonsense, my dear. I'm looking forward to working with you. Liked you the minute I first clapped eyes on you! You'd better run along now and dress for dinner. We may be far from civilization here, but we still observe the amenities. We'll talk further after dinner, yes?"

Jesse smiled and nodded. At last she'd be able to continue her research. She took her typewriter case and valise and vanished down the hall to her appointed bedroom.

It was a large room, she noted approvingly, with its own tiled bath and comfortable sitting area by the windows. The rocky islands out to sea were touched with pink, and the sun made an ever widening glittering gold furrow in the waves of Desolation Sound. The smoky purple haze had deepened; Vancouver Island was lost behind its veil. The south windows offered an equally interesting view; they looked right out into the forest, now dark and shadowed, with the occasional tree trunk scalloped in sun gold. A window seat, below which were cupboards, ran the length of both south and west windows. Plush pillows and a great many throw cushions, betasseled and hand-stitched, completed the arrangement.

As in the rest of the house—or as much as Jesse had seen of it—the decor here was basically the same. The convent she'd grown up in had been designed in like style, though it was much simpler and far more conservative, and it, too, belonged to the Victorian era. But here at Clifftop there was an added flavor of Tudor and Gothic and, as a lighter touch, the occasional Grecian shape. It was startlingly beautiful, Jesse thought, and most definitely in the best of taste.

She had no time to stand and stare though. Dinner downstairs with the family beckoned—and with it a showdown with His Highness Mr. Bensen Everhart. Her knowledge of him so far told her he would not be amused.

"SO YOU WRITE BOOKS, do you?" Dorothy Jorgensen had a thin high voice. She had introduced herself as Bensen's fiancée, and no one had negated the claim. Her father's roots, she informed Jesse, were entwined in the "landed aristocracy." He'd been born in Lund, a tiny village some twenty miles down the coast that had been settled in the late 1800s by Scandinavian fishermen, both captains and common deckhands alike. Dorothy went on to say pridefully that her great-grandfather had been one of the fishing-boat owners. The Jorgensen family now owned not only an extensive fishing fleet, but their own packers—ships, Dorothy condescendingly explained, that were actually canning and processing plants that followed the fleet. In addition to their fishing interests the Jorgensens had also acquired a silver mine near Clifftop. Dorothy was quick to add that whenever her father came up from Vancouver to attend to business—which he did regularly—she accompanied him to visit Bensen and his family.

Jesse listened politely to the woman's proud monologue. Dorothy Jorgensen sat right across the dinner table from her, and privately Jesse wished she didn't. Every time she looked up from her plate, she had to look directly into those frozen blue eyes.

Miss Jorgensen was exceptionally pretty, though, Jesse had to admit. Pure blond hair fell to her shoulders to curl with meticulous carelessness. She wore false eyelashes so well that most people might think they were real, and the elegance with which she carried up-to-the-minute fashion wasn't lost to Jesse's appreciative eye, either. Although the woman had thin shoulders and rather thick hips, she did know how to dress so that her figure appeared its most attractive.

"She writes mystery novels, not just *books*!" Mrs. Everhart answered before Jesse had the chance. She reigned at the head of the table in formidable splendor. "They're very good, too." Sweeping her eyes around the table, as if to defy anyone to argue the point, she added, "For a writer of her young age, her reviews are excellent."

Bensen Everhart sat at the foot of the table, to

Jesse's right. She glanced at him now out of the corner of her eye. The expected showdown had happened only minutes earlier. Without preamble Mrs. Everhart had informed him that Jesse had come to interview her and she was *not* his expected secretary; moreover, Jesse was here at her express invitation. Thereafter had followed a not too subtle argument between Bensen and his grandmother about the inadvisability of having invited her at all.

To Jesse's immense surprise Bensen had lost the argument. Because of strategics, she supposed. Outnumbered by six females, Bensen couldn't make too much of a fuss, nor could he indulge his temper while at the dinner table. The situation didn't sit well with him, obviously. Now his jaw was so tight Jesse wondered that he could eat at all. Her brief dispute with him still rankled.

"If you'd had the sense to tell me right away you weren't Miss Smith," he'd said coldly, "I could have done something about it. Now it's too late, and I've lost a day!"

"You haven't lost anything," Jesse pointed out, "because *I* did the work. And I did try to tell you, but you were in too much of a...a *hurry*—" she swallowed the more vigorous word she had been about to use "—to listen to anything I said! After five minutes in your company I was no longer up to explaining anything."

They had glared at each other, then Bensen turned away, dismissing her presence.

"I'm going to phone that secretarial company and give them a piece of my mind. I always knew they were lax, but this no-show is beyond my patience!''

"There's a lot that's beyond *your* patience," Mrs. Everhart had observed waspishly, "and it appears good manners belong in that category. You've been unforgivably rude to my guest!"

This exchange had happened just before Dorothy brought up the subject of Jesse's writing books.

If the family wanted to quarrel among themselves, Jesse thought, fine and good, but she didn't want to be their bone of contention. She picked at the food on her plate—which was poorly prepared—and wondered just exactly what she'd got herself into this time!

"I'm sure your reviews are good," Dorothy picked up the conversational lag, sounding polite but bored. She moved her shoulders in slight irritation as Martha came to take her plate. The housekeeper, who was serving the dinner in a grudging slapdash way, finally caused Dorothy to snap, "That woman's a disgrace! How can she serve food like this and expect anyone to eat it?"

Jesse saw Martha's back stiffen, even though the woman was halfway down the hall. Dorothy had been looking at Bensen as she said this, and now she waited for a reply.

"We'll discuss it some other time," he answered shortly. Jesse saw the flicker of exasperation in his fiancée's eyes. With marked coolness Dorothy turned from him and addressed Mrs. Everhart, the smile on her lips friendly.

"I saw Lily in Vancouver last week. Did you know she was having a show at the art gallery?" Her tone indicated surprise that Lily should have a show anywhere, let alone a gallery.

"Of course I knew," Mrs. Everhart replied with asperity. "She showed me the work she was taking down. I purchased one of the prints. Bensen did, as well. I admire her work."

"Don't you think all this primitive Indian. . .*stuff* is a bit overrated?" Dorothy's tone was sweet.

"You don't approve?" Bensen put in.

Jesse eyed Bensen with ever growing dislike. Even when he was making conversation, he sounded stern. As his head swiveled in her direction, she steeled herself to meet his gaze. The depth in those black eyes seemed infinite. It was a little like drowning, she thought, and as those eyes now registered supremely arrogant displeasure, drowning in a very hot bath.

"Well, darling," Dorothy interrupted the gaze, "of course you can have whatever you want."

"Why, thank you!"

Jesse herself blushed at Bensen's sarcasm. Pity for Dorothy surged up. Indeed, she felt sorry for everyone. The very air seemed fraught with silent battles, with a tension of everyone's making.

Even Shanna, Bensen's sister, wasn't entirely innocent. Although at first glance she didn't appear to be contributing to the fracas, it occurred to Jesse that she might well be doing more than her share. She hadn't said a word throughout dinner. An air of melancholy seemed to envelope her. Her gentle face was entirely unlike Bensen's; she seemed a younger version of her grandmother, with her fair complexion and the kind of beauty Cecilia must have once possessed. But Shanna's expression was shuttered, the soft blue eyes withdrawn. Off in a separate world of her own and seemingly unobtrusive, she was disturbingly *there*, her melancholy flowing out of her and quietly pressing, pressing against everyone else.

Her two nine-year-old children, Samantha and Merit, had inherited their mother's soft blue eyes, and like their mother neither had said a word. Identical twins, their dark hair styled in page-boy cuts, they ate their dinner with exquisite manners, if not joy.

Jesse couldn't decide if the family was continually at odds or if this was an extraordinary day. Her own nerves were fraying, and she wasn't even involved! She would have liked to cut short her discussions with Mrs. Everhart. In fact, she was almost sorry now that the haughty old lady was so absolutely set on her staying for a lengthy visit. And who was Lily, Jesse wondered as she stole another look at Dorothy while Dorothy's attention was wrapped up in Bensen.

"I understand correctly, then, that you're going to write grandmother's biography?" Dorothy broke another grim and growing silence.

"No, I'm planning a novel set in this locale at the turn of the century, and Mrs. Everhart's knowledge will be a great help."

"Another mystery?" asked Dorothy, gracefully rejecting her dessert, of which she'd had a spoonful.

"Of course it won't be a mystery," Mrs. Everhart

broke in with her own show of condescension. "It's going to be a grand *sweeping* story! Isn't it, Jesse?"

"I hope so." Jesse ventured a brief smile, but no one else did. With an inward sigh, she realized Bensen was staring at her. Was another dispute growing on the tip of his tongue?

"You're not very certain of yourself," observed Dorothy, who had been eyeing Jesse's plain and inexpensive white dress. The stark whiteness of the material subtly highlighted the golden beginnings of her tan. She wore her chestnut hair as ever, hanging straight and thick down her back almost to her waist.

"I'm never certain of myself until a book is written and sold," Jesse answered lightly.

"I gather that as this is your first effort away from mystery, it's also your first serious piece?" Everything Dorothy said managed to be vaguely insulting.

"Why, yes," Jesse replied evenly. "It is rather important." She had no desire to be the pivot of conversation. The thought of a long drawn-out evening discussing her proposed book with Mrs. Everhart— with Bensen and Dorothy listening—was enough to make her lose her appetite altogether.

It seemed that whenever Dorothy came to visit, the whole family made an evening of it; even the twins were allowed to stay up later than usual. Not that this privilege seemed to make them any happier. While everyone else had coffee and liqueurs in the dimly lighted salon, Samantha and Merit had hot chocolate and health-food cookies. The cookies were burned on the bottom, and the twins pecked at them half-heartedly. Their solemn eyes rested on whoever was speaking at the time. Jesse, remembering her own rather boisterous upbringing with twenty other convent orphans, suddenly saw that a family could be a liability instead of a blessing.

Dorothy steered the after-dinner conversation into matters foreign to Jesse, subtly leaving her out. As Shanna seldom spoke and as Bensen's hooded eyes brooded unwaveringly into the small fire burning in the grate, Mrs. Everhart was left to deal with Dorothy's society gossip.

Jesse sat quite still so as not to call attention to herself. Bensen had made it abundantly clear that she was here on sufferance, and she didn't wish Dorothy's attention to swing back to her unwelcome position. She didn't want to have to answer questions about her life so that Bensen's fiancée could make a gentle mockery of it, nor did she want to handle further probings into her writing career. Growing up without a family had made her a very self-sufficient, independent and private person. She saw no point in sharing personal details with someone she didn't like, and although she'd known Dorothy for barely more than an hour, Jesse felt quite certain she didn't like her. To her mind, Dorothy and Bensen deserved each other.

She was aware of Dorothy's veiled scrutiny and knew the woman was curious to find out more about her, to pick her apart should the occasion arise. But Jesse had had enough. Pretending reluctance, she rose from her chair and asked to be excused on account of being tired by the long day she'd had.

A flash of annoyance crossed Dorothy's face, but

Bensen didn't even look up. The firelight flickered over his proud and aloof features, painting highlights and shadows on the long lean black elegance of his dinner suit. He was slouched in casual ease in a large armchair, with an aura of relaxation one would expect of a panther. Mrs. Everhart seemed so disappointed that Jesse assured her they would begin researching first thing in the morning. Shanna chose this opportunity to shepherd the twins upstairs, and as Jesse turned to leave, Bensen curtly nodded goodnight to her. For a few taut seconds the impassive black eyes held hers before they were drawn back to the fire. He was paying absolutely no attention to the conversation continuing around him.

As Jesse walked alone through the darkened hall toward the staircase, she distinctly heard Bensen's angry words.

"Why couldn't you have talked to her in Vancouver? Why did you have to invite her here, grandmother?"

"Because I felt like it!" Mrs. Everhart snapped back. "If you don't like it, then stay out of her way! *I* consider her charming."

"But don't you think," Dorothy interrupted in dulcet tones, "that to invite a stranger into the house is asking for trouble? After all, who is she? I don't want to harp about the family silver, but there are a great many pocketable valuables about, and—"

"Nonsense!" came Mrs. Everhart's imperious voice. "You're too suspicious, Dorothy. That's your problem!"

"You *could* have made arrangements to see her in

Vancouver!'' Bensen obviously wasn't ready to let the subject drop.

Jesse ran up the stairs two at a time, not wanting to hear another word.

"This book had better be worth it!'' she muttered to herself as she shut the door to her room. She crossed to the windows and threw them wide, as if the fresh night air could dispel the climate of tension.

About an hour later Jesse was surprised to hear a knock on her door. Uneasy, wondering whether it was Dorothy coming to request a chummy tête-à-tête or Bensen in search of argument, she had at first wanted to pretend she was asleep, so it was with warm flooding relief that she opened the door to find Shanna there.

"I'm not disturbing you?'' Shanna asked in a rather timid way. She seemed to be making an effort now to overcome her shyness. Jesse hastened to welcome her in, puzzled that Shanna and Bensen could come from the same family and yet be so different.

"You're not disturbing me at all,'' Jesse replied warmly. "I was putting away my things. I don't like living out of a suitcase, even if it is just for a few days.''

"Just for a few days?'' Shanna echoed. "But grandmother said several weeks at the very least. Bensen doesn't like company, and that's why—'' She broke off suddenly, her cheeks flushing.

"He was so angry?'' Jesse finished, smiling faintly.

"Well...I think so.'' She bit her lip in embarrassment. "Even if—if he didn't make you welcome, I'd like to."

"You don't know how much I appreciate that!" Jesse returned, feeling much better at Shanna's words. "You don't get much company?"

"Dorothy comes, naturally. She's been dropping by ever since I came back here. Sometimes Bensen has meetings with the forest ranger or with his woods foreman...but no one else visits. It—it's so remote here, you see."

"Of course," Jesse agreed, not understanding at all.

"Oh, and there's Lily. But she lives a mile away, at Bliss Landing. She's a Kwakiutl Indian—that's the name of the tribe who live around here. She's grandmother's special friend, I guess. Bensen likes her, too!" Shanna's last words were spoken as though Lily were the only person Bensen did like.

Away from her brother and grandmother, Shanna seemed almost eager to talk and occasionally even smiled. Jesse wondered how someone as gentle and sweet as Shanna could have survived all these years with a family as willful and headstrong as she wasn't. And where was her husband? What had happened to the man who'd given her the name of Lazzer?

Shanna had picked up a piece of Jesse's lingerie—a nightgown—and was running the delicate peach lace through her fingers while Jesse watched her. Suddenly she dropped the wispy silk thing, as though it had burned her fingers—which made Jesse curious to know where her mind had been. With her missing husband, perhaps?

"I hope you like it here!" Shanna burst out, abruptly returning to the present. She seemed taken aback by the impulsive force of her words and added, "I mean, it would be nice if you stayed awhile. It takes a long time to write a book, doesn't it?"

"I wasn't planning to write the book here," Jesse explained. "A few days' time is all I need for the basic research." With alarm she saw Shanna's face register sharp disappointment. She felt terrible herself, as though she were deserting a friend in need. Yet she barely knew Shanna.

"Is...ah, was Bensen upset today over something?" ventured Jesse, cautious about broaching such a delicate family matter.

"Not that I know of. Not that he would tell me even if he were."

"Then why was he so grim?"

"Grim?" Shanna echoed, looking at Jesse with wide eyes. She shrugged. "That's not grim; that's his nature. He's been like that for as long as I can remember."

Apparently Shanna accepted this explanation as the truth, but Jesse wasn't satisfied. The two women amiably bid each other good-night, and Jesse was left to ponder the disturbing influences the Everhart family seemed to tolerate willingly.

THINGS DID NOT PROGRESS as Jesse had imagined they would. The next day Mrs. Everhart professed herself too ill to do more than talk to her for a bare hour. Jesse had the distinct feeling that Cecilia Anne wasn't being entirely honest. But why her hostess should want to prolong her stay in this manner was beyond understanding. Unless it was to provoke Bensen. At first thought that seemed ridiculous, yet on second thought quite probable. Why had Mrs. Everhart made no mention to anyone of her expected guest? Was it because she knew that unless Jesse actually arrived, she wouldn't get her way? And why had Mrs. Everhart wanted her to come to Clifftop when she could have seen her in Vancouver, as Bensen had said? Was this arrangement meant to needle Bensen, or was it for some other reason? And if so, what? Jesse's head swam.

With Martha as guide, distant and dour, she was shown to the attic where the family journals were kept. Cecilia had told her these would be invaluable for glimpses into the day-to-day life of almost a century ago. Grudgingly Martha now dusted and swept a little area for Jesse to use, then arranged a lamp on her table. The housekeeper moved very slowly, and since she muttered complaints as she worked, Jesse got to hear rather more than she wanted to about "inconveniences." She was feeling grim, too, by the time the housekeeper had finished—grim *and* stubborn. She would get what she came here for—if it took weeks—and damn the rest!

She was glad to find the family journals were all Cecilia Anne had promised they would be and more. They were indeed invaluable, and Jesse wondered why they weren't in a museum or a university. However, she was not even going to suggest such a thing before she herself had had time to pore over them. Her proposed book would be marvelous with such

brimming life and action-packed history! Unless she
made a complete botch of it, she knew she had an
assured winner. And no one else had discovered these
journals. They held all brand-new detailed information, and they were in her hands! Jesse blessed her
good fortune and the hunch that had prompted her
to accept Mrs. Everhart's invitation. But looking at
the array of journals suddenly made her think her
visit might very well stretch to weeks. . . .

She spent the remainder of the day in the vast and
mostly dark attic, browsing through the stacks of
journals, noting the time spans they covered and
sorting the ones she wanted from those that were too
recent or contained material not needed.

She felt quite comfortable nestled in an old
cushion-covered wicker chair. The quiet and the utter
peace, the sense of removal from the world in
general—and the tension downstairs in particular—
were perfect conditions for her research. Moreover,
she was out of Bensen's way. It was unlikely, Jesse
decided, that they'd trip over each other while she
worked up here. She had opened some of the attic
windows, which were tall and narrow, and a pleasant
breeze now wafted in; she had a lovely view, too—
just a sliver, not enough to distract her. The journals were many and heavy, and she saw no point in
dragging them down to her bedroom only to have to
drag them all up again later, despite what Martha
said.

She spent the greater part of the next three days in
the attic, reading reams and reams of notes into her
tape recorder. She'd decided to tape rather than type,

for that would save time. The plot of her proposed book had not as yet taken a solid form in her mind; she was still molding the characters, trying to decide on their foibles and strengths. But as she studied the fascinating views of people who'd long since come and gone, the basics of the plot slowly seemed to fall into place. The deeper Jesse delved into the first journal, the more excited she became. She willingly spent all her spare hours up in the attic, and the only people who invaded her haven were Martha and Shanna—Martha to inform her that dinner would be on the table in half an hour and Shanna to share a cup of coffee over small talk.

From what Shanna had said, Jesse surmised that Bensen spent ninety-five percent of his time behind the closed door of the library, so that no one saw much of him, either. And Cecilia was still "ill" and keeping to her suite of rooms. Jesse wondered what life here must be like for Shanna, with no one for companionship other than her children and the taciturn housekeeper. From other things Shanna had said, Jesse received the impression that Shanna was completely under her older brother's thumb.

On Friday, as Jesse was looking for the second journal in a particular series, she came across a slim untitled volume. It seemed to be packed from cover to cover in small precise longhand, yet there was nothing to indicate its contents. Curious, Jesse took the book over to her lamp. Her eyes skimmed down the first page. In a sort of daze she sank down in the worn wicker chair and read on, puzzlement changing to amazement. Two pages later she realized what she held in her hand—a personal diary belonging to Bensen. The frustration, pain and anger that rose from the yellowed pages made it entirely impossible for Jesse to put the book down. She was so caught up in it she didn't even appreciate that she *should* put it down.

She judged Bensen to have been about seventeen years of age when he'd written these pages. Gradually a story unfolded to reveal that his parents were seldom home; they'd left him and Shanna in the care of their grandmother and a succession of housekeepers. None of the housekeepers stayed long because of the remoteness of the area and because of the difficulty in pleasing Cecilia Anne Everhart. She was always formally referred to as "grandmother," and no hint of warmth or love showed in her dealings with either Bensen or little Shanna. She appeared for the most part to be a bitterly sad woman, her emotions frozen by some cataclysmic event. On Bensen, then, rested the responsibility of raising Shanna, nine years his junior.

Bensen's grandfather, Samuel Everhart, had died tragically a year after his grandson's birth, and from what the diary said, it seemed that Bensen's father, Perceville, had been wasting away the family fortune from the day he'd gained control of the company. From various references throughout, Jesse understood that Bensen had been looking after the family business of logging since the age of fifteen or sixteen. He seemed fully aware that the empire his grandfather had built was falling apart as more and more capital vanished into the money pots of foreign places. Instead of funds being invested into the com-

pany to keep it prospering and up to date, Perceville
and his wife had chosen to live the high life else-
where. Years of neglect—sixteen years, in fact—had
all but emptied the family coffers.

And far from having everything he desired, it appeared the teenaged Bensen had had trouble keeping
good food on the elegant dining-room table, trouble
paying the housekeepers' wages, trouble keeping a
fast-growing Shanna in clothes. His grandmother
had taken none of this responsibility; the housekeepers went to Bensen with their questions, and he'd
had to deal with them all while his parents, Bensen
wrote, were off in "one damn fancy playpen after
another." How he'd hated them for abandoning
their responsibilities! The "playpens" mentioned
were Monte Carlo, Las Vegas and Rio de Janeiro.
Obviously Bensen's parents had been gamblers. . . .

Jesse read on, excited by these discoveries and
oblivious of the passing time. She'd flipped through
almost half the book when one page in particular
caught her eye.

Funeral. . . she was reading about a funeral, and it
was Bensen's eighteenth birthday. With a shock she
realized it was his parents' funeral that he was
recording with such uncaring detachment. They had
been killed in a plane crash in the Andes, on their
way to Rio after a week's visit home. A little farther
on she read:

Grandmother hardly ever leaves her rooms anymore. Percy was her favorite son, I'm sure of it.
Ever since we got that telegram, she's been like a

ghost. She's willing herself to die. I can feel it; the whole house feels it.. . . I'm calling the doctor tomorrow, and I'll force her to see him. Later I'll figure out a way to pay him. I noticed his house needs new shingles.

Shanna's been crying again and won't tell me what's wrong. I guess the kids at school have been giving her a rough time. I thought things would be better since I beat up on Jackie, but I guess he's been at her again. But this time she won't tell me; the last time she did, I came home with a black eye. Jackie hates my guts and is taking it out on Shanna. Says my dad ripped his dad off on wages. How the hell am I supposed to know those things?

I've been searching through the wage dockets, but they're such a mess even that bookkeeping course doesn't help. I've been trying to keep it a secret that we're flat broke, because if that gets out, the rest of the men will quit—and God knows I need them! I'll be working through the night so I can get the number six boom down the river in time. It's dangerous with just us two handling all those logs, but thank heaven for good ol' loyal Jake. I don't know why he hangs on. He knows we're almost washed up! And another thing, it must be almost time for Shanna to get brazziers and things like that. But how on earth. . .?

Jesse looked up from the pages and stared off into the far reaches of the dark attic. *Well!* was all she could think of at first. Reading Bensen's diary certainly had put a different light on things. He had had precious little happiness in his life, judging by this account. No wonder he was so harsh.... And it also explained why he bossed Shanna and why she accepted his word as law, why there was the continual tension with just that touch of animosity between him and his grandmother. Though an orphan, Jesse's life now seemed heaven when she compared it to Shanna's and Bensen's. At least she had had Sister Theresa to love her, as well as the kindness of the other Sisters. The Everhart children had had nothing.

Today, of course, things were radically different—at least financially. The family fortune had been built up to even greater heights than before; its wealth and stability were well known. Jesse, who read the financial papers regularly and even had some stock invested in the Everhart firm, knew that to be a fact. Just this year they'd completed an office complex nearly fifty stories high in downtown Vancouver, a soaring wing of concrete and glass, competing for architectural elegance with the large bank buildings and the most expensive hotels. Jesse had had occasion to pass the new high rise often, for a good friend of hers owned a small music store on the same street. And when she thought of the energy, will and sheer strength required not only to recover the Everhart company's losses but to advance the business, Jesse felt not only amazement but a growing respect. She had no doubt Bensen was responsible for the firm's shift in fortunes. At the age of thirty-six, he now commanded an empire. Her head was buzzing so with all the implications and new insights that she missed the light tread on the stairs.

"You're late for dinner, Miss Smith-Jones."

Jesse's eyes swung from the old-fashioned crib she was staring at to Bensen, standing at the head of the attic stairs. His expression was enigmatic, his face shadowed outside the small circle of the lamplight. He came slowly toward her with his catlike tread as he added, "Martha forgot to call you."

Suddenly guilt possessed Jesse. The diary—he was bound to see it! A stab of real fear shot through her, and she quickly slipped the book beneath her. Bensen checked himself in midstride, then continued to pick his way through the boxes and scattered furniture. He stopped a few feet from her, his sharp eyes narrowed slightly on her slender figure in the chair.

"What do you mean by working up here?"

"I like it here, thank you," Jesse retorted, struggling to maintain an even tone.

"There's plenty of room for you downstairs." The coldness of his tone sent a shiver down her spine.

"I don't want to work downstairs."

"Because of me?" His faint smile was decidedly sardonic.

"Why should you bother me one way or another?" Both their voices were becoming frostier and frostier.

"Grandmother is of the opinion that you would be more comfortable downstairs." He was watching her like a cat about to pounce. Jesse swallowed.

"I'll thank her for her concern," she returned sweetly, turning away from him deliberately to end the conversation. When he next addressed her, his manner was deceptively soft.

"What are you sitting on?"

"S-sitting on?"

"Get up."

"No."

"Get up!"

"Don't you dare touch me!"

His laugh was short and unpleasant as he grasped her wrist and yanked her up out of the wicker chair.

"Some gentleman—"

"I've never said I was a gentleman!" He held her easily at a distance, a disdainful curl on his chiseled lips. "C'mon, hand over what you're hiding. Couldn't keep your claws off some little item, is that it?" The lips curled still more; the eyes were cruelly amused.

"No, that's *not* it!" Jesse snapped. She threw the diary at him and in the same moment wrenched her wrist free. "I don't have to steal 'pocketable valuables' or anything else!"

But Bensen wasn't listening to her. He was staring down at the little diary in his hands, and the color had fled from his face.

"Why the hell were you reading this?" The words were so quiet yet so packed with rage that they seemed to scream at her.

"I—I—I didn't know what it w-was," Jesse stammered. "Bensen, please believe me! I—I just started reading it, and then I c-couldn't put it down! I wasn't prying! I—as soon as I started reading it, I got all caught up in it and...and...." Her voice trailed off. How could she explain what was impossible to explain?

He was standing over her now, his fathomless black eyes condemning her every word. Anger simmered along the powerful lines of his taut muscular frame.

"Bensen, I'm sorry!" Tears blurred her vision, and there was nothing she could do to stop them. She hadn't cried in years, and here he'd provoked a flood when there was really no reason to cry at all! She couldn't understand it. "I know I shouldn't have read it, but—but it was just *so* interesting that...."

As the warm flush covered his pallor, she knew she'd said the wrong thing. Desperate, she searched her mind for something to add, but nothing would come. She tried to pull herself together and got absolutely nowhere.

Some of his trembling rage seemed to diminish as he watched tear after miserable tear course down her cheeks. She bit savagely into her bottom lip to stop its telltale quivering. Why, oh *why* hadn't she put the book down as soon as she knew what it was! She *should* have—it was only right that she should have. She would be furious, too, were the positions reversed....

"Well...." He continued to stand over her, looking with anger and embarrassed uncertainty at her bowed head, seeing just the wealth of gleaming chestnut hair, the edge of thick lashes lowered to hide tears that wouldn't be hidden as they dropped from her chin onto her blouse. "Well," he began again, then shifted awkwardly. "I thought I'd lost this book. I didn't know it was up here." He cleared his throat, impatience surfacing. "For heaven's sake, will you stop crying!"

"I'm t-t-trying to."

"You're not trying hard enough!"

"I'm trying as hard as I can! Will you leave me alone!"

"I wouldn't have thought you were the type to dissolve into tears, Miss Smith-Jones. Is that your real name? It sounds ridiculous!"

"It was given to me because I didn't have one of my own! Is that all right with you, Mr. Everhart? Orphans that are left on doorsteps don't usually come with name tags!"

There was a split second of quiet before Bensen said tiredly, "Will you *please* stop crying!"

"I'll stop when and if I please!" Jesse breathed raggedly, wishing she could stop that instant.

"If I had my way, you'd be out on your ear, Miss—Jesse! It's only for my grandmother's sake that I'm allowing you to stay. But believe me, if you ever dare interfere again in what doesn't concern you, you'll be out so fast you won't know what happened!"

"Are you always this pleasant to guests?"

"Guests don't usually read my diary!"

"If it'll make you feel any better, I'll give you mine to read!" Jesse held her breath, hoping he wouldn't say yes and, in another way, hoping he would, because then at least they would be even.

He made a sound in his throat of complete derision. "I wouldn't dream of butting in where I wasn't wanted.'' That put her firmly in her place. ''Whenever you're ready, dinner is.'' His voice was glacial, his glance flickering down and up contemptuous. Then Bensen turned on his heel and left—with his diary. Jesse could barely hear the steps creaking as he vanished downstairs.

The tears stopped almost as soon as he was out of sight. Ashamed because of what she'd done, humiliated because she'd been caught, Jesse still couldn't help but feel secretly glad that she'd read Bensen's diary. It explained so much....

CHAPTER TWO

THE ATTIC SOON BECAME Jesse's private domain. Martha haphazardly cleaned away more of the dust and cobwebs, and Jesse spent most of her days there locked in solitary study. From early in the morning until dinner, after dinner until late in the evening, Jesse perused every page of the wonderful old family journals—thereby not seeing much of the family. Shanna came up to visit her, of course, and Cecilia allowed Jesse one half hour in the morning and one half hour in the afternoon for interviewing, but not more than that. Still professing herself to be ill, she mainly kept to her suite.

Bensen Jesse saw only at dinnertime, and even that was too much, as far as she was concerned. The lack of emotion in his black eyes unnerved her, and the cold ruthless cast of his face kept everyone else on tenterhooks around the dinner table. There was always a soft communal sigh of relief when he excused himself and left to disappear into the library, but it was only when the door shut behind him that they allowed themselves to breathe freely.

Jesse thought he shouldn't work so much; she was sure exhaustion was partly responsible for the sternness and rigidity of his manner. When Shanna pointed out to her that she, too, was keeping the same hours, Jesse didn't explain why her situation was different. She wanted to leave Clifftop as soon as possible, and her few days had already stretched to more than a week. If it hadn't been for the journals, Cecilia's procrastination would have driven her mad and likely would have driven her from Clifftop, as well. She had so many questions to ask, plus certain matters from the journals that needed clarifying, that one hour a day was the same as being offered a bowl of grapes, only to have it snatched away after sampling one.

"Jesse, Jesse are you there?" Shanna's voice preceded her up the attic stairs late one morning. She came bursting into the darkened space with an unusual display of excitement. "I just had to show you! I know you like this sort of thing, I mean—" She stopped to catch her breath and deposited a large flat box in Jesse's lap. "It's for grandmother. Open it! She's so hard to please I had to send to Paris for this. She'd *better* like it!" Shanna's excitement was infectious. The more Jesse hurried, the more her fingers fumbled, and she started to laugh.

"There, it's open. Good heavens!" Jesse breathed as Shanna eagerly whisked out a confection of silk and lace.

"It's even nicer than the pictures!" Shanna exclaimed. "Violet is grandmother's favorite color. Violets were her wedding flowers," she explained. "Violet is such an unusual color that it's hard to find, and—hold this while I find the coat." She thrust the peignoir into Jesse's hands and dug farther into the tissue paper. Jesse let her fingers slide through the exquisite material as she inspected the workmanship, to find it perfect.

"I'm sure Cecilia will love it—I know I would! What's the occasion?" asked Jesse.

"Didn't I tell you? It's her birthday today, and I've been expecting this package for weeks!" Almost reverently Shanna lifted the matching dressing gown from the box. Jesse was totally silent in wide-eyed admiration.

"Well...my goodness!" she finally said, and Shanna giggled. "I understand she's hard to please, but if she doesn't like this...!"

"She's almost impossible when it comes to presents." Shanna smoothed the collar of the gown.

Jesse was suddenly dismayed. "I don't have a thing to give her."

"Don't worry about that. We—we don't make any fuss over birthdays," Shanna said quickly. She seemed more subdued as she added, "We just give presents—usually at dinner. That's all. Bensen doesn't like a fuss, you see."

"I...think so. You never give birthday parties? Not even little ones?"

"Well, n-no. We never had them when we were little, and...." Shanna's soft voice faded away. She was looking at Jesse in slight perplexity.

"That's no reason not to have a party now," Jesse pointed out with easy logic. "It would be fun, wouldn't it? Sam and Merit would love a party. Oh, and you could invite Lily, couldn't you?"

"But—but we don't know anyone else. I mean,

don't you have to have lots of people for a party?"

"Of course not! Bensen's gone somewhere, hasn't he? He wasn't at dinner last night—"

"He's away in Vancouver. Do you think we could get everything ready in time? What do we have to get ready? I-I've never arranged a party before." Shanna's cheeks colored delicately. She looked half embarrassed and half frightened.

"How about a cake? Do you think we could coax Martha into baking a cake?"

"We-ell...she doesn't like any extra work. But couldn't we—I mean, we do have some recipe books, and I'm sure if we do exactly as they say, we could come up with a cake. What else do we need?"

"Let's see...."

Heads bent together, they used a sheet from Jesse's note pad to jot down the details. Suddenly Shanna seemed overcome by a mood of sadness.

"No," she said gloomily, "we can't have a party." Her expression was utterly serious.

"But why?" Jesse gazed at Shanna in alarm. She had begun to like Bensen's sister very much, despite her efforts to remain uninvolved.

"Bensen doesn't like parties," Shanna murmured, as though it were law.

"Why does Ben—" Abruptly Jesse stopped, then said thoughtfully, "I can understand that. Lots of people don't like parties. But he's away, isn't he? So he surely won't mind if the rest of us have a party. He wouldn't be so mean as to deprive you of a little fun, now would he?"

"Put like that...well, no...I—I guess not."

Shanna looked doubtfully at Jesse. Then she brightened a little. "Sam and Merry would *love* a party! We could surprise grandmother...and Bensen doesn't have to know. It'll be all over by the time he gets back tonight. I've got to call Lily and to ask Martha—come on, Jesse, we've a lot to do!. How long does a cake take to bake?" Shanna was already halfway down the stairs, and Jesse paused only long enough to switch off her electric typewriter.

Seated at the small round salon table, Samantha and Merit were almost feverish with the novelty of the occasion. Their contained little faces looked fit to burst with excitement. Shanna, flushed and with her honey-blond hair mussed, gazed with supreme satisfaction at the birthday cake she and Jesse had just finished decorating. The twins squirmed in their chairs, and Shanna put a finger to her lips in caution. They nodded solemnly, their eyes enormous, and concentrated on the hardship of sitting absolutely still.

"What do you suppose is keeping her?" Lily whispered. Her liquid black eyes and wide humorous mouth had instantly endeared her to Jesse. Shortly before she'd arrived that afternoon, Shanna had taken Jesse to see the prints and paintings that her brother and grandmother had purchased from Lily through the years, and now Jesse was slightly in awe of the older woman. Her face, with its wide cheekbones and long straight nose, had only feather lines in the smooth bronze skin, making her appear much younger than her fifty-five years, but her hair, which hung in a thick cascade all the way down past her waist, was liberally streaked with gray.

"She's coming!" Martha trod heavily into the salon from the hall, moving faster than Jesse had ever seen her move. The word *party* had had a magic effect on her: she'd put on a clean apron, arranged her bun into a tighter knot at the back of her head and had hardly muttered at all about the additional work. "Light the candles, quick!" she urged. "Now *where* did I put those matches...?"

Mrs. Everhart's haughty querulous tone could be heard from the hall. "Where is everybody? Isn't tea ready yet? Did I come all the way downstairs for nothing? Martha! Martha!"

Shanna nervously fingered the tablecloth; the twins seemed to shrink into their chairs, their sky-blue eyes turned apprehensively toward the door. Martha fumbled and dropped the matches before she lighted all the candles on the cake. Quickly Lily pulled a lighted candle from its surface and ignited the rest just as Mrs. Everhart arrived at the doorway.

The silent seconds seemed to stretch into eternity. Jesse felt a film of perspiration break out on her forehead. Was her idea of a party going to be a miserable flop? As the seconds grew, still grandmother stood by the door, rigid, speechless.

Jesse's heart plummeted. Gathering her wits in a last-ditch effort, she poked Shanna sharply in the ribs, and even though she didn't feel happy, she smiled widely. She shot a quick encouraging look toward the twins. As if on cue, their timing perfect, everyone suddenly cried, "Happy Birthday!"

"Bless my soul!" Grandmother's voice was so

blankly astonished that it made everyone laugh. "This...if I...you shouldn't—oh, bless my soul, what's going on?"

"Well...it's a party. For you," Shanna said shyly, anxiously. Jesse wouldn't have been surprised had Shanna's fingers been crossed under the table. Hers were.

"You're not m-mad, gramma?" quavered Samantha. Abruptly she closed her mouth, as though frightened at having spoken out of turn.

"Mad? *Mad?* I'm delighted! And you should have said angry, not mad," she corrected. "Heavens, I'm not so old that I can't enjoy a party! Always use correct English, my dear. A party! This is simply grand!" She beamed at everyone. The twins' excitement burst.

"Mummy and Jesse made the cake! And Martha made the sandwiches! Merry and I helped!" The words bubbled out of Samantha.

"There are eleven violets and nine roses and seven daisies on your cake, gramma."

"You don't say! No one has ever had a birthday cake as...as lovely as this one! Eleven violets!" Grandmother dabbed at her eyes with a lacy perfumed handkerchief. She smiled indulgently at the twins, and they, overcome at this unusual attention, subsided in shyness in their chairs, both holding their hands tightly between their knees.

"Do you want your presents now or later, grandmother?" asked Shanna, not quite hiding her eagerness. With her cheeks so rosy and her hair untidy, Shanna didn't look old enough to be the mother of nine-year-old twins, Jesse thought to herself.

"Why, I'll open them now; otherwise I'll be too excited to eat!"

Martha placed a tray of gift-wrapped boxes on grandmother's lap and then stood back, her hands folded over her ample bosom. The downward droop of her mouth was less pronounced. The twins chewed energetically on their bottom lips as their great-grandmother opened their present first. Her white hands, thin and long and veined, trembled as she lifted off the cover of the little box. Carefully she took out two rounded polished stones on which were painted a blue bird and a swallow. After thoughtfully inspecting the painted stones, she looked up at the twins, who were holding their breath.

"They're lovely!" she commented. The twins breathed once more. "It must have taken quite some time to paint all this detail. Really, they're beautiful!"

"Mummy said you could use them for...for...." Merit looked to Shanna for help.

"For paperweights," her mother supplied, looking at that moment very happy.

"How thoughtful! Come, give gramma a kiss!"

Shanna need not have worried that Cecilia Anne would find fault with the peignoir and dressing-gown set. At the twins' urgings she even let herself be persuaded to slip on the coat over her dress, then sat down again looking slightly self-conscious but very feminine and lovely. Although the violet color was rich, it didn't pale her delicate complexion; rather, it emphasized her fair coloring and brought a shimmer to the dark brown eyes.

Out of long habit Cecilia Anne made no move to invite Shanna to give her a kiss, but she sent her granddaughter a kinder glance than was usual. Lily's present of a water-color set with five sable brushes was received with mingled surprise and pleasure.

"You used to paint a long time ago," Lily smiled. "You should take it up again."

"We-ell...." Grandmother fingered the sable brushes with a gentle knowing touch. "It's been so long...."

"I didn't know you painted," said Shanna softly.

"I don't know if I still can...."

"We'll help you, gramma!" Merit exclaimed. "Won't we, Sammy?"

"Can we, gramma? It's lots of fun!" Then she added more shyly, "If you want us to?"

"That would be lovely! I shall need your expert advice."

At these words the twins lighted up like Christmas trees, and Mrs. Everhart laughed aloud at their expressions. After the unexpected chuckle everyone was quiet for the barest of pauses, surprised and a little awkward at finding themselves happy.

"I got you something, too," Martha broke in. From the kitchen she brought out a small earthenware pot in which bloomed a cluster of wood violets. She thrust this abruptly into Mrs. Everhart's hands and stepped back, scowling and trying to appear nonchalant.

"Martha! How sweet of you!"

The housekeeper blushed with pleasure while her

scowl deepened. "Just found 'em in the bush," she said gruffly.

"You must have searched for a long time, Martha. Thank you."

"Just stumbled over them one day. Well...shall I bring the coffee?"

"No—we'll have champagne!" Mrs. Everhart cried. "Will you see to it, Martha? I'm ninety-five today, and *that* calls for a drink! Bring seven glasses. One for everybody, even the twins. They can have one tiny glass each. What do you say to that?" she questioned the twins. Grinning, the two heads bobbed up and down vigorously. "You'll remember not to gulp?" she charged sternly.

"Oh, no, gramma!" they said together in hushed tones.

As Martha hurried away for the champagne, Jesse spoke up. "Mrs. Everhart, my best wishes will have to do for now...I haven't a present."

"Of course, my dear." Grandmother bent her head in gracious acceptance, then added more sharply, "Didn't I tell you to call me Cecilia?"

"Oh, yes. Cecilia."

"The party was Jesse's idea," Shanna put in generously. "So she does have a present after all."

Jesse's cheeks grew pink as everyone showered her with smiles. She was glad when Martha returned with the bottle of champagne; the resulting flurry of activity took everyone's attention off her.

"Why aren't you sitting down, Martha?" Mrs. Everhart demanded imperiously.

"She said it wasn't her place, gramma," Merit piped up.

"Mummy and Jesse set a plate for her, but she took it away again," added Samantha.

"Bring it back!" Grandmother ordered. Martha, flustered, began shaking her head, but grandmother waggled a finger in her face. "This is my party, and you'll do as I say!"

"Oh... yes, ma'am!" Martha Potkins flushed red.

By that time Lily had pushed another chair up to the table and Shanna was back from the kitchen, bearing another place setting.

"Isn't this exciting?" she asked of no one in particular.

"It's been ages since there was a party here," Lily commented.

"Perhaps too long, eh?" Grandmother raised her glass with a flourish. "Samuel—my husband," she added for Jesse's benefit, "used to bring people up from Victoria and Vancouver by boat for our parties. What parties we had then! And when all the boys were alive... before they went away...." The momentary sadness passed, and Cecilia Anne smiled at the gathering around the table. "Let's drink a toast to a foolish old woman!"

There was another toast and another; the party gradually grew noisier and noisier and more spontaneous. The twins chattered and giggled, and as no one hushed them or bent stern eyes upon them, they grew less inhibited. Shanna's air of melancholy had vanished for the time being. Grandmother, laughing as though she were young again, the bitterness and sadness at bay, turned out to be quite merry. Lily knew just what to say to draw Martha out of her dour shell, and when the housekeeper laughed, all of her plump rolls under the big white apron seemed to laugh with her. Jesse's rich sherry eyes danced and sparkled as she joined in the general amusement.

No one noticed a solitary figure coming quietly down the hall. Bensen Everhart stopped just outside the doorway, half hidden, watching. He turned silently to go, and the slight movement caught Jesse's attention. Her eyes flashed toward the door, and their gazes locked. The smile died in Jesse's eyes. An odd little twinge of fright fluttered with her heartbeat.

Shanna, laughing, turned to look at Jesse; her eyes widened and slowly followed Jesse's stare. Then one after another everybody at the table looked toward the doorway, and as they did, the laughter and the giggles faded until there was silence.

The sudden hush affected Bensen. He pulled his eyes away from Jesse's to see everyone staring at him: Shanna and the twins with naked apprehension, grandmother with the look of a dawning argument and Martha with huffy dislike.

"I was just leaving," he announced smoothly. Jesse noticed that he slipped a small gift-wrapped package back into the pocket of his tailored business suit.

"Leaving?" Lily stood up. She wore the only welcoming smile. "This is a birthday party, not a hen party. Come on, sit down!"

"Sit here, Bensen." Jesse sprang up, offering him

her chair. She hurried for another, which she placed between the twins—as far from Bensen as possible.

Bensen still hovered in the doorway, tall, dark, aloof and oddly handsome. Jesse wished that he would join them, that he would just for once unbend sufficiently to become one of the family.

"Sit, Bensen!" commanded his grandmother, sounding angrier than she meant to. "Please," she added in softer tones with a wry half smile.

He came forward and sat down in Jesse's chair, large and very male in the female gathering. Somewhat grudgingly Martha brought him a plate, a delicate coffee cup and a champagne glass.

"Now the party's complete." Lily smiled, filling the awkward quiet. She raised her glass. So did everyone except Bensen, and the whole party teetered in the balance of success or resounding failure, awaiting Bensen's seal of approval.

"We—we've been having such fun," Shanna hesitantly remarked to her stern brother. She was quite pale now. "We just decided to have the party a couple of hours ago. It was Jesse's idea...."

Jesse was wracking her brains for some way to revive the party spirit. If it turned out to be a failure, it would be her fault and might bring the family into even greater and deeper division. When Bensen's eyes swung her way at Shanna's words, Jesse frowned slightly. With perfect equanimity she met his eyes.

"Had we known you'd be back in time," she said calmly, "we would have made bigger sandwiches. They're not really man-sized, are they?" She held out the platter with the dainty bite-sized morsels. Bensen stared at her for a second longer with compressed lips, then he helped himself to about six of the confections. Jesse continued in a cheerier tone, "I think we've just enough time to drink another toast before Cecilia blows the candles out. They're getting low, aren't they?" Bensen's silence had induced such nervousness in her now that she had to clasp her hands together to keep them from their telltale shaking. She glanced at the twins, one on either side of her, smiling reassuringly.

Merit looked at the candles and nodded, then stole a peep at her uncle. Samantha, made courageous by the champagne, giggled. She tried to stop and then giggled all the more, setting her twin off. "Gramma has to tell her boyfriend if she doesn't blow them all out!" Samantha gasped. "That's what Jesse said!"

Another bubbling giggle erupted out of Samantha and spread to Merit. Lily encouraged grandmother to take a deep breath, and Martha, with a quick glance at Bensen, pushed the cake closer to Mrs. Everhart. The package Bensen had removed again from his pocket suddenly fell to the floor. As both he and Shanna bent to retrieve it, their heads smacked together. Bensen moaned in mock pain, and now Shanna recovered her earlier joy, giggling along with the twins.

"I'd forgotten what a hard head you have!" laughed Shanna, holding her temple and diving under the table for the package.

"What is it? What's in the box?" grandmother queried, not to be left out.

"Your present." Bensen gravely took the package

from Shanna and passed it to his grandmother. His thick straight hair was mussed now, too, and he didn't look half as stern and unapproachable as he usually did.

"This is like Christmas and Easter rolled into one!" grandmother chuckled, her fingers trembling as she tugged on the ribbon. "This is simply grand! Whose birthday is next?"

By this time everyone was half out of his chair trying to see inside the box as Cecilia Anne opened it. Jesse secretly watched Bensen and saw a flicker of concern pass over the large dark eyes. She smiled impulsively, thinking that there was some human feeling left in him after all.

"Why, it's—it's...oh, Ben, what a lovely surprise!" Mrs. Everhart lifted a delicate brooch wrought into a crest.

"What is it? What does it mean?" the twins asked as one.

"I haven't seen this for—why, for more than seventy years!" cried grandmother, holding it up so everyone could see. "It's my family crest! My family crest from home, from England! I've always wanted a copy but somehow never got around to—here Lily, take a closer look. Isn't it lovely?"

"Grandmother, quick!" Shanna jumped up. "The candles are melting!" Complete bedlam reigned for a few minutes.

Bensen surprised everyone by being rather charming. As he took part in the festivities, they forgot that originally he hadn't been welcome and now warmly included him. Whenever he laughed, they grew happier, for he didn't laugh often, and Jesse decided the sound of the deep rich male tone among all the feminine chuckles sounded very nice indeed. The sparkle had crept back into her golden sherry eyes, making them seem as brilliant as gemstones. Across the table Bensen's glance strayed toward her and lingered. She became aware of his steadfast gaze, noting how one corner of his chiseled mouth curved pensively upward. A pink flush stained her cheeks. She blinked and looked away, feeling a new sort of nervousness overtake her.

Some time later the sharp rat-a-tat-tat of high heels on the beautiful hardwood floor penetrated through the sounds of the party. As the hurrying footsteps neared the salon door, the merriment petered away, to stop entirely when Dorothy Jorgensen appeared. She walked slowly now as she approached the table.

"What is this?" In the unnatural silence her high voice seemed almost shrill.

"A birthday party for grandmother," Bensen said smoothly, his dark face once again a mask, the black eyes alert and slightly narrowed.

"I wasn't invited!" It was an accusation. Dorothy's blue eyes swept around the table. Her eyebrows rose as she saw Lily and then rose much higher when she saw Martha casually sitting beside her employer as though she were one of the family.

"We didn't know you were coming," Jesse tried to explain. "We planned the party only this afternoon and never thought you could be here in time."

"Daddy dropped me off." Dorothy's tone was cold and unforgiving. With growing dislike she stared at Jesse, then she snapped at Bensen, "Why are you having a party?" When he answered with a warning frown, she turned her back on him and walked disdainfully around the table to drop a small package into Mrs. Everhart's lap.

"I'll get a chair for you." Bensen's voice was like silk that overlay razor blades.

"Don't bother!" Dorothy retorted. "I don't really have time to stay. Daddy's going back to Vancouver soon. I just popped up to bring the present," she sniffed, then added, "I didn't know *you* were here!"

"I came back early," Bensen replied disinterestedly.

"You could have told me!"

The twins' heads turned in unison as they watched first Dorothy, then their uncle.

"Does it matter?" The words could have cut through ice. "Didn't you tell me you wouldn't have time for a visit today? Weren't you going to a flower show or some such thing?" Jesse swallowed convulsively at his tone.

"That's not the point! I don't know why *I* was left out when...." Dorothy looked point-blank at Lily, then at Martha and lastly at Jesse.

"We didn't mean to exclude you," Jesse protested, trying to rescue the situation. "We only decided to have the party a couple of hours ago," she repeated. Her tentative smile was met with a cold stare.

"Well, I'm going," Dorothy said curtly. "I *had* left my plans open in case I decided to stay—" her eyes darted toward Bensen "—but I don't feel like it now.'' She walked past him to the doorway. ''Good-bye!'' she flung over her shoulder. Obviously she was too incensed even to stay and watch Mrs. Everhart open the present she'd brought.

Everyone listened to the sharp tapping of Dorothy's high heels fading down the hall. In the dismayed silence Shanna stood up, telling the twins it was time to go upstairs. Puzzled and disappointed, their eyes flickered toward their uncle before they left on Shanna's heels.

''I, uh, have some work to do.'' Bensen paused for a moment. He nodded to his grandmother and to Lily, then turned and stalked down the hall to the library. He never once glanced at Jesse, making her feel absurdly responsible for the altercation between him and his fiancée.

''Can I give you a hand, Martha?'' Dispiritedly Jesse stood up and began gathering plates. Lily took Cecilia out on the lawn to sit on deck chairs, and that was the end of the party. Martha's mouth was pulled down low at the corners, and Jesse's shoulders drooped as they cleaned up without saying a word, each busy with her own rather morbid thoughts.

Although the party had ended unpleasantly, Jesse felt it had cemented her relationship with the family—or at least with the female members of the family. In the days that followed they paid frequent visits to the attic while Jesse was hard at work with her copious notes. The twins came up quiet as mice the first time and shy, but by the second visit their youthful buoyancy had won over. They were so severely trained in good manners that they never overstayed their welcome, so Jesse began to look forward to her discussions with them. Shanna continued to come—more often now—and was always anxious not to disrupt Jesse's work. Then, as her confidence grew, she popped up whenever the notion overtook her, sometimes to say only a few words. Martha regularly cleaned the attic—more regularly than was necessary—and while she was vacuuming and dusting, she dispensed a running commentary on how difficult her life had become since she'd started working for the Everhart family. And grandmother, saying the exercise was good for her now that her "illness" had passed, came upstairs to sit for hours.

"Gramma gives us a kiss only at Christmastime," Merit said to Jesse during a visit shortly after the party. "She must have been really pleased to kiss us both, don't you think?" The twins waited wide-eyed for Jesse's answer.

"Do you think she loves us?" Samantha asked gravely another time. "She's not like other grammas.... The other kids at school have grammas who bake cookies for them. Our gramma never does."

"Yeah, and they get butter tarts, too," Merit added. "Gramma never bakes butter tarts."

"We-ell..." Jesse paused, searching her mind, "not all grammas are the same, just as not all people are the same." They eyed her dubiously.

JESSE PRESSED the play button on her tape recorder and settled back to listen as Mrs. Everhart willingly delved into her memory. "Back in 1903, when I arrived on the coast, we stayed in Vancouver for the first few months while my Samuel arranged his logging contracts. Money was tight for us then, and so we couldn't afford one of the hotels along Hastings Street. Instead Samuel rented a one-room log cabin for us on the North Shore. At that time there were perhaps only ten of these little shacks scattered along the shore; the rest was all forest and bush, and one traveled back and forth downtown by ferryboat. No bridges then—the Lion's Gate Bridge wasn't built until 1938, and after that West Vancouver opened up. But I'm getting away from the point.''

Jesse smiled encouragingly. "Don't worry, any information may be useful. Besides, I'm enjoying it.''

"Hastings Street was the center of town,'' Mrs. Everhart continued. "It boasted three-story *stone* buildings, while plain dirt tracks branching out led right into the forest. In the wintertime the sea of mud between the boardwalks on Hastings was unbelievable! I remember when Samuel took me shopping. He was always going off to talk to this man or chat with that man, and I'd stand there in the rain, patiently waiting and waiting. The fashion was long skirts, and my hem would soak halfway up my legs! I'd get so angry that I'd often go shopping by myself. To get from one boardwalk to another, I'd simply wait for some likely-looking fellow to come along and ask him to help me over!''

She chuckled, then added, "They never refused, either. That was when Samuel would get angry. Oh, how he would storm at me! Hastings Street was always so busy I never had any trouble finding some broad-shouldered candidate. That's where all the fashionable hotels were, and all the shops. That's where the men outfitted their packtrains before setting off for the Klondike and the Columbia.''

Jesse felt transported back in time to those earlier days as Mrs. Everhart rambled on. Really, the woman was a gold mine of information! More than ever, she was confident her novel would be a success.

"The shops were so full of everything imaginable that the goods spilled right out onto the boardwalk!'' the old woman went on. "There were sides of venison and beef and pork hanging from the rafters—and fowl, too. Pheasants and wild ducks and geese. There were kegs of salt pork and bolts of material and fresh vegetables and women's hats. Usually in the back of the shop was a small apothecary, where one could get witch hazel and rose water and headache powder. I loved to go shopping. You see, I was nineteen; I'd just arrived from England, and I'd never been shopping like this before. My family was impoverished, but we still had our butler, and he made all our household purchases.

"One butler and one cook...that's all we had left of the sixteen servants Wentworth Hall needed. I was the eldest daughter, so naturally papa was pleased when the wealthy stranger from Canada offered for my hand. Samuel had come to England to visit relatives he'd never seen and to open the market for his Canadian lumber. Mama was overjoyed that a gentleman of his good family—and of his means—should desire me, for although I was a beauty, I had no dowry to speak of, and my prospects were very poor. Also, there were three younger sisters who needed husbands, as well, and at nineteen I was almost considered as being on the shelf. But you see, now I'm far from the point again! What exactly was it that you asked? You know, dear, talking with you is doing me a world of good! I'm glad I managed to persuade you into staying longer. As I said, there's no point in your rushing off before you've had the chance to go through all those journals!''

Jesse didn't mention that she'd been through one too many—Bensen's. He never came up to the attic, nor did he involve himself in any discussions with her. In fact, he went out of his way to avoid her, and Jesse scrupulously did likewise. That was why she continued to work in the attic, despite the urgings of the womenfolk of the house, who insisted she'd be more comfortable in the library.

But Jesse preferred to be much farther away from Bensen's headquarters. He made her grit her teeth and count to ten more often than not, and Jesse figured that he liked to have his den and the neighboring library to himself. The library door was frequently closed, and since he almost always worked while he was in residence, the door was almost always shut.

It was the middle of the afternoon before Jesse and Mrs. Everhart ended their taping session. Mrs. Everhart had retired for a nap, assuring Jesse that she'd enjoyed herself immensely. Jesse continued to work quietly for a short while, cross-referencing some notes to that day's tape. When she finally went downstairs, she was surprised to find Shanna sitting close by the library door on a step near the bottom of the staircase. The library door was, as usual, closed, but today angry voices could be heard coming from inside; Bensen's and another man's. Shanna's white face and the way she crouched against the wall made Jesse sink down on the stair beside her.

"What's going on?" she asked in an alarmed whisper. When Shanna didn't answer, Jesse took one of her hands and rubbed it between both her own. "What is it, Shanna? What's the matter?"

"It's Ray." Shanna's whisper was distraught. "He's in there with Bensen. Every time he comes, they fight."

"Who's Ray?"

"Ray Dunbar. He...he's the forest ranger in this area. He...I...we...Bensen doesn't like him," she finished miserably. "Every time he comes they fight."

"Why?"

Shanna opened her mouth, but at first no words came out. She cleared her throat nervously, then stammered, "Well, you see, I think it's me."

"They fight over you?"

"Ray and I...we've been...well, seeing each other. I knew Bensen wouldn't like it—I just knew!"

Jesse assimilated this new information before asking gently, "Are you in love with Ray? Is it serious? I mean, do you want to keep on seeing him?"

"Yes," Shanna answered softly. "Yes."

The muffled argument in the library now rose to a crescendo. Jesse wished she could hear at least some of the words distinctly. Perhaps she could help Shanna. If only she knew the cause for the argument.

"Have you told Bensen how you feel about Ray?"

"Oh, no! How can I when—" Shanna waved a hand toward the library. "It's the same thing all over again." Her eyes closed, and a solitary tear slipped out from under her lashes.

"What do you mean, it's the same? What's the same?"

"It was the same with Stu...m-my husband." Shanna swallowed. "Bensen hated him, too. He warned me against Stu, but I wouldn't listen."

"What happened to Stu?" asked Jesse uneasily.

Inside the library the voices raged on. It was a macabre backdrop for Shanna's next words.

"He died five years ago. At least I think he did. The body was never positively identified as Stu's. But who else's could it have been?" She sighed and leaned against the stair at her back.

Jesse was shocked, but Shanna hurried on, as though the words were being forced out of her. "Bensen told me Stu was no good, but I wouldn't listen. He said Stu was after our money. It might have looked as though we had some, but all we had really was a decrepit logging company and this great big old house. Stu convinced me to elope with him because we couldn't get Bensen's and grandmother's approval. I was eighteen and had just inherited a small bit of money from my mother.

"Immediately after Stu and I were married in Vancouver, we flew to Mexico for our honeymoon. I wanted to go straight home after the ceremony, but I'd given Stu all the money, and he wouldn't hear of it. We were gone for as long as my money lasted—

which wasn't long—and by that time I knew I was pregnant.

"When we came home, Stu got some money out of Bensen to buy us a little house and—and to set us up. For a whole year we lived on money that Bensen managed to scrape together for us, though I didn't find that out till later. Stu never worked—he was a logger, or he used to be—but he explained getting the money somehow, and I was satisfied. Then finally Bensen offered Stu a job in the company, a good one, and told him he'd have to start supporting me himself. Stu refused the job. Said it was beneath him. He'd work for a few days at odd jobs and then spend everything at the pub. We lost our house and moved into this—this shack far out in the bush. Then Stu started bringing bottles home. He'd get drunk and sit for hours raging against Bensen for not giving us money—Bensen was struggling to save the company and didn't have an extra dime. But Stu would get angrier and angrier thinking about it, and he'd take it out on me. When he was like that, he used to—to hit me. Sometimes I'd run out into the bush just to get away from him. I never saw Bensen and grandmother then; I was too ashamed. Things went on like that for quite some time. I—I couldn't get up the courage to leave. I felt I couldn't come home after—well, after . . . and I had no money, nowhere to go and two little children."

"Oh, Shanna, how terrible for you," Jesse breathed; genuinely moved. "Did nobody know what was happening? Couldn't someone have helped?"

"Bensen did. One day he just dropped by. It was the morning after one of Stu's big rages. I—my face was bruised. Bensen went nuts. When Stu came home, drunk again, Bensen and he had a fight. Stu kind of flew across the room. He crashed into the wall, then slid down to the floor. I thought—but he picked himself up and shouted something like, 'good riddance' at me. Then he ran for his truck and roared off.

"About an hour later, when Bensen and the twins and I had left after I'd gathered together a few of my things, we...we...he drove his truck right off the cliff. It was on the rocks thirty feet down, smoldering."

Shanna's voice had sunk into such a soft choked whisper that Jesse had to lean close to hear her. "The doctor refused to put a positive identification on the...the body, although it had to be Stu...." Shanna's whisper trailed off. She didn't say anything more for what seemed a long time, then she went on. "I've learned to respect Bensen's judgment. I couldn't go against him again. He never even said, 'I told you so.' I'd be *afraid* to go against him because he'd probably be right again! And yet...."

Jesse sat in a dazed silence. Her mind was reeling. It seemed to her that the Everhart family had had more than its fair share of trouble. Inside the library the argument continued. It rose and fell and rose and fell, increasing Jesse's agitation. Shanna was a bit more subdued now. White and with a strange listless calm.

"I've been thinking," she went on, "about that

conversation we had. Remember when you asked if Bensen was always the way he is now and I said yes? It's been so long since he's been any other way that I had forgotten. When I was little, he was mother and father to me. But when he was about sixteen, seventeen, he started changing. He didn't have as much time for me anymore because he'd started looking after the business. When our parents died, he had to take over. He...he kind of turned into a machine—just work, work, work. No time for...for fun. Oh, he still took care of me, but it wasn't the same. Our closeness disappeared. I wish there were some way to bring it back, but some things can never be recaptured, can they?'' She was quiet again for a moment.

"He was so bossy about Stu that I eloped more to defy him than anything else, I guess. And then Stu was so handsome. He had these bright, bright blue eyes and thick black lashes and curly hair—oh, Jesse, you wouldn't believe how beautiful he was! And he was such fun—at first." The tragedy was written on her gentle face. Jesse couldn't say anything; she just gripped Shanna's hand tightly. "And now...now I don't know what to do," Shanna finished.

"You should tell Bensen how you feel about Ray. Talk to him about it," Jesse urged. "You made a terrible mistake once, but that was years ago."

"Oh, I couldn't! At least not yet. There's nothing—I mean, I don't really know how Ray feels about me." There was wistfulness in Shanna's whisper.

Jesse thought then that she'd like to meet Ray Dunbar. In that instant the furious voices in the library stopped. There was a moment's silence. Shanna and Jesse heard Ray speak up and heard Bensen's brusque answer as an indistinct muffle. The sound of heavy footsteps came toward the door. In one swift movement Shanna stood and ran upstairs. Suddenly the library door opened before Jesse had a chance to collect her wits. She was caught with one hand on the library wall and the other on the banister, straightening up.

"What the hell?" Bensen Everhart glared at her.

"Who's this?" asked Ray Dunbar, a tall loose-limbed man. Jesse's eyes took in the sweep of light brown hair across his forehead and the keen gray eyes that were assessing her with surprised curiosity. "Who are you?"

"This," gritted Bensen, "is Miss Jessamine Smith-Jones. Unleashed on my doorstep by my grandmother! It seems I can't turn around without stepping on you, Miss Smith-Jones."

"I wasn't doing what you think I was doing!" Jesse snapped back at him, stung. Ray Dunbar looked interestedly from one to the other. "As a matter of fact, I was talking to Shanna."

"Oh? Crouched on the stairs when there's an abundance of chairs in the house? And I don't see any evidence of Shanna!"

Jesse gave Bensen a baleful look. She turned to the other man, inquisitively eyeing him up and down. He had a nice full mustache and a short neatly trimmed beard.

"You must be Ray Dunbar." She smiled warmly at him then, and a sudden burst of mischief lurked at the corners of her wide red mouth. "This area's forest ranger—I've heard about you!" Bensen shot her a sharp questioning glance. "I'm very pleased to meet you." Jesse held out her hand, and Ray Dunbar graciously gave it a firm handshake.

"Likewise."

"If you were hoping to get some spicy information for your book, forget it. I have a dislike for people who listen at keyholes." Bensen's thick brows were gathered together like storm clouds as he surveyed her. Abruptly he turned to Ray. "I take it we're finished?" It was a curt dismissal.

Jesse saw the tightening of Ray's square jaw as he replied vigorously, "Yes, for the time being." The forest ranger bowed his head slightly to Jesse and smiled at her. "It was a pleasure meeting you, Jesse. I hope we'll meet here again." With a hard angry look at Bensen he strode off down the hall to the French-door entrance.

Jesse heard Bensen mutter to himself, "You won't meet her here again, not if I can help it!" before he arrogantly slammed the library door shut in her face.

Staring at that closed door, Jesse thought Bensen deserved a telling kick in the pants—and she would dearly love to administer it!

CHAPTER THREE

"I'D RATHER GO by boat," Jesse protested. "The *Shaman*—"

"Nonsense!" Mrs. Everhart waved her hand dismissingly. "Bensen has the car, and there's no reason not to go with him. Not when you're both going to Vancouver at the same time. Besides," she added almost teasingly, "it'll give you a chance to get to know each other." Suddenly she seemed sad. "Do you really have to go now? I've become rather attached to you. I'm afraid you won't come back."

"If you really want me back, then I'll be back," Jesse promised with a gentle smile. She, too, had become rather attached to the feisty old woman. "But I do have to go." She nibbled on her bottom lip consideringly. She did have to collect her mail—she was expecting news on her last mystery novel and another royalty check. Plus she had banking business to see to; had to give her car a run, for it didn't like to sit too long; and had to check on her apartment, which she'd lent to a friend of a friend as a favor. "But I *really* don't want—"

"If it's because you think you can't get along with Bensen for seventy-odd miles and two long ferry rides," Mrs. Everhart interrupted, "don't bother your head about it. The twins are going, as well—to see their dentist and doctor. So you'll have plenty of company!"

Jesse couldn't quite keep the relief out of her voice. "Oh, in that case...." She excused herself and went to see why Shanna wouldn't be accompanying them.

"I'd love to the next time," Shanna told Jesse. "It would be great fun going with you! Bensen never has the time to take me anywhere. Whenever I travel to Vancouver with him, I spend most of my time in the hotel room. I've only been a couple of times, and I'm a little nervous about venturing out alone, you see. I'm not used to cities and—and what to do. But really I can't go this time. Ray is coming, and with Bensen gone I'll have the chance to...to...."

"Say no more." Jesse was smiling widely now. "You don't get to see him very often, do you?"

"No. I hope Bensen doesn't make your trip miserable. He hardly talks at all, you know."

"I don't know *what* he has against me."

"You stand up to him all the time. He's not used to that."

THE TWINS were ecstatic Jesse was coming with them. During the daylong trip to Vancouver they chattered endlessly to her, but to their uncle they seldom addressed a word. Jesse couldn't help but wonder at this.

Other than, "The washrooms are around there," or, "Do you want milk or orange juice?" Bensen expressed no interest in their existence. He expressed even less in Jesse's, but she didn't mind that at all. Somewhat stiffly she shared the front seat of the Mercedes with him, while the twins sat in the back, their natural exuberance dampened by their uncle's presence.

Bensen seemed oblivious to the effect he was creating, yet whenever his black eyes flickered in Jesse's direction, their usual indifference held a touch of mockery. Jesse found the whole situation slightly uncomfortable. It was all she could do to cloak her uneasiness in his company with an unruffled exterior. Not a nervous person, Jesse found her nerves were fluttering wildly every time he did happen to say something to her—which was silly, for his few remarks were of the most impersonal sort. However, she had agreed to this trip, and she wasn't going to allow Bensen to spoil it.

Late that afternoon the big black Mercedes, plain except for gleaming chrome trim, swept up before the Four Seasons Hotel in downtown Vancouver. Attendants were whisking away the newcomers' luggage before Jesse had a chance to realize her valise was gone.

As she said goodbye to the twins, they gazed at her reproachfully with tremulously pouting lips. She couldn't even coax a simple farewell out of them on the assurance that she would soon be seeing them again. Their candid eyes told her they thought she was deserting them, and Jesse sighed with a combination of exasperation, helplessness and pity. She didn't want to leave them with their forbidding uncle, either, and briefly toyed with the idea of tak-

ing them home with her. If Betty what's-her-name
was ready to give up her apartment, she thought,
there would be room for them both. Jesse was beginning to wish she hadn't lent her apartment. Not
wanting to raise the twins' hopes unnecessarily, she
figured the best thing to do would be to go home first
and see what could be done. She could always come
back later to collect the children. Her mind made up
now, she stepped to the curb to hail a taxicab.

"Where are you going?"

Jesse gasped at Bensen's imperious tone. "I'm going home," she returned hotly. "To my apartment.
Where do you think I'm going?"

"Haven't you lent it? It would be rude just to walk
in on the new occupant, don't you think? Telephone
first. I'll drive you over after. Sam, Merit, come
along now."

And with one firm relentless hand on her elbow he
shepherded her and the twins into the hotel. Jesse
was flabbergasted by his cool assumption of com-
mand. She wasn't used to being ordered around—by
anyone! However, there was some common sense in
what he'd said, so she submitted, inwardly fuming.

With a minimum of ado Bensen escorted the trio to
the twenty-seventh floor, where the Everhart firm
permanently maintained a suite of rooms. Bensen's
office complex was in Vancouver, and it appeared
that the hotel staff had a healthy respect for their
regular visitor. He was met with instant recognition,
while Jesse was treated to a great deal of furtive
curiosity. This only served to annoy her further. Did
they think she was one of his lady friends?

Once in the elegant luxurious suite, which held many personal touches, among them some good pieces of Canadian art, Jesse went straight to the telephone, knowing where it was from her earlier visit with Cecilia Anne. The line was busy, and she hung up, eyeing the twins in amusement. They had rushed to the spacious windows and were pressing against the glass as they excitedly peered down at the busy glittering rush of cars and pedestrians twenty-seven floors below.

Bensen shrugged off his suit jacket, slung it carelessly over the arm of a blue velvet chair and flexed his shoulders. Jesse, watching him through the mirror, swallowed convulsively. For some reason the huge hotel suite didn't seem large enough for the two of them. Although she was tall, Bensen always seemed to tower over her, and as her eyes skimmed the breadth of his powerful shoulders, a shiver inexplicably ran down her spine. He certainly wasn't magazine-type handsome, Jesse thought to herself, but his virile masculinity and aura of raw elemental energy were at times overwhelming. She wondered if Dorothy thought so, too. No doubt she did. Was that the reason she put up with him?

As Jesse peeped at him through a wing of her chestnut hair, still covertly using the mirror, she watched him pick up an extension and dial room service. He asked for two glasses of milk and a pot of coffee with *two* cups. That pleased her, though at the moment she couldn't think why.

When Jesse finally got through to Betty, she wished she'd taken a phone in another room for more privacy. A problem had arisen. Betty, the girl she'd lent her apartment to, explained that her mother and two younger sisters were visiting. Jesse couldn't understand how they all fit into her small one-bedroom apartment, but there certainly wouldn't be room for her, as well.

Patiently she listened to Betty and continued to watch Bensen through the mirror. He'd sat down at a wide oak desk by the windows, had opened his brief-case and was already poring intently through a sheaf of official-looking papers. The smoke from his thin cigar swirled up over his dark leonine head.

Feeling distracted, Jesse inquired whether she could at least drop by that evening. Betty apologet-ically replied that as her mother and sisters were in town, she was hosting a small family reunion that night—in Jesse's apartment. Jesse now began to worry seriously about her apartment. Bensen didn't appear to be listening, so quietly Jesse made arrange-ments to visit Betty the following morning. As she replaced the receiver, she decided to use a phone in one of the bedrooms. Surely one of her friends could put her up for a single night, she thought. Gathering her purse, she headed in that direction, but before she'd taken more than two steps, Bensen was looking at her questioningly.

"And what's the plan now?" he queried, obvious-ly fully aware of the problem.

A flash of irritation seared through Jesse, but she replied mildly enough, "I'm going to stay at a friend's place. I have several who have extra room."

"There's room to spare here," Bensen stated, his

dark gaze resting on her face. "No need to bother your friends."

"But—"

"Oh, Jesse, Jesse, *please* do! Oh, say you will!" the twins cried, rushing away from the windows and hopping around her, their uplifted faces eager and pleading.

"Quiet!" Bensen commanded. "It's Jesse's decision." One corner of his mouth lifted in mirthless cold sarcasm as he continued to eye her. "With you here I won't have to provide a baby-sitter." His voice was indifferent as his gaze left her to drop back to his papers. "Sam, Merit, you show Jesse the sleeping arrangements. We don't want her to feel her privacy will be threatened if she does decide to stay."

The twins, of course, missed the implications of his last words, but Jesse did not. Intense irritation once more prickled along her spine. She glared at him. The twins had danced off ahead, calling excitedly for her to follow. Jesse still hesitated.

"I think it would be best if—"

Bensen was staring at her now. One brow arched a fraction. "No need to fear for your virtue...you're not my type," he said softly, the jet eyes narrow as they slid over her.

"How reassuring!" Jesse flashed. "Spoken like a true gentleman!"

"I told you once," he shot back, "I'm no gentleman."

"I believe I'm fully aware of that. You're not my type, either, but *that's* not what I was concerned about." Her creamy almond skin was flushed, and the sherry eyes sparkled with angry golden light.

Sighing, Bensen gathered up his papers and impatiently began drumming his fingers against the desk. "Then what *are* you so concerned about?"

"Not about us, about other people. You have your reputation to think of, as well as Dorothy and the twins to consider. Malicious gossip isn't fun."

"I've weathered worse gossip than this is likely to provoke. And I didn't think you cared a great lot about other people's opinions."

"I don't, but—"

"And I don't, either. Besides, the twins get under my skin when they mope, and you know very well they'll start moping the second you walk out that door. So it's settled." His tone was adamant.

"Fine!" Jesse gritted her teeth and started after the twins.

"They've taken a great liking to you," he continued, talking to her back, and just as she left the room, she heard him mutter, "although I *can't* imagine why."

There were two bedrooms besides the twins', and Jesse chose the one they said Shanna used. The maid had already unpacked her valise, and her two pairs of shoes stood by the foot of the bed, polished and shiny. With one twin tugging on each arm, Jesse was shown where everything was and was importantly informed that uncle's bedroom was on the other side of the sitting room. That made her feel somewhat easier. The farther away, the better!

"JACOB'S AWFULLY NICE!" Merit enthused to Jesse the next morning as they all sat in the restaurant, breakfasting.

"I thought he was funny." Samantha picked up the subject. "I like funny men. He laughs a lot. He made you laugh, didn't he, Jesse?"

"Yes, sweetheart, he did. But don't put such a big piece of pancake in your mouth all at once like that, Sam; you might choke on it."

"And who is Jacob?" Bensen queried. It was the first contribution he'd made to the conversation that bubbled around him as the twins relived the night they'd spent with Jesse and her friend.

"Is he your boyfriend, Jesse?" Merit asked. "He's handsome enough to be your boyfriend!"

"He's a very good friend of mine; I've known him for years, but no, he's not my boyfriend," Jesse answered both questions at once. Then to Bensen she said, "Jacob and I took the twins to see a movie last night, and then we went for dinner. We were all hungry again afterward. They were up past their usual bedtime, but they were too excited to sleep anyway, so I didn't think it would matter." Bensen merely nodded disinterestedly, and that made Jesse frown for a moment.

"Is he the one who has the music store, or is he the carpenter?" Samantha asked.

"He's the one who owns the music store, Sam, and it wasn't a carpenter; it was a cabinet maker, and that's someone else."

"What's his name? Is *he* your boyfriend? He called you twice last night, didn't he?"

Jesse's cheeks grew a little pink under Bensen's sudden regard. She wished for once she could know what was going on in his mind by looking into his eyes. Usually eyes were so telling—but definitely not with him.

"You seem to be very popular," he commented dryly.

"Is he your boyfriend? Is he?" prompted Samantha. "You're awfully pretty, Jesse. You've *got* to have a boyfriend! Can we meet him?"

"She's probably got two or three," Merit put in, making Jesse feel even more uncomfortable. "We won't have time to meet them all, Sam; we're going back this afternoon."

"Quiet, girls!" Bensen said sternly. "There's no need for the whole restaurant to learn the ins and outs of Jesse's busy love life. Furthermore, mind your manners and don't pry. If Jesse wants to tell you who her boyfriend—or *boyfriends*—are, she'll tell you."

He looked at her with a kind of grim amusement, and since Jesse's head was down, she missed the glimmer of curiosity that had entered the jet black eyes. "Don't dawdle, Sam, eat up! Your appointment is in thirty-five minutes. Merit, use your napkin, not your hand. You eat well enough at home; why can't you here?"

"They're just excited, Bensen." Jesse didn't think he had to sound so stern and condemning. He made the two little girls nervous; he was so large and dark and forceful that he made *her* nervous! She swallowed when he met her eyes.

"When I want your opinion, I'll ask for it." The words lashed out with quiet yet heated impact.

"*I'm* the baby-sitter, not you, so don't tell me how to handle them!" Jesse replied in precisely the same manner, suddenly furious. "They behaved themselves perfectly last night, but with you around they get nervous. And it's no wonder, the way you snap and growl. Cecilia Anne was right when she said you act like an angry bear!"

The twins' mouths dropped open in shock. Owl-eyed, they stared at their uncle to see what his reaction would be. Jesse was sorry now she'd lost her temper, but he was so rude at times.

Bensen was glaring stonily at her. "It's not a very good idea to argue in front of children." His low voice was taut and accusing.

"Would you like to argue over there?" Jesse retorted, nodding her head toward the restaurant entrance.

The black eyes glittered into hers, and it took all of Jesse's considerable willpower to keep her gaze steady and unrelenting.

"More coffee here?" The cheery voice of the waitress broke in upon them.

After breakfast Bensen drove the twins to the complex that housed their doctor's and dentist's offices, where he gave them precise instructions on what to do and where to wait for Jesse when they had finished. His tone with them now was tempered by a finely controlled mildness that Jesse knew he didn't feel—something the twins also seemed to sense. They scampered off quickly, glad to be away from him.

Jesse and Bensen continued on alone to her apartment. She knew he was driving her home not to be helpful but to check up on her, to see what part of town she lived in and what her life-style was like. This irritated her, too, for he could have found out by asking her. But, she told herself, he probably wouldn't have given her the benefit of the doubt, even if she had told the truth. He seemed to have an incredibly low opinion of her, and she couldn't imagine what she'd done to deserve it.

Like the twins, she was glad to escape his company and made no effort to hide her relief when he dropped her off. He, of course, noted it and gave silent reply with a mockingly derisive smile—which almost sent her temper skyrocketing again.

The rest of Jesse's morning was spent carrying out her various business errands. To her amazement her apartment was in fine shape, despite its many occupants. Betty apologized again for the inconvenience her visitors had caused, but when Jesse saw that her many plants were still thriving and well watered, she told Betty not to give it another thought. Whenever Jesse went away for any length of time, she had to hire a plant-sitter, and some of them were none too conscientious. And she couldn't complain about anything else; her apartment, with all its foliage, its gold rattan furniture and jungle-hued cushions, curtains and carpet, was clean and tidy. Basically it was just as she'd left it.

At eleven-thirty sharp Jesse collected the twins and congratulated them mightily on their good reports from the dentist. They had a clean bill of health from their yearly doctor's examination, as could be expected, and Jesse stowed away both doctors' comments in her purse to give to Shanna.

As they had an hour to spare before meeting Bensen for lunch, Jesse took them on a drive around the scenic shoreline, happy to show them the beautiful city that was her home. They were crowded in the front seat with her, sitting on the very edge, their hands grasping the dashboard and their heads spinning from side to side in a vain effort to see everything at once. They'd never ridden in a convertible, and they were ecstatic.

Jesse was surprised and a little dismayed at the many things the twins had never done before. The outdoor life they led at home was definitely good for them, but she wondered whether raising them in so sheltered a manner was equally good. Shanna had led a distinctly sheltered life; she knew no other. But Bensen knew. Still, he had no time and, seemingly, no interest. The poor darlings, Jesse suddenly thought, have never even been to a zoo!

They met Bensen at his office as planned, and soon they were sitting in an outdoor restaurant in Stanley Park. Large bright umbrellas shaded them from the fierce heat of the late-June sun, and their view was of English Bay. Freighters lay peacefully at anchor, waiting their turn in the shipping docks, and sailboats, their multicolored sails bellying full, flirted between their mammoth cousins. They skimmed over the gently rippling sky-blue waters, tacking into the wind so that it looked as if they might topple right over into the sea. Jesse sighed with exquisite satisfaction. Bensen ate in brooding silence as she pointed out the beacon at Lighthouse Park to the twins, showed them where they'd driven along Spanish Banks just half an hour ago and named the circling ring of mountains to the north—flat-topped Holly-burn and the sharp twin peaks of the Lions and Grouse, whose ski runs lighted up every night to resemble a large glittering bow tie high above the city.

"Way, way up there," Jesse pointed, "there's a restaurant called the Grouse Nest. You have to take the ski lift to get up there, but once you're there, you can see all the way to White Rock and the States on a clear day. Would you like to go with me sometime?" The twins sputtered in their eagerness to agree. Jesse felt Bensen's quick glance in her direction, yet she didn't look at him. She preferred to pretend he was not there at all.

Then, deciding to gamble, she looked down at her crab Louis salad and said casually, "The zoo's not far from here. Perhaps we should go there after lunch before heading home."

Her words had an electric effect on the twins. All their activity stopped; they didn't so much as move a muscle. Jesse slowly looked up from her salad into Bensen's frigid coal-black eyes.

"There's no time today," he stated bluntly.

The twins' disappointment had an almost physical effect on Jesse. She could feel their hurt, and it prod-ded her on. "Girls, if you're finished eating, why don't you run to that telescope over there and take a look at the ships. Here are some dimes. You drop them in the slot, then you'll hear a click. That means you can turn the telescope in whatever direction you want and the eyepiece will open. Now don't fight over who goes first.''

"There isn't time," Bensen repeated once the children were safely out of earshot. His harsh voice grated on Jesse's ears.

"If there's no time today," she challenged, feeling brave, "when is there going to be time?"

"I'm a very busy man, Miss—"

"Oh, cut the miss business! It would take about an hour. Is your time so precious that you can't give even one hour of it to the twins? They're your nieces, your *family*!" Well, she'd put her foot into it now!

"My sense of family responsibility happens to be very strong. I'm the one who makes sure they're all provided for!"

"I hate to rehash an old, proverb, but, 'Man doesn't live by bread alone.' Don't you care at all for their happiness? Don't you *want* them to be happy? They're children, for heaven's sake! They're only nine years old! Just because you had such an unhappy childhood is no reason to make them unhappy."

"It's Shanna's duty to see they are happy, not mine."

Bensen's cold brittle tone warned her not to continue, but Jesse was in too deep now to let go. She pressed on, her voice urgent and appealing. "It's not a duty to make someone happy; it's a pleasure. You're their father image. Are they to think all men are like you? Where are your *feelings*? Can't you forget business for one hour?"

"You're trespassing into what doesn't concern you! I told you before not to interfere!" he gritted.

"I know, but. . . they look up to you. And your responsibility to them as head of the family is not only to see that they have enough food to eat. They need warmth from you, compassion, understanding. And yes, love!"

"Love is a highly overrated commodity as far as I'm concerned. Now if you're quite finished with your missionary work. . . ."

"You're impossible! You're as stubborn as an ox, and you have blinkers on just like a horse!"

"A bear, an ox and a horse! What next?" Had he not been so angry, it would have been funny.

"The zoo—that's what's next! And you should try some missionary work yourself. Be a little charitable for a change!" She had striven to remain cool but was by now totally lost to the heat building inside.

"I give to a great many charities, most of which are undeserving."

"Yes, you give, and you give money. But none of yourself—none of your stupendously precious time!"

"Will you keep your voice down? For the last time, *no zoo*! And keep your busybodying nose out of my affairs! I tolerate you, that's *all*, Jesse."

"Oh, you make me so mad I could cry!" And she looked like she just might start. The wide-spaced sherry eyes were filling with furious tears. She couldn't help it.

"For heaven's sake!" he groaned, dropping his forehead into his palm. A shaft of sunlight slanting down through the umbrellas fell over his head, and in the intense light the thick black hair shone blue. Jesse stared at him.

"Please, Bensen, please?" she appealed, not knowing how alluring she sounded. "Only an hour. They think you don't like them. Please, Bensen, let's go to the zoo." She was reduced to begging—something she'd never thought she'd do with him.

"And I'm stubborn? *I'm* stubborn! I've never met anyone like you before!"

"Don't spoil their trip for them this way. They've had such a good time till now." Jesse's voice was as soft as the touch of a rose petal against a cheek. "They've been so good; they've behaved like angels. Please, Bensen?"

He looked at her, exasperated to the end of his endurance.

"All right!" he growled. "To the zoo we go." That was added so ferociously that several of their fellow diners looked up in alarm.

Jesse bit hard into her bottom lip to stop the smile of marvel from spreading. She didn't want to push her luck. Her eyes, though, were shining with such radiance that Bensen looked away, thoroughly disgruntled.

"Well, come on, then," he snapped. "If we're going, let's go!"

"Yes, Bensen," Jesse murmured meekly, gathering her purse. She stood up, slim and elegant in her cool green silk dress. When one of their fellow male diners gazed appreciatively in her direction, Bensen glared at him, too.

"Sam, Merit!" Jesse called to them with such a happy lilt in her voice that Bensen shot her an intent perplexed glance.

"Yes, girls, *do* come along," he drawled, his gaze again traveling over Jesse's face. In the sunlight her eyes appeared more gold than brown, and he stared, a half frown running a line in his forehead. Shoving his hands into his pockets, he added, his tone as dry as three-day-old toast, "We're going to the zoo."

Within seconds Samantha and Merit were at his side, and Bensen found himself surrounded by three beaming females. He looked down into the twins' eager eyes, into their silent smiles of delight. The black eyes flashed again to Jesse, and then he cleared his throat. "Shall we go?" In an aside he muttered to her, "You're downright weird!" as if he couldn't think of any other adjective to describe her.

Jesse was too happy to be offended. She choked back the giggle his comment had provoked and said, "You should try it sometime. It's fun being weird."

Samantha and Merit were about ten paces ahead of them. Bensen sauntered alongside, his hands reposing in his suit pockets, his tie pulled loose and the collar of his shirt open. The deeply tanned face was impassive, but a trace of irritated boredom lingered in the dark eyes. Jesse felt he was towering over her again as she stole a glimpse at the aloof face above her head. He didn't seem quite relaxed. She thought he seemed a bit like a big black cat, slightly stiff in unfamiliar surroundings. Instantly she wondered what he would think if she dared add panther to her list. The thought tugged her lips into a rueful smile.

A crowd of people thronged the zoo, as much a sight as the exotic animals. Peacocks raucously screeched from the lower branches of trees; seals honked and squealed, and a mighty splash came from the aquarium, where the huge white beluga whale was putting on a show. Farther up the tree-shaded path monkeys jabbered and howled. There were baby strollers by the score, and tribes of happy chocolate-and-ice cream-cheeked children shouting to their friends and dashing about. There were fat people and thin people, young lovers and tourists with cameras banging against their stomachs.

Just ahead of Jesse and the Everharts a popcorn vendor sang out his wares, and behind them an ice-cream man on his three-wheeled bike jingled his bell. Two teenagers on roller skates executed daredevil stunts, swirling by on either side of Bensen and Jesse. Bensen stopped by the popcorn vendor.

"Do you care for this stuff?" he asked her, being determinedly pleasant.

"I couldn't eat another thing, Bensen."

"And I suppose you two have plenty of room left," he remarked dryly to the twins. A moment later he deposited large butter-stained bags into their sticky fingers. "Don't you *dare* get sick!"

Bensen was nothing if not thorough. The twins saw every part of the zoo there was to see, and it took a lot longer than an hour. They visited every single animal; Bensen was leaving none out. He even made sure his nieces read the inscriptions posted along the way, saying to Jesse, "They might as well learn something while they're here." They fed the squirrels that ran right up their legs and the geese that crowded around them, snapping the food bits out of their fingers.

Peanuts, licorice, ice-cream bars, potato chips, popcorn and more disappeared into Samantha and Merit at an astonishing rate, considering they'd just had a hearty lunch. They were consuming hot dogs from which mustard and relish dripped when they at last reached the polar-bears' quarters.

The bears yawned and stretched and lolled in the sun. One swatted at a bluebottle fly, his ponderous paw slowly sweeping the air. Another opened one eye to peer at the crowd, then settled down to sleep again.

"It's a crime to lock these animals up!" Bensen commented.

"Well, yes, it is," Jesse agreed, her eyes going up to his face. "But if they're born in the zoo, it's not so bad for them. It is a meager life, but...I don't think they're unhappy."

"Is it necessary for everyone and everything to be so damn happy around you?" Bensen demanded, his answering look sharply sardonic. He obviously didn't expect her to respond, for he turned away and stared implacably at the polar bears. Jesse tugged at his sleeve.

"Bensen, why don't you try to relax? Unbend a little and you might have a good time. You work so hard, and for so long you've done nothing else, maybe you've forgotten having fun can be fun."

"This isn't my idea of fun!"

"Then what is?"

He frowned at her but didn't answer, his lips curling impatiently.

They headed for the penguins next. There were only the monkeys to see after that, and then the zoo's sights would be exhausted. Bensen looked around on the way to the penguins, finally saying, "What? No ox?"

Jesse laughed involuntarily, and when her eyes flew to his face, there was a faint cast of a smile on his lips. Her heart turned a complete somersault. She answered impudently, "There's one fine example here; there's no need for more." When he took her arm to steer her clear of a baby stroller, his grip was tighter than necessary, but Jesse didn't mind. Again she glanced up at him. Their eyes met and held for a moment, then both of them quickly looked away.

The monkeys in their cages were quiet, preening and cleaning one another or languorously nibbling on apples and bananas. When Jesse explained to the twins that they could be induced to "talk," they didn't believe her, so she cupped her hands around her mouth and mimicked their high-pitched call. Bensen shook his head, fleetingly cast his eyes skyward and sighed.

An elderly gentleman on the other side of the large cage repeated what Jesse had just done. With her encouragement the twins tried. Some of the monkeys sat up and took notice. One began chattering excitedly from its perch, then zigzagged throughout the cage in huge crazy leaps and swings. Two others began the howl, and then one by one they all joined in, until the area rang with their cries. Beside themselves with this novelty, the twins clapped and howled back again and again. "How-ha...who-ha...oow...hhow-hhaaa!" Jesse averted her face so that Bensen wouldn't see her laughing.

That was the final perfect touch to the twins' day, the maraschino cherry on top of the ice-cream sundae. After that they were content to be led to the car, where they collapsed on the back seat, stuffed full of goodies and quite a lot dirtier than when they'd started out that morning.

With a satisfied look at them over her shoulder, Jesse sank gratefully into the soft cool car seat. She closed her eyes and murmured sweetly, "Thank you, Bensen!"

He grunted an indistinguishable reply.

Back at the hotel Jesse deposited both the twins in the bathtub in their room and then took a quick cool shower herself in her own bathroom. She dressed in narrow cream slacks and a vivid blue blouse for the return trip, finally deciding to wear her high-heeled sandals. With Bensen around, she reasoned, it couldn't hurt to be a few inches taller. She hurried the twins on, not wanting to stretch Bensen's good temper any longer than necessary, and in haste packed their things and her own.

"I've left the clothes you're to wear on your bed," she called to them, walking toward the sitting room to check for left-behind possessions. She was trying to fix the catch of her blouse at the back of her neck, but her long hair kept snagging on the hook. "No fooling around, girls, hustle now!" she called again when she heard their giggles.

Bensen had just put down the telephone receiver. "I've ordered some coffee," he announced to Jesse. "I take it you could use a cup?" Briefly his eyes ran down her slender figure in the fitted cream slacks and the loose brilliantly colored blouse, which she was still trying to close. He gathered a stack of papers from the desk and allowed his eyes to travel over her again before slipping the papers into his briefcase. Then he checked the desk drawers and locked some of them. When he returned to Jesse, she was still working on the catch, her survey of the room complete.

"Here, let me help," he sighed.

"Oh, thank you, Bensen." Jesse swept aside her mane of chestnut hair and turned her back to him. "I don't know why they always make the hooks so small!"

"Your coffee, sir! Ohhh! *Ex-cuse* me!"

The waiter stood in the open door, gaping at the scene. "You said not to knock, Mr. Everhart. You said to hurry. I'm *so* sorry! I had no idea—I mean...." He was embarrassed, but there was a sly smirk beginning to appear on his mouth.

"Just put down the coffee!" Bensen ordered curtly, his hands settling on Jesse's shoulders and holding her stationary. For a second his fingers flexed against her skin, burning warm through the blouse...then his hands dropped.

Jesse quickly stepped away from Bensen, and her hair slid back into place. She frowned at the waiter, who mistook the meaning of her expression and grinned knowingly, trying to cover his embarrassment.

As Bensen slipped some bills into the man's hand, he said obsequiously, "I hope you've enjoyed your stay, sir!" He shot another look of male admiration in Jesse's direction.

"That will be all, thank you!" she snapped at him, beginning to blush deeply. She'd known all along something like this was bound to happen. How stupid when there wasn't even the remotest possibility that...that...the door closed behind him.

Bensen was eyeing her keenly. "Drink your coffee, Jesse," he said in a tone of voice quite kindly for him.

The twins regarded their uncle with a great deal more approval on their way home than they had done earlier in their journey. The afternoon rush hour was just beginning as they threaded their way through the traffic and the bottleneck of Lions Gate Bridge, leaving downtown for the drive through West Vancouver. By the time they'd reached Lighthouse Park and then the town of Horseshoe Bay, cupped in the mountains, the traffic had thinned. Bensen slid the car out of it, heading toward the ferry-parking quay. A ten-minute wait stretched ahead for the ferry to Gibson's Landing.

"And what does *line* mean?" Jesse wanted to find out a bit about logging while she had the opportunity—and while Bensen was still talking to her. "I remember reading something about lines when I... when I was typing those papers for you. Are they sections in the bush?"

"They're small side roads that lead off the main logging road, and they're identified by numbers,"

Bensen replied readily enough. "We clear all our own roads when we go into an area, and each road is carefully plotted and mapped out beforehand to provide maximum efficiency. It's an expensive business, building roads. First we log all the trees that stand in the path of the new road, then continue from there." His expression was vaguely amused as he answered her questions, but Jesse didn't care and pressed on.

"What do you do about the stumps?"

"Small ones a bulldozer can handle. Now knuckle-heads—"

"What's a *knucklehead*, Uncle Ben?" Samantha queried from the back seat. "Is that one of the loggers?"

A grin appeared on his mouth and vanished.

"Well, that's what I think sometimes, but no, Sam, a knucklehead is a tree stump that's so large it has to be blasted out with powder." He paused, and Jesse was wondering what to ask next when he continued, "Every time we cross a stream, the fisheries and forestry department force us to build a bridge so that our activities won't interfere with the salmon spawning and the wildlife. We can't even fell a tree into a stream, and that means leaving some of the best trees behind. Every little dribble of water has to be left inviolate—which can be quite a nuisance. We also have to make sure that any debris dropped into a stream is cleared out immediately—branches bark, twigs, every little thing—or the rangers close us down."

"You mean someone like Ray Dunbar keeps track

of all those things and is constantly checking up on you?'' Jesse asked.

"Every minute of the day. I sometimes think he has eyes in the back of his head. Thankfully he's got a bit of sense—some of the kids they send out here straight from school are so holy they're unbelievable!''

"Well, I don't suppose you're ever likely to see eye to eye. You're on opposite sides of the fence.''

"We're not really. It's in a logger's best interest not to destroy the forest or land from which he makes his living. It's just that some of them see us as the enemy and cost us an incredible amount of time. Of course, you do get loggers who don't give a damn. Generally they don't last too long, though. In our area Ray makes sure of that.''

Jesse found she was tentatively enjoying this first real conversation with Bensen. She made a mental note that they weren't likely to argue if they were talking about logging. If only she knew more about it. . . .

"Girls, look over there!'' Bensen instructed. "See that? I believe that's one of our log booms.''

In the waters of Howe Sound, coming slowly into view, was an immense number of logs bobbing compactly together in the waves, their girths and lengths enormous. A ring of logs chained around the outside kept them all together. Sam and Merit were glued to the car window, and even Jesse, who had seen log booms many times by the Vancouver shoreline, leaned over a little toward Bensen to look out.

"It always amazes me that one little tugboat can

pull all those logs!'' she exclaimed, sinking back into her seat when he turned his head to glance at her.

"One tug can pull ten of those booms," Bensen explained, his eyes running over her face carefully, as though something other than logs had just occurred to him.

"Where are they going?" Merit asked. Jesse was glad his attention was diverted. She licked her lips and smoothed her hair, wondering if she looked all right.

"They're not going far. They're loaded right onto a ship from the water. It's called a barge, although it's really a ship because it has its own motor. There's a crane on the barge that scoops them up. To unload, the barge is tilted to one side by means of air ballasts, and the logs slide off."

Surprisingly, Bensen patiently explained to the twins how air ballasts worked. They were absorbed in what he had to tell them, and he explained it so simply and clearly that they understood at once.

"What a neat trick!" Samantha exclaimed when he was finished. Her uncle flashed her a quick smile. Seeing it, Jesse thought it a pity he didn't smile more often. He looked almost. . .hastily she pushed the unexpected thought away, turning her head to avoid Bensen's gaze.

"It works very well," Bensen agreed gravely, eyeing Jesse's averted profile.

By the time the first ferry trip was over, Samantha and Merit were asleep. Jesse and Bensen continued a desultory conversation, mostly about logs and related matters, each of them studiously polite lest they inadvertently step on the other's toes. And although Bensen didn't say so in actual words, Jesse had the impression that he'd come to terms with her stay at Clifftop. He wouldn't make her welcome, but neither would he push her out the door. Which was good, for there were many more journals she'd yet to study.

Joyously Shanna hugged the twins, crouching so that she could get an arm around each.

"Oh, mummy, mummy, we had a wonderful time!"

"We went to the *zoo*, mummy!"

"You *what*?" Shanna stared at them in disbelief and looked anxiously at Jesse.

"Yes, mummy, we did, really!"

"Uncle Ben and Jesse took us to the zoo!"

"He did?" Shanna echoed in amazement and bewilderment.

"Yes, Shanna, it's true." Bensen said gruffly, "Strange, I know, but true." He cleared his throat and frowned slightly. "Hadn't they better be going to bed? They had a late night yesterday, too."

With another perplexed look at Bensen and an eyebrow-arched glance at Jesse, Shanna took the two little girls by the hand and prepared to lead them upstairs. The twins eagerly expounded on their trip, and the usually quiet, rather somber hallway was filled with their excited voices. All the noise brought their great-grandmother from the salon.

"Ahh! So you're back! You're late, aren't you? What are you two girls so chirpy about?"

And the story of the zoo and the movie and a million other things poured out of them—but in a more subdued way, for gramma was held in awe and with a great deal of respect for her sharp tongue. The slightly cold set to her face relaxed as she listened.

"Stop, stop!" she protested finally, chuckling and holding up her hands. "You can tell me the rest tomorrow, all right? Good heavens, I didn't realize that I missed you!" She patted both their dark heads and waved them imperiously off to bed with orders not to giggle all night long.

"I'm glad to see you're back, Jesse. I thought Bensen might have put you off so much that we'd never see your face again. Don't glare at me like that, Ben; you know very well what a foul temper you have."

"Hello, grandmother," he said wryly. He picked up his briefcase, leaving Jesse's valise on the floor, and went into the library, closing the door behind him.

"Well, my dear," Mrs. Everhart looked at Jesse from head to toe, "so you had the wherewithal to put up with him. Good show!" She actually laughed. "I thought you did, and I'm never wrong. Join me for a nightcap. It's been terribly quiet here the past two days. Could hardly get a word out of Shanna. And then she disappeared somewhere last night. Very curious. Wouldn't tell me where... said she went for a walk," Cecilia harrumphed. "I may be ninety-five, but I'm not stupid! So you and the girls dragged Bensen through the zoo, eh? I'm sorry I missed that. *Martha!* Where the devil is that lazy good-for-nothing? I could use a hot cup of coffee, and you're looking a little peaked. Bensen's doing, I suppose. We'll have some brandy if—*Martha!*''

THE NEXT DAY Mrs. Everhart slipped up to the attic to talk at some length, giving Jesse exactly the kind of information she needed. Jesse sat rapt, listening to her, and in the middle of the morning, when the twins came up to see her, they were as quiet as mice, wide-eyed in absorbed attention at the stories that fell from their great-grandmother's lips. Mrs. Everhart had a sharp memory for all her years, as well as an astringent wit, which made the bygone era sparkle with life. Shanna came up to talk to Jesse, and she, too, was caught in her grandmother's spell. In no time she was perched on a box, chin in hand, her eyes riveted on Cecilia Anne's aged face.

No one except Jesse seemed to hear the creaking of the attic stairs as Bensen came bounding up them, two at a time. Her heart beat rapidly as she wondered what she'd done this time. Bensen's explosive sigh of relief at seeing her took her completely by surprise. She looked from his face to the rotted piece of wood he held in his hands. What on earth was afoot? By this time his presence in the attic was marked by everyone, and he was commonly gaped at.

''I was walking around the house,'' he explained, breathing heavily, ''when this piece of wood came crashing down from that little balcony up here. Dammit Jesse, I thought you were fooling around on it!''

''I didn't even know there was a balcony from the attic,'' Jesse protested irritably. Did he always have to make her sound like a nitwit?

"Good thing, or you'd have been on it!" Bensen retorted, directing a shriveling glance her way. Jesse didn't bother to say he was probably right; instead she frowned mutinously at him.

He'd dropped the chunk of railing by Shanna's feet and was striding over to one of the narrow sets of windows. Two cumbersome packing crates blocked the tall panes, and Jesse was about to say he'd never be able to move them himself when he did.

She felt a slight choking sensation in her throat as she witnessed this effort, the muscles rippling along his back and arms. He could probably lift her right off the ground with one hand, thought Jesse, swallowing to ease the constriction that wouldn't go away. She struggled against a sudden sense of complete confusion, her eyes straying to the floor. When she looked back, Bensen had opened the windows and was cautiously testing the balcony.

"It's ready to go anytime," he stated, turning around. His eyes fell first on Jesse, and inexplicably she blushed. She could feel the color welling up in her face, could do nothing to stop it. His gaze narrowed on her, then swung to encompass everyone present.

"Nobody goes out there, do you hear me? *Nobody!*" To the twins he added grimly, "If I catch you so much as looking in this direction, I'll tan your hides, understand?" Frightened, they hastened to assure him they wouldn't, Shanna echoing their words.

"You don't have to tell me," grandmother snapped. "I hate balconies, especially at this height."

Bensen turned to Jesse, and she hastily said she wouldn't dare.

"You," he said to her, coming closer, "have to promise. I know what you're like! Now give me your word you won't do it just to thumb your nose at me."

Jesse's mouth, which had dropped open, shut. "What a thing to say! I'm not completely without sense, you know. All right, all right, I promise," she conceded when he took a threatening step her way. "Cross my heart." And she did so.

"I'll tan your hide, too, if I find you breaking your word." His black eyes stared her down, seemed to swallow her up into them.

"Just you try!" Jesse sputtered, furious at his overbearing tone, uneasy because of his menacing expression.

In a milder but mocking voice he returned, "It would be easy enough." His gaze whipped intimately down her slender feminine form. Jesse, remembering the way he'd moved those packing crates, wisely remained silent. Her eyes, though, flashed golden fire across the space. As Bensen watched her, one corner of his mouth slowly quirked in a real smile.

"I'll have Joe fix that as soon as he gets back," Bensen said over his shoulder, heading for the stairs, "but that won't be for a couple of weeks. By the way, Martha's wondering where everybody is. It's lunchtime." And he disappeared.

The afternoon passed more quietly than the morning had done. Jesse and grandmother continued alone through history. After about an hour Cecilia's monologue drifted into more personal matters concerning the family and the twists and turns the years had wrought.

Nathan Everhart, who had been Cecilia's father-in-law, had come to Canada in the 1860s, and his choice of free land had been the Everhart homestead on the British Columbia coast. There he'd based his dream of a logging empire, and there he'd married a beautiful Haida girl. During his lifetime the family business never reached the heights he'd aspired to, but his son, Samuel, inspired by the same vision, brought his father's dream into reality. Cecilia's memories of that happy period were especially vivid.

"We had four boys," she continued, a lingering sadness evident in her voice. "Four beautiful boys: Nat, Byron, Andy...and Percy. The Second World War stole the eldest three from me. They died, all of them, and I never saw them again. They were all so young. Younger than Bensen is now. Percy was the only one who didn't go. He didn't pass the medical examination. Nat, Byron and Andy—they were strong husky fellows; they looked just like their father...quite similar to Bensen, actually. Percy looked more like me. He had my small build, and nothing would fatten him up. And Lily, poor Lily! She and Andy were to have married as soon as the war was over. One by one the telegrams came. To this day I can't stand the sight of a telegram," she added bitterly.

"All I had left was Percy...and my Samuel. One day the woods foreman came into the house shouting...." She sighed very softly, then went on in a vigorous mode, "Damn that Samuel, he just wouldn't wear a hard hat! Said it was a newfangled thing and he was having no truck with it. They were felling a tree, and...and he...it...." For a moment she couldn't speak.

"They called it a widow maker," Cecilia said finally. "That's what the foreman called it. Never did find out exactly what that meant in bush language, for the meaning to me was clear enough. Oh, Jesse, my dear, the years haven't been kind. Don't fall in love with a man unless you can't help it. It's been more than thirty years, and I still miss him!" There was a catch in the old voice and a pause before she resumed.

"Then young Percy runs off and gets married to this flibbertigibbet society miss with nothing in her head but stars. I refused to go to the wedding. Neither of them had my blessing. And I was right, too. If Percy had been at home where he belonged, tending to business instead of flying from one gambling den to another, he'd be alive today. When I received that last telegram...I felt destroyed...for years. I wanted passionately to die, too. Everybody else had gone; why not me?

"I was barely aware that Bensen and Shanna were alive. Poor little tykes, I wonder what it must have been like for them.... As it turned out, I realized once I was back on my feet again that they were grown-up. Bensen had raised Shanna all by himself. Had done a pretty good job. But he was overprotective. Of course, she always was a shy quiet sort of girl. I remember Shanna's seventeenth birthday.... I sat down and had a talk with her. And do you know, she didn't have a clue about the wide world out there. She hardly knew what men were for. Of course I understood Bensen's difficulties in explaining... everything to her...."

Suddenly her tone became vehement. "It's Bensen's fault she eloped with that rat! He practically forced her into it because he was so bossy. He meant well; he tried hard. But he pushed *too* hard. I might add that Mr. Stu Lazzer's demise came as a welcome. That shocks you, does it? But if you could have seen Shanna after he was through with her...well! It's done now. When Shanna and the twins came back here to live, it woke me up a little. You can guess Bensen wasn't much company. Having those two little girls around started me living again, and...I don't know why, but lately things are looking up. I'm ninety-five, and I feel better now than I have for years!"

LATER THAT EVENING, after dinner, Jesse was on her way to the salon to join grandmother, Shanna and the twins when she noticed that the door to the library was open. On impulse she walked in and then, after a moment's hesitation, cautiously approached Bensen's den.

She was so quiet that at first he wasn't aware of her presence, and she had an opportunity to study him. He was working, of course, the dark head bent over lists of figures and pie-shaped graphs, a slim gold pen in his hand. The hand was long and lean and brown and looked very strong. The lowered profile was clearly etched by the flames in the fireplace behind him—the Everharts suffered no shortage of firewood or fireplaces, and Jesse had found she rather liked their tradition of lighting a fire in the evening. It was warm and cozy and suited the mansion. Now the bright flames illuminated the line of his broad forehead, the strong nose, the sensitive mouth and the firm jut of his chin.

He was wearing a simple plaid shirt, the cuffs rolled back and the neck open; over the powerful width of his shoulders the plaid pattern seemed to go on and on. His narrow denims were faded almost white in spots, with the side seams still a dark blue. He looked relaxed and at ease, at home in the room that, after she had had a quick look around, Jesse realized reflected his character.

There was the rich dark gleam of solid wood paneling, a spectacular British India rug that shouted with vibrant color. Everything possible was made of wood: the desk, the file cabinets, the bar, the bookshelves. But it was not just common furniture. The wood had been beautifully carved, its many different grains combined with unusual flair. The couches and chairs were large and casual. And here, too, Jesse saw the fineness of the art hanging on the walls. The lamps caught her eye—such delicate antique brass that they looked almost out of place in the masculine room. Yet somehow they fit perfectly, as if Bensen's precise, mathematical brain had worked out the exact finishing touch. The room seemed alive.

Jesse's eyes swung back to Bensen and the sinewy tapering length of his body. Her slow wishful sigh was barely audible, but he heard, and his head came up to see her in the doorway.

"What's a *widow maker*, Bensen?" Jesse asked, coming into the room. She had his complete attention now.

"It's a branch—a large one—that simply snaps off the trunk of a tree and comes straight down. Nobody knows why or how; it just happens. Dangerous as hell, too. More men have died that way. Why?"

"Grandmother was telling me about...your grandfather. She said that's how he died—because of a widow maker. She didn't know exactly what that was; she'd never wanted to find out."

Looking him full in the face, Jesse could see he was tired. Lines of weariness showed at the corners of the large black-lashed eyes and around the mouth. She knew he'd been out for most of the day and wondered where he'd been and what he'd done. Bensen pushed himself away from the desk and leaned against the high back of his chair.

"I'd heard that," he sighed. "She never talks about him. She talked to you?"

"Well...yes."

He frowned. "It seems you've wormed your way into her confidence in an admirable hurry. She won't discuss family matters with her own family, and yet she spills the beans to you, a complete stranger."

"You're mixing your metaphors!" Jesse snapped back. "And your grandmother and I have—well, we've sort of become friends, I suppose. What's wrong with that?" she added in fierce challenge.

His black eyes measured her. "I didn't know the

old besom had it in her to be friendly,'' he finally commented.

"If that's how you think of her, then it's no wonder you two don't get along, is it? It's hardly surprising she won't talk to you."

"Do you ever keep quiet, or is that mouth on spring hinges?"

Jesse put both hands on his desk, leaning toward him in angry emphasis. "You just can't stand being told anything, can you? Oh, you're so good at telling other people off, but when it's your turn, you don't like it. Well, that's good, because now you know how it feels. I suppose you're going to throw me out of the house now?"

He slapped both hands on the desk, too, and leaned over it so that their noses were mere inches apart. "It crossed my mind. Don't push me too far, Jessamine, or you might find yourself with more than you bargained for!"

"I'm made of sterner stuff than you imagine. I can be as tough as you. I learned how to handle bullies a long time ago, and you don't scare me."

"Want to see?"

The slight space between their angry faces was so charged that it seemed to crackle with electricity. When it seemed the tension couldn't be borne another second, Bensen suddenly grinned. The big broad smile burst across his face like a ray of sunlight. Jesse straightened up and moved away from him in alarmed surprise. What on earth was he up to now? She eyed him suspiciously—which provoked an even wider grin.

"Well, that got the adrenaline going," Bensen commented, his tone full of amusement. "Thanks, I was almost going to sleep over this work!" His wave encompassed the paper-strewn desk. He watched the anger draining from Jesse's face, from her body. "If I need waking up in the future, can I call you in for a little fight?"

She had to smile; she couldn't help it. Her smile, however, was a little reluctant. "We can always pick up where we've left off," she suggested.

"That suits me fine. It was just getting really interesting...." His voice had softened to a drawl, and his gaze held hers arrogantly. "Only time will tell how interesting. I'm tempted to find out right now...but I do have work to do."

"Should you be working this late?" The words seemed to just slip out.

"What?" His eyebrows shot up.

"I mean, would you like a—a cup of coffee or something? The twins are having cocoa, and I could...." Jesse's voice trailed away as a slow cynical lazy smile spread from one end of Bensen's mouth to the other. "Well, I just thought..." she said defensively. Self-conscious color stole into her face.

He eyed her pensively, stirring a disquiet in her that spread and spread. It seemed as if the blood in her veins had suddenly decided to reverse direction. She was about to turn on her heel and leave when he murmured, "I'd love a cup of coffee." The tone was sincere, yet it held a gentle mockery. Jesse turned back to see that he was still faintly smiling. "Martha's such a termagant I'm afraid to go into her kitchen, and her takeout service is none too good."

"She's doing something to the stove, I think," Jesse was striving to behave normally.

"She fixes things that work until they break. I might as well call the repairman right now. Always takes him at least a day to get here."

She grinned, "Call him right away!"

Jesse left to make a pot of coffee, aromatic and strong. While Martha grumpily watched, still fiddling with the stove elements, she poured brandy into five large glasses, added the coffee and then carefully scooped chocolate ice cream into each. Martha's eyes were growing bigger as Jesse grated squares of chocolate on top of that, finally putting the five appetizing frothing glasses on a salver. She left one on the stove for Martha, and with a cheery smile at the housekeeper's disconcerted face, she slipped through the kitchen's saloon doors. She left three more of the glasses in the salon, then took the last one to Bensen.

He gazed appreciatively at it when she placed it on his desk. Hardly waiting for a thank-you, Jesse left him alone with his work. In fact, she left in such haste that he stared after her quizzically, a little disappointed.

THE FOLLOWING DAY was as sunny and hot as the ones before—and as enticing. Jesse spent the morning in the attic on her fifth round of studying the family journals. But after lunch, when she went up the narrow curving stairs to the lofty darkness of the attic and took a look around, she saw how the sunlight spilled in through the tall windows. She recalled Shanna's mention at lunch of going salmon fishing.... The idea of work with that beckoning prospect was suddenly unthinkable. Abruptly Jesse turned and ran back downstairs.

Perhaps Shanna was still rather naive about the world in general, Jesse thought later, but where water, boats and fishing were concerned, she was an old practiced hand. Jesse was full of admiration for the way Shanna handled their twenty-foot motorboat and the way she'd selected their fishing spot between some of the smaller sea-washed islands of Desolation Sound.

"We'll find some here," Shanna had said, and that was that.

The twins weren't novices in the art of fishing, either; they had their hooks baited with live herring and their lines in the water before Jesse had even stopped looking into the bait pail at all the squirming, wriggling, four-to-five-inch herring.

"Ah, maybe I'll suntan first," Jesse gulped, glancing up at Shanna, who was grinning.

"Good idea," Shanna agreed guilelessly, her eyes dancing with laughter. She threw Jesse a plastic bottle of suntan lotion, having finished applying a liberal coat everywhere that her bathing suit allowed. Jesse shrugged out of the terry-cloth top and dropped it on the deck, rubbing the lotion onto her legs first, then working her way up around her bikini. The hot sun on her skin was absolutely marvelous; she felt as though she must be in heaven, with the circling pattern of islands and sea all around her, the mountains thrusting high above them to the east, the water and the wide clear sky exactly the same shade of summer blue. Far, far above her an eagle swooped and soared through the mountain air currents. Such perfect serenity and incredible solitude, Jesse thought. There were no other human beings in sight, apart from their own little group.

Jesse stretched out on the deck like a cat, sighing with pleasure. "I can't believe I almost spent the day working!" she murmured.

"It's too nice a day," Shanna agreed, coming to join her on the smooth warm wooden deck. She held a herring in one hand and her lead line, with its two hooks, in the other. Jesse squinted, ready to close her eyes the instant anything unpleasant happened. In one fluid movement Shanna had the small fish baited, one hook through the nose and the other through its dorsal fin. Jesse watched it sink down, down, into the crystal-clear water.

"Salmon go for wounded herring," Shanna explained apologetically, adding, "Jesse...?"

Just the tone of Shanna's voice made Jesse look up at her.

"Uh-huh?"

Shanna spoke softly, though the twins were out of earshot. "Remember I told you about the last time I saw Ray? When you were in Vancouver?"

"Uh-huh. He seems like an awfully nice guy... from what you've told me, anyway. And Bensen doesn't scare him."

"Would you do me a favor? A big, big favor? *Please?*"

"Well, what is it?"

"Ray wants to see me again. Tonight. Would you—I mean, could you—keep Bensen busy when Ray comes? Grandmother will be out of the way, but Bensen—I don't want to tell anyone yet; I don't even want anyone to know. If things do get... well, serious, then eventually I'll have to face Bensen, but I just couldn't stand any arguments about it right now."

"How does Ray feel about keeping things secret?"

"He doesn't know that I—that I haven't told anyone. I've always managed to get away somehow. But Bensen will be home tonight for sure."

"Where are you going to go?"

"There's a lodge on Kinghorn. It's really cozy. It should be full of tourists this time of year, so there'll probably be a live band. It's like a real date, Jesse. I'm being wined and dined, and I—I rather like it!"

Jesse grinned in reply to that. "Are you so sure Bensen would object? I think he kind of likes Ray, as a matter of fact—in his own peculiar way."

"I really want to go tonight." Now a note of urgency entered Shanna's soft low voice. "I even have a new dress. And I don't want anything to start tonight off on a bad foot. This is awfully important to me. Will you do it? Please? I know it's asking a lot, but I'll only ask you this once."

Shanna's pleading eyes were too much for Jesse, and she supposed she could always bear another argument with Bensen if it came to that. Still, she felt a faint sensation of butterflies in her stomach as she sighed and agreed to Shanna's request.

Suddenly the tip of Shanna's rod dipped sharply, and her attention shot to the water. Excitedly Jesse got up on all fours to peer over the side, spotting the fish in waters the sunlight barely penetrated. With a jerk the fish took the line out, speeding off into the deep.

"He's close!" Jesse cried. "He was almost under the boat! Oh, my gosh!"

Shanna cranked back hard on the rod to catch the hooks firmly, then let the line spin out as the salmon dived deeper. It was a running fight—reel in, spin out; reel in, spin out—and Shanna valiantly held the rod tip up.

"Grab that hand net and bring him in, will you?" she directed Jesse. The splendid two-foot-long spring salmon was thrashing against the side of the boat. With unpracticed movements Jesse hung over the side and tried to bag him, but the tired fish darted out of reach. Expertly Shanna played with him, reeling him in closer to the boat until at last Jesse caught him and triumphantly heaved the bouncing net onto the deck.

"It's so beautiful!" she exclaimed, staring wide-eyed at the glistening silver-scaled fish. Her long braided ponytail fell forward over her shoulder as she bent to examine it.

"Not so close," Shanna warned. "I have to kill it right away."

Jesse quickly retreated, watching from a distance. After a well-aimed blow on the head with a gaff, Shanna grasped the fish under the gills with one hand; with a knife in the other hand and a flick of her wrist she had the fish open from head to tail. Two more flicks of the knife and the entrails fell cleanly into the water. "There! It's ready for the ice chest. Do you want to tuck him in?" She handed the fish to Jesse, her eyes dancing merrily.

Jesse cleared her throat and seized the fish. She tossed it into the ice chest, patting crushed ice all around and over it. Then, straightening up, she spied the bait pail. She cleared her throat once more and asked, "Where'd you put my pole?"

CHAPTER FOUR

SHANNA PRECEDED JESSE into the kitchen, where she gave the day's catch—seven spring salmon—to Martha, with instructions on how to prepare them for supper. The rest were scheduled for the smokehouse. Jesse mixed long cool drinks and, leaving Martha with a basketful of salmon and a drink to sustain her through the dinner preparation, went out onto the stone terrace.

Outside, she and Shanna sank into chaise longues to enjoy the late-afternoon sun. Its heat flooded down over them and radiated up from the granite floor of the terrace. Jesse pulled aside one strap of her bikini and saw with pleasure that she'd achieved a nice toasty golden brown tan. And then she smiled a little when she thought that tonight Bensen would be eating a dinner she had helped bring home. The smile still lingered on her mouth when the estate jeep came into view from around a bend in the shaded forest road.

Speak of the devil, Jesse said to herself as she watched the jeep hurtling toward them over the rocks. From their vantage point Shanna and Jesse watched Bensen park the jeep; then he vaulted out and came striding up the gravel path toward the terrace steps. He's been out in the bush again, Jesse thought, judging by his clothes. His denim jeans, faded and close-fitting, were stuffed into the top of scuffed Kodiak boots whose laces were only half tied, and his sleeveless T-shirt was dirty.

Jesse's earlier and complete relaxation vanished with a snap, and she wondered where she'd left her terry-cloth top. Suddenly she felt very bare and wondered further whatever had possessed her to buy such a terribly skimpy bikini. When she looked down at herself, the bits of white material seemed to have shrunk in the most alarming way.

Bensen's abrupt stop at the head of the terrace stairs when his eyes first alighted on them was purely a reflex action. One hand held a battered clipboard and what appeared to be a mangled sawblade; the other he pushed through his straight black hair, brushing it back off his temples. It swept forward again in a blue black wave as his eyes jumped from his sister to Jesse's long supple form, seemingly relaxed against the chaise longue. His gaze was too straightforward by far. Jesse's whole gold-tanned body felt like a heat rash. She was sure he'd assessed every curve and contour in those endless seconds.

"Well, it's good that some of us work for a living," he finally said, much to Jesse's relief.

"I caught your supper for tonight, so you've no cause for righteous indignation," she returned, glad to be talking so that she didn't have to think about the utterly new physical unease he'd touched off. She'd worn this bikini many times before and had never felt prudish about it until now. Going out on a limb, she added laughingly, "You'd better be nice to me, or I'll tell Martha to cook yours in a special way."

"Blackmail! I'm not surprised. What exactly did you catch? Or do you know?" Lazily his eyes continued their perusal of her body.

"A five-and-a-half-pound spring salmon, so there!" Jesse fidgeted, wishing he would look away from her revealing bikini top.

"Has the repairman showed up yet?"

Shanna didn't answer, so Jesse said, "No, not yet. So it's barbecued salmon outside tonight." Did he have to stare like that?

"Martha will have to try really hard to spoil that. Good. I'm starved." Bensen suddenly grinned at Jesse, and before she could collect her thoughts, he'd disappeared through the French doors.

Shanna turned to make sure her brother was out of sight and out of earshot. "You know, I think going to the zoo did Bensen some good," she said in a half whisper to Jesse. "Doesn't he seem a little different to you? I mean, did you see that smile? I wonder why he smiled like that?"

"I—I don't know," Jesse replied, confused herself. "But don't hold your breath; he didn't enjoy the zoo one bit. Gosh, I don't envy Dorothy. In fact, I think I admire her. Can you imagine being married to someone like him?"

"Good Lord, no! It would be absolutely awful. I wonder how he ever managed to be pleasant enough to propose?" She giggled suddenly. "Can you imagine him? 'My darling—'" she pressed a hand to her chest " '—will you do me the honor of becoming my wife?' "

"Do you think he'd do it like that?"

"How else? Can you see him in a mad adoring passion, suddenly sweeping Dorothy up in his arms?"

Jesse hesitated. "No, no... but can you see Dorothy being swept up? She's not the mad passionate type herself."

"That's so. I wonder how they ever got to the point—well, I'm sure it's more like a business venture to Bensen than anything else. He probably weighed all the pros and cons, used mental graphs and came up with a mathematical yes. And she's more than willing, even though I can say almost for certain she's not in love with him. It's not that she wants his money," Shanna added hastily. "She's got enough for two lifetimes. What do you suppose attracted them to each other?"

Jesse ticked off the points on her fingers slowly. "Well... he probably considers it's time he married—heirs, you know. And Dorothy does come from the same background, so he doesn't have to worry about her hounding him for his money. Plus Dorothy *is* very pretty."

"Uh-huh... the kind of face you'd see in a shampoo commercial."

Jesse looked at Shanna with surprise, then a glimmer of a smile showed on her wide lips. "I wonder why they haven't set a date?"

"Dorothy wants to, but I get the idea Bensen's in no hurry. Now that he's made up his mind, I think *he* thinks it doesn't much matter when. And he's always

so wrapped up in his work that he keeps putting settling the details off.''

"Does that make her mad?''

"You bet! But nobody pushes Bensen, so....''
Shanna spread her hands wide.

"You're damn right!''

Both Shanna and Jesse jumped at Bensen's clipped
voice. Almost at the same time they half rose in their
chaise longues to turn to face him.

He stood surveying them from the library doors
with his hands on his hips in a cool kind of anger.
With a sinking heart Jesse saw that his eyes were
directed mainly toward her.

"We...uh,'' Jesse stammered, blushing red. She
felt that not only her cheeks had changed their hue.

"Do you think you're qualified to discuss my personal life? Are you going to start trying to rearrange
that, too? I wouldn't if I were you!'' The black eyes
pinned hers in a frightening manner, and Jesse could
think of nothing to say to defend herself. She seemed
to be unable to think at all and certainly couldn't
decipher the flashing multitude of messages he was
sending her.

"I—I think I'll go get dressed,'' Shanna murmured. She favored Jesse with a half-apologetic,
half-beseeching look and quickly ran past Bensen.

Vexedly Jesse watched Shanna go. Then reluctantly
her eyes returned to Bensen's face and the narrowed
eyes. She moistened her lips before saying, "I have
never even remotely considered rearranging your personal life.'' She forced herself to add in a perfectly
even noncommittal drawl, "It's of no interest to me.''

Slowly she turned her back to him and prepared to lay back into the chaise longue, her braided ponytail swinging over one shoulder.

"You deserve a nose at least twice as big as the one you've got!"

When her head whipped around, he had gone. Jesse felt a sudden prickling of tears behind her eyes. She didn't like it that mere words should have this quick, unexpected power to hurt. She didn't care what he thought of her, she really didn't, she told herself.

And yet, Jesse realized, this incident, unfortunate as it was, coming just when they were almost getting along, might serve a useful purpose. It would be easier now to provoke another argument with him. She had to keep him occupied somehow for Shanna's departure with Ray later on. Just one little word from her now was likely to set him off. Useful or not, it didn't make Jesse very happy, and she had to remind herself she didn't give a damn about Bensen Everhart's opinion.

She was more nervous than she had expected when, after supper, the hour of Ray's arrival approached. She'd been up to see Shanna and had helped her dress for the occasion. Up in Shanna's bedroom she'd felt fine. It wasn't hard to be distracted from her own problems. Shanna was so excited; she looked absolutely gorgeous with her honey-colored hair, her soft sky-blue eyes sparkling. And her dress was just right, Jesse considered; it suited Shanna perfectly and heightened the effect of innocent sensuousness. If she didn't knock Ray Dunbar off his sturdy feet, Jesse decided, it wouldn't be any fault of Shanna's.

Now, hovering uncertainly downstairs in the hallway, Jesse felt positively panicky about "keeping Bensen busy." How on earth would she manage that? What should she say? Picking a fight suddenly seemed to be a very difficult and dangerous thing to do. Her mood couldn't have been more antiwarlike. Still, she had promised Shanna.... Rubbing her palms together, Jesse cautiously approached the library door. She was almost tiptoeing.

One step farther would have carried her through the door. But then Jesse stepped back. She'd made Shanna swear not to delay for one extra second when Ray came for her. Looking at her watch—synchronized with Shanna's—she saw there was still a few minutes' grace left to her.

What would be her opening line? Should she bring up this afternoon, or should she set off on a new tack? Jesse wandered abstractedly over to the mirror and once there saw that *her* dress was all wrong for the occasion. The rather thin clingy material of her shift wasn't fit for battle. Again it seemed to reveal rather too much. Another glance at her watch showed she had no time to run upstairs to change.

Without realizing it, she was literally wringing her hands as she once more approached the library door, one dreading footstep after another. Maybe she would say something about the attic balcony. That bright idea fizzled out as she remembered his violent threat. She didn't mind going to bat for Shanna, but enough was enough. She had no more time to lose....

"I'd like to talk to you." Her voice was peremptorily accusing. Her nerves were leaping.

Bensen looked up, startled, and Jesse steeled herself. For several tense endless seconds he simply stared at her. Slowly one of his eyebrows lifted.

"Please do." He dropped the gold pen on the desk and leaned back in his big chair. Calmly, steadily, the black eyes watched her, intrigued. "I take it this is not just a ploy to stay awake?"

"I-I-I'd like to know why you're always picking on me." She thought it wiser not to let him get a word in after that faltering start and so raged on with scarcely a pause for breath. "And don't deny it. You've done practically nothing but shout and scream at me since the first day I arrived!"

Was that the sound of the jeep? She itched to look at her watch but of course couldn't. "What on earth have I done to you that I should merit such treatment? I'm your grandmother's guest; I've tried to stay out of your way, but you continually harass me!" Jesse felt like a fool saying such things. Yes, it definitely was a jeep. Please, dear God, let it be Ray. "You really are a boor!"

"After all that, *I'm* supposed to be picking on *you*? Sounds like the pot calling the kettle black. Just who do you think you are to come storming in here, to make foolish stupid accusations! Have you lost your head?"

"It's still on my neck, isn't it?" snapped Jesse, trying to whip up indignation.

"Perhaps it should be knocked off!" Suddenly Bensen rose from his chair and circled the desk. Jesse's eyes widened, but she held her ground.

"Are you threatening to knock it off? Case in point. You couldn't have proved my words to be true more clearly. You certainly aren't a gentleman. A—a caveman is more like it!"

"What's got into you?"

That stopped Jesse for a moment. She stared a little blankly at the large dark man towering over her. Was that a door closing? "Me? I just don't like being picked on all the time, that's what. And I don't like being yelled at. Nor do I like being threatened. And furthermore, you had the nerve to accuse *me* of eavesdropping. What were you doing this afternoon? Don't you know it's not polite to sneak up behind people to listen to their private conversations?"

"You seem to forget yourself!" Bensen gritted. The black brows had gathered together like storm clouds, and Jesse hoped she hadn't gone *too* far. "This happens to be my house, not yours, and I can behave any way I please. If you don't like it, leave! I've noticed you don't appreciate being told what to do, so don't try it on me. What's the matter with you?"

"I'm perfectly fine, thank you."

"There's something not quite right. Why are you picking this fight with me?"

"Picking a fight?" Jesse hoped her scornful laugh sounded convincing. She had her back turned to him so that he couldn't see her face. "You're the one who's always stirring up things! It's all right for you to pick a fight, but nobody else can, is that it?"

"Why are you looking at your watch?"

"Wha-at?" She spun around, sending her silky

chestnut mane rippling over one shoulder. "I wasn't. I mean, don't change the subject!" There it was, faintly—the sound of the jeep starting up, revving.... "You don't seem to realize that I've asked you to explain a few things, and instead of giving me one good answer, all you've done is argue in return."

"This, obviously, is getting us nowhere," he growled, coming closer. "And I *wasn't* eavesdropping."

"Then what were you doing?"

"I have a right to walk about in my own house, don't I? I happened to need a book that just happened to be close to where you two were sitting. Dammit, what am I doing even trying to explain it to you? It's none of your business!"

"How I'm treated is my business." Noise from the jeep had dwindled away. "Well, there's no point in trying to come to an understanding. A rational conversation is a no-go with you!" Jesse shrugged in what she hoped was a disdainful way. She brushed her hair back with a sweep of her hand and started for the door, her chin held high.

"Now just wait one minute!" Bensen's large hand clamped over her shoulder, and he forced her around. "Don't think you can just walk out after that display!"

"What am I supposed to do? Bow a couple of times first?" Her chin went up farther—and not only because she had to tilt her head back to look at him. The amber eyes were glittering into his. Fear hammered against her chest.

Bensen's tone sank to a warning low. "There's

something going on...there's something fishy about this whole little gambit of yours. One minute you're dying for a fight, and the next you're in a crazy hurry to go. Look at me, Jesse," he ordered. "What are you trying to do?"

Jesse shivered. The tip of her tongue moved out to moisten her lips, which were suddenly very, very dry. "N-nothing. You're imagining things...you—"

"Answer me, Jesse!"

"I'm not going to say another word."

"That'll be the day! For the last time, what are you up to?"

She stood glaring back at him in mute defiance, while little panic explosions started going off within her.

"That's not going to get you anywhere." He took a threatening step toward her.

"No...no, Bensen! Please...I'm not up to anything, really I'm not. It's just th-that... ummm...." Jesse put a hand to her forehead. "I have a headache."

"Now I *know* something's going on. Dorothy's the type that gets headaches, but oh, no, not *you*. Dammit, you rile me! You're going to tell me just *exactly* what you're up to if I have to squeeze it out of you!"

"If you weren't such a tyrant, things like this wouldn't happen in the first place. Don't touch me! If you lay one finger on me, I'll make you so sorry—*Let me go!*"

In struggling to free her wrist, Jesse only managed to twist her arm. Bensen drew her closer, bringing her suddenly within an inch of his chest.

"You little hellcat!" he gritted, the set of his mouth just above her head vehement, the depthless black eyes endlessly burning. Jesse stared back with wide eyes, the breath choking in her chest.

Numbly, vaguely, she sensed the change in the tension between them—a change that seemed to build rapidly of itself, that swept up and around the two of them, blotting out their anger with a feeling just as intense while mounting, mounting, toward an unforeseeable crescendo. Her nerves leaped and quivered, very much alive. Irresistibly Jesse's gaze was drawn to the smooth brown cheek, the imperious curve of his mouth. Her lips parted, she felt dreadfully short of air. The skin on her nape tingled.

The still hooded eyes were intent upon her face, and although Jesse tried to avoid them, they drew on her like a magnet, compelling her to meet his gaze. The moment she did, clear realization dawned like a physical shock, and they both knew. With a gasp Jesse twisted her wrist free from his suddenly loosened hold. She stepped away from him as though burned and stood rubbing her wrist, staring a little wildly at him, her knees shaking with pure fright over what might have happened. Furious color flooded her cheeks.

"I think I heard a jeep," he stated coldly, his voice harsh. Abruptly he turned away from her, starting for the door.

"It's already gone."

He swung around, the eyes narrowing familiarly. For a few more seconds he continued to survey her. Then he said quietly, dangerously, "So that's it. You were sent to keep me occupied while Shanna slipped out the back door, weren't you? That's the only explanation for your absurdity!''

"It could be something entirely different." Her voice was shaking.

His contemptuous glance dismissed that notion. "Do you know where they've gone?" Bensen went to his desk, where he picked up his wallet, slipping it into his back pocket.

"You're not going to follow them!" Jesse was aghast.

"What do you think I'm going to do? Stand by while some leech sneaks Shanna out of the back door? What the hell's the matter with the front, may I ask?"

"They didn't sneak. Anyway, *he* didn't—and he didn't know Shanna did. And why do you suppose she's sneaking in the first place? Because she's convinced you wouldn't let her go if she did ask. She's afraid of you."

"You expect me to believe that? What crap! I just want to protect her—she knows that! She's too trusting to—''

"For heaven's sake, Bensen, Shanna's a grown woman! She *can* go out on a date, with or without your approval. Don't you trust her judgment at all?"

"Then why the hell all this secrecy?"

"I've already told you. Listen, for a change, instead of giving orders. Shanna was afraid you wouldn't let her go at all or would cause such a fuss that it would ruin everything. After all, it's only a date—it's not an affair or a proposal or. . .or anything definite yet. You might just scare the poor guy off with all your suspicions and demands. Don't you see? She doesn't want you to interfere. And she thinks you've got something against Ray, even though I tried to tell her that I think you actually like him. Do you see now? If you go chasing after them and ruin their date, she's never going to forgive you and—"

"Ray? Ray Dunbar? She's out with *him*?"

"Yes. I thought you knew they—"

"This is the first I've heard of it. But why should she think I've something against Ray? I've never said anything to her about him."

"Remember that time you thought I was listening at keyholes? Well, Shanna *was*. She was convinced you two were arguing about her that day. She said to me, 'It's the same thing all over again,' meaning what happened with Stu."

The stunned look on Bensen's face made Jesse wince. She saw the tinge of gray underneath the healthy bronze tan and knew then that he blamed himself. Without conscious thought Jesse went to him and put a hand on his arm.

"Bensen...." With an irritable shrug he shook her hand off. Jesse stepped back quickly, a touch wounded. "Shanna wants to tell you, Bensen," she persisted, "and she will—in her own time. Give her that time. If you want her to tell you sooner rather than later, just drop a few hints about Ray. Say that you like him or that you admire the way he does his job—anything. But it's got to be nice. She really does believe you have something against him."

"Because we sometimes have differing views when it comes to logging? That's to be expected."

Jesse sighed. "She doesn't know it's business. You're always in the library with the door shut, and no one can hear what's going on, just that you're having what sounds like a terrible fight."

"Does it really sound that bad?"

"It sounds like a prelude to fisticuffs."

"That's ridiculous!"

"Maybe, but that's the way it is."

Bensen ran a hand through the black thickness of his hair. For a while he stared abstractedly at her. "We'd better say nothing of this. You'll act like none of this ever happened. And he'd better have her home by one! Two, anyway. Let her think your ploy worked. I'll invite him to stay for supper, or some such thing. Too bad Martha's such a lousy cook; I hate to put anyone who's unprepared through an experience like that. Not that he'll be thinking of the food if he's interested in Shanna...."

"Then you really don't mind?" The eagerness spilled from her voice, and Bensen frowned angrily.

"I'm not an ogre!"

"Well—" Jesse took two steps backward "—sometimes you act a little like one."

Bensen stood eyeing her somewhat grimly. "Don't tell me you're afraid of me, too." Taunting sarcasm hid the genuineness of his question.

"Don't flatter yourself that I care enough ever to be frightened of you." She glared at him from afar.

"Well, then, if that's the case, perhaps you'll leave me in peace." He gestured sharply toward the door of his den. "And if it's at all possible, *try* to keep your nose out of my affairs in the future. I'm sure I can muddle along well enough on my own." With a scalding glance her way he settled his long frame behind his desk and picked up the slim gold pen.

Jesse edged toward the door. She was glad that matters had come off as well as they had and, not expecting too much, was eager to be gone. But at the door some devil took hold of her. She turned impetuously and leaned back into the room, one hand on either side of the doorway. The words tumbled out in a rush.

"Whether you believe me or not, everyone here *is* afraid of you, from your grandmother right down to the twins. You're either working and locked away from everybody, or you're giving orders and snapping angrily. I'd think you'd see that a bit of kindness would go a long way with Martha's cooking skills—she did wonderfully at Cecilia Anne's birthday party. And I don't blame Shanna for the way she thinks of you. It's not her fault she's misinterpreted your overprotectiveness. And it *is* overprotectiveness. Shanna's a woman and not the little girl you once knew. And I say 'once knew,' because you don't know her anymore. You're always too busy. And of course the twins appreciate your giving them those horses—they were ecstatic. But the biggest gift in the world doesn't go as far as a smile would. And I know grandmother's always poking at you, but I think that's because she resents being under your thumb. There, I know that I've gone too far, that I'm meddling in what doesn't concern me, that I'm a busybody—as you've told me several times—but I don't care!''

With that parting shot, Jesse spun about and ran through the library, sure now she really had gone too far. Why did she have to open her big mouth? She really wouldn't blame Bensen if he kicked her out of the house this time. Putting her cool hands to her hot cheeks, she burst out into the hall, almost running smack into a man in overalls.

"You Mrs. Everhart?" Bushy eyebrows rose to a peak as he shifted his tool kit.

"No!" Jesse replied with such vehemence that the man took a step backward. "I—I mean—"

"Who are you?" Bensen demanded from right over her shoulder. Jesse took a nervous little jump away from him.

"I came to repair the stove. Couldn't get here till now because—"

"Oh, that's wonderful!" Jesse exclaimed, grasping his hairy arm. "Come right this way." Tugging him along with her, she led him quickly away from a smoldering Bensen to the stove and recalcitrant Martha. She felt his eyes bore holes into her back as she scurried all the long way down the hall.

She knew neither of them would ever forget this evening.

THE NEXT MORNING Jesse was more than a little surprised to discover the library door ajar. Quickly poking her head in the room, she saw that Bensen was in his den, that door open, as well. Stunned, she hurried on to the terrace, where the female members of the family were having coffee, hardly daring to wonder at the significance of those open doors. . . .

Jesse hadn't had a chance to see Shanna yet, for, having had a late night, she'd slept in. The glowing pink of her cheeks and the happiness behind the blue eyes at once answered Jesse's curiosity.

Shanna looked at her now with a wide conspiratorial smile. "Good morning," she said brightly.

"Morning," Jesse replied a little more evenly, a slow smile lighting her face. She winked at Shanna to let her know everything had gone as planned. No need to worry her, Jesse decided.

"You weren't home last night," grandmother said to Shanna without preamble. "Where were you off to? You've been out a couple of times lately. . . ."

The twins looked around at everyone, silent and agog to hear more of this adult conversation.

"I—I think I'll go take Bensen a cup of coffee," Jesse put in. This time Shanna could do her own explaining. She poured a cup of Martha's wicked black coffee and left before Shanna could say a word to her. Bensen's sister was staring after her with some perplexity when grandmother's voice sharpened, so that Jesse could still hear it on her way through the library.

"What's the matter with your ears?" the old woman was demanding. "Where did you go last night? Don't you think it's time to let us in on your secret?"

Jesse bit her lip and grinned. A half smile still lingered as she quietly slipped into the den and put the steaming cup down on Bensen's desk. Its surface was littered with small tiles of wood, each a different color and grain. She tilted her head closer to get another quick look before leaving, but the movement swept her hair forward, and it tumbled over Bensen's shoulder in a shining swoosh. With a sharp intake of breath Jesse pulled her hair back as Bensen impatiently turned in his chair. Somewhat warily she eyed the dark stern features.

"Relax," he muttered, passing a hand over the roughness of his unshaven chin. "I don't bite this early in the morning." He cast a cursory glance over her, and the hooded eyes gave nothing away. Even so, Jesse felt relatively safe.

"I put cream in the coffee because it's really strong. What are you doing with those?" She nodded at the tiles, deciding to hazard a question.

"They're samples, the finished products. I'm choosing which to send where with our overseas salesmen."

"They're all so beautiful, how do you decide?" Jesse moved closer to examine the small thin squares of wood. While she looked at them, Bensen looked at her. When he spoke again, it was with a slight drawl.

"By what each country's asked for, naturally."

"Oh?"

"Japan's asked for yellow cedar—some of these—" he pointed out a little separate pile of tiles "—and black cedar—those over there. Yellow cedar's the most expensive—almost worth its weight in gold. The black is cheap lumber, mostly sent to pulp mills for paper. One order from England calls for spruce—this pile—and it usually goes to make furniture. This white hemlock, as well.''

"You can tell which is which just by looking at them?'' Jesse scanned the vast array of tiles incredulously.

"I've been doing it for years.'' He paused, and Jesse continued going through the tiles. "Are you extending an olive branch?'' he asked abruptly.

Her head jerked around. For a moment she seemed on the edge of flight but managed to master the overpowering impulse. She looked back at him, the sherry-amber eyes wary and slightly wider than usual. "Would it hurt if I were?''

Bensen didn't answer. Jesse might have been mistaken, but it appeared to her a smile hovered at one corner of his sensuous mouth. Then he said, "How does Shanna seem to you this morning? Is she up yet?''

"She looks wonderful. Go out and see. She's having breakfast outside with grandmother—Shanna's being put through the wringer!''

Now Bensen really did smile. Jesse wished it could have lasted longer. "She doesn't suspect anything?'' he asked.

"No, I didn't let on. She thinks everything went just as we'd planned.''

Bensen let that pass. "I expect to see Ray sometime today. Do you think it would be rushing things if I asked him to stay for dinner?''

"No. I—I...no. That sounds great.'' Jesse found she was almost gaping at him, so she shut her mouth and composed herself.

Bensen shot a quick sharp look at her before picking up one of the tiles to run his thumb over the smooth surface. "It would help if dinner weren't too awful. Could I ask you to, ah, keep an eye on things? Martha would fall out of her tree if I started giving orders in her kitchen."

Jesse swallowed before replying, "How about a big ham? I know there's one, and I'll do my best to get it into the oven whole before Martha gets her knife into it. She does try, you know. Well, sometimes," she qualified.

"Yeah. That's what worries me. Anything good to eat on the table out there? I'm starved."

"Actually, there are some really fine butterhorns—believe it or not; they aren't burned or anything. There's tea, too, if you'd rather. Martha's coffee is like a punch in the stomach today."

"What does that signify, I wonder." He came around the desk, and they started for the door together.

Jesse smiled up at Bensen. "Do you mean, does the state of her coffee point to her state of mind? We'll have to keep an eye out and see." The dimples in her cheeks grew deeper with amusement.

Bensen was gazing down at her, and the strange expression in his eyes caused a flare of mental confusion. She continued on just a little ahead of him and walked out onto the terrace, blinking—but not because of the brilliant sunlight. Bensen pulled a chair over to the table and set it between grandmother and Shanna.

"Jesse tells me the butterhorns are good," he remarked, ignoring the rather surprised looks he was getting. He eyed the table and went for the butterhorns. In one bite he demolished half a pastry. He was behaving as though he joined the family every morning. Shanna cast an oblique look at Jesse, who shook her head in reply and shrugged ever so slightly, trying to tell Shanna she didn't know what had got into Bensen, either.

"Wonderful weather," he continued blandly, "isn't it, grandmother?"

"Oh, yes, fine. Hot, though." She tapped her teaspoon thoughtfully against the tablecloth. "Have another butterhorn. Best when they're fresh."

"I can't believe Martha actually made these. Mmmm!"

Grandmother's and Shanna's suspicions were growing. Shanna reached for the coffeepot. "Jesse, let's go see if Martha's made some more."

Once in the hall Jesse and Shanna whispered at a furious rate back and forth. Jesse denied knowing anything about anything, and indeed it was true—she didn't understand Bensen one bit. But one thing she was sure of: Bensen wasn't setting any traps with his mild manner. He might be domineering and abrasive and a million other things, but he certainly wasn't malicious. So she calmed Shanna's fears and, to prepare her, told her Bensen expected to talk to Ray today about business. As far as she knew, Jesse informed her, Bensen and Ray got along quite well, except for minor arguments about business. Shanna's dubious expression made Jesse sigh.

"Come on," she finally said, "we'd better get

back to the table before everybody wonders what we're doing.''

Bensen popped the last of another butterhorn in his mouth as they sat down. He had been talking with the twins, and he gave the two women scarcely more than a glance. "So you girls approve of your horses? The vendor told me they were gentle, but you never know. They haven't been biting or acting up, have they?''

"Oh, no, Uncle Ben.'' Samantha breathed. "Daisy's the best horse in the whole world!''

"And so's Ribbons,'' added Merit. "We can keep them, can't we? And the other two—Taffy and Bobbin? They're all such friends, Uncle Ben. It'd break their hearts if you took them away.''

"Yes, sure, you can keep them all. They'd just go the knackers if we gave them away.''

"It's nice to have horses around here once more,'' Cecilia interjected. "They help keep the lawn down, too.''

"Did I see you up on Taffy the other day, Jesse?'' Bensen's question caught her off guard, for she had been engrossed in puzzling over him and staring at his mouth—which she'd come so close to kissing only last night.

"Oh, ah, y-yes. She's old, but she's great. I was never too good at galloping anyway. A nice gentle walk is more my style. And she doesn't have that annoying habit of turning for the barn as soon as she's left it.'' Jesse fervently hoped her eyes didn't show any of what she had been thinking as his gaze lingered on her.

"Well, I'd better get back to work," he announced. "I'm expecting Ray this afternoon. We've a lot of points to cover, so I thought I'd ask him to stay for dinner. If we've the evening, as well, then perhaps we can get everything wrapped up today. That all right with everyone?"

Grandmother dropped her teaspoon with a clatter. Shanna had tensed like a coiled spring at the first mention of Ray. Now she sat rigid in her chair. Jesse kicked Shanna's bare leg under the table.

"Ah...ah..." Shanna floundered. She sent Jesse an agonized look. "I-I'd like that. I mean, Ray's a nice—umm...yes, I'd like to have him for dinner," she finished in a rush, confusion turning her cheeks a guilty pink. She avoided her brother's eyes. Bensen pretended not to notice anything was amiss.

"Fine." He smiled around at everyone, then left them alone, disappearing into the library.

"What's going on here?" grandmother asked sharply. "Now Shanna, explain to me again where and why you went for such a long walk last night."

"It was...it was just a walk, grandmother, nothing to explain." Shanna looked hard at Jesse and with a slight nod of her head indicated she wanted to speak to her in the house. This time Jesse took the coffeepot, and they went indoors.

"What's going on?" whispered Shanna fiercely. "There's something fishy here; I know it! Why is Bensen so nice all of a sudden? He hasn't...he isn't usually...Jesse, what happened between you two last night?"

"Nothing," Jesse returned, whispering, too. She

avoided Shanna's searching gaze. "I don't know, but didn't I tell you he thinks Ray's okay? This just proves it, that's all. So when Ray comes today, just act perfectly natural with him. Bensen will soon get the message."

"I don't know...things have sure picked up here all of a sudden. Jesse, have you told me everything? I just have this feeling that—"

"You know everything there is to know. Everything's fine! So why are you worried?"

"I—did you have a really terrible fight last night? Is that why Bensen's...well, being so nice this morning? Asking the twins about their horses and everything? Oh, Jesse, I'm sorry. I knew it would be hard, but.... Was he really awful?"

Jesse remembered her argument with Bensen and the strange thing that had flared up between them. If, during those seconds when he held her arm, if he'd bent down and kissed her, she would have kissed him back, and they had *both* known that. She wriggled uncomfortably. Whew, thank God it hadn't happened! Jesse cleared her throat to rid herself of the peculiar choking sensation. "Ah, no, he really wasn't too bad. Considering that I went in waving red flags. Don't give it another thought, Shanna. I'm not going to."

Jesse took the coffeepot and herself off to the kitchen, while Shanna wandered back out to the terrace, obviously deep in thought and wondering about a whole lot of things. Once in the kitchen Jesse set the wheels in motion for supper that evening. With gentle coaxing and cajolery she convinced Martha that this and this and this would result in a splendid supper if it were prepared in such a way. She somehow made the woman believe it was entirely her idea. Jesse didn't begrudge the time and effort this took. She felt "off" in some way and knew that concentrating in the attic would be hopeless. So she puttered away in the kitchen with Martha, partly to keep an eye on things and to forestall any change of mind in the cook and partly to keep herself busy and out of Shanna's and grandmother's way. She'd answered enough questions recently. Later she'd escape with the twins for another gentle ride on Taffy.

JESSE POPPED HER HEAD through Shanna's bedroom doorway. "Are you ready? Let's go down and try to convince the men to have cocktails with us. I've just been in the kitchen and Martha's doing fine. She's grumbling, but she's doing fine." Jesse didn't mention she'd also seen the door to the library still open and she'd heard the murmur of voices within. "Come on."

"I-I'm not quite ready yet," Shanna replied, running the brush through her hair once more.

"You are so; you look perfect."

Shanna began rearranging the perfume bottles on her dressing table. "You go ahead. I'll be down in a minute."

"Oh, for heaven's sake, stop dithering about. Come on!" Jesse kindly eyed Shanna's apprehensive face. "What do you think of my dress?" she asked, trying to get Shanna's thoughts off herself.

Jesse was wearing high heels fastened with the tiniest of straps, sheer silk stockings and a silky backless summer dress that was a shade lighter than her eyes.

Shanna gave Jesse a tip-to-toe look. "Oh," she moaned, "I wish I looked half as good as you!"

Jesse laughed merrily and pushed Shanna out the door.

"But you do the talking, okay?" Shanna whispered urgently as they started down the stairs together.

"All right, but don't you dare run off and leave."

They could now hear the murmur of men's voices from the library. Two more steps down and they caught Bensen's suddenly sharp words.

"Dammit, Ray, the men start at daybreak out in the bush! All logging stops at ten. Do you have any idea of the amount of money we stand to lose if you cut our operations back further?"

"And you know very well that down line seven it's too dry. One little spark and the whole country's up in flames. Section 108 is already ablaze! What the hell do you expect me to do? Perform a rain dance?"

"None of my men smokes when there's a fire hazard on. They know they'll lose their jobs on the spot if they're caught. You know we've never started *one* fire."

"Not that can be proved!"

"Are, we suddenly responsible for campers? You can't stick the blame on us, because it's not our fault 108 blew yesterday."

"Not your fault? You were laying in an extension on line four. Dynamite, powder, gasoline fumes everywhere. Then there's the men smoking and the cook shack and—"

"Look, I went up there myself yesterday and checked everything after shutdown. I don't know how the hell that fire got started, but I do know it wasn't started by us!"

"See?" Jesse whispered to Shanna. They were standing where they'd crouched the other time. "See? It's business." Shanna expelled a long shaky sigh.

"Why do they have to shout?"

"Well, I guess it's pretty serious. Forest fires—"

"It's too late now to talk about whose fault it is," they heard Ray snap. "Any men you have to lay off we can use for firefighting. We've got three water bombers over there now trying to contain that blaze so it doesn't spread to 109. You know what trouble we'd have if it caught."

"Don't I! But I still say shutting down 102 is premature. We're out by ten now. Shut down, closed down, locked up tight. There's still dew on the grass at ten in the morning. Do you know how many men you've already put out of work? What do you suppose I tell them? What—"

"Excuse me," Jesse interrupted airily, "but dinner's going to be on in a minute, and we thought you'd like a drink first. Care to join us?"

Both Bensen and Ray Dunbar swung around, their discussion forgotten in that moment. Shanna was so nervous that Jesse couldn't help feeling it.

Bensen's black eyes flickered from his sister to take in Jesse. "Yes." A little crooked smile shaped his mouth. "Coming, Ray?"

Ray didn't seem to have heard him. "Hello, Shanna," he said happily.

"Hello, Ray."

Bensen wrapped his hand around Jesse's arm and pulled her slightly back so that they followed Shanna and Ray across the hall to the salon. His hand stayed there, warm and firm. "What's your guess as to dinner?" he murmured, bending his dark head down to hers.

"It's turned out wonderfully. Martha even surprised me. If you get a chance, compliment her. And please, be careful with Shanna, she's—"

"You wouldn't be trying to tell me what to do, now would you?"

"Never." Jesse gulped.

Bensen gave her a sharp sardonic smile and stood staring down at her. "You're looking very lovely."

Jesse's eyes widened, and she stared up at him. His words plus the change in his expression upset her. When would he let go of her?

"I didn't think you noticed such things," she finally responded.

"That and a whole lot more," drawled Bensen, watching her closely, one corner of his mouth turning up.

The room seemed terribly stuffy to her, and she wished Shanna weren't in such a deep discussion with Ray, for she would dearly have loved to go to her. And what was Bensen referring to when he said "and a whole lot more"?

Apparently Bensen liked the quandary he'd put her in, for he smiled suddenly, his teeth gleaming white against the teak bronze of his face. He was standing close to her, much too close, looking down, his hand warm on the soft flesh of her upper arm. Even in her high heels Jesse was still shorter than Bensen and had to look up into his face. She felt her sense of time vanish; she was oblivious to the passing seconds. His fingers moved on her arm in a little soft caress.

The spell was broken by Martha's gruff announcement, "Dinner's ready now."

The meal went by without a hitch. The honey-baked ham was succulent, the roasted potatoes tender and appetizing, the garden-fresh green beans perfection. Grandmother was in an ebullient mood. It was clear she liked to have company for dinner. It was also clear to everyone that Bensen and Ray basically got along well together. Jesse could see Shanna relaxing under her very eyes. She was a totally different person from the quiet moody melancholy girl Jesse had met at her first dinner with the Everharts.

Dessert, a baked Alaska, took everyone by surprise, when Martha brought it to the table with a flourish. Martha was complimented by everyone, from Bensen down to the twins, and it was easy to see that under her I-don't-care attitude she was bursting with pride. Jesse hadn't been too worried right from the start, for she'd seen the cook put on a clean fresh apron that afternoon, and that was always a good sign.

As they were sipping their coffee and liqueurs, Bensen said appreciatively, "If I had room, I'd start eating all over again. From start to finish." His eyes found Jesse's, and she knew he was thanking her for her hand in the dinner's preparation. She smiled back readily, thinking that he was tremendously handsome when he wasn't frowning.

"Did you really want to go over those things tonight, Ben?" Ray asked. "There's an excellent band at the Kinghorn Lodge, and I thought Shanna and I might take in the evening there."

Jesse heard Shanna's muffled gasp and saw the sudden sharpening of grandmother's brown eyes. She wondered how Bensen would react now. She didn't have long to wait.

"There's no rush; we can do the rest tomorrow or the day after." Bensen grinned at Ray and then smiled at a startled Shanna. Everyone began to rise in concert from the dining table.

"I'll keep the twins amused," Jesse offered. "I'm a great baby-sitter."

"We're too old for baby-sitters!" Merit protested.

"I know. That's why I volunteered," answered Jesse. "If it were *really* a case of baby-sitting do you think I'd have asked for it?"

Merit giggled happily at that, then asked, "Are you going dancing, mummy? Are you?"

"We-ell. . . ."

"Yes," answered Ray, "she is. With me." He added gently, "Do you mind?"

"Oh, no! You've a nice mustache," Merit laughed, "I'm sure it's all right."

"Have a good time," Bensen put in, his eyes on his sister's face. He turned to Ray, saying, "Just take good care of Shanna, and don't get home too late."

That caused Shanna to send Bensen an indignant look, but in Jesse it produced a much different reaction. Shanna might not know it, but she was very lucky to have Bensen and grandmother. Nobody had ever said those things to Jesse. It wasn't that Sister Theresa hadn't cared about Jesse after she grew up; it was just that by then she'd had a whole new batch of children to love. She simply hadn't had time to spend with someone out of her charge.

Jesse felt a lump torn in her throat. It would have been nice just once, just *once*, to have someone there to say, "And don't get home too late." It gave one a feeling of belonging, and she had never had that in her entire life. She'd always belonged only to herself.

After Shanna and Ray had left—through the front door this time—grandmother said cheerfully, "Now I know why Shanna's taken such a fancy to walking in the forest. I didn't think she could be that interested in trees! It's the ranger! Pleasant fellow... seems as if he has a good head on his shoulders. And he doesn't let you boss him around, Bensen. That's good! Well, good night, Ben. Good night, my dear. Sleep well. That was a lovely dinner. We should have company more often." It was amazing, Jesse thought, watching her ascend the stairs, that she could look so frail, yet be so vigorous. "Send Martha up to me, will you?"

"I'd better go see where the girls have got to." Jesse turned to go, but Bensen stopped her. Martha brushed past them to follow Mrs. Everhart upstairs.

"They've gone out to see Shanna and Ray off. Hey—what's the matter?" His hold on her arm tightened, and his other hand came up to lift her chin, his touch surprisingly gentle. "You're looking sad,

Jesse.'' His dark head tilted to one side as he studied her face. ''What's the matter?''

Unknowingly he wasn't helping her sudden sadness; he was making it worse. She felt very weepy now.

''Nothing, nothing's the matter.'' What *was* the matter with her? ''I've got something in my eye, that's all.''

''Here, let me have a look....'' He bent down closer, and Jesse panicked. His mouth was just too near hers for comfort. She twisted her head away, and turning quickly so that her full skirt swirled out against his legs, she rushed up the stairs.

''I've got some eye drops,'' she called down to him. ''They always work best.''

With a decided frown Bensen watched her until she'd disappeared around the landing.

CHAPTER FIVE

A SLIGHT WIND had sprung up off the ocean, and it skeined Jesse's hair out on the breeze. The rush of air felt cool and delightful against her bare skin after the pressing heat of the day. There was no one about—Bensen was telephoning in his den, Shanna and the twins had gone off somewhere on the horses and Martha was snoring in a hammock. Grandmother was in the salon, reading a novel in the cool dimness of the house. Jesse felt peaceful and quiet and lazy. She meandered around the garden, listening to the wind in the treetops sighing and rustling and whispering, the boughs creaking as they rubbed against one another; the mewing of the sea gulls; the quick high-pitched chattering of unseen squirrels.

Suddenly she felt an icy cold hard jab in the middle of her back. She sprang forward and at the same time looked over her shoulder. A grizzled, dirty old man stood holding a long-barreled shotgun. It was pointed directly at her.

"Now I've got ya!" he shouted. "Thought you'd get away with it, did ya? Ha, ha! Got ya right where I want ya. Right in my sights." He wiped his mouth and stubbly chin with a filthy tattered sleeve. "Dirty thievin' varmints! I'll teach ya; I'll teach ya to try to grab from ol' Bob. Bob's real smart, he is! He knows when he's been took!''

Jesse was trembling from head to foot. "What are you talking about?" she demanded. "Who are you? Can't you point that gun somewhere else?"

"You betcher, me lovely, right at yer liver! Richest seam I ever found, and you here with that big house an' all try to swipe it. I'll show you what ol' Bob's made of!"

"Oh, please don't! There must be some mistake. I'm sure we can sort it all out!"

"You ain't thievin' from me, you ain't. I ain't a goin' to sort *nothin'* out!"

"Bensen! Bensen, help!" She tried to speak more calmly. "Bensen will see that you're reimbursed for—for any, uh, losses.''

"Reim—what? You tryin' to confuse me? You tryin' to toy with ol' Bob?" He stepped closer and poked the cold barrel of the gun at her stomach, jabbing it in a couple of times. Jesse thought she'd faint. The gun was cocked.

"J-just one minute. I'll go get someone who can help you get back whatever it is. Please don't shoot, please. I'll be right back. Please put down your gun, Bob." So saying, Jesse cautiously backed up several steps; then, when it looked as though he wouldn't shoot, she turned and ran. She flew into the house crying, "Bensen...*Bensen!*"

She charged straight to the den and startled Bensen as she clutched both his arms. "Bensen!" she gasped gratefully, trying to catch her breath and spill out the story at the same time.

Automatically his large hands settled on her hips, and he drew her closer to him. "Hey, hey, easy now, Jesse, honey. You look as though you've a gun to your back."

"I do! I mean, there *is*!" As quickly as she could, she told him what had happened in the garden.

"You stay here," Bensen ordered, heading for the door. Abruptly he stopped at the wall dividing the hall from the library. He pressed some panels, and a section of the wall silently slid open to reveal a whole bank of guns—hunting rifles, shotguns, revolvers.

Jesse watched in amazement as Bensen selected one of the larger rifles and slung a belt of cartridges over his shoulder. With an odd look in her direction he sped out and down the terrace steps. Jesse moaned—and then tore after him. There was no way she was going to stay in the house!

Her heart quaking, she followed Bensen at a safe distance, staying right behind him so that he wouldn't see her. He strode with long easy steps over to the man who called himself Bob. A film of perspiration broke out on Jesse's forehead.

"Well, I'll be darned!" she heard Bensen saying. "If it isn't old Bob! Where've you been all this time?"

"Here an' there; here an' there." Old Bob, cocking his stubbly chin, sized up Bensen with gleaming calculating eyes.

"You say I stole something from you. What is it?" Jesse shivered in the hot still air.

"My claim, you ol' geezer, that's what. My claim!"

"I see. Well...let's both put down our weapons and talk this out, real sociablelike. No need to get hurt, either one of us. Let's put our guns down, both at the same time now."

Their eyes on each other, the two men slowly bent and laid their guns down in the grass. Just as slowly they eased up again. Jesse sighed and wiped her hand over her forehead.

"Where is this claim?" asked Bensen.

"Gopher Mountain—you know, that belly of rock that sticks right out an' looks jest like a gopher head. I put a marker on it, and it's gone. You plannin' to jump my claim? You think mebe ol' Bob's not smart enough ta know?"

"Let's see...that'd be Section 103, probably. We were logging in that area a couple of weeks ago. Would your marker have been a cairn—a pile of stones?"

"That's it; that's it all right! Ha, ha! Do you do know 'bout it."

"Why, sure! My foreman called me. Said some of his men knocked the stones over hauling out a tree. Real sorry about that. Knowing how you prospectors feel about things like that, I hustled up there and hammered in a yellow flag on the exact spot. Didn't you see it?"

"Well, shore I seen it. Couldn't help but see it there bright as day. I figured somebody was a tryin' to hustle in on me, that yeller flag an' all."

"If I'd known it was your claim, I'd have put your name on the flag. But how could I tell? I figured whoever owned it would find it same as he left it.

Easier to spot, too, with that flag. It was just as you left it, wasn't it?"

"Well, shore, that it was. So you put that there fer me?"

"That's right, Bob."

"Well, that ain't so bad. I didn't know fer shore, though, so's I came with my gun. Niver can tell when folk're gonna turn sour on ya."

"That's so. Well, now, you old geezer, care for a drink?"

"Hey, like that real fine, I would. You're lookin' right good, Ben."

"So're you. Need a bath, though."

"Ain't you tellin' the truth! I can smell my own stink a mile away."

"The creeks are pretty cold for bathing. Come on up to the house. We'll have you fixed up in no time."

"That's right kind, right kind. You betcher I will! Who's the purdy little lady? Didn't know ya got yersel' a woman, Ben."

"What?" Bensen looked over his shoulder to see Jesse standing uncertainly a short distance away. He sighed and shook his head. "That's Jesse. And she ain't mine. I mean, she isn't."

"You did yoursel' real smart, ketchin' her."

"Er, she's—"

"Yep, real smart. Say, if'n I git this claim comin' good, I might be thinkin' of marryin' mysel'. I may be old, but I'm a tough ol' geezer, you betcher! Niver bin married. I think I got mysel' a rich one there on Gopher. Women, they like a house and purdy things.... Mebe now I kin git some."

"You have some woman in mind?" Bensen was keeping his face straight with an effort, then he couldn't suppress his grin any longer.

"Not a particular one. And 'course, not one as young as yourn. But Gopher, now, that's the best I ever seen in all my born days. Wouldn't that be right smart, me comin' in rich as old as I am!"

"You're thinking gold?"

"Shhh! Not so loud, not so loud. Them trees has ears, don't ya know."

"You're right. Listen, if you need any help—you know how rumors spread—you call me. I've got men out of work, and I could send you a couple just to keep an eye on things. You know what the smell of gold's like."

"Might jest do that, Ben. Say, I'm right glad I came 'round here. Real nice seein' ya agin, Ben. An' it's bin a long time since my last whiskey."

Jesse turned and hurried into the house. She went to the salon, poured two generous helpings. of whiskey and placed both glasses and bottle on the table in Bensen's den. Then she raced up the stairs two at a time, pulled some towels out of the linen closet and set them in a conspicuous spot in the large upstairs bathroom. She started running a bath, rummaging next through the medicine cabinets. When she'd found a razor and shaving cream, she added them to the towels.

The men were entering the house as she came down, their guns now resting casually in their hands as if they'd been out hunting together. Bensen was laughing uproariously at some story Bob was in the

process of telling. Coming to the finish, Bob slapped
Bensen on the shoulder and roared, too, but seeing
Jesse, he sobered, the bright eyes glinting at her from
under salt-and-pepper brows.

"Fergive me, Jesse, ma'am, my words ain't fit fer
purdy little ears like yourn."

She raised one brow and smiled. "I've heard some
salty stories in my day. Carry right on." Privately she
thought he'd have some wonderful tales to tell.
"There's whiskey in the den, and your bath is upstairs ready anytime you are."

"My, but if you ain't a sight fer sore eyes, Jesse,
ma'am! All soft an' sweetlike."

"Thank you, Bob."

"Say, Bob, I noticed you don't have your pack,"
Bensen put in. "Lost it?"

"Yep, dang ol' fool that I be. Lost it crossin' Flet-
cher Creek in the spring rush. Nearly lost me, too!"

Jesse smiled again at Bob, then left the men to go
to the kitchen. If she was right, old Bob would be
staying for supper, and it was time to hustle Martha
out of her hammock.

Jesse sidled back into the library, itching to listen in
on Bob and Bensen, yet not certain of her welcome.
The moment Bob spotted her, he nodded her in.

"That bath still hot? It's gotta be hot to get this'n
offa me."

"It's boiling."

"Heh, heh. I'll run on up an' jump in." Old Bob
tipped his head back and poured the whole glass of
whiskey down his throat. Smacking his lips, he
bounded up.

"I, ah, just saw Martha," Jesse said tentatively, looking Bensen's way. He understood and nodded. "Bob, won't you stay for supper?" she invited. "We'd love to have you."

"Geez, an' here I was a hopin' you'd ask. I'll be so bright an' shiny ya won't recognize me when I come back down, Jesse, ma'am."

When he had gone, she turned to Bensen and half whispered, "What has he got to wear? If he gets back into those filthy rags, he'll. . . ."

"You want to dress him, too?" There was a small sardonic smile on his lips.

"Well, I just thought. . .and if he lost his pack. . . ." Her voice dwindled away into silence as Bensen continued to watch her contemplatively. She began to feel terribly self-conscious then and longed to get away from him, but she couldn't move.

"You want to take care of everybody who comes within your range, don't you?" His amusement couldn't hide what Jesse thought was derision.

"I do not!" she protested hotly. "It's just that—"

"I know; I know," he interrupted her, smiling openly now. He got up, and as he walked past her, he brushed one finger carelessly over her cheek. "It's just that you're 'all soft an' sweetlike,' as ol' Bob said." The smile widened into a grin at her surprise. He strode to the bottom of the hall stairs and shouted up them, "Hey, Bob, you wouldn't take it amiss, now would you, if I offered you some clothes?"

Bob's grizzled head poked around the landing. "We's frien's, ain't we? Why should I git all uppity, seein' as how my duds ain't fit to wear? I've bin wearin' 'em since spring, heh, heh. Naah, that be right fine with me. I'd give ya some of my britches if'n ya needed 'em—an' if'n I had 'em.''

DINNER THAT EVENING turned out to be a riotous affair. Grandmother cackled over Bob's stories; the twins sat round-eyed at his descriptive language. Bob used both hands and his knife and fork to emphasize the finer points in his dialogue, and Jesse fell in love with him. He was just about the nicest old man she had ever met. Martha hung about in the background, and occasionally her disapproving expression melted into a laugh as Bob related the shenanigans he'd been up to and skirmishes he'd been into since last they'd seen him—more than a year ago.

They were nearing the end of the main course; Jesse had already finished and sat with her chin in her hand, gazing across the table at Bob. He was half out of his chair as he described a barroom brawl he'd been involved in.

"Pow! An' smack! That big bloke jest flew over th' table, an' me an' Cappy there ducked an' came up swingin'. Next I know Cappy dives under th' bar, an' next thing bottles are whizzin' through th' air. Heh, heh. I grab me some as they're a flyin' past, an' stuff 'em in my pack. An' Joe, th' barman—he sees me an' comes a lungin' at me. Now Joe's big, real big—an' mean! I figger it's lights out fer ol' Bob wen this other pucky little fella jumps right on Joe's back from behind, an' down they both go. Crash! Th' table breaks, an' the chairs break—Joe's real big, ya see. Then Cappy—he comes slinkin' through all the fists flyin' and arms flailin'. He grabs me by the collar an' says, 'Cops! Red-jackets! They's a comin!' Well, now, I ain't particler 'bout spendin' the night in jail, so him an' I lights out th' back way, an we run. Gosh, we run like th' devil's after us'n. We run clear through th' town—it were Tenedos Bay—and we run clear into th' bush an' don't quit till we's halfway up the mountain!''

Jesse thought she'd heard the front door closing but ignored it.

''We-ell, wen we gits to our camp, why, we have us'n a party! Drunker'n skunks we got. Drank till the moon set. An' then Cappy—he's heard that if'n ya drink lotsa water, ya don git a hangover next day. So off he waddles down to th' creek, and he gits down and sticks his head in an' is a gulpin' away, and th' next thing I know he's gone! Heh, heh. Fell right in!''

Suddenly Bob stopped short. Jesse's eyes went from him to Shanna sitting beside him; they were both staring at the door behind her. Shanna did not look pleased. And then Jesse recognized the sharp tap-tap-tap of Dorothy's walk.

Old Bob doffed an imaginary hat as Dorothy entered. ''Well, now, how-de-do, ma'am,'' he said and settled back into his chair.

''Hello,'' she said to everyone, ignoring Bob. She went over to Bensen, stooped down and kissed him sweetly on the mouth. ''Hello, darling. I just flew up with daddy for a short visit. Can't stay long, though. He'll be back for me in about two hours. There's an emergency of some sort in one of the new shafts, and he wanted to see personally what was going on.''

"Dorothy—" Bensen's hand stayed on her waist "—I don't think you've met Bob. . . ."

Jesse watched in anger as Dorothy's blue eyes coldly traveled up and down old Bob. How dare she be so insulting!

"Oh?" Dorothy raised one brow high. Pointedly she moved the chair Bensen had placed between him and Bob closer to Bensen before she sat down. Fastidiously arranging her skirts, she ran her eyes around the table, alighting finally on Jesse.

"You're still here," she said with finely measured charm.

"Yes, so it would seem," Jesse replied equally sweet. She couldn't help it, but her temper was rising. She tried not to look in Bensen's direction, and as he sat to her immediate right at the foot of the table, that was fairly hard to do.

Grandmother and Dorothy started a desultory conversation that lasted through dessert. No one else spoke much; Bob had lapsed into a strangely quiet mood. Jesse sighed inwardly, her appetite for the sweet gone. When Martha brought out the coffee and brandy, Bensen rose and announced that he and Bob would have theirs in the den.

As Bob left the table, he said, "Thankee, Jesse fer invitin' me to supper. And thankee Cecilia an' Shanna. A right pleasure, right pleasure. Martha, them steaks were divine!" He bowed courteously and bobbed off after Bensen.

"You invited that—that hobo for dinner?" Dorothy was aghast. "Isn't that. . . just a little bit forward of you? I can't imagine—"

"If Jesse hadn't, I would have," Shanna interrupted, her gentle shy manner gone. "Bob's not a hobo. We've known him for years, and he's a friend of ours."

Grandmother started to speak, then looked flustered when Dorothy got her word in first. "All the same, it's not really proper, is it? And that language. How can you let those innocent darlings—" she waved her hand at the twins "—sit through a whole dinner of that? His filth isn't fit for their young ears. If I were their mother, I certainly would not—"

"You're not their mother!" Shanna snapped. "Listening to Bob is learning about life. And Bob would never do anything to hurt them—or us."

"All the same," Dorothy insisted with a gentle smile, "he's not someone the twins should know. *I* wouldn't want them associating—"

"Bob's got as fine a character as any of us, including you Dorothy." Grandmother at last managed to squeeze into the heated conversation. "He may be rough and ready, but he has a good heart. I will not hear another word against him in my house!"

A heavy silence descended. Dorothy pursed her lips, then smiled expansively at grandmother.

"Of course, forgive me," she murmured. "I was just shocked that a guest in your house should have the temerity to invite another guest for dinner." Her laugh was silky. "I've been so busy lately—you just won't believe it, Cecilia, dear—or I'd have been up to visit a lot sooner. I was elected president of the

Women's Music Society for our chapter, even though I didn't think I should receive the title. It was pressed on me! And you won't believe whom I met last week. He's—''

Jesse looked at Shanna, and Shanna looked at Jesse. Shanna made a small grimace, and Jesse felt a terrible overwhelming desire to giggle. She rose hurriedly and gathered some plates together. Dorothy watched her, still speaking to grandmother. Then she spoke to Jesse.

"You've begun helping out about the house? How thoughtful of you. But I suppose you think that's only fair, considering how your visit has lengthened. I'm sure everyone appreciates what you do to help.''

"Martha does,'' Jesse answered with perfect equanimity, smiling right back. She left with her hands full.

Shanna was close on her heels, her hands too laden with dishes. She called over her shoulder to the twins, "Sam, Merry, you both help, okay?'' And they all trooped down the hall together.

Martha was groaning over the stacks of dishes she had to wash and muttering complaints under her breath, so Jesse took the coffeepot and went out to refill all the cups. Grandmother's and Dorothy's first—with more saccharine-sweet smiles—and then Bensen's and Bob's. She was entering the library when she heard Bob's hoot of laughter.

"So's ya got yersel' two! *Two* women! Ha, ha, ya ol' geezer you!''

Jesse stopped in her tracks.

"No, no." Bensen was trying to explain, "Jesse's, ah, a friend of the family, nothing more."

"Harrumph! What's that ya say? Why, I'd ruther hev that Jesse girl any day. With them nice big gold eyes. Th' other one looks like she's a peepin' out of glacier chips, an' I niver could stand them false eyelash things. Look like they's spiders when they's off. Like they could stand right up an crawl off when you wasn't lookin! Naah, you listen ta me, son, I've seen a good many women in my day—" Jesse was creeping out of the library "—good'uns an' bad'uns. Go fer that Jesse; she's—"

"I know, I know, 'all soft an' sweetlike.' But she's got a mouth on her that just doesn't quit!"

"Heh, heh. She's bin a talkin' back now, has she? Ya need a woman 'round th' house with a bit o' spunk to her, you betcher. Ain't no fun without that! You listen ta ol' Bob now...."

Jesse could hear no more, for she'd safely reached the library door. She stood in the hall, blushing and shaking her head. A friend of the family, was she? That was a new one! Straightening her shoulders and tossing her head so that her mane of chestnut hair fell back over her shoulders, she headed for the kitchen.

Jesse had to pass the salon doorway to reach the kitchen, and as she neared it, Dorothy's high voice wafted out to her, more strident than usual.

"When is Jesse leaving?" It was quite obvious that Dorothy didn't care whether anyone overheard her or not.

"When she finishes what she came to do," grandmother replied, and Jesse had to strain her ears to hear that.

"You don't think she's...how shall I put it, overstaying her welcome?"

"Dear sweet heaven, no!" This Jesse heard clearly, for Cecilia's tone had risen. "I enjoy her company, and so does everyone else here!"

"Everyone?" Dorothy's nuances were not hard to grasp. Jesse gritted her teeth. "I suppose she's entertaining enough in her own way. Although her manners—well, she doesn't come from a good family, does she? And one can always tell, by so many... *little* things. Has she done any work at all on that book of hers? I can't see that it would be much of a success, after all—"

"That's quite enough!" grandmother cut in, her tone acid. "You may not like the book when it's finished, my dear, but I can assure you that your tastes aren't everyone's!"

"That's true," Dorothy laughed. "I suppose we can't *all* be intellectual sorts."

"No, indeed not!" returned grandmother. Her voice sank, and Jesse missed the next part. The trouble was, now she didn't want to pass that door—not for anything. She decided to go out the front of the house and around through the garden to get back to the kitchen. She spun around, bumping right into Bensen behind her.

"Ohhh-h!" she gasped, and clutched at the coffee-pot—which had almost escaped her grasp.

He put out his hands to steady her.

"H-h-how long have you been there?" Jesse whispered fearfully.

"I've had an earful," Bensen whispered back. His mouth looked tight, but there was a vivid sparkle in his eyes that made Jesse think he was secretly laughing.

"I didn't mean to listen, really!" she defended. "I was going to the kitchen, but I couldn't—I couldn't go past that door after—"

"Shhh!" He grasped both her arms as Dorothy's voice once more floated out of the salon.

"Don't you think it's time you put an announcement in the paper, Cecilia? That Bensen and I are engaged, I mean. It wouldn't be proper if I did it, and I really think it should be done quite soon."

"I'll put it in when Bensen tells me to," came grandmother's dry reply. "And shouldn't you have a ring before that announcement goes in?"

"I can't imagine why Bensen is taking so much time choosing one. I could just scream sometimes."

"Scream at him, my dear, not at me."

"Yes, well, perhaps you could remind him. After all, it would be to your advantage if the wheels were put in motion." Dorothy's voice was like honey itself.

In contrast, grandmother sounded downright unhelpful. "Would it really? How do you mean?"

"Why, isn't it clear? When I'm mistress here, you can relax! It takes a lot of energy to run this household, and I'm sure it must tire you terribly. After all, you are getting on in years, and I'm sure there are plenty of times you'd rather rest than see to everything. I'm sure you do all that you can, considering your...well, infirmity, and I don't suppose Shanna's much help to you. So the *sooner* Bensen and I are married, the better.''

"And what are some of the improvements you had in mind?"

Perhaps Dorothy couldn't tell, but both Jesse and Bensen knew that grandmother was up to no good using that suddenly warm encouraging tone.

"First thing, that Martha definitely go. I've said to Bensen many a time—"

"I know, I know, carry on."

"Second, I'm sure you'd feel better if there were a qualified nurse here. After all, at your age one never knows when...and if we could find a suitable comfortable nursing home, I think you'd be much happier there. You'd have company your own age. Just think of the fun you could have! Third, it's a sheer disgrace the way Shanna lets those twins run about like *savages*! I know of an excellent private school that would soon bring them up to snuff."

"Do you, my dear."

"If I sent along a letter of introduction that would pave their way, of course."

"Of course!"

"Yes. And then...the solution to Shanna is more difficult. But I'm sure I could find someone suitable to marry her. Bensen shouldn't have her on his hands. It must be terribly trying for him, the poor darling."

"Yes, the *poor* darling."

Jesse pressed a hand to her mouth. She didn't

know whether to be horrified at what Dorothy was saying, or amused by the whole situation. Amusement, though, seemed to be winning the battle, for giggles were rising in her throat. She didn't dare look at Bensen. She couldn't imagine what he thought.

"That's basically it," Dorothy continued, supremely confident. "There are other minor things, too, of course. The whole place needs redecorating, for example. But what do you think of my suggestions? Do you see the wisdom in them?"

"Wisdom my hat!" Grandmother's words were clipped. "You are a stuffed shirt, Dorothy Jorgensen, that's what you are. And you'd better revise some of your hoity-toity plans if you figure on moving in here with me!"

"There, there, please don't overexcite yourself. You know that at your age it's terribly unhealthy."

"That's the fourth time you've told me how old I am... my *dear*!"

"Well, I didn't mean. I only want to—I have the feeling I'm being insulted!"

"Took you long enough to catch on!"

"We'd better get out of here," Bensen suddenly whispered into Jesse's ear. "One or the other of them is going to erupt out of there any second."

Pulling her after him into the library, he shut the door and leaned against it, laughing silently, his wide shoulders shaking. Jesse stared at him in wonder. She had thought he would be furious, absolutely furious. She had expected him to go charging into the salon to lecture Dorothy. And there he stood in stitches! She bit her lip as the laughter that had been building in her ever since dinner came bubbling out. Bensen looked at her, and she tried to stop.

"I'm sorry," she gasped. "I don't mean to laugh at your fiancée but...but—" a spasm of giggles overcame her "—I'm sure she really is quite nice, but...but...." Jesse urgently cleared her throat. "Umm...would you like some coffee?"

"That's what I was going for." Bensen sobered, too, but at the corners of his mouth a smile still threatened. He was watching her with those penetrating black eyes. "Don't you know you're not supposed to eavesdrop, Jessamine?" he teased.

She slanted a glance at him through her hair, then quickly looked away. "I, umm, don't think I should say another word at the moment."

"You've something on your mind?"

"I've a great deal on my mind, but I—I don't want to meddle."

He laughed softly, and something in his laugh alerted Jesse. She threw another glance up at him, suddenly realizing that his eyes were fastened on the low neckline of her dress, on the rounded swell of her breasts. Her lips parted as she took a deep breath. She felt extremely light-headed, all at once aware they were standing much too close together. Every nerve in her seemed to be vitally alive to him, to his strength, to his maleness. She took another deep breath, but that didn't help. Desperately she wished Bensen would stop looking at her like that.

"Bensen...."

"Jesse?" His voice was low and soft.

"Nothing. I—I mean, I'd better go."

Neither of them saw Bob peeking around the door of the den at them.

"Perhaps you should." Now there was something almost rueful in his smile as he stepped away from the door to open it for her. She brushed past him and headed down the hall toward the kitchen, looking neither left nor right as she passed the salon. She'd entirely forgotten to give Bensen and Bob their coffee. . . .

MARTHA, SHANNA, with Merit on her knee, and Jesse, with Samantha on her knee, were having a cozy chat in the kitchen when Bensen's head appeared above the saloon doors.

"I've asked Bob to spend the night," he said as he advanced into the kitchen. "Can we get a room ready for him? He needs new supplies, picks and axes and things like that, so I'm taking him down to Vancouver with me in the morning." He shoved his hands in his pockets and looked around at the female gathering.

"If by 'can *we* get a room ready,' you mean can *I* get a room ready," Martha said sourly, "I suppose it can be done. Which one?"

"Something handy," Bensen shrugged.

"None of them's handy," Martha grumbled, shifting out of the chair.

"Bensen?" came a high familiar voice. "Bensen, is that you?" Suddenly Dorothy entered the kitchen. She went over to Bensen and slipped an arm through his, smiling sunnily up at him. "I thought I'd stay overnight. You *are* going to Vancouver tomorrow, aren't you?'' Bensen nodded. "Then you can take me," she continued. "I've just told daddy I'm staying over. I've hardly had a chance to see you at all!" She pouted prettily. "I thought we could at least have the rest of the evening together, darling."

"So that's *two* bedrooms now, is it?" Martha scowled.

"Er, yes," Bensen answered.

"Two?" Dorothy's high voice rose higher. "Why, who else—"

"Bob," clipped Bensen.

"What?" Jesse didn't think Dorothy's voice could get any higher, but it did. "You mean to tell me that...that dirty old man is staying *here*? Bensen, do you think it's wise to encourage—"

"Your bedroom will be on the opposite side of the house, Dorothy. I'm sure you'll be quite safe." He pulled his hands from his pockets, and her arm slipped out of his. Then, with a hand on her back, he steered a reluctant Dorothy out of the kitchen. She was trying to catch Shanna's eye.

"Should the twins be up this late?" she asked, her voice trailing. "It's ten o'clock."

"I'm not staying if that woman comes to live in this house!" Martha said fiercely once Dorothy and Bensen had gone. "Not with the likes of her!" she added, rustling out of the kitchen.

Shanna gave a long drawn-out sigh. "Sometimes...." She stopped as grandmother wandered in.

A moment later Bob joined them, and then Martha returned. The evening ended in a kitchen party that lasted late. At the close of it Shanna showed Bob to his bedroom, and Jesse settled grandmother in for the night since Martha seemed asleep on her feet. She had also had a fair bit of plum wine—which had made her a jolly companion, to the surprise of everyone.

Upstairs grandmother asked Jesse for her novel—she suffered from insomnia, but refused to give up coffee—which she'd left in the salon. Jesse smiled and went to get it. With the house now dark and hushed, she tiptoed down the stairs. A dim light was burning in the salon as Jesse quietly entered. She found the book where grandmother had told her it would be, picked it up and reached to turn off the lamp.

It was then that she saw Bensen, sitting absolutely still in a chair by the fireplace. Frightened, for she hadn't expected anyone to be there, Jesse stood clutching the book. She stared at him, her heart pounding as his dark eyes probed hers. Then he sighed slowly and eased his tall length out of the chair.

"It must be late," he said, his eyes resting thoughtfully on her from across the room.

"It is," Jesse replied very quietly.

"Did you have a good time tonight? It certainly sounded like you did."

"I—yes, we had a grand time." For a moment Jesse had the impression Bensen would rather have been with them, laughing in the kitchen, than with Dorothy. Then she shook her head slightly. Just because she knew where she would have been, had she had a choice, didn't mean Bensen would have made the same choice. Dorothy was his fiancée, after all. It only made sense that he would want to be with her. What had they done all evening, she wondered, closeted together in the den? For no reason a shiver, a tickle of apprehension, ran up her spine. She struggled to appear calm, despite the sudden tightening in her chest.

"Bob's quite the fellow, isn't he?" she asked a little lamely.

"He's a good friend—but a tough customer if he's crossed."

"I gathered that." Jesse sensed neither of them was really speaking what was foremost in his mind. They seemed to be hedging about a bush, skirting the real issue, but for the life of her she couldn't pinpoint what that was. He had always puzzled her, and now she was feeling thoroughly perplexed by her own reactions to him. He looked as he usually did, distant, aloof—rather arrogant, actually. A tall dark lean whip of a man—a tough customer, as he had said of Bob. These backwoods men, it seemed, had quite a lot in common in some ways. And suddenly she didn't think Dorothy and this man standing so tensely still made a good match at all.... It seemed a dreadful waste of a fine man.

Jesse felt rooted to the spot. Why couldn't she just say good-night and leave? The lengthening silence between them was becoming thicker. His unwavering gaze locked hers for what seemed an interminable moment. The utter quiet held only the sound of the clock ticking and her heart beating under her ribs, pounding and pounding until it filled her ears.

Something was happening to her focus, to her, in the dim soft light; it seemed that Bensen was right over her instead of several yards away. She blinked but the impression wouldn't go; his face was inches from her own and coming closer, as if...as if.... The sharp intake of her breath abruptly awakened her to the reality. Bensen hadn't budged an inch.... She blinked again, the sherry-amber eyes wide and confused.

"Jesse," his voice, low and intense, startled her. "Go to bed. Now. Or we could both be sorry in the morning."

"Good night, Bensen," she said shakily, turning on her heel and half running from the salon.

More sedately now, she crept up the curving stairs to her bedroom. But her thoughts were still in something of a swirl. There seemed to be all kinds of things suddenly that needed clarifying. In her room, she sat on the soft cushions of the window seat and brushed her long hair, feeling oddly awake. Something was changing between her and Bensen; somewhere, somehow, their relationship had changed.

Perhaps she'd grown used to his ways and had found that his bark was worse than his bite. And there had even been times when he was almost pleasant to her—such as tonight, when they'd stood together in the darkened hallway outside the salon. She'd almost had the impression that he liked her, too. Was she mad? And then there was that really odd feeling that he'd been about to kiss her just moments ago. Bensen? It couldn't be! There weren't any grounds for believing that. He'd said she wasn't his type, and he certainly wasn't hers. She *was* mad. It *was* all in her mind.

She stared out the window. A moon full and round like a silver dollar shone against a backdrop of deep royal-blue sky. Jesse smiled, an oddly unhappy little smile. That was it—she was suffering from lunacy. She switched off the lamp and climbed into bed.

She lay down, quiet, and stared up at the shadowy ceiling. She turned on her right side, cuddling into the soft eiderdown quilt. The moon seemed to slide by, and a quarter circle of silver showed in a high corner of the casement.

A pool of silver light fell on the carpet and grew slowly, stealthily, bigger. What was Bensen doing now? Was he still awake, too? He was taking Dorothy to Vancouver tomorrow, and Bob was going with them. A slight smile hovered on her lips as she wondered who would get the front seat of the Mercedes—Dorothy or Bob?

Jesse's thoughts continued to torment her. What had happened tonight with Bensen, she realized, was an exception. Or was it? There was that other time...there were several other times when.... The moonlight crept up the leg of a chair and spread slowly, slowly, across the carpet to the edge of her bed and then over the coverlet. Somewhere far in the depths of the forest an owl hooted, and it was a faint puff of sound.

THE NEXT MORNING Jesse wasn't wondering about anything; she was hard at work in the attic immediately after breakfast. Clear broad daylight had worked its magic, and she was enjoying her research. Breakfast had been fun, too, with Bob and the family, especially since Dorothy had had breakfast in bed—something Martha complained about bitterly.

Jesse hadn't been at work for more than half an hour when grandmother came up as promised to recount more of her adventures. Hard on her heels came Bob, trying—unsuccessfully—to sidle in unnoticed. He grinned sheepishly.

"Do join us, Bob," grandmother said dryly, her pure white head tilted to one side and a small smile twitching her lips.

"Jest thought I'd like ta listen in. Won't disturb ya, no sirree. I'll jest sit here quietlike. That Dorothy person shore takes a deal of time gittin' hersel' ready to go. It's them eyelash things she wears, I'll betcher. First she's gotta ketch 'em, an' then she's gotta paste 'em on! Heh, heh. Hope she don' grab a spider by mistake, heh, heh, heh." Bob slapped his knee. He'd at last settled himself in an old creaking chair. "Carry right on now; don' mind me."

Grandmother started speaking. Before long, Bob interjected, "That reminds me, that reminds me! D'you recall. . . ."

Jesse, her eyes alight with excitement, switched on the tape recorder. She nestled back into the wicker chair to listen.

The twins crept in and settled on a packing crate side by side. Jesse glanced over at them and, for a moment, couldn't tell them apart. The expression on their faces was exactly alike; they glowed with an avid curiosity. Then Shanna tiptoed in, smiling

quickly at Jesse before she sat down on an old chest.
They made a rough circle now, cozily arranged in the
dim attic, bright gold sunlight spilling in in narrow
shafts from the windows.

"My very first Christmas here...." Grandmother
was silent for a second, then laughed. "I had no
money of my own left, not a penny, and I was heart-
broken that I'd nothing to give my Samuel. Being so
young—and rather foolish, I imagine—I took it very
seriously that I had no gift for him. And I knew he
had something for me, for he would hint and grin
and then go all mysterious.

"One morning, about two weeks before Christmas, he hinted again, those black eyes of his sparkling, and I couldn't bear it. As soon as he left, I
burst into tears. Lily's mother found me crying."

"Lily's *mother*?" Samantha said incredulously.

"Shh!" Her twin nudged her. "Did she help you,
gramma?"

Grandmother chuckled. "In more ways than one,
Merit. Samuel, your great-grandfather, had asked
her to give me a hand about the house. He thought
she might help me adjust to the life here. I was alone
all day, you see, half frightened out of my wits by
that incredible forest. I needed to make friends, too.
There were hardly any other Europeans around here
at that time, so I had to make my friends among the
people who—then—seemed utterly foreign and
strange to me."

The old woman paused, and Jesse's attention
drifted to Shanna, whose blue eyes suddenly seemed
sad. Was she remembering her own brief marriage,

those lonely months spent in the bush? The sound of grandmother's voice claimed her once more as the old woman resumed her story.

"Well, Lily's mother found me crying, and although we didn't speak the same language, eventually the story came out. She thought hard for a few moments, then got my handbag and my walking coat and motioned for me to follow. I had never ventured out into the forest without Samuel, and I was frightened, but my need to get a present was stronger. She took me straight to her village. To say I was terrified, overwhelmed, wouldn't be saying enough. I was literally shaking in my boots. Their dress, their houses, their food—my eyes must have been popping from my head.

"But I followed her and followed her right into one of the lodges, bending down to get through the entrance. She sat cross-legged in front of an old woman very respectfully, and I watched what she did and did the same. What looked like a very lovely piece of leather changed hands. Lily's mother then pressed it into *my* hands. I didn't know how to thank her—nor, at that time, what to do with it. For that matter, I didn't know how to thank the old woman. So I bowed three times very deeply to her and then twice to Lily's mother, only not so deeply. It seemed I had done the right thing.

"Through some pretty elaborate sign language she asked me whether I could make something with the leather that would please Samuel. I had the wonderful idea of a vest and, when we were home once more, took one out of the closet to show her what I meant."

"How did you sew the leather, gramma?" Merit put in.

"Lily's mother showed me how to sew with sinews," the old woman answered. "When the vest was all together it looked wonderful, but I wasn't yet satisfied. I motioned to Lily's mother that I wanted to add beadwork as I had seen among her own clothes. My untutored fingers made what looked like a dreadful mess to me at first. Several times I was close to tears again, but she was incredibly patient with me, and together by Christmas we managed to have the vest complete."

"And what did grandfather say?" Shanna asked eagerly.

"He was taken entirely by surprise, and he loved it, if I do say so myself. He wore it all the time. After he died, I packed it away. It never wore out."

"You packed it?" Shanna asked. "Where?" In her voice was subdued excitement.

"I—I...in one of the steamer trunks I brought over with me. It should be up here somewhere." Slowly grandmother stood, letting her eyes drift over the accumulation of crates and boxes and trunks. "It was the old kind, wooden with brass and leather straps. It—could that be it?" She sounded excited now, too.

Soon, with everybody's help, the trunk was pushed and pulled out of its place, quickly dusted and opened, and the contents spilled out to at last reveal the cherished vest.

It was a work of beauty—no doubt about that, Jesse thought. And it was still wearable, the leather smooth and pliant, the beadwork glistening with an array of colors. The sinews, too, were all still intact.

"I remember him wearin' that vest, you betcher." Bob was nodding his head emphatically. "Looked like a king in that vest. Yes sirree! That vest was the envy of all them who seen it."

Grandmother held it in her hands, her fingers running over the many beaded patterns in which could be seen intertwined both Indian and Victorian designs. "It's hard now to believe that we got all this done in two weeks," grandmother mused. "Ah, well...."

"So this is why the house is so quiet!" Bensen stood at the head of the attic stairs. "Bob, ready to go? What's that?"

And the whole story of the vest was recited again to Bensen, this time with Bob, Shanna and the twins fitting in pieces of the tale whenever they could get a word in edgewise. Jesse sat back and watched the expression on Bensen's face as he repeatedly eyed the vest. Quietly grandmother gave it to him to examine.

"That's the most beautiful vest I've ever seen!" he said, turning it over in his hands. Cecilia started, looked sharply up at Bensen, and the pale color of her cheeks heightened. She held out her hands for the vest, and Bensen returned it to her. "And what did *your* Christmas present turn out to be?" he asked.

"Oh, didn't I tell you? It was a horse. A three-year-old Arabian. Samuel knew how I loved horses—we'd always had them back home. After I got that horse, I went out in the bush more often; I wasn't as frightened, you see. What a beauty he was...like

black satin. Samuel had to pay a fortune for him.
Had him shipped up from San Francisco.''

''He must have been madly in love with you, too,''
Shanna said, smiling at her grandmother.

''Yes.'' Cecilia Anne smiled complacently. ''He
was.''

''Where on earth has everybody got to?'' Dorothy's cry came echoing up the attic stairs. ''Are you
up there, Bensen? Bensen! Where is everybody?''

For a moment no one answered, and then everyone
answered at once. Dorothy came up hurriedly.
''What's everyone doing in the attic, for crying out
loud.'' Her eyes fell on Jesse, and she murmured,
''Oh.''

Jesse wondered what that meant. Bob had been
right about glacier chips, she decided.

''Well, Bensen?'' Dorothy went to him and
touched her hand to his arm to get his attention.
''Aren't we ready to go? What's the holdup?''

Jesse thought she might have heard Bob snort, but
when she glanced over at him, he was looking perfectly innocent.

''And what's all the fuss about anyway?'' Dorothy
persisted.

Bensen looked down at her by his shoulder, and
Jesse wished she could see his expression. Then he
said, ''Grandmother was showing us a vest....''
And briefly, very briefly, he explained.

''How nice,'' Dorothy replied after he had finished. ''Now can we go? Oh, by the way, I think I
saw Lily coming up the drive.''

''Lily?'' Grandmother beamed. ''I'll have to show

her this. She would remember it. She loved it when she was little. Used to sit for hours on Sam's knee playing with all the beads.''

Dorothy had already been heading purposefully for the staircase, but now she turned. "Is it really true that Lily was going to marry your son, Andrew? I heard that somewhere.... Oh, yes, daddy told me. It's only a rumor, surely. I can't for a moment believe you would actually condone such a marriage, Cecilia!''

"No? Why?'' There was a curious note in grandmother's tone, and Jesse's eyes quickly flicked over to her.

"Why, she's...she's an....''

"An Indian?'' Bensen supplied for her. "You've noticed, then.''

"Don't be absurd! Of course she's an Indian. That's why....'' Dorothy's voice trailed off, as though there were no need to explain further.

"Why what? Explain yourself!'' Grandmother's voice was as fine-edged as a knife.

"We-ell, *your* son getting *married* to an *Indian*?''

"Lily was a charming girl then, and she's a charming woman now. I heartily gave my blessing,'' grandmother snapped. "After all, why shouldn't I?'' Her voice suddenly became airy, although when Jesse looked more closely at her, she saw the old eyes were razor sharp. "My Samuel was half Haida.''

Dorothy's astonishment could not have been more apparent. Jesse almost felt sorry for her; she had royally put her foot in her mouth.

"That's right.'' Bensen, Jesse saw, was grinning.

He slid his hand down Dorothy's arm. "That makes me Indian, too. Never thought you'd become engaged to an Indian, did you now?"

"You...you're...." Dorothy quavered, just barely above a whisper, swallowing and staring hard at Bensen.

"A savage," Bensen supplied once more. A laugh rippled through his frame. "Shanna here, as well, although you'd never think it to look at her." His tone was pleasant and conversational, and Jesse's eyes narrowed as she watched him. When he turned of a sudden and shot a look her way, she was startled.

"But why didn't you tell me!" The words exploded from Dorothy. She stopped and said more quietly, rather lamely, "I...I mean, you should h-have...."

"Told you?" Bensen added helpfully. "Would it have made any difference?"

Everyone's eyes were riveted on Bensen and Dorothy. Jesse held her breath. It seemed an awful moment. Old Bob shifted in his chair, and the resulting creak sounded very loud in the intense quiet.

"No. I—no! But why did you keep it from me?" she finished suspiciously.

"Is it commonplace to reveal one's ancestry for several generations back when one is introduced? Besides, I thought you knew. It's not exactly a secret we've Haida blood in our veins." Bensen sounded so highly amused that Jesse studied him keenly. He *was* smiling, but not exactly with amusement. The twist in the sensuous lips was ruthless. Jesse couldn't help shivering. She thanked her stars she wasn't Dorothy.

"Tha's right! You're a Haida, yes sirree. Tall an' skinny. An' that *nose*!"

"Yes...but only one-eighth Haida." Dorothy recovered her aplomb. "Shall we go now? We don't want to get home too late. I suppose you're coming with us, Mr., uh, Bob?"

"You betcher!" Old Bob bounced out of his chair.

After they had left, there was a gloomy silence in the attic.

"It'll be a fine day when she moves in!" grandmother spat out, grimly staring after them. "Well, I'd better go meet Lily. Now where did I put it? Ah!" Cecilia gathered up the vest and then picked her way through the attic to the stairs.

Jesse and Shanna were left staring at each other. Merit tugged at her mother's arm.

"Mummy, were Uncle Ben and Aunt Dorothy having a fight? Were they? Were they, mummy?"

"I, uh—" Shanna glanced quickly back to Jesse "—well, um, I suppose sort of a...a...."

"Fight," Jesse said, and grinned.

CHAPTER SIX

LATER THAT WEEK Bensen and Ray had another heated argument in the library—with the door open. This time the females of the household didn't blink an eye. If one was in the hall and strained her ears just slightly the occasional swear word could be heard, mixed in with ten-o'clock deadlines and the laying off of twenty men. There was talk of such-and-such a creek blocked by debris, plus some to-do about reseeding logged areas.

Jesse, approaching the library for a book that Mrs. Everhart had told her would be useful for background material, learned that the government supplied the seedlings and the personnel. The logging companies, however, were responsible for leaving the area clean and cleared, so that the reseeding might progress unhindered. Bensen's angry reply to Ray made Jesse decide to search out the book a little later in the day. Retracing her steps, she saw Shanna hovering in the salon doorway; she was looking mightily pleased with herself. The two young women had a quick whispered consultation before Jesse went back upstairs to the attic.

An hour later, as Jesse passed the salon doorway, she saw that Shanna and Ray were there, their low tones a murmur. Ray's arm was wrapped tightly around Shanna's waist, and the tender expression on his face as he looked down at her made Jesse hurry past. Cautiously, as though she were walking on eggs, she entered the library. Bensen was in his den, and her fleeting glance at him showed a tight mouth and furrowed brow.

Jesse absorbed herself in looking for the book—which, Cecilia had said, could be almost anywhere. She decided to start methodically at one corner of the room and, having carried the small library stepladder over, began searching from the top shelf down.

A short while later Shanna entered the library, and seeing Jesse there, she smiled gratefully at her. Bensen noticed Shanna had come in; he stood up from his desk and came into the library, too.

"Bensen," Shanna began before he had the chance to say anything, "Ray and the twins and I are going out for the day. He's in the salon now, using the phone." She stopped and eyed her brother warily. When he made no comment but merely nodded, Shanna cleared her throat and clasped her hands together. She shot a quick glance over to Jesse, standing very quietly on the ladder. "And we—I'm going out with him again tonight. We-we're going to the lodge, I think."

Again Bensen didn't comment, but he nodded. His dark aloof face registered neither pleasure nor displeasure. Shanna looked at him uncertainly, not knowing whether to leave it at that or say more. She waited a moment, then half turned to leave.

"Is it serious, Shanna?" Bensen asked abruptly.

Shanna swung around and gazed at him with wide eyes. "How should I know!" she exclaimed, as though Bensen had asked her if the moon were made of cheese. And with that and a rather saucy smile she left.

Jesse had turned to the books to hide her grin, but she heard Bensen's explosive sigh behind her.

"Jesse!"

Her face straight and carefully blank, she turned to face him, for once looking down at him and liking the effect. From her height she saw the top of his head and the thick gleaming wealth of raven hair, a stray lock falling over his high forehead.

"What did she mean by that?" he demanded, frowning irritably at her. "You're a woman; perhaps you can decipher what she said. And don't look as though you don't know anything about anything."

"I think she means you're to keep your nose out of it," Jesse replied spiritedly. Stung out of watching her choice of words, she immediately regretted her answer. Bensen's lowered brows now shot up as he stared at her with cold annoyance and a certain angry cynicism that curled the corners of his beautiful mouth.

With slow deliberate steps he advanced; he put his hands in his jean pockets, stood at the foot of the ladder and glared up at her. "There are some days, Jessamine!..." he warned distinctly, then stopped and continued to glare at her. His lips compressed over what he had been about to say. With a final meaningful glance he turned on his heel and strode off to his den, slamming the door behind him. Jesse sighed; she stuck out her tongue at the closed door in the exact second that it reopened. Bensen leaned out, one eyebrow lifting at the sight of her fastly disappearing pink tongue.

"Two can play that game," he commented disparagingly.

Embarrassed, she replied tartly, "Oh? Well, let's see yours, then."

He blinked in surprise. "Sorry, it's not my style."

"You're afraid only for your dignity."

"And you've just lost all of yours!"

She shrugged. "That's all right; dignity gets rather heavy if one has to carry it around all the time."

"Meaning?" He returned to the foot of the ladder, his eyes glittering into hers.

She shrugged again, saying casually, "It was merely a statement of fact; no need to take it personally."

"Ha! And I guess frogs don't like water. Do you have any more pithy facts you'd like to share while we're at it?"

"I'm saving the rest for a rainy day."

He stared up at her, then snapped, "You've got the fastest mouth in the West."

Feeling a suddenly intense desire to reach down and touch his hair, she swallowed tightly and said very sweetly instead, "Thanks, Bensen, you've perked me right up. Here I was practically falling asleep. A little tiff with you gets the adrenaline going every time." So saying, she turned away from him and went up two more steps on the ladder, pretending to ignore him, pretending to concentrate on her search for that errant book. A quiet minute passed— and another and another. He was still there.

"What are you doing?" She twisted around to look down at him, her nerves vibrating at high pitch.

Slowly his gaze wandered upward from her bare legs over the curves of her body to at long last meet her eyes; that gaze had the blood pounding in her ears.

"Doing? I was merely observing the wonders of Mother Nature. I have a scientific bent of mind, don't you know?" His black eyes held a dancing taunting sparkle.

"You were looking up my dress!" she retorted suspiciously.

"Me? Not *me*! I may have many faults—I'm sure you have them cataloged—but looking up ladies' dresses is not one of them."

"Oh, go away! Leave me alone!" was all she could manage. Her cheeks were burning, and she was wondering what he had thought while surveying her figure so minutely.

"Actually, I had a question to ask you. But I'm afraid it's slipped my mind." A lopsided grin grew slowly on his face. He retraced his steps, returning to his den. In the doorway he shot her one more vivid look before disappearing inside.

Jesse decided to postpone her search for the book. Without wasting any time, she retreated to the attic.

LATER THAT AFTERNOON, after Ray and Shanna and the twins had gone off fishing, Bensen's woods foreman arrived at Clifftop by motorboat. The attic windows were open, and Jesse heard a little of his and Bensen's conversation outside before the men retired to the library. From the few words that drifted upstairs she surmised the forest fire in Section 108 had spread. Dan Cameron was in charge of all operations "out in the bush," and he had sounded worried to Jesse.

A while later, finished with her work for the day, Jesse stole downstairs from the attic. She noticed that Bensen and his foreman were still closeted in the library, and since Ray, Shanna and the twins were due back at any moment, she thought it best to warn Martha there might be two extra mouths at dinner. Martha, to her surprise, bore the news with fortitude; she listened patiently as Jesse made tentative suggestions for the repast. In a roundabout way, Jesse conveyed to the housekeeper that if dinner were half decent, it might, it just might, keep Bensen's bad mood from growing worse. Martha replied with a sniff but went willingly enough to work once she had armed herself with a fresh white apron.

An iced cucumber soup, elegantly served, and thick juicy salmon steaks from Shanna's and Ray's catch, did improve Bensen's mood, and everyone set to with a hearty appetite. Cecilia Anne, loving company, was in high spirits, and since the master of the house was terse, uncommunicative and preoccupied, she kept the conversation rolling. Fortunately any gloom that threatened to descend because of the forest fire was averted.

Over dessert, a light egg custard baked in a caramel glaze, topped with dollops of whipped cream and slivered almonds, Ray made clear his intention of taking Shanna dancing at the lodge. There was a small well-satisfied smirk on grandmother's lips at

this news, and her brown eyes regarded Ray shrewd-
ly. He bore her scrutiny without batting an eyelash,
and to complete the good impression he had made on
Mrs. Everhart, he smiled calmly at her. Jesse, remembering Merit's comment, thought he really did
have a nice mustache.

Bensen diplomatically and rather absentmindedly
gave his blessing, and Jesse just about laughed aloud
at Shanna's reaction of joy and relief.

In her opinion, Shanna was one of those few and
far between people who were innately gentle, and seeing her so happy now made Jesse feel warm all over.
It was a pity, she thought, that her brother didn't
share any of her qualities.

Shanna, her eyes alighting on Jesse and then wan-
dering to Dan Cameron, very casually announced,
"Why don't you join us, Jesse? And you, too, Dan?
After all, it is Saturday night."

"Good idea!" Ray joined in. "There's nothing
more we can do tonight about that blaze. It's out of
our hands now."

"You're right about that," Dan Cameron grimaced. He was a powerfully built stocky man who,
despite his aggressive appearance, was actually a
relaxing person to be around; he had added his own
calming words to the dinner conversation.

At Shanna's suggestion Jesse had, all in a mere second, thought, no, at first, and then, well, why not.
An evening's entertainment appealed to her. And it
wasn't as though she and Dan would be having a
date.

"You two run along and get yourselves dressed,"

Martha stated, plodding into the dining room. "Don't you worry about those dishes. Leave them for me; I ain't going dancing!"

Jesse felt her first tinge of excitement—a night out! By chance her topaz eyes met with Bensen's jet gaze, and she caught her breath. His eyes were cold, and they glittered like black diamonds in his teak face. Jesse blinked with the shock of it. Gone was her impression that Bensen did, on the odd occasion, like her. The feeling of being at Clifftop on sufferance instantly came flooding back. Now, in a mood of mingled defiance and sharp return of dislike, she glared back at him. Her light voice not betraying her emotions, she said, "I'm looking forward to the pleasant company."

Almost everyone at the table missed the nuance. Bensen did not, and neither did Cecilia. One delicate white eyebrow quirked up as she glanced back and forth between her grandson and guest. Only Shanna, saw the secret smile trembling on her grandmother's lips and a kind of wicked satisfaction in her eye as she watched Bensen grit his teeth.

THE LODGE AT KINGHORN, situated on the rocks overlooking a small cove, was a combination hotel and local meeting place. If, in these wilds, one wanted a night out, one went there.

Built of immense notched logs, the lodge had been weathered gray through the years. A wooden deck served as its porch. When the Everhart speedboat arrived, the party of four had to search for an empty berth. It was the same as looking for a parking space in a jammed lot, Jesse thought.

Fiery Passion. Forbidden Love. Free.

A Contemporary Love Story

LOVE BEYOND DESIRE
RACHEL PALMER

...At his touch, her body felt a familiar wild stirring, but she struggled to resist it. This is not love, she thought bitterly.

PRIDE AND DECEIT WERE
WHAT THEIR HEA...

Yours FREE with a home subscription to
SUPERROMANCES™

Now you never have to miss reading the newest **SUPERROMANCES**... because they'll be delivered right to your door.

Start with your free *Love beyond Desire*. You'll be enthralled by this powerful love story... from the moment Robin meets the dark, handsome Carlos and finds herself involved in the jealousies, bitterness and secret passions of the Lopez family. Where her own forbidden love threatens to shatter her life.

Your free *Love beyond Desire* is only the beginning. A subscription to **SUPERROMANCE** lets you look forward to a long love affair. Month after month, you'll receive four love stories of heroic dimension. Novels that will involve you in spellbinding intrigue, forbidden love and fiery passions.

You'll begin this series of sensuous, exciting contemporary novels...written by some of the top romance novelists of the day...with four every month.

And this big value...each novel, almost 400 pages of compelling reading...is yours for only $2.50 a book. Hours of entertainment every month for so little. Far less than a first-run movie or pay-TV. Newly published novels, with beautifully illustrated covers, filled with page after page of delicious escape into a world of romantic love...delivered right to your home.

Begin a long love affair with **SUPERROMANCE**.
Accept *Love beyond Desire,* free. Mail the card
below, today.

SUPERROMANCE
1440 South Priest Drive, Tempe, AZ 85281.

┌─Mail this card today.

FREE! Mail to: **SUPERROMANCE**
1440, South Priest Drive, Tempe, Arizona 85281

YES, please send me FREE and without any obligation, my
SUPERROMANCE novel, *Love beyond Desire*. If you do not hear
from me after I have examined my FREE book, please send me
the 4 new **SUPERROMANCE** books every month as soon as they
come off the press. I understand that I will be billed only $2.50 per
book (total $10.00). There are no shipping and handling or any
other hidden charges. There is no minimum number of books that
I have to purchase. In fact, I may cancel this arrangement at any
time. *Love beyond Desire* is mine to keep as a FREE gift, even if I
do not buy any additional books.

CI047

Name	(Please Print)

Address	Apt. No.

City

State	Zip

Signature   (If under 18, parent or guardian must sign.)

This offer is limited to one order per household and not valid to present
subscribers. Prices subject to change without notice, offer expires
December 31, 1982.

Printed in Canada   **SUPERROMANCE**

A compelling love story of mystery and intrigue... conflicts and jealousies... and a forbidden love that threatens to shatter the lives of all involved with the aristocratic Lopez family.

←Mail this card today for your FREE book.

Inside she saw that the logs had mellowed to a warm golden hue. A fire crackled in the oversized fireplace, while scores of people sat on the plump chesterfields around the windows or on the assortment of wooden chairs around sturdy wooden tables. A dart game was in progress, and through a double doorway Jesse saw that the two pool tables were busy. There were people everywhere she looked, and a great many of them seemed to know one another. The hubbub of voices was in the high decibels, and the lodge's patrons circulated freely as conversations flew from one table to the next.

Ray found a table with three empty chairs, and with a shout across the room soon a fourth chair was on its way, passed overhead from one table to the next. Guitar strings twanged experimentally on the PA system. A crashing drumroll effectively drowned the voices and captured everyone's attention. The heartthrob of a country violin launched a familiar country-music tune; boots stomped on the plank floor, high heels tapped; fingers snapped. Neighbors continued their conversations at a shouting level. Some rather ripe language came floating past, and with a look at Jesse Dan Cameron grinned.

Jesse was having a wonderful time; she'd been introduced to a lot of people and had danced with several men, as well as with Dan. It seemed to be expected of her, and she was happy enough to comply. Shanna was delighted with her popularity.

Jesse, resting for a round, leaned back in her comfortably worn chair and sighed happily. She took a small sip of wine, closing her eyes for a moment to let the music and sound sink into her. Again someone tapped her shoulder, asking her to dance. Jesse hadn't been introduced to him yet, and they chatted a little. He was Lily's nephew, as it turned out, and he owned his own fishing boat—a trawler. Soon he had a chair airlifted over to their table.

Dan complained, "Sitting next to you, Jesse, is the same as sitting next to a honeypot in a room full of bees!"

Sipping on wine and listening to the interesting chronicle of that year's fishing season, Jesse was perfectly happy and at ease. But suddenly she had the precise feeling that something was missing. The annoying niggling feeling wouldn't go away; further probing showed it wasn't something that was missing but someone—Bensen. What was he doing now? Why hadn't he come with them?

With a sharp pang Jesse remembered that no one had invited him. No one had even suggested Bensen should join them. And then, despite her annoyance with him, she leaned over to Shanna and asked her why not. Shanna's reply was to look at her as though she'd gone daft. When Jesse defended herself by saying they should at least have asked him, Shanna seemed vaguely upset.

"But Jesse, I don't think Bensen likes having a good time. You know how he is."

BENSEN WAS STILL UP when Shanna and Jesse walked through the front door side by side; they were laughing and giggling together and didn't immediately see him as he came out into the hall from the library.

"Brr-r-r, it gets chilly out there at night!" Jesse exclaimed, shivering and rubbing her bare arms. "I wonder if there's still a fire in the salon?"

"If you'd worn something decent, you wouldn't be cold!" Bensen announced crisply, narrowing his eyes in a mocking head-to-toe inspection. He turned to Shanna. "Have a good time?"

"Oh, yes!" Shanna replied. She looked at her brother's stern countenance for a second longer, then at Jesse. "Well, I, um, think I'll go to bed."

"Me, too!" murmured Jesse. But as they went past him, she impulsively stopped and shot a quick glance up at the dark remote face. "I wish you'd come with us." It was out before she had a chance to think. "I—I mean..." she stuttered, a pink tinge spreading over her cheeks. "Y-you probably worked all night...." She sounded completely inane, and she despised herself for it.

"Jesse danced all night!" Shanna broke in, smiling more warmly than she usually did at her brother. "You should have seen her. Everybody, simply everybody wanted to dance with her. Dan was quite put out by it."

"Adding more boyfriends to your list?" Bensen quipped, all sardonic amusement, the edge in his tone now sharply pronounced.

His arrogant expression sparked her temper. " 'Variety is the spice of life!' " she snapped, goaded into saying it.

"Oh? You should know, I suppose," Bensen retorted.

"And what's that supposed to mean?" cried Jesse.

With an open mouth Shanna's head jerked from one to the other.

"I think you know," he drawled unpleasantly. "I'm well aware things in the city aren't as tame as they are here." Jesse felt as though he'd slapped her. "Still, I wouldn't be surprised if you were off to the lodge every night from now on. Just try to keep the fights down to a minimum. The local men aren't as forgiving, and they tend to form territorial rights far more quickly than in the city."

"Oh, now I'm glad no one invited you. You would have sat there criticizing me all night long, I suppose. What do you want? To see me in tears? Well, Bensen, you'll have to try harder than that." Her voice quavered at the end. Now both Shanna and Bensen were looking at her, equally startled. Jesse gulped and continued in a firmer tone, "I had an absolutely lovely evening, and you just had to go and spoil it, didn't you!" The prickle behind her eyes was gone now, and she was furious again. "And I was feeling sorry for you because you were left behind! How—"

Abruptly Bensen reached for her hand, but Jesse jumped backward. In one swift movement he stepped forward and caught both her hands in his. He clasped her fingers tightly so that she couldn't twist free. "Jesse, I'm sorry," he said gently. Shanna's jaw dropped still more. "Jesse, look at me. I really am sorry." He bent his head in an effort to see her face, which she held averted. "You're not crying, are you? Jesse, I didn't mean it," he persisted, bending around even more to look into her face. But she deliberately turned it from him.

"You're a beast!" she said woundedly to the wall.

"If you say so."

Her head moved quickly, and the thick chestnut hair fell down her back. Her face, now upturned to his, was radiant, and the sherry-amber eyes were sparkling. "Will you come with us next time?" An open challenge.

Looking down into her eyes and still holding tightly on to both her hands, he hesitated. Shanna, standing in rigid surprise on the bottom stair, glanced back and forth between them.

"Were you really feeling sorry for me?" Bensen's tone sounded incredulous, and a doubtful smile turned up one corner of his mouth.

His eyes were suddenly too piercing for Jesse to bear. "We-ell. . ." she hemmed.

"Yes, she was," Shanna put in.

Jesse was beginning to feel a bit foolish now. Her cheeks burned under Bensen's interested stare. "It-it's not pleasant when one feels left out, that's all. Why are you staring?"

Bensen grinned at her, a wide full smile, his black eyes suddenly warm. Jesse's knees felt weak. Hastily she pulled her hands from his and said primly, "Good night, Bensen."

"Good night, ladies. Sweet dreams!"

Shanna shot her brother a dubious look. She peered at Jesse in the dim light as they went up the stairs together. As soon as they had cleared the landing, she said almost accusingly, "You two get along!"

"We do?"

"Bensen's never said sorry before. I've *never* heard him say that!"

"You see? There's still hope!"

"You like him!" Shanna exclaimed, sounding so amazed that Jesse wanted to giggle. "I mean, I do because he's my brother, but you don't have a reason. You do actually like him, don't you?"

"We-ell. . .sometimes," Jesse hedged. "Sort of."

"Good heavens, I can't think why. He's just what you said—a beast!"

"Well, yes, but I just felt rather badly about tonight. We didn't even think of him. And he really might have felt left out."

"I don't think Bensen has feelings like that."

"That's just it. He's human, too. He worries about everybody, but nobody ever worries about him. He's got a lot of responsibility to carry, and sometimes it must get pretty heavy."

"Jesse, are you all right?" Shanna asked tentatively.

"Of course, why?"

"N-nothing, er, nothing." Shanna kept on peering at her, her bewilderment growing. "Bensen's always taken care of himself, believe you me. He doesn't need any of us to do that." Her soft voice seemed to admonish Jesse to care for herself first of all.

"Yes, but everybody needs to feel wanted and. . . and. . . ." Jesse couldn't find the right words to express exactly what she meant, and she could see she wasn't making herself clear to Shanna. "Gosh, I'm tired. That boat ride and all that fresh air have done me in."

"It's those stairs that do it to me." Shanna yawned. "I swear that cliff gets higher every time I climb it! Jesse...?"

"Yes?"

"Ah, nothing. See you in the morning."

THE FOLLOWING EVENING Shanna and Ray went out again, and this time they told no one where they were bound. The twins, in the throes of romantic conjecture, were still wide-eyed at bedtime, and Jesse, tucking them into their beds, decided to read them a story in hopes of putting them to sleep. She settled into a chair, her back to the door, and put her feet up on Merit's bed.

Within half an hour the little girls were at least lying quietly in their beds. Ten minutes later Jesse noted the soft sound of their regular breathing. Quietly she closed the book. She stood up, tucked Merit's arm under the covers and then turned to Samantha. As she drew the blankets up, the little girl stirred, and her eyes blinked sleepily.

"Jesse?" she said, her voice sounding very young and defenseless in the deepening blue twilight. "Is mummy going to marry Ray? Is she?"

"I don't know, darling. Would you like to have a dad?"

"I think so. I don't remember mine. I don't know what it would be like."

"I never had a dad, either, so I can't tell you." Jesse placed a gentle hand on the little girl's forehead, brushing back her dark hair. Then she straightened up.

And her heart jumped in her throat, for Bensen stood leaning against the doorjamb. She had no idea how long he'd been there. At her startled look he quietly entered the room. He, too, bent over Samantha's bed.

"Go to sleep now, Sam, and don't worry about your mummy," he whispered. "She'll be all right; Ray will take good care of her. Everything will be all right; just wait and see." His voice was so kind and reassuring that it brought a lump to Jesse's throat. She blew Samantha a kiss and then left the bedroom, Bensen following behind her. In a hurry she went upstairs to the attic, even though she didn't feel like working. Bensen, with a long glance after her, went back downstairs.

Jesse worked for another hour on her notes, and then, yawning and stretching, she shuffled her papers into neater piles. She clicked off her typewriter and the lamp and found her way to the attic stairs in the dark. It was only half-past ten—too early to go to sleep—and she wasn't really tired anyway. The thought of reading a book or watching television didn't appeal, either. She felt oddly restless. As she still hadn't found the book Cecilia had told her about, she decided she might as well continue her search.

In the library she discovered that she could, by leaning over, catch a glimpse of Bensen working at his desk in the den. Despite his civil manner to her earlier, she'd sensed his mood was not good. Now she saw him slouch back against his chair and stare off into space for several minutes. Moments later, when she peeked at him again, he was running an impatient hand through his hair, which flopped back on his forehead in blue black disarray. The next time she leaned over for a look the gold pen was flowing smoothly over the paper, but soon she saw him fling the pen across the desk, saw his broad chest rise and fall with a mammoth sigh.

Jesse sat down on the stepladder, her fingers wedged between the pages of a book. What was the matter with Bensen? What was he worried about? Shanna? But everything was going so well it couldn't be Shanna. Everybody else was fine. Business? Somehow she knew he wasn't the type to worry about business. He would do what he thought best and leave it at that; worrying took precious time that could be spent in action. What, then? What, what, what? She wished she could just go and ask him. But of course he would think she was meddling again, and she would *not* stick out her nose one more time. Jesse sighed, vexed, and halfheartedly resumed her task.

She'd combed two shelves when she inadvertently noticed the book in an area she'd already checked. Chiding herself for not having paid attention earlier, she pulled the sought-after book from the shelf. She leafed through it quickly and, satisfied that it would be helpful to her, closed the glass doors that kept dust from the books. A moment later she put away the stepladder, intending to retire for the night. She had to steel herself not to look in the den as she started for the hall.

"Jesse?"

She stepped back into the library with a great leaping beat of her heart. There she hesitated an instant, calming her quivering nerves before heading toward the den.

"*Jesse...?*"

"Yes, Bensen, I'm coming," she said serenely, and stepped inside.

She tried to remain tranquil as his coal black gaze probed hers for what seemed a long time. He obviously had something to say to her, yet he seemed uncertain how to begin. That made her apprehensive. Would he hint that her stay at Clifftop had lasted long enough? She sat down on the arm of a chair close to his desk, quietly waiting.

"Jesse, is it serious between Shanna and Ray?"

"Wha-at?"

"You must know more than I do. You're always talking and whispering together, and to me she won't say a word. Do you know? Is it really...serious? That's all I'm asking you. I'm not digging for secrets."

Jesse studied the dark face before her, the wealth of black hair, the strong line of nose and mouth. An impervious face. "I'd say yes, it is serious," she answered after a moment. "I know Shanna's in love with him, and I think Ray's very much in love with her."

He waved a dismissing hand. "And what about the twins?"

"They seem to have accepted him. And from what I see, I think he could be a good father to them. He cares for them; it's obvious. Anyway, what makes all the difference is that Shanna and Ray really do love each other.''

"Love!'' Bensen ground out the word. There was a quick derisive twist to his lips. "We all know how long that lasts! I don't want her to go through another heartbreak.''

"Ray's not Stu!'' Jesse argued. "I never knew him, but I've seen pictures of him, and if I had to go on appearance alone, I'd pick Ray any day. Oh, I know Stu was incredibly good-looking,'' Jesse added when Bensen's eyebrows rose mockingly, "but it's what's behind the eyes that counts, and he gave me the creeps.''

"And I expected a rational opinion!'' Bensen said witheringly.

"Ray's not a drunk; he's not a shiftless laze; nor is he a womanizer. And he doesn't expect Shanna to fight his battles for him. You can't discount their love. I think it's real—and steady. And *that's* the important thing.''

"You might think romantic love is the be-all and end-all of existence,'' Bensen said scornfully, "but I know better. Day-to-day living is one hell of a lot rougher than fancy nights out!''

"Well, of *course*, Bensen! Don't you think they make a good pair?''

"She should get married again. She's young and beautiful, and she should start a new life of her own....'' Bensen sighed—just a whisper of sound that Jesse barely heard. "She's been moping and mourning and locked up here for long enough....''

"She's liked being here, Bensen, despite everything. It's her home. She does love it. I—I guess it'll be pretty lonely here once Shanna and the twins are gone...." Jesse's voice dropped off.

Her eyes, resting on Bensen's rugged chiseled features, widened a fraction. All at once she knew what was bothering him. The big strong self-sufficient man who needed no one had suddenly realized he cared for his sister and his nieces more than he'd thought possible.

"This place will be an absolute *tomb*!" he sighed. "I—you've noticed that grandmother and I don't get along too well." There was amusement in his tone now, but it was a grim amusement, and there was a bleakness in the jet eyes that wrung Jesse's heart. She fully understood what he meant. This big stone mansion empty, quiet, the halls echoing...living here alone with a cantankerous old woman who didn't particularly like him, perhaps because he reminded her so much of her Samuel. But Jesse knew Bensen wouldn't appreciate her compassion. He would throw it back in her face. And yet she couldn't help how she felt. Had she been more comfortable with him, she would have gone to him and put a hand on his shoulder...or—or something. She shook her head to herself and straightened her shoulders. No, that would definitely not do.

"You could always marry Dorothy," she said encouragingly, "and bring her here and have loads of children. Then...then..." she faltered. Bensen did not appear especially pleased with her solution. She stared at him in consternation.

"Yes, well, it's a thought," he finally said, his

voice cutting. "With those wide hips of hers she would have no trouble bearing children." He kept right on, ignoring the shocked look on Jesse's face. "That is, after all, what I want. The perfect solution would be children without a wife, and fortunately Dorothy has more than enough outside interests. I don't suppose she'd be here much. She doesn't like the backwoods." His lips curved into a humorless smile as his eyes focused narrowly on her face. "You're right about me. See how selfish I am? . . . I'm not a particularly nice person, Jesse."

Was he warning her? And if so, about what? She took a deep breath and held it. The air in the room seemed very still. Suddenly she thought of her own rather slim hips and wondered. And the wondering shocked her more than what Bensen had said. Her body was suffused with red heat, and she desperately wished Bensen would stop watching her so keenly, his eyes now dangerous black slits.

"Don't you believe in love at all?" she demanded.

His smile grew. "Certain kinds, assuredly."

Jesse blinked and looked away, tracing the quilted pattern on the armchair with one finger. "Well, I believe in all kinds," she said stubbornly.

"Then why is it you're not married?"

"I-I've been too busy. I had my own life to arrange before I could think of sharing it with someone. And I guess I've been on my own for so long I don't really know how to begin sharing." She didn't know why she was telling him such private facts. Time to change the subject! "For Shanna it's easy. She's a sharing kind of person. She gives all the time."

"Don't you? You've given rather a lot of your time and interest to us—people you hardly know."

"That—that's different." Jesse gulped. Her chin lifted. "And you? Why aren't you married yet? You've had plenty of opportunities, I'm sure. Dorothy's waiting. What are you waiting for?"

"You don't like talking about yourself, do you? Every time I ask a question, you ask me one in return. You wouldn't have a bit of Irish in you, now would you?"

"You just did exactly the same thing. We're sitting here talking and avoiding each other's questions." Jesse smiled, a little crooked smile. "For all I know, I could be Polish."

"You've never tried to find out who your parents were?"

Jesse shrugged. "I was a baby-in-a-basket-on-the-doorstep case. I'm proof that it really does happen. There weren't any clues."

"It doesn't seem to bother you."

"Not anymore."

"You're a lone wolf."

"So are you."

"Would you like a cigarette?"

"Oh, yes, I would." Jesse was glad at the prospect of having something to do with her hands. He offered her one, took one for himself and then came around the desk to light it for her. She was dismayed when her fingers trembled slightly and hoped he hadn't noticed. Around him she seemed to lose some of that self-confidence that had taken so many years to build. Talking with him stirred a sort of apprehensive excitement, sent the blood singing along her veins. What was it about Bensen, she wondered, that made her want to run away to safety, yet held her like a magnet, so that she couldn't go?

Bensen, instead of returning to his desk, sat in the armchair opposite her. He was now much closer to her than earlier, and without the expanse of desk between them, Jesse felt she had just to reach out to touch him. She shifted uneasily on the arm of the chair.

"You were a secretary?" Bensen's ever watchful eyes gazed at her through a screen of smoke. Jesse despaired of returning the topic to Shanna.

"For six years."

"How long have you been writing?"

"For...forever, I guess. About something or other. It's filled a lot of spaces in my life. About four years ago I was finally making enough money at it to quit my job and write full-time."

"You've formed no strong attachments?"

"Oh, well...I have some very good friends."

"That's not what I meant."

Jesse looked at him through a wing of her hair. She moistened her lips. "I—well, no, I guess not."

"Hmmm. Would you like a shot of brandy?"

"Yes, please." Some Dutch courage might help.

Bensen opened the carved doors of a small bar, poured two snifters and handed one to her. Jesse glanced at his hand as she took the glass, careful that their fingers should not meet. He had beautiful hands. Hands that looked as though they should be able to play a piano, except they were tanned to a mahogany brown—which spoke more of the outdoors.

"How's the book coming along?"

Jesse shot him a quick oblique glance to see whether this might be a roundabout way of inquiring when she would be leaving. But Bensen was too direct to employ such means, she decided, and he did appear genuinely interested. Jesse slid into the armchair as she told him a little of what she'd done so far, tucking her long denim-clad legs underneath her. She felt a lot more at ease—eager, in fact, to discuss her work. She truly enjoyed it and was only too happy to share this part of her life.

"With all this rich background material the plot almost fell into place. It was so easy it scared me. But although I've picked it apart every which way, it still holds tight. I think the hero is especially good. He...." Jesse swallowed. She viewed Bensen in alarmed surprise. Her throat had closed over her words, for she had just realized her imaginary hero was a lot like Bensen. *Too* much like Bensen. With a long, powerful, well-knit body and that rugged chin and the brooding black eyes....

Bensen had asked her something. She hadn't the faintest idea what and could only stare at him blankly.

"Didn't you hear me? What is it?"

"Oh, I—I just remembered something important I have to take out of the book." Jesse cleared her throat and, to hide her confusion, took a mouthful of brandy, letting it slide slowly down. "Actually, I should maybe do it right now before I forget...." She was almost up out of her chair.

"No, don't go," Bensen urged. "You've worked

long enough today. Besides, it's almost midnight. The witching hour.'' It was certainly a bewitching smile that he sent her. It completely transformed his face. Fascinated, Jesse sank back into the soft comfort of her chair and wondered whether she would jump off a cliff if he asked her to. But despite these negative sentiments, she had to admit she did want to stay.

It was very still now in the house; Martha and Cecilia had long since gone to bed. And from the surrounding forest outside came a deep breathless quiet that Jesse found strangely soothing. The stereo in the den was set low and wafted a dreamy classical symphony into the night air with the silkiest softest thread of musical notes. On Bensen's desk a pool of light shone, while the rest of the room was in shadow. They sat in that quiet shadow, enjoying the late hour. It was all so very relaxing and comfortable that Jesse wondered why she should feel so vitally *aware*, with an inner kind of awareness that defied explanation and seemed to exist entirely of itself without anything to do with her. Or so it felt. It was just there, and Jesse was forced to bend to its power.

"You were going to tell me about the hero of your book," Bensen prompted. He went to the bar, looking at her over his shoulder. He brought the bottle of brandy back with him, poured more for her, more for himself, and then set the bottle down on a nearby table before resuming his seat.

"Y-yes, well...." Jesse began to describe the hero, leaving out the characteristics similar to Bensen's—which made the description lifeless. She could see he was puzzled, so she amended, "I've just discovered a—a major flaw in his character that I'd never noticed before. I'll tell you more about him when I've, er, rearranged him."

Bensen made a few very observant suggestions for some of the incidents and characters in the novel—which surprised Jesse. He really was interested, and he'd had listened to her every word. That surprised her even more than the clarity of his observations. And she found that talking with him, really talking, was lovely fun. His mind possessed a quickness and liveliness that made her think one could chat with him forever without getting bored.

"So then, of course, the cat's out of the bag, and the heroine goes storming off alone. The hero's brother assumes she's gone over to the enemy camp and hastens to inform the hero. She's licking her wounds in private, and the hero—he thinks of the way she kissed him the last time and sees it as a Judas kiss...."

One small part of her mind diverged from the rest and wondered, all on its own volition, what it would be like if she were to kiss Bensen.... An insidious warmth crept into her limbs. But she shouldn't be having such thoughts about Dorothy's fiancé, she admonished herself.

"Oh, what a tangled web we weave..." Bensen murmured, smiling slightly. "It seems almost too painfully real, doesn't it? So what happens next? You can't leave me with a cliff-hanger like that, Jesse," he remonstrated when she appeared to hesitate.

"This is where it gets complicated. Don't forget, that contract for the fishing trawler still has to be signed and he—the hero—owns part of that strike up by Barkerville. He's getting rich quick, but his money and the sudden power he wields keep him tied to the area, keep him busy; he doesn't even try to locate the heroine. His old flame—remember, she's now the colonel's wife—is showering him with attention, and you can imagine what it does to his ego, because—"

"Before she would have none of his kisses," Bensen ended.

"Yes," said Jesse, and that small part of her mind kept on going its own way.... What *would* it be like if Bensen kissed her? He did have a wonderful mouth, and his chest was so broad and the muscles underneath so powerful.... The tanned mahogany skin would be firm and warm beneath her touch. Jesse was becoming a little alarmed. It had to be the atmosphere in the room, she told herself. It was too close, too intimate, too romantic. The music, the warm red glow of coals in the fireplace, the soft shadows and a man and a woman—alone.

"Jesse?" Bensen's low voice was a deep murmur. Every cell in Jesse's body tensed, and she waited, not quite meeting his eyes, in an agony of suspense. "You seem to have drifted off," he continued, his black eyes fastened curiously on her firelit face.

"I, well, yes." She felt like a babbling idiot. "I was thinking of how to rearrange the hero. It won't be easy, and he was so perfect."

"You haven't told me what's wrong with him—or

very much about him at all, really. I see everybody
else very clearly, but he's indistinct.''

"He was much *too* distinct to start with," Jesse
muttered.

"What? What was that?"

"Oh, er, nothing. I was just...just mumbling
messages to myself." She smiled across at him blandly, hoping none of what she was thinking showed on
her face. "Perhaps I'll go to bed. A good night's
sleep might set me straight on him." Suddenly she
had to get away from him, get away before she
slipped up and he discovered exactly what was going
on inside her head.

There was the barest of pauses, then Bensen
nodded. "Okay. I guess there's no point in waiting
up for Shanna. I'll join you. That is, I'll join you in
sleep—if not in bed." He grinned wickedly at her
startled face, a look of amusement and something
else flashing through his eyes. "Come along now,
Jessamine," he said, switching off the desk lamp. He
used the voice he sometimes used on the twins—a
kind of half-coaxing, half-ordering tone. Only now it
was overlaid with a taunting quality that sounded
rich with laughter.

Jesse got up out of her chair rather too hastily, and
telling herself not to let Bensen rattle her, she determined to remain cool and collected. Or at least if that
were not possible, to appear so.

Only the fire's deep red glow lighted the room
now, faintly outlining the furniture as Jesse made her
way in the dark toward the door. She felt Bensen
following her, sensed that he was very close. If she

just turned around, put her hands on his chest and.... But she kept on walking—almost numbly. They went side by side through the library and out into the hall. When they reached the stairs, Bensen's hand slid under her elbow to guide her through the darkness and the quietness that was now complete. At the top of the stairs, where they had to part company, he stopped. With his warm hand still holding her, he bent his head and whispered in her ear, as if not to break the silence, "Good night, Jessamine."

His cheek brushed against hers as he straightened up. She could make out the glimmer of white teeth. His touch, his presence, filled her head. She could never remember wanting to be kissed and held as much as she did in that moment....

Several days later, with Shanna and the twins out with Ray for a ramble on the four old horses, with grandmother occupied at a game of cribbage with Martha and growing irritable because the housekeeper was winning, and with Bensen out in the bush with his woods foreman, Jesse took the estate jeep and went bumping off on her own. She had decided to visit the small town of Lund, some fifteen to twenty miles south along the coast.

Lund was the seat of the closest municipal hall, and Jesse wanted to examine the historical archives there. The facts, figures and dates in her book had to be correct, and she was taking no chances.

The clerk at the town hall proved most helpful and allowed her access to the record store, which was set up in the basement of the building. Later, when Jesse offered to leave him two pieces of ID in exchange for the loan of a thick tome she'd picked out, he willingly consented. She thanked him warmly and went across to the town hotel to look through the book, for there was no extra space at the tiny town hall for her to use.

The hotel's coffee shop was closed, but the bar was open. Jesse settled into a quiet corner booth out of the mainstream, ordered herself a light beer and set to work. Her list of questions before her, she diligently checked the various information, the thick journal spread wide open and taking up most of the tabletop. There weren't many people in the bar at this hour—a handful of men gathered around a pool table, watching two others having a game of snooker; three oldsters nearby; the barman; and off by themselves, by the one and only window, what looked like a tourist couple. Jesse bent her head back down to the yellowed hand-written ledger in search of answers.

A few minutes later she raised her head for a sip of beer. Her hand stopped, clutching the cold perspiring glass a couple of inches from her parted lips. In utter rigid shock she stared at one of the pool players. Almost directly under the wide green lampshade above the pool table, the man's face was revealed in full light. Jesse could see him clearly, sharply—and for the first time.

It was Stu Lazzer. Never had Jesse experienced such complete mindless fright. She was looking at a ghost—a ghost of a man dead these five years, the victim of a tragic accident. Yet there he was! Every feature, every line, every hair on his head, was the same as in the pictures Jesse had studied. A shiver enveloped her, and with her whole hand shaking, Jesse very slowly set down the cold wet glass she was still clutching.

Oh, my God! Her lips mouthed the words as she stared at the fellow leaning far over the table to reach a shot. He was talking animatedly to his much larger buddy. Transfixed, Jesse heard the sharp snap as the cue hit, saw the brightly colored balls spin out over the green felt.

Thank God Shanna hadn't come with her, she thought desperately. Thank God Ray had showed up to take her off. Ray. Oh, heavens above, *Ray!* Jesse felt as though her mind was exploding in several different directions simultaneously. It just simply couldn't be. And yet the evidence was there before her eyes.

He was most definitely alive. Strikingly handsome in logger's clothes that suited his frame—he was on the slight side—and the worn tight denims, the red plaid shirt and high scuffed boots made him seem like some handsome devil in a magazine ad extolling cigarettes.

Snatches of their talk floated over to Jesse. She heard certain words, phrases, quite clearly, and of them most were curses—rough talk that wasn't un-usual in a backwoods bar—and certainly not in a log-ging camp. Jesse's hair crawled on her nape. *A ghost. . . .* She put a hand on her neck to stop the feel-ing that her hair was standing on end.

She watched every move Lazzer made, watched

every change of expression with a sort of dreadful fascination and futile hope that if he just turned this way or that, she would see that his profile was all wrong, that she was all wrong, that it was just a bizarre coincidence. But each time he turned or moved he cemented her first impression. It had to be him.

No two people, she decided, could possibly look so similar, especially with a face like Stu's. She saw him mouthing off to his companion; it looked as if they were placing bets.

And then, very clearly, she heard his friend's exclamation. "Hell, Craig, you son of a bitch!"

It was as though his buddy's words had touched a match to a firecracker. Stu spun on his friend, lashing out at him viciously. Jesse found it a strange sight to see so large and powerful a man cowering before someone half his size. His head was bowed; he was shuffling his big feet while Stu—Craig? *Craig!* His friend had called him Craig. Then it wasn't Stu Lazzer! Jesse wilted against the corner of the booth. The most incredible sense of relief descended upon her. But if it *was* Craig, then why, *how*—the resemblance was so true.

Jesse's fixed stare must have made itself felt, for the man's head suddenly swiveled in her direction. For a second he narrowed his eyes. They were blue. She could see that from where she sat—a deep, startling blue, just exactly like Stu's eyes staring up from a photograph. For a second those eyes stared back at her. Then he winked flirtatiously, confident of his attractiveness, before becoming absorbed in lining up his cue.

Jesse felt hot at being seen. Then she felt cold. And then she felt sick. She gathered her long list of questions and her short list of answers, shut the yellowed ledger and slid cautiously out of the booth. She made a beeline for the door, and once outside, she gasped for air.

With a backward glance over her shoulder to make sure she wasn't being followed, she shivered again in the hot July sunshine. She hurried across the street to the jeep. There she rubbed her arms, trying to warm up, trying to get rid of that stunned hit-over-the-head sensation. It was just by chance that she remembered to return the borrowed tome. She would have left her ID behind had not the clerk run after her with it.

"WHAT ARE YOU STARING AT, Jesse?" Merit asked. She turned in her chair to look at the wall behind her, where Jesse's eyes had been fixed for so long a time.

Jesse blinked, and it brought the dining table into focus. Old Bob had left earlier that day, and she was vaguely aware of his absence; otherwise everything seemed normal.

"Are you feeling quite well?" grandmother asked solicitously. "You haven't been yourself all evening."

"That's so, Jesse." Shanna looked at her with concern. "You've hardly said a word all through dinner. Did something happen in Lund? I can't imagine anything ever happening there."

"Perhaps it was the road," Cecilia said when Jesse didn't answer but looked, uncomfortable and embarrassed, from one face to the next. "That's a devilish road. The bumps, those cliffs straight down to the water, those hairpin curves. I would feel quite dizzy. Is that what upset you? Did you see a bear? They're quite common around here, you know.''

Jesse swallowed and wondered if she should agree to the bear, but Bensen spoke up before she had the chance.

''Perhaps—'' he paused until he had her attention ''—perhaps she did something to the jeep and is afraid to tell me because she figures I'll take her head off?''

Jesse registered the mocking smile flitting around the corners of Bensen's mouth. A small sigh escaped her.

''Did you, Jesse? Scratch a door or bump a fender? Tell me. I promise I won't get angry. Really, I won't. Come on, tell Uncle Ben all about it.'' Despite his taunting, his putting her on the spot, there was an underlying kindness in his tone. The black eyes were glittering with mischief as they baited her.

Now everybody was looking at her. Jesse cleared her throat. She glanced around the table.

''I—I, umm, was just thinking about. . .business. I should go into Vancouver again soon, and. . . .'' She looked at Bensen, and to her at that moment he seemed safe, comforting, so very strong and endlessly capable. Maybe, she was thinking, she should tell him about Craig to help restore her peace of mind.

''Is that all? Just business?'' Shanna laughed with relief. ''Bensen's going in tomorrow—Bensen, didn't I hear you saying that to Ray? You wouldn't mind, would you, Ben?" Then she seemed alarmed. "Oh, Jesse, you're not finished here yet, are you?"

"I, umm...." Jesse peeped at Bensen.

"Of course she's not finished yet!" Cecilia announced with royal disdain. "We've just barely got past my first Christmas here!"

"It's a long trip," Bensen put in smoothly. "I'd be glad for some company." Immediately everyone's attention turned to Bensen.

"Can we go, too?" Merit piped in. "Can we? Please, please?"

"Oh, yes, please? We'll be terribly, awfully, good. Honest we will!" Samantha promised. "Can we, mummy?"

"Er, it's 'may' we, and you'll have to ask your uncle."

"And you'd better ask Jesse, too," grandmother added.

Jesse looked again at Bensen, and he shrugged. "We-ell..." she said thoughtfully. The twins' wide-eyed silent appeal to her did the trick, and besides, she had some of her own reasons for wanting more company. "All right," she finally agreed.

She wanted to tell Bensen about her afternoon in Lund yet somehow couldn't find words to phrase it sensibly. And of course, Stu was dead, so she'd really seen Craig, whoever he was.... Jesse couldn't help feeling acutely uneasy once more.

But if she went to Bensen, he might think she was meddling. And how would she bring up the subject?... "I thought I saw Stu Lazzer in the Lund pub this afternoon...." No, that sounded ridiculous, and certainly Bensen would think her completely crazy.

So she said nothing to anyone, hoping that the mysterious Craig would hurry up and leave town and never, never come back. She had a moment's worry about Shanna finding out somehow, but there was no reason to suppose the stranger would come to Clifftop. Besides, Jesse told herself, Ray was going to be close by for the two or three days she and Bensen would be gone.

CHAPTER SEVEN

"YES, BETTY, I think I understand." Jesse paused. "No, I'm not upset." It was almost exactly the same scene as the last time she had come to Vancouver with Bensen and the twins. She was on the phone, listening to explanations, while Bensen was already at his desk, going through the contents of his briefcase. The twins were squashed up against the windows in gleeful excitement, pointing out noteworthy pedestrians who strolled by on the busy downtown street twenty-seven floors below.

"No, really, it's all right.... Is she? That's nice." Jesse had her back to the room and was facing the mirror; she could see everything that went on behind her. Bensen snapped his briefcase shut and started opening some mail he had collected at the front desk of the hotel. She watched him as she listened to Betty's voice. "Yes, of course...it *did*? Three new flowers? Terrific!" Pause. "Oh, good." Pause. "No, that one's the Areka palm; the Ti plant is the one in the corner beside the bookcases." Pause. "Yes, I'll see you tomorrow morning. I'll be bringing along two friends of mine. I'm kind of responsible for them for a couple of days."

Bensen glanced up from a letter, and Jesse wasn't

quick enough in looking away. He raised an eyebrow as he caught her eyes in the mirror. Jesse blinked in sudden confusion.

"No, your sister can stay," she went on. "Yes, really, it's quite all right. I'll see you tomorrow, around ten. Okay, bye."

When she turned around, both Bensen's eyebrows rose in an unspoken question. Jesse nodded, then did a double take, for there was the oddest smile on his face. He went back to reading his letters, and she hurried down the hall to the bedroom she'd used last time. She threw her purse on the bed and stepped into the bathroom to freshen up after the long drive and the two ferry rides between Vancouver and Clifftop. That accomplished, she returned to the sitting room in time for tea.

Joining the twins, she gazed out the windows and viewed the conglomeration of high rises. She stared at the sea on either side and the green wooded patch that was Stanley Park. Across the inlet the patch ended at the North Shore mountains. Jesse felt as happy as the twins were excited to be back.

Immediately after tea Bensen left for his office. He had told Jesse he would most likely be working late, and she felt free to make several telephone calls to various friends. She also spoke with her literary agent, her stockbroker and her bank. She was just about to leave the suite with the twins in tow when the telephone rang. Hoping it wasn't Dorothy wanting to talk to Bensen, she somewhat reluctantly picked up the receiver with the strong feeling it *would* be his fiancée. How would she explain her presence? . . .

"Hello, Jesse?" It was Bensen. She smiled in sweet relief.

"Bensen!" Her voice was warm.

"Have you made any plans for tonight?"

"Well, I was going to take the twins for a walk down in the mall and let them see a bit of downtown. Then I was going to stop for dinner and find an early movie they'd like to see. After that, nothing. Why?"

"What time are the early shows over?"

"Oh, eight-thirty, nine o'clock."

"Fine. I'll arrange for the baby-sitter. She'll meet you in the coffee shop. And you meet me at—" he gave her the address "—at nine-thirty. I'll be there by then."

Jesse was well acquainted with the restaurant. It was one of the finer eating establishments in town. For a moment she could think of no reply, so surprised was she.

"Are—are you taking me to dinner?" she finally asked.

"Yes, of course."

"Oh, I see. Thank you for telling me." Jesse was met with silence. She waited for his reply, not quite certain how she felt about this rapid turn of events.

"Will you come?" There was nothing in his voice that gave her the least inkling of how he felt.

"Oh, umm, yes."

"Good. See you later." And he hung up. Jesse put the receiver down slowly, bemused. He had sounded different just then—as though, as if, he'd been smiling. People's voices always sounded different when they talked through a smile, she thought. But oh, dear heaven, she had nothing to wear for the occasion tonight!

"Jesse, aren't you coming?" Samantha popped her head back in the suite. "The elevator's come and gone!"

"Who were you talking to?" Merit bounced in beside her twin. "Your boyfriend? Gosh, you sure look pretty, Jesse. Did he say something nice?"

Jesse blushed. She turned beet red and knew it, for the color was clear enough in the mirror above the phone. She grimaced at the twins and said, "Out!" They obeyed readily enough but wouldn't stop pestering her about the mysterious caller. To stop them, she finally turned their minds on a different track by suggesting a shopping spree. She didn't tell them, however, that she had a particular motive in mind.

WITH THE SHOPPING and the downtown tour complete and the bags and parcels left at the hotel, Jesse took the twins to dinner. While they ate—between talking and chattering—she sipped coffee and tried to maintain some kind of order. Actually, she was glad to be busy right up until the last moment. That way there was no time to think.

Luckily, the choice in movies was swiftly made. Theatre Row—that downtown street only a block from their hotel—was lined with one movie house after another; the twins, though, unanimously voted for the sequel to the science-fiction movie they'd seen there the last time.

Shortly after eight-thirty, talking all the way about the film's high points, the trio walked the short distance to the hotel. The twins' were beginning to lag; the surfeit of excitement and fun had made them ready to call it a day. Jesse, on the other hand, felt as though she were just commencing. Far from being tired or sleepy, she was starting to feel twinges of real nervousness, rather like what she'd experienced on her very first date.

On entering the hotel, she was pleased to find the baby-sitter—Bensen had arranged for one through the hotel service—on hand and awaiting them in the coffee shop. She seemed a comfortable trustworthy woman, and understood at once that the twins' reluctance stemmed not from a dislike of her or naughtiness; rather, they considered themselves too old for such nonsense as baby-sitters. Jesse took the twins immediately off to the bathtub, popped them both in and then gave the woman instructions and the restaurant's telephone number. Finally, trying very hard to subdue her happy anticipation and nervous excitement, Jesse herself went off for a quick bath and a change of clothes.

When Jesse reentered the sitting room almost half an hour later, the twins were in pajamas on the divan, one at either end, their feet in the middle, sharing a blanket. Mrs. Petty, the baby-sitter, sat knitting placidly, and everyone seemed to be getting along fine. With the television on and with ten different channels to choose from—around Lund and Bliss Landing there were only two—and with a great bag of treats to share between them, the twins were supremely content. Jesse, however, was not prepared for their reaction when they first saw her.

Merit sat bolt upright and screeched, *"Wow!"*

Samantha uttered, *"Go-osh!"* with such feeling that Jesse looked down at herself.

"Gee, and I hate brown! It looks smashing on you, Jesse!"

"Ooooh, I didn't know you were so beautiful, Jesse. Wow! I hope mummy lets us dress up soon. I'm going to wear brown, too!"

"No, you're not, I am! We can't both wear brown!"

"We won't be going out with the same man, silly."

Jesse, instead of lifting a finger to stop the growing argument, laughed because she felt so wonderful and their appraisal had made her feel that way. Earlier she hadn't been so sure, but now....

"Oh, yes, Miss Smi-Smith-Jones." The baby-sitter, like many other people, had trouble with her last name. "You do look very elegant!"

The chestnut-colored dress, with its spaghetti straps, slightly full top gathered by a thin belt and narrow skirt was made of a delicate material that sheened in the light. It suited Jesse's willowy frame and golden summer tan to perfection. With slim very high heels of the same shade, a tiny matching bag and a loosely knit mohair shawl, she appeared extremely chic and beautiful—quite a change for the twins, who were used to seeing her in jeans or a simple cotton dress. Small gold earrings and a necklace of amber beads were her adornments. The thick straight hair hung silky and shining in a stream down her back.

She kissed the twins goodbye, smiled at Mrs. Petty and went to the door amid a chorus of, "Who are you going out with? Who? When will you be back? What will we tell Uncle Ben? *Who*, Jesse?" and a final, "Don't be too late!"

She stepped into the elevator, an uncontainable ear-to-ear grin bursting on her mouth. Finally someone had said that to her! It really did feel very nice. Her nervousness was gone.

Jesse sat in the back of the taxicab with the door open, the setting sun slanting through the windshield and one slender foot resting on the pavement while she searched through her bag for the cab fare. It was a good thing the bag was small, she thought in amusement. She looked up with the bills in her hand and saw Bensen, standing tall and dark on the sidewalk. He was staring at her, Jesse thought dizzily, as if she were the last woman left alive on earth. He paid the driver and, taking Jesse's hand, helped her out. Quickly he shut the door, then turned around to gaze at her admiringly. Jesse smiled serenely. Her feet were already off the ground as he eyed her a second longer before taking her arm.

"I'm glad you came. I thought you might, you just might, change your mind." His soft drawl was pleasant.

"I never gave it a thought."

His face split into a grin. "Are you trying to put me in my place?" He was looking down at her—only tonight, because of her very high heels, he didn't have to look down so far.

"That's one new thing I wouldn't like to try!" Jesse returned his gaze, her sherry eyes sparkling in the fading light. A light summer wind rustled under the street canopy and wafted a cascade of chestnut hair over Bensen's black-suited shoulder. For the barest of seconds he paused. Then his hand came up close to her throat as he swept the tresses back and over one bare arm. Leaving a trail of heat, the hand moved slowly down to the small of her back.... The doorman bowed them in. Bensen's warm hand stayed lightly and possessively around her arm all the way to their secluded table.

And as they were shown to the table by the maître d', Jesse thought to herself that this wasn't a date, not really.... But then, what was it?

The restaurant wasn't as fancy as some and put on no big displays, but its most important feature, the food, was excellent, as was the service. The decor was dark and restful, unobstructive and in simple but very good taste. Jesse settled into their tucked-away booth, placing her shawl and bag on the soft cushion beside her. Bensen was conferring with the maître d' about their dinner and their choice of wine. From time to time he asked her a question, and after her full day she discovered she now had a healthy appetite. The maître d' was hardly gone before he returned with Bensen's first wine selection.

It was a crisp, very dry white wine that delighted Jesse's tastebuds on the first sip. The maître d' slipped away on soft-soled feet. Suddenly they were alone, and Jesse looked over the top of the wineglass rim at Bensen.

"I'll bet you never thought you'd go out for dinner with me that afternoon you first arrived at Clifftop," he murmured, his eyes glinting in the dim warm light.

A slightly wry smile hovered at one corner of his mouth. "I wasn't at my most charming, if I remember correctly."

The eyes drifted over her face, the shining fall of hair swept back over smooth golden shoulders, the amber necklace resting in the hollow of her throat, the swell of breasts under the silky clinging chestnut fabric. His gaze returned and dwelt for a long moment on the softly rounded rose mouth.

"For once I can agree wholeheartedly with you," Jesse smiled. She felt disturbingly light-headed. "If the *Shaman* had still been there, I would have been down those endless stairs so fast all you would have seen was a streak!"

"Did I scare you that badly?"

"You looked awfully big and awfully mean—and the way you pounced on me from behind...."

"I can see I made a lasting impression—but not a very good one!"

"Our acquaintance has been a little, er, turbulent." *And what is it going to be after tonight,* she suddenly wondered.

"A little turbulent? Admit it now, Jesse, we fought like cats and dogs. And if I know you—"

"Yes, well, perhaps I'm more used to you now." The corners of Jesse's mouth curved up. He gazed at her pensively. "And then, of course," she continued, "I didn't aid my case when I read your diary." Her smile grew.

"That's true," Bensen drawled. "But after I thought about it, I realized I'd have done the same thing in the same situation. I'd have picked up your diary and read it—read every last word. Something tells me it would be worth it!''

Jesse laughed slightly. ''In my case it was, even though I was terribly embarrassed, I'm still glad I did it.'' He looked a bit disconcerted at that, and it made her laugh more. ''I understood the situation better after that,'' she added soberly.

Then, curious about how he'd made the leap from a penurious schoolboy hemmed in on all sides by problems—and big problems at that—to the lumber magnate he now was, she cautiously drew him out. She didn't want to be accused again of being nosy.

Over hors d'oeuvres, Bensen explained it hadn't been a leap at all. It had been a slow climb, inch by inch, to a position at the top. Years of working into the night; of working Saturdays and Sundays; of utilizing all the strength, wit, common sense and raw energy he could find in him to plod steadily onward. He'd had to tackle all the endless annoyances, setbacks and bottlenecks while, of course, keeping pace with the competition. Payday after payday he'd watched the checks flow out to office employees, loggers, cat operators and chokermen. Overhead costs, building requirements, equipment payments, insurance rates and government taxes had to be settled, too. Then, figuring out the sum left over, he'd put aside an amount for next month's operating costs, finding nothing left with which to pay his own meager salary.

''Business,'' Bensen said, ''is a hell of a lot of fun. You get a lot of hell and some fun.'' His eyes seldom left her face, and when they did, it was to wander over the rest of her until Jesse felt as warm as toast, inside and out. It was an entirely new sensation, despite the fact she had gone out with plenty of men.

Their dinner arrived, and with it a full-bodied fruity red wine. When Jesse's glass had been replaced and the new one filled, he decided to ask a few deft questions of his own.

"But you should know that," he began. "You run your own business, as well. It's entirely different, but it's a business nonetheless. You're at once boss and employee. You've hired yourself a salesman—in your case, an agent; you have a distinct cash flow; you have a product-market balance—which, I'd say, is working for you." Bensen didn't give praise lightly, and Jesse took this as a compliment. "I'll bet you have assets in the stock market, money tied up in investments, directed savings in the bank. Then you have your liabilities and your costs, your overhead. Am I right?"

Jesse stared at him with something like wonder. "Well. . . yes, except you're the first person to see it that way. Almost everyone thinks it's—it's romantic and nothing but fun. It's not!"

"No?"

And he coaxed Jesse into telling about her long years spent writing on coffee breaks, lunch hours and after work in the evenings, when everyone else was out having a good time; the hours and hours she'd read, studying literature; the massive research she'd had to undertake for whodunits, the seemingly endless lean time before she'd had several books out on the market; and the struggle she had experienced to gain acceptance in the literary world.

"I almost phoned the critic who wrote my first review because I was so angry! Nobody would want to read the book after hearing what he had to say. The first printing didn't sell too well, and I blamed it all on him. For some reason the publisher decided to put it through a second printing, and then it sold very well. So I forgave the critic finally, after three terribly long years. You know, thinking about what he said still gives me a sharp pain." Jesse realized she was rattling away to Bensen as though she'd known him for years. How long had she talked, disclosing things about herself she never offered even to some of her good friends? A small frown nicked her brow—she was a listener, not a talker!

"You probably have that review tucked away somewhere," Bensen put in, "and every now and then you take it out and read it."

Jesse said with a small reminiscent smile, forgetting her resolution to be more reticent, "It's in my diary. It falls out from time to time...sometimes at the *wrong* time." Bensen smiled slowly at her. "I'm thinking of having it framed, along with the best review I've ever had. I'll hang them above my desk to remind myself not to take anything too seriously."

"I'd like to see where you work."

"Y-you would?" Jesse gazed at him with parted lips. "The twins and I are having coffee tomorrow morning with Betty—at ten. Are you free?"

"I'll come up with you when I drive you over. Are you sure you've had enough to eat? How about the dessert menu?"

"Oh, Bensen, no. I'm certain I don't have room."

"Coffee and liqueurs, then?"

"Ummm. And a cigarette?" She certainly needed something to bring her back to solid ground. She wanted to stay here forever, just like this. It was a dream; it had to be. They hadn't argued once, not *once*, all evening. There hadn't been one awkward moment; one subject had led to another and another. It was the best date she'd ever been on in her whole life, she decided. Her blood felt as light and bubbly as wine; she felt good from the top of her head to the tips of her polished pink toes, and she knew she looked good. Bensen's black eyes held a wordless message that had pitched her into a breathless excitement right from the start. But somewhere out there, beyond their private present world in far-away reality, she knew there was a woman called Dorothy....

"You," Bensen drawled in his deep cynical tone, "look like a cat full of cream." There was a potency, a vibrancy, under the words that sent a warm delicious shiver down her spine.

"Perhaps that's because I feel like one." She paused for a moment, her topaz eyes clinging to his. Then she just *had* to know. "Bensen, doesn't Dorothy mind your going out for dinner with other women?"

The black brows raised arrogantly. "Why should she mind? It's none of her concern."

"B-but—but...."

"But what?" There was the barest of smiles on his mouth as his eyes watched her intently, then dropped down to her lips in unmistakable emphasis. When he looked back into her eyes and saw the confusion he'd aroused, the smile deepened on his sensuous mouth. Jesse took a long breath, her mind in turmoil. What was happening to her?

"But aren't you engaged?" she persisted. "*I* would mind if we—if you... oh, gosh, I'd better not say another word!" She closed her eyes in embarrassment—and abruptly opened them again, for Bensen had taken her hand.

Under her alarmed gaze he turned the palm upward, and with a warm teasing insistency his thumb moved slowly over the sensitive skin, moved up to the line of her wrist and then back into the hollow of her palm. His depthless black eyes studied the expression on her oval face, watched the way her mouth parted as the sensations tingled across her skin.

"Were you going to say if *we* were engaged, you would mind my being with another woman? Jessamine?"

Her eyes flew up to his face—and just as quickly returned to her lap. She shook her head wordlessly, unable to trust herself to speak. Things were progressing with such speed, in such a dangerous direction. And the way he used her name, as if it were an endearment.... Her heart was thudding in her breast, slowly and ponderously, like the swing of a heavy pendulum.

"Oh, Jessamine, if you only knew how lovely you are! But you're blushing, as though this were your very first date."

Jesse couldn't explain what she was feeling. Her lashes remained lowered, making deep shadows on her cheekbones. And his thumb persistently and enticingly continued its exploration of her palm. She hadn't the strength to pull her hand away. She felt swamped, helpless, caught in the grip of something much stronger than herself.

"How many boyfriends do you have, Jessamine?"

Startled, she stared up into his lean ruthless face. He looked like he meant to find out, one way or another. Her eyes darkened to a smoky topaz.

"And how is that your concern?" she asked softly, lightly, her poise returning at last. Her laugh was low and silvery. "Checking out the competition?"

"I want to know how many men you've been to bed with."

She gasped, her eyes wide with anger and shock.

"I'm not going to apologize for being so direct, so don't look at me like that, Jessamine. I want to know. I told you backwoods men don't beat around the bush."

"I have absolutely no intention of telling you!" She tugged at her hand, but his fingers had closed around it like a steel vise. "Why on earth should you want to know such a thing! That's strictly private information as far as I'm concerned. I don't kiss and tell, and furthermore you've no right to ask!"

His chuckle was low and sent myriad disturbances through her bloodstream. The color on her cheeks deepened. He gazed in intent appreciation, then suddenly turned quite serious.

"There was a bad experience, wasn't there?" he prodded gently. "You frighten so easily. You withdraw at the slightest hint of anything personal. But you're so enchanting and desirable I find it hard to believe you don't— What happened, Jessamine, that frightened you so badly?''

''Nothing happened.'' She choked over the words, panicking that he should sense so much about her. Her body was one taut line; she felt as though she couldn't move.

''Don't lie to me, Jessamine. I'm going to find out.''

A long trembling sigh escaped her. She had no doubt he would inevitably do just as he said. She swung her head down and to the side so that a wing of chestnut hair hid her face. ''He—he was married.'' Bensen had to lean forward to catch the faint words. ''I didn't find out for months.'' Her tongue ran over her suddenly dry lips. ''His wife told me. And she was so nice.'' There was anguish in the quiet simple phrase. ''I felt like the lowest, the worst. . . . He told me—he'd asked me to marry him, and I had visions of children and, and. . . .''

Somehow Bensen had taken hold of her other hand, too. The warmth and tightness of his big brown hands disconcerted her still more. She took a deep steadying breath.

''But that was a long time ago.'' The sound of her voice, much calmer, was reassuring. She slanted a quick oblique look at his face, expecting to see something other than the boundless understanding and the expression that made her feel dizzy and light-headed all over again.

''How long ago?''

''Almost three years.''

''And you're over it now?''

"Oh, yes." She smiled at him, not hiding now.

"And there's been no one—no one serious, I mean—since then, has there?"

"No..." she said softly, her sherry eyes studying him, wondering how he did it. He should be working for the government questioning spies! "Are you satisfied now?" she asked a little tartly.

"Not entirely." He grinned, seeing her eyes widen in alarm. "But for the moment I am. You were very strictly raised, weren't you?"

Jesse eyed him warily, feeling electric undercurrents in the air that she hadn't consciously noticed until then. It was just like those other times. Now looking at him across the table from her made her again think he was a dangerous man, a tough customer. But she no longer wanted to run away. She wanted to stay with him, to stay within the circle of whatever it was they created every time they were alone.

"Don't go and hide, Jessamine. It was just a simple question, that's all. Look at me, Jessamine, and answer me."

"Y-yes, I was. Can you imagine being raised among nuns as being any other way?"

"Is that what gave you your untouched look?"

"I don't know what you mean."

"Perhaps you don't, but men notice it all the time. It certainly didn't escape my attention. That innocent air with your looks, Jessamine, is one hell of a combination." The black eyes ravaged her face, her lips, her throat. She felt just as if he'd touched her. Everything inside her seemed to be quivering—but not from nervousness. Was this the Bensen she knew? What was he doing to her? *How* did he do this to her? And what else did he mean to do.. . .

"I'm not innocent," she insisted. He was going much too fast.

"And yet you look as though you've never been properly kissed in your whole life."

"I've been kissed lots of times!"

"Perhaps not by the right man."

Was he teasing her, playing with her? She couldn't tell. Why couldn't she read him as accurately as he seemed to read her? "I don't believe in—in that nonsense about a Mr. Right, and I didn't think you did, either. You told me as much when we were discussing Shanna and Ray. Oh, that doesn't mean I don't believe in love. But there isn't a prince charming in the whole wide world. Actually, now that I think about it—" a small frown hovered on her brow "—Ray does seem to be Mr. Right for Shanna. Perhaps occasionally it really *does* happen!" She shrugged her golden shoulders. "What do I know?"

"I must be getting old," Bensen drawled cryptically, "reaching my second childhood." His eyes slowly, languidly, traveled from the top of her dress, where the soft swell of her breasts began; moved up to meet the puzzled question in the luminous amber eyes. "I'm starting to believe in fairy tales," he answered. Jesse saw his faint smile and the distinctly dangerous gleam far in the depths of the jet gaze. "Drink up, Jessamine, I'm taking you home." His tone at the end was as soft as black velvet.

They had lingered so long over the meal that it was

late when they left the restaurant—nearing midnight. As soon as they stepped outside, Jesse unfolded her shawl and was placing it around her shoulders when Bensen, behind her, slid his hands underneath her hair and lifted it out from under the shawl. Her hair slipped like silk from his hands. When she'd felt his touch, she'd stopped, unable to move a muscle, and he'd stepped closer, until now she could actually feel the heat from his body.

"The car, Jessamine," he reminded her, an arm sliding around her waist, the hand settling in the curve between her hip and her rib cage. He held her against him as they walked to the curb, where his black Mercedes stood waiting. Jesse felt warm and shielded from the night's chill. Dreamily she thought there wasn't anything impersonal or courteous to his touch, as when a man holds a woman's arm to help her across the street or through a door. No, it suggested nothing of courteousness.

On the way from the restaurant to their hotel, neither Bensen nor Jesse said much. But it made no difference to the winding, quicksilver heady tension, that nerveless and yet fully complete awareness of self and the other.

When they entered the suite, Mrs. Petty was steadily knitting and watching television. While Bensen paid for her service and ushered her off to a taxi, Jesse disappeared into the bedrooms to check on the twins. She straightened out the blankets, careful lest they awaken, and then on impulse, because their mother was so far away and she was sure Mrs. Petty hadn't done it, she bent down quickly and kissed them both. For the first time, as she gazed at the twins from the door, she felt a twinge of envy for Shanna.

When finally she turned away, she noticed most of the lights in the sitting room were switched off. Only one small lamp burned somewhere in the room down the hall. She hesitated, wondering if Bensen were getting ready for sleep, when he suddenly appeared... minus his black dinner jacket, minus his beautiful dark silk tie. The collar of his white shirt was open at the neck, and the cuffs were rolled carelessly up to his elbows, revealing the corded muscles of his tanned forearms. Jesse blinked, watching him approach her. She studied the long black length of leg; the narrow male hip; the widening torso sheathed in white; the deeply tanned vee of his chest, smooth and muscular; the bottom column of throat; and the large pitch black eyes that regarded her steadily. The eyes seemed to draw Jesse up into them as he came closer. Something inside told her to be careful, to look after herself before she looked after anyone else. Was it Shanna's voice?

As though he did it all the time, he ran a hand around her waist. Then he turned her back into the darkened room, glancing over first at each twin. The warm pressure of his hand slid down to her hip, and the fingers curved into the softness of her stomach as he quietly shut the door. He started down the hall, still supporting her, flicking off the light switch as they passed.

His cuff links and tie, gold watch and slim black pocketbook lay in the light of the one remaining lamp. To Jesse it was all like a dream. He turned her to face him, a hand on either side of her waist. She was intoxicated by his very nearness, by the caressing touch of his hands.

He bent his head. It seemed that an eternity passed before his lips first touched hers, softly, very softly, warm and achingly sweet, burning their imprint into the curves and the rosy roundness. The unexpected tender quality of his kiss undermined all her inborn resistance; under the soft touch of his mouth her lips parted with innocent willingness and sudden hunger for more. It was much, much nicer than she'd ever dreamed it would be.

With a muffled groan she just barely heard, he slid one hand around the small of her back to close the gap between them while the other moved sensuously through her hair to cup the back of her head. At last, at last, long last, the strong arms were around her and the solid broad smooth chest was beneath her fingers. Under one hand she could feel the heavy pounding of his heart. It vibrated through her blood, an echo to her own heart filling her ears. Her body felt as light as whipped cream as she sank fully against him. The searing heat of his gentle mouth caused a corresponding lick of flame deep within her; the hard taut muscles of his thighs and torso against her sent her senses into an erotic storm.

There was a giggle from the hallway, then a twittering childish peal sounded in the air before being abruptly muffled.

Startled, Bensen and Jesse turned toward the doorway, his arms still around her and one hand tangled in her hair. Merit had her hand clapped over her sister's mouth, while Samantha's cheeks were puffed and her mouth was screwed up tight to contain a spasm. For several blank seconds Bensen and Jesse stared at the two small tousle-headed pajama-clad figures in the doorway.

Then Jesse stepped away from Bensen, her body feeling cold where he had touched her, and Merit's hand dropped. Samantha's giggle dwindled into the hiccups.

"We—*hic*—wanted to make sure you were—*hic*—home."

"What were you doing?"

Jesse looked at Bensen, feeling her cheeks start to burn. He looked at her and smiled slowly.

"I was kissing Jesse good-night," he answered Merit gravely.

"I've seen good-night kisses, and that—*hic*—didn't look like one! *Hic!*"

"Give yourself a few years, Sam," Bensen said dryly. "Now jump back into bed, or you'll lose precious beauty sleep. Good night!"

"*Hic!*"

Bensen grinned.

"Come on, Sam, I'll get you a glass of water and then tuck you in." Jesse turned in the doorway, her hands on the small shoulders. "Good night, Bensen."

His eyes held hers just long enough to start another delicate pink tide sweeping over her neck and face. He didn't say anything to her, but his slow wicked half smile made Jesse pivot and hurry the twins ahead of her down the hall. She forestalled their questions with a, "Shhhh. . . it's time you two were in bed; it's time I was, too."

THAT ONE KISS changed nothing and yet changed everything. When Jesse woke early the next morning, the sun was still in its accustomed place, the static Prussian blue of summer sky domed the city, sea and mountains just as it had always done, and Jesse realized reality had been the kiss and not the dream. It had finally happened, and now she needn't wonder any longer what it would be like to kiss Bensen Everhart. As her mind drifted off to last night, the muscles across her stomach tightened, and a spiraling thread of excitement wound through her.

Simple chemical reaction, Jesse decided, climbing out of bed. He did something potent to her; he always had, and the kiss was just final proof. It had felt as though she'd suddenly been plugged into a two-hundred-and-twenty-volt socket. . . and yet had anything really changed?

Jesse stood at the floor-to-ceiling windows of her bedroom, clad in a wispy shorty nightgown, and looked out over the slowly awakening city. She nibbled on her bottom lip, a frown chasing over the smoothness of her forehead. What was going to happen next? Where was life leading her? Should she step out of the picture while there was still time to get away safely? Would Bensen *let* her step out? And where did Dorothy fit into this?

The die was cast. She could no more step out of the picture than she could step out of life.

Later that morning, but still at an early hour, Jesse was seated on the sofa in Bensen's office with a twin on either side of her, her long legs crossed and the hem of her cream linen suit not quite covering the appealing curve of her knees. The long chestnut hair was up in a ponytail to take it off her face and to keep her back cool, for the day was already gathering a tropical heat. Past the smoked-glass windows of Bensen's office the city below sparkled and glinted with white-hot sun, but inside in the spacious room it was cool and the soft, almost unnoticeable whir of the air conditioning soothing.

The other side of the room was a hum of activity...Bensen on the phone, Bensen issuing clipped precise orders to executives who flowed in and out the immense double doors of his office—gold cedar doors that were carved and polished to a glasslike finish. The steady clicking of typewriters could be heard every time those doors swung open.

For five minutes straight Bensen talked to a company lawyer, giving instructions that made Jesse's head swim. Occasionally she would look out the windows, but her gaze returned irresistibly to the man behind the splendid desk, his dark head to one side, the high forehead partially hidden under the sweep of raven hair, his long brown fingers against his lips in concentration. Here he seemed truly at home; he might almost have had his feet up on the desk, Jesse thought to herself, except that he didn't. There was an economy of action, of speech, of expression, and yet he managed to appear incredibly relaxed.

From time to time the black eyes drifted over to the

sofa and Jesse, drifted up the length of shapely leg from ankle to knee, roamed farther over the curves under the cream linen suit up to the well-shaped head exposed by the ponytail of falling chestnut silk, the twins on either side of her like summer poppies in their carmine dresses. Every now and then their eyes would meet, and Jesse's head would fill with thoughts of lovemaking. She couldn't help it. She was sitting there in his office melting with desire for him and hoping it didn't show.

JESSE RODE THE ELEVATOR up to the twenty-seventh floor; she was alone and closed her eyes sleepily, dreamily. It was very late; she had no idea of the time. The twins, she supposed, would have been asleep for hours, and Bensen, too, would long since have gone to bed. She wondered with whom his business dinner this evening had been. Dorothy, by any chance? Would he classify her as a business dinner?

Outside the door to the suite Jesse searched in her evening bag for the key, yawning delicately and thinking that Bensen's choice in companions didn't matter one way or another to her—really, it didn't. She let herself in quietly. Seeing faint light in the sitting room and thinking it was very thoughtful of Bensen to leave it on for her, she rounded the corner to switch it off.

"Where the hell have you been?"

She dropped her bag in fright. Bensen swung off the divan and stood up in one quick motion. He was very wide awake and on the coffee table before him stood a half-empty bottle of whiskey and a glass. The ashtray was full of butts. Jesse stared open-mouthed at him.

"Do you have any idea of the time?" The fury in his low tone was unmistakable. Jesse blinked and continued to stare helplessly at him, frightened and astonished beyond words. Bensen in a wild temper set all her nerves to screeching at once.

"Do you?"

Jesse shook her head, trying to clear her thoughts. "No-o...." Her voice was just above a whisper. She hadn't moved.

"It's three o'clock. *Three* in the morning! Where the hell have you been?"

"I—I was out with a friend."

"Dressed like *that*?"

Bewildered, Jesse looked down at her ice-pink brocade dress. It was strapless, with a tight bodice and skirt that fit her figure like a glove. Two slits ran up either side of the skirt to show the beginning curve of thigh.

"Well...yes. Jacob took me to a concert."

"I've yet to see a concert that lasts till three in the morning!" Bensen ground out the words, his white teeth visible. The black eyes flamed across the room.

"W-we went to dinner afterward. We talked and talked. I haven't seen him in such a long time that—"

"You *talked*? Dressed like that? I don't believe it."

"I always dress up when I go to a concert!" Jesse exclaimed, two spots of color forming on her cheeks. "Just about everybody does. And Jacob's never been the groping kind, if it's any concern of yours! He's a gentleman, and besides, he's been a friend of mine for years and years, and I can go out with him anytime I please! And who cares what time it is? I'm not one of the twins; I don't have to be in bed by nine-thirty!''

"A friend? Just what kind of *friends* do you have?"

Jesse bent, picked up her evening bag and threw it at him as hard as she could. The little bag with its pale pink glass beads went sailing through the air, releasing its contents as it flew. Bensen caught it with one hand and dropped it on the coffee table beside the whiskey bottle. He came slowly toward her.

"Well?"

"Damn you, Bensen!" The emotion-charged words were out before she knew it. She was breathing raggedly, and her hands were clenched at her sides. "There are times when I hate you!"

"I sat here hating you for three hours. I've got the jump on you, Jessamine! I was just about ready to start phoning the hospitals and the police. I've been going out of my mind and all you can say is, 'Damn you, Bensen!' " He stopped right in front of her, and Jesse's vision was filled with the breadth of his chest. She felt faint, suddenly weakened by her outburst. To look up at him would put her in too vulnerable a position, so she glared through her lashes, holding her head with maximum dignity.

"There was no need to wait up for me," she gritted. "If you hadn't noticed, I happen to be an adult and—"

"To my regret I noticed it too much."

One of his hands snaked up and curved around her chin, forcing her head back. In the same instant his mouth covered hers in a mad passionate ruthless kiss that sent shock waves reverberating through her system. A small cry strangled in her throat. No man had ever attacked her like this before, and she pushed against his chest, panicked by his pagan urgency.

"Oh, no, you don't!" he muttered under his breath as she struggled for her freedom. He swept her protesting hands away and jerked her against him, his strong arms crushing the breath from her body as they pressed her into the hard planes and angles of his. Gathering her hair, he tilted her head back, smiling slightly, deliberately, into her furious topaz eyes. And then his mouth descended over hers with a masterful intent and consuming purpose that stole her breath and forced her lips apart. His devouring passion closed over and around her, binding her to him, while his mouth continued the plunder of her soft rosy lips.

A moan caught deep in Jesse's throat, and a shudder rippled through her, releasing the angry tension of a few minutes earlier. Her toes in the pink satin evening slippers curled. In her bloodstream a wildfire of desire was mounting. Her body turned pliant within the steely circle of his embrace. Letting go of her hair, he pressed her hips against him...and Jesse's hands slid up his shoulders, feeling the warm coiled muscles beneath her fingers, touching, feeling the firm flesh to assuage the need within her. She clasped him tightly, the pink nails of one hand indenting his shoulder while her other hand slid into his raven hair, loving its soft thickness, loving to be able to touch it at long last.

When he raised his head just a little bit to be able to see her, she whispered, "Please, Bensen, don't stop." When his lips didn't immediately touch her own, her eyelids fluttered open to see a deep glow of fire in the black eyes. They roamed possessively over her face, a smile of male content on the imperial mouth. She quivered inwardly at that look.

"Jessamine, my Jessamine..." he murmured huskily, and his mouth kissed her eyes shut, lingered over the curve of her cheek and jawline.. "I won't have you going out with other men." A mutter and another kiss. "At least not men I don't know." And his lips continued to the pale pink shell of her ear. His tongue touched the sensitive inside, and then he started to nibble on her earlobe.

"I'll introduce you to Jacob," Jesse breathed, her heart thudding in rhythm with his. Her fingers curled in his hair as his mouth pursued its hungry path.

"He didn't kiss you?"

"No..." Jesse gasped as one hot kiss after another was pressed all the way down the side of her neck. Her skin shivered with delight.

"Why not?"

"We—we don't do that sort of thing."

"He's a fool."

"You'd like him."

"Maybe...." Bensen swung her up into his arms and carried her to the sofa, raining kisses on her face and throat. Both of Jesse's hands were wound through his hair, and her arms were twined around his neck. When he laid her down, they stayed, for he sank down beside her, his body half covering hers. He claimed her inviting parted lips with a simmering passion. In Jesse's inner vision the world melted out of sight. Mind, body and soul were concentrated on the man and what he was doing to her, the feel of him, the touch of him, the warm breath mingling with her own.

Then the dark head was beneath her cheek, and the brush of his chin, nuzzling between her breasts, was pushing down the top of her dress. The imprint of his hot mouth against the soft rounded swell followed, and the smooth sensitive skin under his mouth became milky white as his lips passed the tanned line of her bikini. A long brown hand helped the dress down farther and then slid slowly over her stomach, warm and caressing. Her dress had crept up, and one long shapely leg was exposed by the skirt's side slit, the material falling apart just at the line of her hip so that Bensen's hand moved unhindered along the soft inside curve of her silk-stockinged thigh.

Desire flooded her whole body with languorous heat. His breath was heavy and ragged, and the warmth of it tingled over her bare breast as his lips moved in a sensuous circle around the tip until it hardened under the hot moist touch of his mouth. The gentle biting of his teeth provoked a shudder that rippled down the length of her body, communicating to him instantly so that his hands tightened, desirous. His arm around her back tightened, supporting her pliant length against him as one hard-muscled black-clad thigh slid between her legs. More of his weight shifted onto her as he raised his head, the black eyes burning with passion while they ravished the dreamy cast of her face, the swollen rosiness of her love-drugged mouth. Her amber eyes shimmered as they gazed unwaveringly into his.

"Bensen, I...." Her voice was a low appealing whisper, and when it trailed away, he kissed her very softly, barely touching her lips with his. "I thought I wasn't your type."

He groaned, and the deep male sound was arousing to all of Jesse's senses.

"I've been wanting to take your clothes off ever since that first day, when I saw you typing and dancing at the same time!" There was a soft knock at the door, neither of them stirred, choosing to ignore it. "You were wearing tight jeans and a red-and-blue plaid blouse." Jesse blushed under his steadfast hungry gaze. She couldn't think straight, and the blood was pounding in her head and along her veins, beating out the timeless rhythm of love and desire. In a state of breathless confusion, bemused and totally wrapped up in the man and the moment, she didn't hear the second knock. But Bensen's head moved up sharply.

With a muffled curse he swung off the couch. He grabbed his suit jacket, which lay over the back of the divan, and bringing Jesse abruptly to a sitting position, he wrapped his jacket around her shoulders. A click sounded in the lock, followed by the slight swishing sound of the suite door opening.

"Sir? Mr. Everhart, your coffee's finally here." The bellhop's voice came floating from the small anteroom. There was the faint jingling of china and silver and the door closing. "Sorry it took so long. I knocked twice, and you said you were alone, so I thought I'd just bri—" Gasp. "Bring. . . ." He stared in complete dismay, his mouth agape. "Oh, no!"

Jesse clutched the front of Bensen's jacket tighter around her, her neck and cheeks flaming red under the bellhop's goggle-eyed stare. Bensen growled something and took the tray from the stunned man's hands, whipping it down onto the coffee table so that everything rattled and jumped.

"Here!" he said, slapping a few bills into his still outstretched hands. Then, jerking the man out of his trance, he snapped, "Do you think you could go now?"

"I'm so sorry! I never thought—that is, you've never had a woman—I mean, you've always been alone before, and I just thought you were working and—" The door shut on the bellhop's next words.

Jesse stood up, shocked and trembling, her fingers still grasping Bensen's jacket tightly shut around her. Her bare breasts rubbed against the silk lining, heightening her awareness of her near nude state, and fresh color washed over her cheeks. She looked at Bensen mutely with wide bewildered eyes, as though she'd just woken up.

He stood just inside the sitting room with his hands in his pockets, watching her steadily. The dark face was an implacable mask, but the black eyes glittered. Jesse took a shuddering breath. As he came toward her, she involuntarily stepped back, strangely frightened. She was yearning for him, yet the very strength of that yearning rattled her more than the demanding desire she saw in his jet eyes.

"I knew something like this would happen," she said wretchedly, turning from him to adjust her dress. Her fingers were shaking with such unstrung nerves it seemed to take forever before she was once more fully clothed. Outside the windows the million night lights of Vancouver twinkled, unchanged.

He had stepped up behind her, and now his hands brushed against her shoulders as he slipped his jacket off. Her skin shivered at just that small touch, and she curved her shoulders forward. The slight movement brought out a frown between Bensen's brows. He dropped his hands but stayed where he was.

"What do you mean? The lovemaking or the interruption?"

"What happened?" she moaned, her thoughts a distracted whirl.

"I think it's called the birds and the bees," he answered roughly, sweeping her hair aside and planting a searing kiss on her nape. When she gasped and would have drawn away, his arm encircled her slender waist and drew her firmly back against him. Partly to get away and partly because his mouth was evoking the most profound sensations, Jesse wriggled within his clasp. But he held on tight, and his other hand slid around her ribs to cup her breast and hold her even closer.

"Bensen...." She tried to talk to him through her breathless dizzy condition. "We must be sensible. We—we shouldn't be doing this...I don't think. Bensen, stop that. There's a—a reason why, but I can't think of it at the moment...ohhh-h...Bensen, no, wait...we...really shouldn't...be doing...this.''

"Do you always talk so much?"

"I'm trying to make it clear—"

"You are; you're making perfect sense, darling."

The hand around her waist slid down between her hip bones, caressing and creating a delicious warmth that spread and spread like ripples in a pool.

"I want to kiss you all night long," he murmured, "and all day tomorrow, that night and the day after and the night after, forever. A man could get lost in you Jessamine...." His mouth continued its erotic teasing on her highly sensitive skin. "Do you think the twins would be surprised to find you sleeping in my bed?"

"Dammit, Bensen, who says I'm going to sleep in your bed?"

He turned her slightly in his arms so that she was leaning back on one of his shoulders, looking up into his face. One black brow was slightly raised, and there was a faint dangerous smile on his mouth.

"You might as well know now that I'll kiss and hold and touch you any chance I get." Jesse's heart leaped with a clamor of warning signals. "And that we'll be caught at it simply because we'll be doing all or some of those so often...Jessamine."

"Oh, you think so, do you?"

"Don't you?"

Jesse intended to bring up the subject of Dorothy and the ringless engagement, but looking up at Bensen now, she knew that if she didn't go to her own bed soon, she wouldn't be going at all. He overwhelmed her, and it was rather terrifying that someone should have so much control over her. Her thoughts were filled with him morning, noon and night, it seemed. He could do things to her that no other human being had ever done—and he was engaged to another woman! Damn, why did the world always have to be so complicated?

"And don't try being cool and standoffish, because I'll catch you one dark night and kiss that protective shell away inch by inch. I mean that, Jessamine."

"You don't waste much time, do you?"

"With you, Jessamine, I've wasted too much time already. I should have put down those letters and kissed you as I wanted to that first afternoon." He paused, a slight grin altering his expression. "But that might have shocked you." He bent his head and kissed her hard and quick, leaving her in no doubt that he intended to carry out everything he'd said to the letter.

"Good night, Jessamine."

He dropped his arms abruptly and moved off toward his bedroom just beyond the sitting room. He flashed a final smile wickedly over his shoulder before closing the door behind him.

CHAPTER EIGHT

THE LONG TRIP home was laced with the same quick silver tension that became more acute at odd moments. Jesse, wary of Bensen's every move toward her, dared not be cool and distant and, as a consequence, ended up being perfectly natural with him. But that had its pitfalls, as well, for all of a sudden she would find that she'd reached out and touched him, and once she even caught herself wanting to brush the hair off his forehead but stopped herself just in time. The head wind on the Earl Cove to Saltery Bay ferry blew it into his eyes, making her impulse all the more irresistible. And right after she'd stopped herself, his hand had slid around her waist, as if it were the most normal thing in the world to do; he did it so casually that neither of the twins noticed. The pitch-black eyes held a hint of slumbering passion in their depths that made Jesse lick suddenly dry lips and wish he would look somewhere else.

On the last lap of their journey, after lunch on the ferry, Jesse found herself thinking of how she'd described Clifftop to Jacob as home. It was strange, but for the time being she did consider it home. *Home!* As if she had a place there, as if Cecilia were her grandmother, Shanna her sister, and Samantha and Merit her nieces.... And Bensen? He didn't fit in anywhere but occupied a place all his own. What was the matter with her? It wasn't as though she'd fallen in love with him; it was only that he was, in truth, one of the most fascinating men she'd ever come up against. He intrigued her, that was all. And she *was* attracted to him....

They arrived at Clifftop a scarce hour later. As soon as the car's wheels stopped, the twins shot out of the Mercedes like arrows and ran shouting toward the house, daring each other to take the terrace steps four at a time. Jesse watched them go with a wry smile and turned to see what Bensen was doing, one hand already opening her door. But instead of being on his side of the car, he was sliding over. Then his arm was around her shoulders and his mouth closing in on hers. Gasping in surprise, she pulled away from him with one fluid movement that carried her through the door, which she shut in his mocking grinning face.

It appeared that Shanna had been about to go out riding, and in short order she convinced the twins and Jesse to join her.

"You weren't planning on *working* today, were you?" she asked Jesse in mock horror.

"I guess not! An excursion on Taffy sounds like just the thing after spending the whole morning locked in that car," Jesse replied, setting her valise on the floor and stretching. She stopped in midstretch, for Bensen's glance over her figure was like the touch of his hand.

Shanna's eyes flew to Bensen, then to Jesse again.

"Yes...I know what you mean," she murmured sympathetically. "Well, let's go—"

"You're right, Jesse," Bensen interrupted. "A ride sounds like just the thing. I'll join you all."

A small silence fell in the hallway as everyone sent him quick surreptitious looks.

Then Merit spoke up. "But Uncle Ben, there are only four horses, and there are five of us!"

"You two little folk will have to share, then, won't you?" Bensen grinned down at the twins, a mischievous charming smile that always got its way. "Go on, get cracking—I'm not going to wait all day for you ladies to change!"

The twins dashed toward the stairs; Shanna, with a puzzled look over her shoulder at Jesse and Bensen, ran up after them. Jesse picked up her valise and was about to follow when Bensen stopped her with a slight touch on her arm. She turned back to face him, on her guard.

"All those plants you have in your apartment..." he began, and she waited, eyeing him and wondering what was coming next, "I like them. We could use some here, don't you agree?"

"Ahh, well, yes, I—I suppose so."

"Um-hum. It would make the place less bare and more alive. Would you do me a favor, Jessamine? Would you look after it?"

"Oh, ahh...yes, of course, Bensen." She couldn't hide her astonishment. "You—you mean order them from Vancouver? But how would we get them here?"

"I'll take care of that if you'll have them delivered to this address." He took a small business card from his pocket and scribbled on the back of it. "That's one of my warehouses. Give them instructions on how to care for whatever you choose."

"You mean I should just order whatever I want?"

"That's it." The black eyes were sparkling down at her. "You know plants, obviously, since you own a thriving jungle. And I like your taste. Hurry up now. We've got a date in ten minutes behind the barn!" He chuckled at her baffled expression, gave her a little shove toward the stairs and added in an undertone, "If you hadn't noticed, Jessamine, we're alone, and if you keep on staring at me like that, I'll kiss you, and then perhaps we won't go riding at all. Go on, beat it!"

Jesse was tugging on her denims when there was a slight knock on her door.

"Come in!" she called out.

"It's me, Jesse." Samantha came in, stuffing her shirt into her jeans.

"What is it, honey?" Jesse turned around to pull a T-shirt over her head.

"I thought I'd better tell you you don't have to worry about Merry's and me telling anybody we saw you and Uncle Ben kissing."

Jesse swallowed in shock and surprise. She'd forgotten all about that.

"Mummy said when two people kiss it's private, and nobody should go around talking about it."

"You told your mummy?" There was a slight edge of panic to Jesse's voice.

"Oh, no! But she said that when we saw her kissing Ray, and it's the same thing, isn't it?"

Jesse gulped. "Yes, it is, Sam. Your mummy's very wise. Hey...thanks."

"Oh, you don't have to thank us; it's just good manners," Samantha answered seriously. She turned to go, then pivoted on her toes. "Do you *like* kissing Uncle Ben?"

"Oh...ah...if I answer that, will you promise to keep it a secret?"

"Can I tell Merry?"

"Well, okay, but *only* her."

"Cross my heart and hope to die!" Samantha flew over to her, and Jesse dropped into a squat so that they were eye to eye.

"Yes, I do," she whispered.

"Go-osh!"

"My feelings exactly," Jesse muttered to herself as Samantha ran from her bedroom. Quickly she braided her hair, took a flying glance at herself in the mirror, pulled on the riding boots that she'd collected from her apartment and was out and down the stairs at a fast clip.

"I don't have to tell you young folk to take it easy—on those horses you couldn't do anything else! When will you be back?" grandmother asked of everyone, following the group onto the sunlit terrace. Martha hovered behind her.

"In time for tea," Bensen replied, rolling up the cuffs of his shirt.

"I'll be waiting." Grandmother's brown eyes were actually twinkling. Jesse took a second look at her, then a third.

"And I suppose you'll all be hungry enough to eat

a—never mind," Martha sniffed. "I worked all morning; there's no reason I can't work all afternoon, too. Work, work, work..." she grumbled as she shuffled away into the house.

When Bensen unnecessarily helped Jesse up on Taffy, one of his hands stayed curved around her thigh; neither Shanna nor the twins noticed, for they were on Jesse's other side, and he knew it. A corner of his mouth was curved up in a suppressed smile as his hand moved slowly and sensuously back and forth.

"Stop it!" Jesse hissed at him.

"Make me." He grinned into her flashing eyes.

Although Jesse tried to keep pace with Shanna and the twins, Bensen somehow managed to cut her off and force her into last position when they had to go single file down a narrow wooded path. He checked his already slow horse so that they dropped behind. Jesse was mouthing words at him under her breath, but her pulse was racing. The path, however, was too narrow for more than one horse; dense shrubs and underbrush made any divergence impossible.

Jesse clip-clopped along impatiently behind Bensen, while up ahead Shanna and the twins moved out of sight. Shafts of sunlight filtered down through the forest roof, and as Bensen passed from greeny gold shadow into the light, Jesse, watching him, sighed softly, feeling a certain helplessness overtake her.

The path meandered down and around and up. She breathed the moist mossy scent of the forest, relished the pungent musk of the pine-needled earth, and when she passed a huckleberry bush, reached out to pick some of the fruit. The small translucent red berries melted in her mouth, at once tart and sweet. She reached for more, but Taffy had plodded out of range.

The trail continued up and up until they entered a cedar forest. The trunks, massive and reaching high, high into the sky were limbless, except at the top, where their heads met to show only a lacy patchwork of sky. Under the green cathedral ceiling the air was cool and sweet smelling; the underbrush had melted away, and the forest floor was bare but for a thick carpeting of needles and jeweled green moss. Jesse saw just a flash of blue from Merit's shirt far ahead on the path before that, too, winked out of sight. The beat of her pulse quickened as she realized how isolated she was from the main riding party.

Before she knew what he was up to, Bensen had expertly turned Bobbin broadside on the trail and was already reaching for Taffy's reins. Her horse wasn't quick enough, and she was too inexperienced to outmaneuver him. With a couple of slight tugs Bensen had Taffy docilely pulled up beside Bobbin. Jesse dug in her heels, but it had absolutely no effect.

"Did you come riding just to do this?" she asked crossly. One of his hands settled on the saddlehorn between her legs and the other twined her long braid around his wrist.

"Of course," he murmured. "If I don't get a chance, I make one." His mouth was an inch away from hers.

"Bensen, for goodness' sake, what about Dorothy?"

"What about her?" His mouth descended in a

long delicious demanding kiss. When he'd finished, Jesse had forgotten her question. The hand that had been on the saddlehorn was now freely roaming over the taut muscles of her stomach and then roaming farther.

"You *are* the groping kind!"

"Better get used to it."

She dug her heels in hard twice, and Taffy heaved into a stumbling start. Bensen gave a slight yank on her braid before he let go, and she could hear his soft laughter behind her as she urged Taffy into a lumbering trot.

When she came out into the little clearing where Shanna and the twins were waiting, wondering what had happened to them, her cheeks were still flushed. Shanna sent a questioning searching look before glancing past to Bensen's bland expressionless face. Sam and Merit, whispering and giggling together, sent them secretive looks. Jesse's embarrassment increased.

Shanna edged her horse close to Jesse's and whispered, "Have you two been fighting again?"

"Wha-at? Oh." Jesse cleared her throat, trying to appear natural. "No, not—not exactly," she qualified. "But let me lead the way, will you?"

AFTERNOON TEA passed calmly enough, with Martha's butter tarts the main attraction. Bensen had gone to his den, and grandmother and Martha were listening to the twins' version of their Vancouver holiday. Shanna was telling Jesse about her last date with Ray when she stopped abruptly.

"Somebody's coming," she said, listening closely. "Hear it? That's the trouble with that cliff—you can't see who your guests are until they're right on the doorstep!" She grimaced, then brightened. "Perhaps it's Ray. Or Dan. I think he's sweet on you, Jesse. It wouldn't be Lily; she usually walks over. Oh, *damn*, it could be Dorothy."

"Dorothy," Jesse muttered despondently. She was the last person she wanted to see. She found herself gripping the arms of her chair as they waited for someone to appear at the cliff head. Sure enough, it was Dorothy.

"Having tea *al fresco*?" she asked rhetorically, running up the terrace steps. "Anything left over for me? Hello, Cecilia." Dorothy stopped and kissed a wrinkled white cheek. Martha grunted and stomped off into the house. Jesse, easing herself out of her chair, smiled blandly at Dorothy and began gathering plates and cutlery.

Dorothy ignored Jesse and smiled at Shanna instead. "What's this hot gossip I hear about you and—who is it, Ray Dunbar? It isn't true, is it?" Her high laugh trilled in the calm late afternoon air. "The things one hears!"

"And what if it is true?" Shanna asked quietly. She wasn't smiling.

"Well, you're not exactly a matched set, are you? I don't mean to be a snob, but he's not what one could call well-off. Oh, I know he's got that small house, and daddy tells me it's rather charming, but—" she gestured at the mansion before her "—it's not the same, is it? You're used to... to the better things in life, and he—well, darling, he *is* just the local forest ranger. Not husband material at all!'' Dorothy settled herself complacently in Bensen's vacated chair and reached for a butter tart.

The twins were watching her with wide eyes, intent upon what she was saying.

''He'd be Shanna's husband, not yours, so I don't see what difference it makes to you!'' grandmother said acidly while she turned a charming gracious smile upon Dorothy.

Jesse said nothing as she continued gathering plates. She felt as tense as a compacted spring. Only an hour ago she'd been enjoying Bensen's kiss.

''Shanna's practically my sister,'' Dorothy said smoothly. ''Of course I'm concerned that she should find just the right match. A—a man of good background, of good standing in the community. A man of means!'' Dorothy popped the last of the butter tart into her mouth and reached for another.

''I don't know why this sudden drive to find me a husband,'' said Shanna in her soft voice. ''When I want a husband, I'll take care of it. I think I can handle that much on my own!''

''Of course, dear. But you didn't do so well last time, did you?''

This remark was met by a stunned silence that Dorothy didn't seem to notice. She munched avidly through the butter tart.

''I've made a few mistakes,'' Shanna finally said with a sort of tense calm, ''but I hope I've had the sense to learn from them. And if I need character witnesses for Ray, I've only to ask anyone around.

Even grandmother and Bensen like him, don't you?"
There was a tinge of desperation in Shanna's eyes as
she looked toward her grandmother.

"He's delightful," Cecilia Anne promptly replied.
"And he's no Milquetoast—which is what I like!"

"Of course he's *nice*," cooed Dorothy, "and he
does have that ravishing smile—" she glanced toward
Shanna with a small understanding simper "—which
would charm any woman. But I don't think Bensen is
at all keen on him. Oh, I suppose he doesn't mind
your amusing yourself with Ray—after all, there's
little enough to do up here—but as for anything more
serious, no. Bensen's dead set against him. If I were
you, Shanna, I'd listen to Bensen. He *knows* what's
best for you. Had you listened to him in the first
place, you wouldn't be in the situation you're in
now!" Dorothy helped herself to another butter tart,
and Jesse viciously thought that she'd better watch
those thick hips of hers. She would have liked to say
any number of things.

"I hadn't realized my present situation was so god-
awful!"

"It's not exactly ideal, though, is it? Who wants to
marry a woman with two nine-year-old girls? If I
were you, I'd keep my relationship with Ray under
wraps. You can't want word to get around. You
don't want to spoil your chances. So far, despite your
disastrous first marriage, you still have a—a *decent* reputation—which you can thank Bensen for.
But if you persist in flaunting yourself about with
Ray—well, then, you'll just have to bear the conse-
quences. And if you go against Bensen again, don't

be surprised if he's not overly generous with his money.''

"That's enough."

They were just two little words, but the way Shanna said them had everyone looking at her in astonishment. Even Dorothy was momentarily nonplussed.

"There's no need to get huffy," Dorothy finally soothed. "I was only trying to help. After all, I *am* more worldly-wise than you are. But if you won't accept my advice, then all I can say is I've done my best. Does Bensen know your attitude? If not, he'd better."

"He's in the den," Shanna retorted, looking down at the nails of one hand. "You can tell him all about it!"

"I've always taken your part in the past, Shanna, dear," Dorothy said reproachfully, gently, "but this time I don't think I can." Slowly she stood up, brushing the crumbs from her skirt.

"I don't mind."

Dorothy, looking down at Shanna, who was still studying her fingernails, sighed. She reached across the table to pick up another tart before she turned decisively, as though she'd just made a weighty decision, and walked off toward the library's open French doors.

"Bitch!" Shanna muttered, looking after her. "I'm clearing out if she comes here to live."

"And I just might go with you!" grandmother added heatedly.

"It looks as though Bensen has an insurrection on his hands," Jesse murmured wryly, not quite realizing she'd been heard until she saw the sharp gleam of amusement in Cecilia Anne's eyes.

Shanna helped Jesse clear away the rest of the dishes—Martha was not putting a foot out of her kitchen. They left grandmother with her self-appointed task of trying to cheer the twins out of their sudden uncommunicative gloom and started up the staircase together, each wrapped in her own thoughts. They'd gone barely two steps before Shanna put a hand on Jesse's arm to stop her. "Shhh...listen," she urged, a finger to her lips.

From the library came the muffled sound of an argument. Even with allowances it was definitely an argument: Dorothy's shrill high tone angrily remonstrating, Bensen's deep short growl in reply. Shanna looked at Jesse, and Jesse looked at Shanna.

"Damn it, I wish we could hear what was going on!" whispered Shanna. "These old walls are so thick...shhh."

They both stood stock-still, straining their ears.

"Oh, gosh, *hurry*!" Shanna grabbed Jesse's arm and dashed up the stairs. They flew around and out of sight onto the landing just in time. Peeking around the balustrade they saw the library door being wrenched open.

Dorothy stalked out, her face set in cold anger. As she battled to regain her poise, several different expressions altered her features before a more normal one took its place. She turned on her heel to face Bensen, who was leaning in the doorway, and flung some words at him in a taunting provocative way, obviously playing the coquette.

He replied, and like lightning Dorothy's hand came up and swung out. Her whole body was behind the slap that never made it, for Bensen suddenly caught her wrist. He waggled a finger in her face, saying something more, and the two women above could see his cold grin at Dorothy's bottled fury. Jesse shivered on the landing, her heart in her throat. Then abruptly Bensen pulled Dorothy to him and kissed her deeply. Jesse stood watching, frozen. She saw Bensen's hand moving down from the small of Dorothy's back and still that kiss went on. Jesse nearly choked. Only an hour ago Bensen's lips had been on hers and his hand had been caressing her curves....

Dorothy was melting in Bensen's arms, her smile up at him all pink and pleased. Beside Jesse, Shanna snorted in quiet disgust. They watched as Dorothy and Bensen moved off down the hall toward the front door. His hand was on her waist; he was saying something to her, and she was giggling in the most charming way.

"Well!" Shanna muttered, sitting down on the bottom stair of the next flight, "*that* didn't look so good! If he thinks he's going to put the pressure on by using her against me!... Oh, and I wouldn't put it past him!"

"But—they *were* arguing!" Jesse protested quickly.

"Uh-huh. Sure they were. *Were*. Didn't you see that kiss? I'd feel a lot better if I hadn't!"

So would I, Jesse thought mournfully to herself. Sighing, she sank onto the stair beside Shanna, cupping her chin in her hands. She could have burst into great watery tears right at that moment. Bensen's heart clearly belonged to someone else. Hadn't she learned her lesson about other women's men? Once she'd been lied to. But Bensen hadn't lied to her. She *knew* he was engaged. So why had she persisted in letting him kiss her, touch her, say things that should only have been said to his fiancée. . . .

"Well, come on." Shanna touched her fingers fleetingly to Jesse's arm and stood up. "There's no point in sitting here."

Slowly, both disconsolate, they went back down the stairs. They entered the library, looked at each other, looked away. They sat down at the large gleaming library table, their movements vacant and automatic, though for different reasons. Jesse glanced into the den. Bensen wasn't at his desk; that meant he was still outside with Dorothy. Doing what, she wondered miserably.

"Do you believe this!" Shanna suddenly sputtered. "Dorothy walked in, was here for maybe ten minutes, and just look at us! How dare she? She may be going to marry Bensen, but that doesn't give her the right to order us all about, to be such a busybody, such a know-it-all! She's just like Bensen!"

"It's no wonder they get along," Jesse commented drearily.

"She's so rude and insensitive. She's just exactly what Bensen needs. He'll get some of his own medicine at long last."

"I just don't understand him," mourned Jesse.

"He deserves all the misery she's going to give

him! He wants a doormat for a wife—that's why it's taken him so much time to make up his mind about her!''

''She's no doormat,'' Jesse agreed.

''They've both got ice water in their veins instead of blood. If I have to go to their wedding, I'll go there 'flaunting' myself with Ray, as she puts it! 'Bensen's dead set against it,''' mimicked Shanna beautifully. ''That snake in the grass! Was he pompously letting me have my way before bringing down the ax? Who does he think he is?''

''A snake in the grass. That does suit him.'' Jesse was remembering what he'd said to her at the hotel about wanting to kiss her that night and all the next day.... Was he the kind of man for whom it was a way of life to have a mistress on the side? It seemed he was. Then what was his opinion of her? Jesse cringed at this thought. It was only her vanity that was suffering so badly, she told herself, burning a hole where her heart should have been....

''How *very* illuminating!'' purred Bensen, stepping out of his den. ''Now I'm a snake! A bear, an ox, a horse and now a snake!''

''H-how did you get in there?'' quavered Jesse, disbelieving and in strident panic.

''I was in there all the time!'' The jet eyes were piercing. ''That old saying about eavesdroppers not hearing any good of themselves has been proven once more!'' His harsh sarcasm stung her unbearably. ''But at least this time you both allow that I'm marriagable. The last time you two were discussing me so cold-bloodedly you weren't even allowing that! I must say it's nice to know where I stand with you both. I suppose you have grandmother falling right in with your opinion. It gives me a really warm feeling to know the people I share this house with think I'm a 'snake in the grass'!''

He wheeled around and walked straight out through the library's French doors. As he passed, the white sheer curtains fluttered. Then he was down the terrace stairs and gone.

"Oh, God, no," uttered Jesse, sinking her head down into her arms with a groan. She buried her head farther. From outside came the roar of the jeep revving, the sharp squeal of protesting rubber.

Jesse's misery increased when Bensen didn't show up at supper time. Nobody said anything about his absence. His empty place setting at the table made Jesse want to choke every time she looked at it. And since it was right by her side, she didn't eat very much. Bitterly Martha complained about the amount they'd eaten and threatened them all with leftovers the next day. Grandmother told her to shut up. Martha harrumphed emphatically and muttered some remark about everything going to seed before retiring to her kitchen.

"Oh, *hell*!"

Everyone's head jerked up to look at Shanna, as if to make sure they'd really heard that word on her lips.

"I just thought of something," she announced, unhappily meeting Jesse's eyes. "It's Bensen's birthday tomorrow."

The following silence swallowed the wretched words.

"Do you think he'll come in time?"

"Oh, for heavens' sake, Merry, that's the ninth time you've asked," Shanna replied, exasperated. "I don't know!"

Bensen's birthday dinner had been warming in the oven for fifteen minutes past the usual dinnertime. Bensen hadn't been home, nor had he called. The four women and the two girls made a solemn depressed group as they waited in the dining room. Jesse sighed unhappily, looking again at the large clock face. Seventeen minutes past seven.

At twenty-seven past a soft tread sounded outside in the hall, and there was a flash of electricity through the dining room before everyone moved at once. Bensen appeared in the doorway, large and dark, his mere presence forceful and aggressive. He ran a hand through his hair, brushing it back, and his black eyes swept over them.

"You're late for dinner, Bensen," grandmother said calmly, going to her place at the head of the table. "Hurry up and wash your hands." He sent her a withering look, but she had her back to him.

The talk at the table was desultory, polite and concerned the most unimportant things. Jesse couldn't meet Bensen's eyes throughout dinner; she kept looking down at her plate. As soon as the meal was finished, Bensen excused himself and disappeared into the library, and everyone's eyes, except Jesse's, followed his progress across the hall.

"Well, at least he's home," grandmother muttered. "That's the first time he's walked out like that. Samuel did it to me a couple of times; he had to be *really* furious. I'll swear you two haven't told me everything that happened yesterday. Now do any of you have any bright ideas for getting him out of that den?''

"If Muhammad won't come to the mountain," Jesse shrugged, "we'll take the birthday cake to him. *I'm* not going in there alone!" she added hastily as everyone looked at her with purpose in their eyes. "Oh, no. We'll all go in with the cake."

"Don't you count on me," Martha blustered. "I ain't goin' near him, him in that evil mood."

"But you've got to," Jesse pleaded. "You baked the cake!"

"You're coming," grandmother decided imperiously. "Go and get your cake. Shanna, get a bottle of champagne. Merit, you get matches, and Sam, you find that package of candles. Jesse will give me a hand with the presents. Where's that Lily? She said she'd be here at eight, and it's eight now."

Bensen, as it turned out, had forgotten all about his birthday, and his blank astonishment broke through the thin icy layer of tension. Lily's steadfast calm had already soothed Jesse's nerves, and Shanna's attitude hovered between resentment and relief.

The outlook for this birthday celebration brightened considerably after Bensen blew out the thirty-seven candles. The unease seemed discharged with his mighty blow, and it was as though yesterday had never happened, almost as though things were back to normal. After several rounds of champagne things grew downright jolly. Shanna's relief was outweighing her resentment, and once Jesse even saw her looking rather fondly at her brother. But she didn't delve into her own emotional state regarding the head of the household. That would keep till later. At the moment it was enough for her that he was back all in one piece. And although her warm smile was a shade reserved, the amber eyes followed him about with a deep secret longing.

The high point of the party came when Bensen opened grandmother's present to find it was the vest—the special beaded vest. To say he was tickled pink would almost cover it, Jesse thought, the longing coming closer to the fore as she watched him slip the vest on. He was so wildly attractive in it she had to draw a long steadying breath.

"You look as good as Samuel used to in that vest," Lily admired. "It fits you perfectly."

"In a way I hate to agree, but you're right, Lily. It could have been made for you, Ben. I'm glad you like it." At the end grandmother's brisk voice was quite gentle.

"Next?" Bensen asked, grinning. "I can take more of this!"

"You look smashing, Uncle Ben!" Samantha beamed.

"Just like in the movies!" insisted Merit.

"Next to Ray you're the handsomest man on earth." Shanna smiled widely at her brother. At that moment it seemed she forgave him.

"Jesse? It's your turn." Bensen's cool black eyes studied her with amusement. A sort of sweet relief poured over her that he was not holding a grudge, and her smile deepened as she looked up at him.

"Whisper in my ear, and I'll follow you anywhere." Her voice was a light teasing dance.

Bensen leaned closer. "Would you care to repeat that?"

Shanna laughed at Jesse's startled expression. "I'm going for another bottle. Don't tell him till I get back. I don't want to miss anything!" She ran out of the den.

"I—I think I'll go help her," Jesse murmured, still gazing wide-eyed at Bensen. She didn't dare say that again, for she knew the next time it would come out with meaning to the words, and there was no way she wanted him to know the extent of her fascination with him. Grandmother was chuckling as Jesse slipped away.

She hadn't gone more than three steps down the darkened hallway when Bensen spun her around and into his arms. She was crushed against the massive chest as his mouth came down with a relentless desire that engulfed her in immediate flame. Willingly, eagerly, she responded, overwhelmingly glad he was kissing her again. The soft urgency of her mouth absorbed all his anger, until at last he seemed drained of it, and the demand on his lips became sensuous, undermining her last remaining reserve. He kissed her until her breath was coming in gasps, and then he raised his head. His lips curled with a satisfied smile as he tipped her chin up to look at her better. Then his fingers on her chin tightened.

"You like kissing a snake?" he said coldly, cruelly mocking.

Jesse's eyes widened. Stunned and unbelievably

hurt, she continued looking up at him for a few more seconds.

She pushed herself away from him, and his arms let her go. For a moment she just stood there, dazed, and then her bottom lip trembled, despite her efforts to control herself. Slowly the large amber eyes filled with tears—her emotional state was too churned up to take *this* on the chin—and the tears spilled over. Shaking her head, thoroughly embarrassed, she put her hands to her cheeks to wipe away the wetness.

"Oh, Bensen, what have you done!"

Shanna's distressed voice woke Jesse from her trance. She took one more look at Bensen's startled face, and a quick glance in Shanna's direction had her flying up the stairs, hurt and ashamed; wanting to get away from everyone, wanting to hide so that no one would ever find her again.

When Shanna knocked tentatively on her bedroom door a few minutes later, Jesse said without opening the door, "Please go away." She managed that quite steadily, even though she was still crying. She couldn't seem to stop.

"But Jesse, you have to come down," Shanna said urgently through the door. "Please! What's everyone going to think?"

"T-tell them anything. I'll," she gulped through a sob, "I'll be back in a while. I'll be all right. Really I will."

"Okay, okay, I'll think of something. Bathe your face in cold water. Oh, Jesse, I'm sorry. Bensen's such a—"

"I'm fine, really. Usually I don't do this sort of thing. . . ."

Shanna went away, and Jesse wept and wept into her pillow. Her heart felt shattered into a million pieces. However was she going to put them all together again? The vision of Dorothy haunted her, jealousy burned in her soul. Her doorknob rattled, and she turned to look in alarm. But she'd locked her door, and finally the rattling stopped. She knew her would-be visitor was Bensen. Her slender body shuddered with a fresh spasm.

The next time Shanna knocked, Jesse had bathed her face, and she let her in.

"If you don't come back downstairs soon, honey, everybody's going to come up here looking for you. I've made all the excuses I can, but they're wearing thin. Come on, Jesse, you can't back down now. You *know* what Bensen's like. Don't let him hurt you so. Fight back—the way you always do! I know he's a beast sometimes, but—listen, the twins are staying up late tonight because it's a special occasion and there's a really good movie on TV. We're going to have a pajama party in the salon. So hurry, get into your robe and join us. It'll be pretty dark; no one will notice you've been crying. The twins are changing now, and I'm going to, as well. I'll be back for you, and you'd better be ready. Okay?"

"Okay," Jesse said miserably, blowing her nose. Going back downstairs to face everybody was the last thing she wanted to do, but if she didn't, she'd have to come up with explanations, and *that* was worse. She'd go and pretend nothing had ever happened between her and Bensen. Damn him anyways.

"Jesse—" Shanna reached for her hand and squeezed it between both her own "—I've been pretty wrapped up in myself lately, so I haven't been noticing much. Are—are you in love with Bensen? I know it sounds really crazy but—"

"No!" Jesse peeked at Shanna and looked into her clear blue eyes and couldn't lie to herself any longer. *Yes, I am,* she cried inwardly. *Oh, God help me yes!*

Instead Jesse tried to smile, then she said, "No, ah...maybe just a wee bit?"

"But how?"

"I don't have any idea *how*," Jesse returned miserably.

"Oh, hell! And he's engaged to Dorothy, of all people! How can he be so stupid? You'd think he'd see through her. I do finally. Ray's just come, and Bensen seems to be pleased. You know what she said yesterday about Ray?" Jesse nodded. "Well, I don't think Bensen had anything to do with that; I think it was all her opinion. I don't really believe Bensen's 'dead set against Ray'!"

"I don't think so, either, and I've told you that from the beginning."

"Yes, well, I'm beginning to believe you *and* him. But why would Dorothy want to stir up a fuss like that?"

Jesse shrugged.

"She's not going to marry Bensen if I can help it. Don't you worry, Jesse, I'll think of something. If we could get you two alone together...maroon you on the boat, maybe...."

"No! Shanna, please."

"Don't worry. Hurry up and get changed now. We'll talk later. Be back in five, okay?"

Jesse closed and locked the door after Shanna had gone. Automatically she stepped out of her clothes and into her dressing gown. She slid her feet into matching mules, brushed her hair and applied make-up to hide as much as she could hide of her recent tears. Then she switched off everything but the night lamp on the bedside table and sat down on the edge of the bed, trying to compose herself for the ordeal ahead.

In the silence of her bedroom came the sound of a key clicking in the lock. With a sort of mingled alarm and horror she watched the knob turn, the door inch open. Bensen slipped in, shut the door and locked it behind him. By the time he was halfway across the room, Jesse had recovered from her fright. She shot off the bed with some idea of making him leave, but his hands clamped on her shoulders, forcing her backward and down onto the bed. Her heart thudding wildly, she pushed against his lowering chest. But he dropped down on top of her, his weight making movement impossible and squeezing the breath from her body.

"You can call me anything you like," he muttered, his arms sliding beneath and around her so that she was aware of every taut muscle in his frame. "Jessamine, I can't leave you alone. . . ."

He claimed her mouth with an unhurried hungry need that demanded a complete response—and received it. Despite her determined resolve to keep her emotions from him—from everyone, for that matter—his warm mouth covering hers permitted her no dishonesty. All her pent-up longing broke free and flowed through her eager lips, through her fingertips curled around his neck, through her body where it was pressed against his. Passion flared in seconds, burned them in white-hot sensuous fire. There was absolutely nothing she could do to stop him, to stop herself; she was being swept along on a tide of feeling too powerful to deny. His tenderly urgent kisses on her mouth, in the sensitive hollow of her throat, his arms holding her pliant body to him, acted like balm on her wounds. Her senses reeled.

When he shifted his weight to open her dressing gown, she made no demur, drugged by his nearness and the touch of his fingers through the thin nylon as he undid the tiny pearl buttons. All the way down her throat his lips and tongue created a wildfire of desire in her blood; his deep husky voice caressed her, his warm breath teasing her skin. She moaned softly when her breast filled his hand, and when his black eyes swept over her face with a fiercely possessive primitive quality, she drew a deep sharp breath. He bent his head again to kiss the raised responsive tip of her breast through the lace of her nightgown, and a delicious urgent heat spread through her. His mouth continued its seduction; her body moved unconsciously against his. The immediate answering pressure made her fully aware of his aroused state. She could feel his belt buckle pressing into the softness of her stomach and thought only of getting it out of the way....

Someone was knocking.... "Jesse, are you ready?" Shanna's call floated through the door.

Jesse felt as if someone had dashed ice-cold water over her.

Bensen swore, and in a flash they were both off her bed. Jesse fumbled madly with the small difficult pearl buttons as Bensen smoothed back her hair, then ran his hands through his own hair. He shook his head, as though trying to wake himself up, finally sighing explosively. The bed was dreadfully rumpled, but there was no time for that.

"Hide, Bensen, *hide*! Quick!" she whispered in complete agitation.

"What?" he hissed back, not quite believing he'd heard her right.

"Hide! Oh, please!"

"Why? What does it matter if Shanna knows?"

"Oh, Bensen, don't argue, not now! I don't want anyone to see us—us kissing."

"For God's sake, why?" he whispered back fiercely, his eyes beginning to glow.

"I'm ashamed to be seen kissing you."

He stared at her for an incredulous second, and then he said, his low undertone suddenly dangerous, "Oh, hell woman, you're going to have to explain that!"

"I will; I will later. Only now *please*—I'm coming, Shanna!"

"Oh, all right!" Bensen stepped behind the heavy fall of the damask curtains. They rippled once and then hung down still.

"I'm ready!" Jesse gasped, opening the door to

Shanna. She dropped her head so that her hair fell about her face as she tied the sash of her dressing gown. Her breathing was dreadfully erratic, and she tried to calm it by holding her breath.

Bewildered, Shanna looked at her anxiously. "Are you really all right? You're feeling okay? You look fine but—"

"Oh, I've never felt better!" Jesse gulped.

"Uh-huh," Shanna replied, gazing at her with a puzzled doubtful frown. "Let's go before you change your mind. If Bensen gives you a hard time, put him in his place. I don't know how you manage to talk back to him so beautifully, but keep right on doing it. Don't lose your cool at this point, Jesse."

"I'll do my best," she murmured, and followed Shanna down the hall and down the stairs.

When Bensen sauntered into the salon a few minutes later, Jesse kept her eyes riveted on the TV screen. He hadn't changed into his pajamas—indeed, no one expected him to—but everyone else, except Ray, was dressed comfortably for bed. The attire made the party cozier. Even Lily, who'd been persuaded to stay the night, was curled up in a big chair, wearing a large fuzzy terry-cloth robe borrowed from Shanna. Martha had on a flaming red-and-blue kimono, and grandmother wore Shanna's birthday present to her. And the movie was definitely a good one—a classic comedy, which was exactly the right medicine for Jesse's shattered nerves.

She would have been able to behave quite naturally had it not been for Bensen, who chose the nearest chair he could find to be close to her. Oh, outwardly,

she supposed, he appeared much the same as usual—
that relaxed slouch, his dark masculine features composed, the thick fall of black hair over his forehead.
But his eyes! The naked desire still burning in them
raised her temperature, quickened her pulse. Jesse
dared not look at him; but she would find herself doing so and then had to pay for it with a light-headed
confusion that made her lose the thread of the movie
or the thread of the conversation every time.

Uneasily Jesse wondered whether the others had
interpreted that look, whether they could sense the
electricity that sparked between them. Shanna
seemed unusually alert and often glanced from her to
Bensen and back again. He obviously didn't care
what the others noticed.

His eyes regarded her with a lazy simmering passion
in their black depths. When he passed her a snifter of
brandy, he ran his fingers lightly over her hand; when
her hair snagged on the button-tufted couch she was
sharing with Shanna and Ray, he was the one who
helped her, taking far longer than was necessary, and
while the fingers of one hand worked on her hair, the
fingers of the other enticingly, intimately, caressed her
nape. Luckily her hair covered what he was doing, but
if anyone were to look closely. . . . In desperation she
turned her head to plead silently with him. He smiled,
and she suddenly realized he could kiss her mouth by
moving only a fraction of an inch.

Her head jerked back to the television set. Her
cheeks were burning under Shanna's and Ray's combined glance. Her heart was thumping so loud she was
afraid everyone in the room must hear it.

Then to make matters worse, Bensen sat down on the arm of the couch on the pretext of freeing her still snagged tresses. His shoulder pressed into hers as he casually bent over her, saying, "Damn it, Jesse, how did you make such a mess!"

He twirled a strand around his finger and gently yanked on it. His breath feathered in her hair, and Jesse shivered a little.

"Do you need help?" Shanna offered, leaning closer.

"No, I think I've got it now," Bensen murmured dryly, smiling crookedly into his sister's rather anxious face. "I'll give it all back, I promise," he added when she continued to look at him searchingly. Shanna, going back into the warmth of Ray's encircling arm, frowned quizzically at them both a moment longer.

"There," Bensen said as he untwined the last strands and lifted them free. Suddenly he scooped up all of her hair in his hands before letting it drop with a swish down her back. "It's all yours again, Jessamine."

He said her name as though he always called her that, so it slid by relatively unnoticed. Then, instead of finally moving away from her, he leaned along the back of the sofa, supported by his hand. He seemed as cool as a cucumber, Jesse thought, while she felt stricken with fever. He was so close she could feel his body heat. Restive, she shifted her position, wanting to sit more upright rather than curled right into him. She put a hand on the arm of the sofa to pull herself up, but her hand happened to curve around his upper thigh. She just left it there. She didn't know what else to do. To snatch it away would look suspicious. She sat there frozenly till it suddenly occurred to her that Ray and Shanna were sitting close together at one end of the sofa, their arms around each other, while Bensen was draped right around her back and she had her hand intimately on his thigh! What on earth did they look like from the other side of the room? Her fingers fluttered once, then her hand slowly crept down into her lap, but she could still feel the imprint of hard muscles tensing under her touch.

CHAPTER NINE

"JESSE, FOR HEAVEN'S SAKE, can't you sit still for five minutes? We have to discuss what we're going to do about Dorothy and Bensen!" Shanna took the coffeepot from Jesse and set it firmly back down on the kitchen table. "You don't need another cup right now!"

"We can't do anything. We can't interfere."

"Why the hell not?"

"Shanna!"

"I mean it. She makes everybody miserable when she pops in for ten minutes. Can you imagine how it will be when she *lives* here? Martha'll go—and she's just getting to be a decent cook! And grandmother—she *loves* to argue with her, so can you see what that would be like?"

"Oh, I wish you'd leave it," Jesse begged, almost in tears again. She felt so guilty, so ashamed of loving Bensen to the point of distraction, despite the concrete fact that he belonged to someone else. And what was to be done about it? Every solution that came to mind seemed crazier than the last...empty gestures much the same as shutting the barn door after the horse had already gone. And she'd always thought she was so sensible!

"I've never seen Bensen look at her the way he looks at you," Shanna went on. "I've never seen him ever look at anyone that way. I didn't know he had it in him; he's so cold mostly. Except when he's fighting with you... or looking at you. I think he might be a wee bit in love with you, too, and if he's not smart enough to recognize that, then all I'm suggesting is a little push in the right direction. Around the house you're only going to get interrupted, and grandmother won't have any goings-on under her roof! But on the boat?" She spread her hands. "I could jinx the motor so that Bensen wouldn't have a clue as to what's wrong. Think of it: all day, just you two adrift, time to sort out Dorothy and—Jesse, how can we leave it?"

The telephone rang then, and as Shanna flew to answer it, Jesse sighed with heartfelt relief. Shanna's idea was too tempting.

She glanced at Bensen's sister now, her ear pressed to the receiver. She saw the horrified disbelief sweep over her face, and then she knew who was calling. When Shanna let the receiver drop in shock, Jesse hurried over at once. The voice still talking on the other end of the line was the voice of her long-dead husband.

"I don't believe it—I don't believe it—I don't believe."

Jesse returned the receiver to its cradle and shook Shanna by the shoulders, snapping her out of it. "It's Stu, isn't it?" she said, grimly. "What did he say?"

"He's coming to see me. He flew into Vancouver this morning from Edmonton, hired a plane to fly him to Lund and will be here in—in thirty minutes, probably less, because he always did drive like the blazes. Oh, God!'' Shanna gasped on a half sob. It took her a few seconds before she could continue in a dazed monotone, ''He said he just wanted a few minutes of my time, that was all. If, after he'd had a chance to speak to me, I decided I never wanted to have anything to do with him again, then he'd disappear, and I'd never see him again. He asked about the twins, but—but I told him Lily had taken them for the day. I had to, Jesse. I don't want them here when he comes.'' As she spoke, she distractedly dialed Lily's number in Bliss Landing. ''I'll decide after I see him whether they should be told he's really alive.''

Jesse listened to her telephone conversation with Lily in agitation. The worst had happened: Craig really was Stuart Lazzer, and he hadn't left town.

''What about grandmother?'' Jesse asked when Shanna had finished.

''We won't tell her—yet. I don't want her here, and you know she'd insist. If we're lucky, her afternoon nap will last till dinner.'' It was as if one part of Shanna had shut down and she were running on pure nerves. It frightened Jesse, and she wished Bensen were present. Tentatively she asked how to get a hold of him when he was out in the bush.

''Oh, no! You're not to call him. No, Jesse. He and Stu were enemies, and I don't want—I just want to see him without grandmother or Bensen around.''

''But wouldn't it be nice to have Bensen close by?''

''No, oh, no! You see, I—'' She stopped, an-

guished, reached for Jesse's arm and held on tight.
"I never told you; I've never told anyone, but I'm
still...sort of hung up on Stu, and I—if he hadn't
died, we could have put an end to...our marriage.
But he did die, and it was never finished. I couldn't
bear to have grandmother and Bensen here because
I'm ashamed of feeling that way about Stu after
everything. You know what she calls him. Ray asked
me to marry him two days ago, and I was afraid to
say yes because...Stu was still there in my mind, like
a faint shadow, like the outline of a ghost. Don't you
see? This is my chance to know for sure. Oh, dear
Lord! And now I wish I hadn't wished to see him one
more time."

"Oh, Shanna!" Jesse groaned in dismay, suddenly
understanding the hopeless melancholy that sometimes still enveloped her, the unfathomable moods of
resignation and depression.

They stayed in the sanctity of the kitchen until Lily
came to whisk the twins away. For a long spun-out
moment neither Jesse nor Shanna moved after they'd
vanished. Then there was a common surge toward
the door, as if by tacit agreement they were prepared
to meet the coming man only in the more formal part
of the house.

Shanna chose the library for the encounter. They
both sat down on the straight-backed Gothic parlor
chairs, waiting. Outside, the sun sparkled on the turquoise waves far below; inside, the gentle afternoon
air was permeated with shock.

Only Shanna's eyes revealed her apprehensive
dread as she waited; her face was expressionless, and

the aura of catatonic calm shuttered over her unnerved Jesse.

"He...should almost be here." Uncertainly Jesse broke an interminable silence. "I guess I should clear out...."

"You're not leaving me alone!"

"I'll be in...the kitchen if you need me."

"Oh, Jesse, please stay. *Please!*"

"But you should see him alone, Shanna. You didn't want Bensen or grandmother, and I'm not even one of the family."

"You have to stay! Don't you see, you never knew him before so—so.... I can't see him alone, Jesse. He's been dead to me for five years. *Dead!* The last time I saw him was in that burning wreck, and if I had to face him alone, I think I'd run screaming from the house."

"The...last...time you saw him?" Jesse stared at Shanna, and Shanna stared back at Jesse, aghast. Her throat felt parched, her lips dry. "If the—the unidentifiable body wasn't Stuart, then w-who was it?" Jesse finally asked.

There was a dreadful pool of silence between them as they gaped at each other, shocked.

A flicker of movement abruptly swung Jesse's gaze to the doorway. Stuart Lazzer stood there. Neither of the women had heard any sound of a vehicle arriving, and his sudden appearance gave Jesse an awful fright. Shanna, who had her back to the door, stared at her in fresh alarm.

"Shanna? *Shanna!*"

The joyful lilting words were bullets in her back.

She reared out of her chair, knocking it over. A small terrified whimper fell from her lips as she clutched at Jesse with both hands, her head swiveling toward the door. She stood beside, almost behind, Jesse, and Jesse could feel the jolts that pulsed through her like a current; Shanna's fingers were digging into her arm, but she hardly felt the pain.

Stuart Lazzer stood braced in the doorway, elegantly, expensively, dressed in a dark blue suit. He carried himself with an arrogant grace that bespoke his self-confidence and his awareness of what a dashing figure he cut, whether in logging gear or as he was now. His head was thrown back, the vivid blue eyes sharp and sparkling under half-lowered lids. He gave Jesse a cursory dismissing glance before focusing those searching blue spotlights on Shanna's gentle tortured face.

In the static split seconds before anyone moved, Jesse looked him over from the top of his curly black brown hair to the tips of his immaculate fine leather shoes. He appeared prosperous, healthy and abundantly alive; a dancing vitality just beneath the surface held a powerful charm, so that Jesse found herself strangely confused by her reaction. She was at once attracted and repelled. She couldn't help but admire his physical graces and that radiating appeal, yet her radar, tuned on high, met with discordant interference. A trickle of fear for Shanna alerted all her senses to the danger this man presented. That first understandable fear inexplicably welled into a flood that engulfed her before it washed away, leaving plain common sense—and a film of cold perspiration on her brow.

"Shanna." This time his voice was softer, some of the joy had gone out of it, to be replaced with a diffidence—an almost, but not quite, pleading note. He crossed the room in a bound, bearing down on the two spellbound women, his sudden impulsive movement frightening them even more. Grasping both of Shanna's hands in his, he continued, his delivery throbbing with passion. "Oh, Shanna, can you ever forgive me?"

Shanna's hands hung limp in his. She looked at him numbly, her face paper white.

He bent his curly head and kissed both her passive hands eagerly, urgently, as if he could instill some life in her that way. "I came to tell you—I had a speech all prepared, Shanna, a perfect speech that I've worked on for *years*, one I was sure would persuade you to give me another chance. But I've forgotten it. Oh, Shanna, you've no idea how I've longed for—*planned* for—this day! That first terrible year away from you—I knew you were much too good for me; I knew I'd done the unforgivable. I drank myself into oblivion every day for a whole year, and at the end of it you were still with me. Shanna, are you listening to me?"

His intensity quivered in the air. He had his back half turned to Jesse, excluding her beyond recall, and she could see his handsome profile and Shanna's full face.

"Shanna, I know I'm hardly making sense; I must sound like a complete fool. But won't you just listen? That's all I have a right to ask. And I have to tell you everything now before I lose my nerve. Shanna, the second year was worse. I wanted you so bad; I wanted to come crawling back to you. But how could I? I'd been a drunk, a good-for-nothing for so long I thought that was all I could ever be. I got picked up one night for creating a 'public disturbance' in a bar. It was a Friday, so I cooled my heels in the slammer till Monday morning. Shanna, I knew then I'd be inside again if I didn't get you back.

"I haven't touched a drop since then, Shanna; I haven't had *one* drink for three-and-a-half years! Back then I set a goal for myself, a stake. I wouldn't come back to you, I wouldn't get in touch with you or bother you in any way, until I had it complete. If you had made a new life for yourself, I wouldn't have wanted to interfere. And when I did come to beg your forgiveness—and that's what I mean to do, Shanna, to beg—I wanted that money as proof to you, to your brother, to your grandmother, that I wasn't after your money. So it had to be a lot. It took me three-and-a-half years, Shanna, but I made it. Sixty thousand dollars. I know it's not a million, but it's enough, Shanna. It's enough to start a little business of my own. It's enough to start *us* again. It's all yours, Shanna. My heart, my life; I'm all yours, Shanna."

Jesse sagged back against the chair, feeling weak and spent. In the great cavernous quiet after his emotion-charged speech she hardly dared breathe.

Bensen's sister dropped her eyes down to their clasped hands; there was still that eerie aura of calm about her. With a slight movement she pulled her hands free and walked away from him, as if in a deep sleep.

"You've changed, Stu." Her voice was thick and strangled, as though all along she'd been thinking her own thoughts and hadn't been paying any attention to his impassioned words.

"Yes. *Yes*, Shanna! That's what I've been trying to tell you. I'm a different man, and it's all because of you."

Anyone hearing him could not have doubted his sincerity, and Jesse found herself wanting to believe him, *hoping* all he'd said was true. Almost convinced, she was teetering in the balance; her sweeping radar, however, sent in a cloud of suspicion. Oh, he was something all right. But what? His eloquence, his apparent frankness, his charming youthful buoyancy made for a powerful combination.

Her thoughtful gaze swung to Shanna, now facing them from across the table. She was a lot more curious about Shanna's reaction to her husband than she was about the man himself. But it was hard to judge Shanna's feelings; she remained shuttered deep inside herself, and Jesse wondered what hell Stu had once played with her to make her retreat so entirely.

"What do you want, Stu?" Shanna's tone was a little more even this time. "Why did you come back?"

"Because I love you Shanna, I always have! I was such a stupid ass. I only hope you'll find it in you to forgive me." He shook his head and rapidly circled the table, stopping short at some distance from Shanna.

"You're my wife!" he exclaimed, throwing out his hands. "Yet my wife in nothing but name now. But

Shanna, I came here to change that. I want you and me and our babies together again—for always!"

"They're not babies anymore, and you forget, Stu, I went to your funeral."

He turned from her then and grasped the back of a chair, his head bowed low and the knuckles of his hands turning white.

"I'm sorry, Shanna," he groaned. "I'm sorry, I'm a thousand times sorry. I'm entirely at your mercy."

"That's a switch." Even though Shanna spoke quietly, there was an acid bitterness to her words. "Why did you let me, let everyone, think you were dead?"

"I was already dead as far as you were concerned, wasn't I? Didn't you tell me that morning you never wanted to see me again? Didn't you say we were finished!" Stuart Lazzer slowly raised his head, and Jesse was in his direct line of vision. He stared at her for a moment.

"Can't you leave us alone?" he suddenly demanded. "Don't you have somewhere to go?"

"She stays!" Shanna replied sharply. "I want Jesse to stay!"

"All right, Shanna, anything you want is all right." He cleared his throat. "As...you remember, I was already roaring drunk by ten that morning. After I left you, I picked up Brian. You remember Brian O'Brian, don't you—the hobo who lived in that shack down by the creek? Nobody ever knew his real name. He was hitchhiking...wanted a ride into town. I let him drive because—well, I was hardly in any shape. I don't remember the accident at all. I must have been knocked out before the truck went over the cliff. When I finally came to, I was lying in the bushes about fifty yards or so away from the wreck. I had no idea how long I'd been there. I was pretty smashed up—cuts and bruises, though nothing was broken." His face and voice were tense, and he kept his head down.

"There was no sign of Brian when I searched, so I figured he must have either got out or been rescued. God, there was nothing left of the truck; it must have been one hell of a fire!" Stuart Lazzer took a long ragged breath. "Anyway, I—I had nothing to stay for. And I figured the...authorities would try to pin the blame for the accident on me. I don't think Brian ever did have a driving license. I couldn't bear the thought of facing you, of facing your brother, of facing the whole town after...everything. So I took the coward's way out and split. Later, much later, I found out there had been a funeral for me. I knew then old Brian hadn't made it. And you buried him and thought you were burying me. Funny, how that worked. If he'd have been an inch taller or an inch shorter than me.... At the time it seemed for the best. I might as well have been dead. That's how it happened, Shanna."

"So it was Brian..." Shanna murmured, closing her eyes for a moment. "I always rather liked him, even though he was a bit strange. There was nothing but a few bones left, Stu." She shuddered.

"And he never had any family...." Stuart sighed heavily again. "Nobody to miss him. I guess the fuel tank exploded, and then I was carrying two saddle tanks full of gas, as well. It's no wonder there was nothing left of him. But at the time I hoped...."

Fascinated, Jesse saw the way his face contorted with suppressed emotion.

Abruptly he swung to face Shanna. He looked at her for a moment in silence, then turned his head back over his shoulder to send Jesse a swift angry glance.

"Shanna—" his voice was gentle "—our past happened a long time ago, five long years ago. You could have married many times, but you didn't. So I'm hoping, *praying*, I still have a chance, however small. I'll take anything I can get, Shanna. But first I have to know that you've...that you're willing to... to...forgive me for all my past sins."

A great well of silence descended over the library. Outside the sun played on the waves....

Jesse hadn't realized how strained she was until she tried to shift in her chair. The heavy pregnant quiet weighed oppressively on her, and she felt a longing to flee, to flee from Stuart Lazzer. Again she wished Bensen were here—or at least within calling distance.

Shanna's hands settled, trembling, on either side of her brow. Desperation glowed in her eyes as she looked toward Jesse, as if hoping she would have the answer. Her lips quivered once, slightly. Then she took a long deep breath that was clearly heard in the aching stillness.

"It was a long time ago, Stu. You're...forgiven. You have my pardon, if it means so much to you."

Shanna looked at him for a poignant moment. Suddenly she turned on her heel and left the library.

A couple of minutes later there was the faint sound of a door being closed somewhere in the house. Jesse hadn't moved, and neither had Stuart Lazzer. Across the table their eyes met.

"And who, may I ask, are you?" he challenged, as though she'd been the one to insist on staying in the room.

"A...friend of the family." Jesse remembered Bensen's words with a flash of relief. "You must understand, under the circumstances I felt I had to stay."

"Perhaps you won't consider it your duty the next time?"

There was an edge to the sarcasm, a warning that caught at Jesse. The vivid deep blue eyes were fixed intently on her, and while she was aware of their attraction, she had at the same time the absurd impression of being focused in gunsights. She rose slowly from her chair.

"Mr. Lazzer, if you do happen to love Shanna, you're not the only one." Her voice was cool and even; she crossed her arms in front of her as she faced him squarely. "I happen to care for her, too. I'll do whatever she wants me to do."

His eyes measured her with a calculating gleam. "I can see it would be worthwhile becoming your friend. I'll have to do my best to get you on my side. You take your...friend-of-the-family responsibilities very seriously, don't you? How long have you been here?"

"Long enough. And you might as well know right now I'm on Shanna's side. I'm for whatever *she* wants. That's all."

"Yes, that's all. For today. It was a pleasure meeting you... is it Jesse? Jesse. It suits you." He had a winning smile, too. "Would you please tell Shanna I'll call her tomorrow? In case she wants to get a hold of me in the meantime, here's where I can be reached."

He placed a small white card on the table and started moving off toward the French doors. In the doorway he paused. Pivoting on his heel, he leaned slightly into the room. "And it's not a question of *if* I love Shanna. I do."

He surveyed her for a moment longer, a whimsical smile lighting his eyes. Then he was gone, and from where Jesse stood she could see him disappearing into the stairwell at the cliff head. That meant he had come by motorboat, she reasoned. Strange they hadn't heard the usual roar of an approaching motor.

JESSE HAD THE UNHAPPY TASK of breaking the news to Bensen when he came home. Shanna couldn't be induced to leave her bed, much less her room. She'd just lain there all afternoon, listlessly staring up at the ceiling or out of the windows and not seeing anything but a kaleidoscope of an inner eye. She wouldn't talk. She wanted to be left alone. Jesse was worried sick.

"Oh, Bensen!" she gulped, meeting him at the door. That wasn't at all how she meant to start. His eyes widened on her for a second, then a slow smile spread across his face.

"Did you miss me?"

"Oh, Bensen!" In boundless relief she fell into the arms that were already embracing her. Her arms went around his neck tightly, and she buried her face in his chest. Pressing her whole body against him was a sweet release from the day's trauma. She cuddled even closer, and his hand wound through her hair and held the back of her head. "And I don't care if Dorothy *is* right behind you!" Jesse muttered, but her words were lost in the folds of his shirt. His arms crushed her to him. Suddenly the urgent pressure changed, and his embrace became gentle.

"Something's the matter, isn't it?"

Jesse nodded, rubbing her face against his shirt. He smelled so nice, and he was so warm and strong...she wanted to melt right into him.

"Come on, then, let's talk." He led her to the den, shutting the door behind them.

"Now out with it." He smiled at her slightly, quizzically, as he sat beside her on the couch. "I'd like to think I got that kind of greeting just because you missed me, but I guess I'm not that lucky. Yet." His eyes, full of warmth and tender humor, studied her face, and then he took her hand reassuringly. "What's wrong?"

Jesse grasped his hand between both her own. Soon the whole story spilled from her lips, from that first second Shanna had picked up the telephone until the moment she'd watched Stuart Lazzer disappear down the stairwell. She talked of Shanna's over-wrought state and what she'd been doing since, and then she told him about seeing Stuart—or Craig—in the Lund pub.

"And he told Shanna he'd just arrived in Vancouver this morning when I saw him here two weeks ago!" Jesse finished. Bensen's dark eyes looked into hers for a long moment, and he sighed, a sigh that seemed to come from his very depths.

"Stuart Lazzer," he muttered.

The way he said the name caused a chill of apprehension to shoot down her spine. Her hands tightened around his as she waited for him to grasp all the implications of the day's events.

"Stu Lazzer." Bensen repeated in the same muttering frightening tone. He stared at the floor between his feet. Then his eyes lifted to her face. "Perhaps he really has changed. You say Shanna gave him full pardon. She must have had some reason to believe...." His jaw hardened. "And he wants her back," he added slowly, almost in a whisper. Cold hatred flashed across his rugged features.

"What are you going to do?" Jesse asked worriedly.

"Do? There's nothing I can do; it's for Shanna to decide. But I'll stand behind any decision she makes. He *really* wants her back?"

"It appears so." She paused, then said consideringly, "Bensen, why did Stu say he'd arrived this morning when I saw him here almost two weeks ago?"

"Tell me about that time in the pub again. Tell me everything you remember. Can you absolutely swear it's the same man?"

"Yes! His face was right under the light." She went through the whole episode again.

"But his friend might not have been talking to him when he said Craig. He might have been talking to any one of the other men there."

"No, I'm certain he was talking to Stu," Jesse insisted. "Stu turned on him right after. Gave the man what looked like one hell of a tongue-lashing. That I remember clearly. He wasn't nearly so charming then."

"Still, I can't see that it means anything. Stuart knew Shanna hasn't remarried, so how would he find that out? He came here on the quiet two weeks ago to check things out before he actually stood face to face with Shanna. So? What's wrong with that?"

"Nothing," Jesse admitted reluctantly. "But it wouldn't hurt, would it, to do some checking up on him in return? Find out where he's been working, make a few discreet phone calls? And just for starters, to have a look at his birth certificate?"

"Jesse, honey, you've been writing mysteries for too long."

"No, Bensen. Does he have any brothers? How about family? Shanna's never mentioned—"

"She hasn't because as far as we know, he has no relatives. An only child; parents died young; raised by an elderly aunt who's gone, as well." Bensen shrugged, then his lips compressed. "It's not that I'm against checking up on him, Jesse. The last time I was in the process of doing just that, I told Shanna. She swore that if I went on with it she'd marry him. So I never did send away my inquiries. She married him anyway. I couldn't do it, Jesse. I promised Shanna, and I keep my word. Besides, if she ever found out, she'd never speak to me again. She's got a stubborn streak in her, too. And she's just *begun* talking to me again—for which I think I have you to thank. After all these years of getting the cold shoulder from her—well, let's just say I'm glad we seem to have signed a truce.''

"You're probably right," Jesse replied. "She wouldn't ever speak to you again. Underneath all that softness and gentleness is a rather strong woman—when she puts her mind to it."

"Exactly. We'll just have to wait and see what happens. It *is* Shanna's life, and if she wants to ruin it by joining with Stu, then that's her privilege. If he *has* changed, perhaps it will even be for the best. She was mad about him, Jesse. She was completely head over heels, swept off her feet in love with him. I've often had the feeling during these past five years that she was still pining for him in some obscure way. *Damn!* I was hoping Ray.... Hasn't she been different lately? So much happier? Still, it's better that Stu showed up now before she remarried...."

Jesse chewed on her lip and thought back to the scene in the Lund pub. Had she seen Craig—Stu—drinking beer that day? She tried to remember. It seemed to her she had. And if that was the case, it meant Stu had lied to Shanna. Perhaps Bensen's hands were tied when it came to checking up on Stuart Lazzer, but hers weren't. If he checked out, there was no reason ever to let Shanna know. But if he didn't....

Jesse was so wrapped in thought she didn't realize Bensen had been staring steadily at her for quite some time. With a start her eyes flashed to his, and she was swallowed into that brimming depthless black. It was quite a shock to her. Her head filled with thoughts of mad passionate love on the couch, and at the same time she wondered whether his gaze was as perceptive as it seemed. A slightly pink guilty flush crept over her cheeks. Her chin moved up a fraction of an inch.

"Jessamine, do I detect a certain gleam in your eye?" he drawled softly, bending closer. His hands slid up her arms to curve around her shoulders, preventing a quick move backward on her part. "Jessamine?" He rubbed his nose against hers in an Eskimo-style kiss. "What are you thinking?"

Jesse swallowed, and her cheeks turned redder. Then she twisted her head to kiss him, thereby avoiding giving either of her two answers. Her soft rosy lips settled on his and clung for a short but infinitely speaking moment. It just seemed to be the best thing to do at the time; she had no resistance left.

"That's the first time you've kissed me," he murmured with a faint upward tilt to one corner of his mouth. "I like it. Do you think we could try that again?"

As she stared at Bensen, she thought that never in her life had she ever wanted to steal anything as badly as she wanted to steal Bensen away from Dorothy.

There was a sharp rap on the den's door, immediately followed by the door swinging open—which gave them no time to draw apart. Martha filled the doorway, surveying their startled faces.

"No snackin' before dinner," she said dryly. "It'll spoil your appetite. And food's on the table, in case you're interested. You haven't time to change, Mr. Everhart, and you know your grandmother will have your hide!"

"I take enough bossing around here not to get it from you, too, Martha!" Bensen stood up and swung Jesse along with him. "And I daresay she won't be thinking about my jeans after she hears the news!"

"News?" Martha questioned suspiciously. "What news? Bad news?"

"It could be. Stick around and you'll hear all about it. I've no taste for repeating it twice."

"It's *bad* news," Martha stated glumly, leading the way to the dining room.

Shanna, Jesse and Bensen stood assembled around the table waiting for Cecilia Anne to make an appearance. The twins were staying the night with Lily, and Martha was hovering by the sideboard, arranging and rearranging bowls on the warming tray.

"I had a wonderful nap, thank you. So charming of you all to ask!" Grandmother sailed into the dining room, smiling at everyone in her cynical way. She was dressed in her notion of proper dinner attire.

"Must you wear those old patched jeans at dinner, Bensen? Are Sam and Merry late again? Shanna, Dorothy's right, you know, in a way you do let them run about like—Shanna? Oh!" Her eyes flew from Shanna to Bensen. "Dear heaven, what's happened?" Her voice had withered to a croak, and she reached for the back of her chair with a frail wavering hand.

Bensen hastened to seat her. He stood behind her with his hands on her shoulders and looked at Shanna, lifting his brows slightly in question.

"No, please, Bensen, you tell her."

His lips compressed momentarily into a harsh uncompromising line.

"Grandmother, Stuart Lazzer is alive. He came to see Shanna this afternoon."

Mrs. Everhart didn't blink an eyelash. She stared straight in front of her while both Shanna and Jesse unconsciously held their breath. In her lap, Cecilia Anne's hands slowly curled into fists until the blue veins were raised and throbbing, then very slowly they uncurled again until they were once more lying passively in her lap.

"You told that *scum* to come here?" she said to Shanna, her tone as cold as stone and as hard. There was a dreadful echoing silence after her words. "As far as I'm concerned, he's dead!"

The harshness in her voice cut like a knife, piercing Shanna's cushion of shock. She slid into the nearest chair, dropped her face into her hands and burst into bitter tears, her slender frame racked with great shuddering sobs. Jesse stood paralyzed for a heart-stopping second. Then she sped to Shanna and dropped her arms around her like a protective shield.

"Don't you mollycoddle her!" Grandmother's voice whipped out at Jesse, and her arms tightened. Shanna turned her head into Jesse's shoulder and wept on, mindless, shattered. "She's a grown woman. It's time she took responsibility for her foolishness!"

"Grandmother," Bensen's voice snapped, "it's not her fault Stuart's alive, for God's sake!"

"It's her fault he dared show his face here! Whom does she think she is, inviting him here!"

"Clifftop is not sacred ground! She's his wife. Sam and Merry are his daughters. He has a right to see them, if nothing else!"

"He has no rights!" grandmother spat out. "This is my home, and I will not—"

"It's Shanna's home, as well!" Bensen interrupted harshly. "And it's Shanna's life. Stu wants her back again, grandmother."

"He *what*?"

"You heard me. And if that's what Shanna wants, that's what she'll get." He paused for a moment, breathing heavily. Then he added in quiet, more dangerous tones, "And you're not to interfere. He's asked Shanna's pardon for what happened, and she saw fit to give it. I'm not saying I would have; I'm not saying you would have. But you're not married to him! Whether they get a divorce or they try living together again is nobody's business but their own. We interfered last time, and look how it ended. We won't interfere again, will we?"

The last two words, for all their quietness, were a distinct warning. Jesse felt the fierce clash of wills between the seated old woman and the younger man who towered over her—a silent acrimonious battle.

"Very well," Cecilia Anne replied finally in frigid

tones. "I won't lift a finger against him. But if she goes running after him again, I shall disinherit her."

Jesse, holding tightly on to Shanna, felt the tremor that raced through her body. She looked helplessly up at Bensen, tears of distress welling in her own eyes.

"Grandmother—" Bensen sank down on a chair next to her, turning so that he was eye to eye with the old woman "—if you do that, you won't have any family left at all. You'll find yourself living here all alone! Shanna's happiness is at stake, not your likes and dislikes! We're barely a family now. Do you want to blow us all apart, or do we stick together?"

"And what would you suggest?"

"I suggest that as head of this family I invite Stuart for dinner tomorrow evening and we behave in a civilized manner. I won't have Shanna finding it necessary to sneak away to see him. Whatever happens, it will happen in the open. Do you understand?"

There was a faint stiff nod of her white head.

"And furthermore, you're going to take back right now what you said about disinheriting her. That's interference after the fact, as good as a curse, and I won't allow it!"

"*You* won't allow it? And who are you to *allow* me anything!"

"Am I or am I not the head of this family?"

There was another terrible distressing silence. Martha stood frozen by the sideboard, holding a lid in midair, heedless of the escaping steam.

"You forget yourself," grandmother ground out

at last. "I am ninety-five, you. . . you are only thirty-seven."

"Are you pulling rank? Now, after all these years? Where were you when Shanna and I were growing up? Who was head of the family then? Who ran this house? Who provided food for the table? Who kept this roof over all our heads? Did you? Did you even realize Shanna and I were alive?"

Another family sore spot, a long hidden wound, was out in the open. Beads of perspiration filmed Jesse's forehead as another spell of silence stretched to the breaking point.

Grandmother turned from Bensen, dropping her eyes. She bowed her white head. "You have made your point." Her demeanor was at once humble, yet infinitely proud, and her aged voice continued with dignity, "I. . . abdicated a long time ago. It seems Stuart Lazzer is not the only one to ask for pardon. I have never been one to make a great display of affection, and that, perhaps, has compounded my mistakes. You had both better know now that despite whatever you may think, despite all my actions in the past, despite the fact that I have never said this before. . . I do love you. Shanna, please discount what I said. I was trying to bully—but only because I'm so afraid for you." She reached a hand to Bensen's shoulder, pulling herself upright. For a short moment her fingers lingered on the beads of the leather vest she'd made many, many years earlier, than she began walking away from the dining-room table. After just a few paces she half turned back toward them. By this time Bensen had risen to his feet.

"And you, Ben, you keep Samuel and all I loved in him continually fresh in my mind."

"If I could change that...." He spread his hands.

"Don't worry." A dry smile flitted about her mouth. "These days it gives me more pleasure than pain." And again she turned from them.

"Ma'am," Martha cried when she was almost at the door, "won't you eat?"

"Eat?" she queried, as if she'd been asked to fly to Mars. "Don't be absurd, Martha!" And she swept from the room.

CHAPTER TEN

DINNER THE NEXT EVENING was not a happy social success. No amount of politeness or effort could chase away the air of awkwardness that hung over the dining-room table, though dinner in a culinary sense was excellent. The twins' absolute correct manners, their cool stiff little faces, shouted their real feelings for anyone who cared to see. Their shock had not yet worn off. Shanna's natural yet grave expression became a tinge embarrassed when, just before Martha served dessert, Stu handed his daughters each a jeweler's blue-velvet box. Duly the twins stated their thanks without a single trace of enthusiasm for the delicate pearl rings inside. In fact, they showed more interest in Martha's trifle.

And there was one particularly uncomfortable moment when grandmother asked Stuart, "And what about your...accident all those years ago? What are you going to do about that?"

"My lawyer's working on it. I knew it would be difficult coming back, but any difficulty was worth just seeing Shanna again."

Shortly thereafter he took Shanna off for a walk in the garden.

"And did I behave in a civilized manner?" grandmother asked Bensen once they had gone.

"I can't fault you." He smiled back at her lazily, the smile reaching his eyes. She sniffed and snapped for Martha to come and refill her coffee cup.

When the telephone rang, Jesse flew to answer it after the second ring, for Martha hadn't materialized and Bensen and grandmother were involved in an animated ripost too interesting to interrupt.

It was Ray Dunbar, asking to speak with Shanna. Jesse felt an anxious tug at her heart as she went to find Shanna, still with Stu in the garden. The thought of having to break in on them, especially after what Stuart had said the last time, upset her even more when she rounded a corner of the house and came upon them kissing.

"Were you hired as Shanna's chaperone?" Stuart asked as he passed her to go into the salon. His manner was at once boyishly charming and unpleasantly sarcastic—which made Jesse feel sharply uncomfortable. She turned toward the kitchen instead of following him into the salon. After hanging about there and getting into Martha's way for twenty minutes, she crept into the hall to see the telephone receiver on its cradle.

A quick peek in the salon showed only grandmother, Bensen and Stuart in desultory conversation. Jesse flitted up the stairs and knocked quietly on Shanna's bedroom door. When there was no reply, she turned the knob and looked in. Shanna was sitting by her dressing table with one hand clutching something sparkly and the other hand over her eyes; she was crying.

"Heavens, what's happened now?" Jesse cried, hurrying over to her. Big tears kept right on sliding down Shanna's cheeks; she compressed her lips in an effort to control herself but failed and dropped her head. It was a different helpless sort of crying, and it scared Jesse. She moaned in agitation, watching the flow of tears.

"Was it something Ray said?" she prompted gently. Shanna nodded her head and rubbed her free hand over her cheeks.

"We h-had a f-fight," she gulped. "He's really angry, Jesse."

"About Stu? But why?"

"Because I didn't tell him. He says I should have told him yesterday. He found out from Dorothy that Stu was back."

"From *Dorothy*? But how did she find out? I don't underst—"

"Dorothy's staying with her father up at the mine. They have quarters there; she didn't go back to Vancouver last time. Apparently it's all over town now that Stu is back. Ray dropped in to visit Lily, and *she* was there and couldn't wait to tell him!"

"Ohhh-h. . . hell," sighed Jesse softly, and Shanna nodded in agreement.

Her hand on the dresser opened, revealing a diamond necklace that slowly slid down onto the table-top.

"Stu just gave me this," Shanna said, looking at it, "out in the garden. I told him about Ray, and he swore he'd make me forget Ray Dunbar ever existed. He said he wasn't going to lose me again—not for anything in the world. He *has* changed, Jesse; there's something not at all the same about him. What am I going to do?''

"Don't let him hurry you into anything! Don't let him overwhelm you into doing what *he* wants! You don't owe him anything, and to date he's been nothing as a father."

"But he *is* their father."

"A bad father is *not* better than no father at all!"

Shanna sighed, rubbing both hands over her brow. "Will you...would you mind terribly saying my good-nights for me, Jesse? I just can't go back downstairs right now. I don't want to see him right now."

"Of course I don't mind," Jesse replied, turning for the door. "Are you going to be all right?" Shanna's nod was not quite convincing, but Jesse felt she was better left alone. She stepped out the door, closing it behind her, and bumped into Stuart Lazzer.

"What are you doing here?" she gasped, sounding rather accusatory in her fright.

Stuart's hand snapped out to grasp her wrist; his eyes narrowed on her face. "Just exactly what are you trying to do?" he asked in a threatening undertone through clenched teeth. "*You* stay out of it! It's none of your damn business what Shanna does!"

Furious, Jesse wrenched her hand free and stood staring at him in surprise. He must have been listening by the door!

"I came to say good-night to Shanna, and that's exactly what I'm going to do!"

Jesse hesitated, then stepped away from the door. She stood there until he had shut it in her face.

JESSE WAS ALONE with Bensen for only a few minutes that evening; it happened when Martha swung out of one of the kitchen's saloon doors and Bensen swung in the other. He stood surveying her for a thoughtful second and then came striding purposefully toward her. Involuntarily she took a step backward to find herself pressed against the sink.

"I've had a feeling.... Jesse, have you been avoiding me for the last half of tonight?"

"A-avoiding you?" she echoed inanely. "Whatever's given you that idea?"

"Don't prevaricate, you know what I'm talking about. And you have some pretty fierce explaining to do, if you'll remember."

Jesse eyed him with a mixture of uncertainty and acute physical unease. Shanna's news about Dorothy being five miles away instead of the expected seventy-five had grown in importance in her mind as the evening wore on. At first she hadn't thought much about it, but then.... It might not mean anything, and it might mean the world. Jesse had been to-and-fro about it ever since, and this sudden confrontation crystallized the massive doubts she'd developed. That night he hadn't come home—had he been with Dorothy?

She wanted so badly to ask about Dorothy. But he had never clearly answered any of her previous questions about his fiancée. She still couldn't understand what the situation was and where she stood. Most likely he wouldn't give her a clear answer, now, either, and all the while they were getting in deeper and deeper. It simply wasn't any good. She shouldn't, she couldn't contemplate encouraging him. It wasn't right, she decided. If Bensen wanted an affair, then he should have one with his fiancée or else break their engagement.

Jesse flipped her hair back over her shoulders in an effort to stall further. Did he have to stand there and keep looking at her in that knowing way? The kitchen light cast his features into sharp relief—the thin nose with its flared nostrils and slightly beakish aspect, the deep-set eyes, the finely drawn mouth. Jesse's stomach fluttered, and she gripped the edge of the sink.

Bensen took an abrupt step closer. "You *do* remember?" It wasn't so much a question as a mocking statement.

His fiancée's name hovered on the tip of her tongue, but she didn't know exactly what to ask or how to ask it. And simply by asking, she would be revealing that her attraction to him went far beyond the physical. She couldn't do it. She couldn't admit to him she was so in love with him that it hurt. Oh, no, that would only increase his hold on her, his power over her, and he had too much as it was.... "I don't want to discuss it at the moment," she said loftily.

Bensen stared at her in outraged amazement. *"Jesse!"*

He took another step closer, and she gripped the sink tighter. "Perhaps we'll discuss it in another fashion..." he drawled, with a sudden grin, advancing and cutting off her only escape route.

"No! No, dammit Bensen! You—you caveman! Hey, that's not fair! Stop it! Oh, please, please don't do that...oh, no, you don't! Take your hand away from there! Dammit, I'm serious! Oh, now you've gone too far!" His hand was not only under her dress at the back but was moving along the lace trim of her panties, edging them aside, his fingers sliding along the intimate bared curve of smooth skin. She wiggled in a desperate attempt to dislodge that tightening hand; she beat his chest; she tried to slap his laughing taunting face and then, when that had no effect, she bit his shoulder. That worked, but with a twitch of his wounded shoulder he caught her face between both hands and kissed her on the mouth, hard.

"Mmmm, you're sweet, Jessamine...'all soft an' sweetlike.' But not too receptive at the moment. Have you been counting my many faults again?"

"You bet! And the nos are stacking up!" she shot back, her mind in turmoil, her body in a turmoil of flagrant desire.

"That's a pity. For I haven't gone *nearly* as far as I mean to go with you. And you can take that any way you please! But let me tell you this: whether you're here or in Vancouver, it won't make any difference. So don't go flying off, hoping you'll get away! And perhaps next time you'll have your explanation ready. I'm dying to hear why you're ashamed to be seen kissing me!" With that and a sharp lopsided sardonic smile, he left her alone in the kitchen.

Later that same evening Jesse went up to her attic and typed out several letters of query concerning Stuart Lazzer, then shortened them to telegraph form—she wanted the answers back *immediately*. Her years of research paid off then; she knew exactly where to send the telegrams for the kind of information she wanted. At supper Stu had mentioned the names of several companies where he had supposedly worked to amass his small fortune, so Jesse composed discreet inquiries to them, as well.

That small incident outside Shanna's bedroom door had put a seal of approval on what she was doing; she didn't feel nearly as guilty about it as she had earlier. When she finished, she had seven neat envelopes ready to be dispersed. The carbon copies of each query she slipped inside a folder on her table, then she clicked out the light and had to stop herself from tiptoeing down to her bedroom. Despite everything she was nervous about the seven letters she clutched in her hand and felt as though she *should* be sneaking about.

Jesse idled so long in her bedroom the next morning that she missed Bensen at breakfast—which was exactly what she meant to do. For two reasons. Her first was that she had the uncanny notion he would know exactly what she'd been doing just by looking at her face—and she wanted those seven letters sent before coming eye to eye with him. Second, she'd had a mainly sleepless night thinking about her future. Her probings deep beneath the surface had turned out to be most alarming.

At every corner she came to in her mind, again and again she had to face the fact that she loved Bensen Everhart. Didn't just like him or find him amusing, interesting, entertaining intellectually beyond the norm; it wasn't just his physical attributes that tossed her into an emotional storm, that laid bare all her desires. No, it was an unexplainable empathy, an unequivocal rightness in being close to him, a sudden frightening belonging to and dependence on someone else.

She found herself involved up to the neck and wasn't altogether clear on how that had happened and, in retrospect, how it had happened with such speed and completeness. She knew emphatically that if he asked her to marry him, she would do so at the drop of a hat. That was the extent to which he'd engaged her mind, her emotions, her desires, her trust. For someone as independent as she, the sudden realization of her need of another person for mere well-being was, indeed, alarming. Especially when she considered that although she belonged to him, he irrefutably did not belong to her, nor did it seem he was prepared to change that one immense fact.

She knew, of course, that morning, as she kneeled on the window seat to lean her elbows on the sill, gazing out to sea, that sooner or later she and Bensen would have to talk. She still owed him an explanation. But with it the subject of Dorothy would come up. Jesse was aware that she had a clear case of cold feet, and that, combined with the conviction that she'd hear something she didn't want to hear, made her want to postpone the inevitable.

But when Jesse finally meandered downstairs, she found Bensen had left the house entirely. Grandmother informed her that he'd gone off somewhere in the motorboat with Dan Cameron and that Stu had whisked Shanna and the twins away for the day according to some prearranged schedule that no one else knew about. That left Jesse plenty of time and more than enough opportunity to take the jeep into Lund to send off her seven telegrams. She told Cecilia Anne she needed more information from the town-hall ledgers—which she did and which she sought out while in the small waterfront town.

The remainder of the day was spent in trying to work on her notes. But she couldn't fully concentrate. Shanna and Stu and Ray—that triangle kept plaguing her mind, as did the one she was involved in to an even greater extent.

A strange mood, a mood of waiting for something to happen, settled over Jesse, and at dinner—which only she and Bensen and grandmother shared—she sensed that they, too, were affected. The very house around them seemed to be quietly waiting.

During dessert a telephone call came for Bensen; as Jesse sat there at the dinner table staring down at her apple pie and rapidly melting ice cream and listening to the muffled sound of Bensen's comments—it was obviously not a social call—she apprehensively wondered whether the call would be the trigger for a whole chain of events.

She was more convinced that this might be so

when, a few moments later, Bensen appeared in the doorway and stopped there, as if undecided. There was a set look to his mouth and a suggestion of anger behind the inscrutable black of his eyes.

And then he rapped out, "Jesse, wait up for me." Without staying for an answer, he rushed off.

Jesse started up from her chair, worried. But by the time she reached the doorway, he had disappeared, and in what seemed only seconds later came the pulsing roar of the motorboat gunned to full power.

"It won't help looking at me like that," grandmother suddenly snapped, waspish, as Jesse returned to the table. "I don't know what's going on, either!"

Jesse was inordinately glad to see Stu Lazzer arrive with Shanna and the twins not more than half an hour thereafter. They, at least, were all right, so whatever was going to happen was not going to happen to them. One worry eased from Jesse's mind.

Stu Lazzer did not stay long; after several charming and respectful remarks to Cecilia Anne, further establishing each of their "stand off and be polite" positions, he sent Jesse a warm carefree smile, squeezed Shanna's hand once and took himself off. Jesse was happy to see him go, was about to reprimand herself for being such a worrywart, when Shanna abruptly said good-night to them and took the twins upstairs.

Grandmother and Jesse were left in the hall, gazing after her in bewildered surprise. They felt absurdly cheated by her quick and uncommunicative departure. All day Jesse had been speculating on the outcome of Shanna's day, had worried for her and over her, only to have her steal away when she did finally arrive. This secretiveness made the whole sense of waiting for something that much more acute.

For two hours—even longer—Jesse and grand-mother sat in the salon, ostensibly watching tele-vision—programs neither of them had ever showed any interest in before. From time to time Jesse would get up and make a circuit of the room. Every time she did, grandmother's eyes would follow her, enduring this display with the sort of enforced patience people often assume waiting for a late train.

Jesse simply knew it wasn't going to be an ordinary phone call from the first ring of the telephone. She sat there, frozen, until the third ring sounded and then dashed to answer. To her quavering hello came a brisk authoritative male voice.

"This is Constable O'Malley of the Lund detach-ment." Jesse turned pale. "Is Bensen Everhart in?"

"No, no, I'm sorry, he's not," Jesse replied, unable to control the quaver in her voice.

"In that case, may I speak with Shanna Lazzer?"

Jesse was now thoroughly scared. "I-I'll get her. Please wait."

With her heart in her throat she flew up the stairs. Cecilia Anne came into the hall, looked at the receiver lying on the table, at Jesse vanishing. Jesse was already knocking on Shanna's door as grand-mother's hand reached for the receiver.

"Shanna, phone!" Jesse announced after the door reluctantly opened. "It's the police!"

Shanna stared hard at Jesse, alarm in her eyes.

There was a quick intake of breath, then with a nervous lick of her lips she pivoted and went to her bed table. Her hand was on the telephone receiver when she whispered fiercely to Jesse, "Take the extension in Bensen's room! Quick!"

Jesse never thought twice; she simply did as she was told. It was the first time she'd had a glimpse of his bedroom, and she had some panic-stricken moments before she found his telephone. She called back to Shanna, hesitated one second more, then lifted the receiver at precisely the same time as Shanna lifted hers in her room down the hall.

"This is Shanna Lazzer." A picture of Dorothy smiled up at her from the dresser. Jesse turned her back to it.

"Hello, Mrs. Lazzer. Constable O'Malley here. There's been an accident in town. Ray Dunbar was found half an hour ago in the alley behind the pub. He's been taken to hospital. He was attacked and beaten—doctor's working on him now." He paused, as if waiting for Shanna to make some reply, but there was only a stunned echoing silence all down the line. "Mrs. Lazzer?"

"Y-yes?" Shanna's voice was just a thread of sound.

"Mrs. Lazzer, Ray Dunbar asked for you before he lost consciousness. The doctor would like you to come into town. Now. He has head injuries, maybe a severe concussion and any stress.... Your presence—"

"Of course I'll come. I'll be there as soon as I can."

"Do you need transportation?"

"No, no, I—"

"Do you have someone to drive you?"

"Um. . . ."

"I wouldn't advise you to drive by yourself, Mrs. Lazzer. Do you know where Ben—Mr. Everhart is?"

"I thought he was home. I—no. . . ."

"Could you leave a message for him concerning the accident? And to give me a call when he gets in?"

"Yes, yes, of course."

"Drive safely now. We don't need another accident. I'll see you in town, Mrs. Lazzer." He hung up the phone quickly, as if to forestall the questions he knew were coming.

Shanna and Jesse met in the upstairs hall.

"Oh, my God! Hurry Jesse! Where the hell is Bensen anyway?"

"Out. . .he took the boat. We'll take the jeep. I'll drive."

"We've got to leave him a note."

"No, no, you two get cracking!" grandmother ordered from down below in the hall. "Put something warmer on, hurry! I'll tell Bensen when he comes. Don't worry about the twins. They'll be all right with me. Hurry now!"

"Jesse, you take care!" Grandmother gave them each a quick fierce, unexpected peck on the cheek and then quite literally shooed them out the door. As they ran to the jeep, they could hear her shouting for Martha.

Jesse stopped the jeep with a protesting squeal of hot tires and a puff of dust in front of the small country hospital. Shanna was already out and running for the doors by the time Jesse had slid out of the driver's seat. She followed at a more sedate pace, arriving to hear the doctor's low-voiced explanation of Ray's injuries. The parietal bone on the left side of the head had been fractured—an undisplaced fracture, he expounded, which meant that although the bone was still together, it was cracked. It was not known yet whether there was any hemorrhaging; these first forty-eight hours were the most crucial. He was being checked every half hour for blood pressure, his rate of respiration, his pulse and the reaction of his pupils to light. Thereafter followed a miscellany of lacerations, cuts and bruises to be found on other parts of his body. Jesse felt nauseated, and she wondered how Shanna was faring.

"The trouble is," the doctor continued, "we gave him the last supply we had of his blood type. He may need more, and we may have to make a rush flight into Vancouver tonight. If that's the case, are you prepared to go with him?"

"Oh, yes!" Shanna answered immediately.

The doctor looked down at her for a pensive second, then said firmly, "Let the nurse here take you to the lounge. There's nothing you can do at the moment. The minute he wakes, we'll call you. I know it's difficult, but please try not to worry too much. His condition has been holding steady, and that *is* a good sign."

"Who could have done this to him?" Shanna fretted to Jesse as they each started on their second cup of coffee. "And *why*? What if he needs more blood,

Jesse? Why don't they take him to Vancouver right now? What will a flight do to him?"

Jesse could only miserably shake her head and wonder where Bensen was now that they needed him.

Constable O'Malley stopped by the hospital to see them and explained more of where and how Ray Dunbar had been found. Apparently he had a lead on someone who might have seen something. He asked Shanna where Bensen was.

"I've just phoned my grandmother, and he's not home yet."

The RCMP constable frowned, nodded and then left them alone in the lounge. The same nurse who'd shown them in came by to report on Ray's condition: it remained the same. A nighttime hush had fallen on the hospital. . . the muted sound of wheels on a tile floor, the soft click of steel on steel, the murmur of voices down a corridor. . . and Bensen! There he suddenly was.

It helped immensely just to have him there. Shanna had barely finished telling him what she knew about the beating when the doctor returned, smiling blandly while he pricked their thumbs for blood samples.

"Just to see if we have a compatible blood type right under our noses," he said, handing the waiting nurse the samples.

After they left, Shanna, with her elbows on the table, sank her head into her hands at this fresh cause for anxiety. Bensen stood beside her, smoothing a hand across her shoulders, and looked over at Jesse.

"Oh, Bensen, I just remembered, you're supposed

to call Constable O'Malley right away. He wasn't too pleased when nobody knew where you were, and—''

"He said *Constable* O'Malley?" Bensen interrupted Jesse.

"Yes."

"That's odd...he's always been Tom to me."

"Maybe he has something to tell you about the accident that he didn't want us to know? Oh, Bensen, what do you suppose—''

"Er, is it Jesse?" The doctor had appeared again. "Could you step this way?"

Bensen wheeled on the doctor. "But—"

"You sit down and have a cup of coffee, Ben. That's all you can do. It's Jesse here we need." The doctor turned and led the way, Jesse following docilely behind. She took a look over her shoulder. Bensen and Shanna were staring after her, and she raised a hand in a quick wave before she was swept into a small examining room.

"You lie down here, honey," the nurse said cheerfully to her. "This won't take too long." Jesse stretched out on the clean white cot. The doctor nodded to her, then left. "It's really lucky, your having type O." The nurse chattered on, drawing Jesse's attention off of the long hollow needle that slid under her skin. "Ray is type O, too. Mr. Everhart's an AB, and his sister is an A—no good at all. Just relax your hand now. Try to lie still, and don't get up. I'll be back in a sec." The nurse patted her arm lightly and disappeared out of Jesse's line of vision. If she turned her head slightly, she could see what looked like a plastic bag hanging by the bedside, slowly filling. The sight of it made her squeamish, and she closed her eyes, trying to relax.

After the procedure was finished, the nurse told her to lie quietly for another ten minutes. At last she was allowed to stand but was cautioned to move slowly. Even though Jesse did, when she got to her feet, the room swam before her eyes for a few bewildering seconds. Her legs felt a faintly rubbery as she walked back down the corridor. Other than that she felt fine.

They waited in the lounge, the minutes ticking softly by on the high white wall clock. Jesse found herself leaning against Bensen; his arm was curved around her shoulders. She was unaware of exactly how that arrangement came about but glad that it had. On his other side was Shanna, with a long arm around her, too. Then suddenly a nurse was motioning for Shanna to come.

Jesse bit her lip, and the arm around her tightened. She turned her head into Bensen's shoulder; she moved closer to him, almost clutching him for a few seconds. His other hand came up to smooth back her hair and, tucking her head under his chin, his arms enveloped her.

"Er, excuse me, Ben?"

Jesse moved slightly out of Bensen's embrace to face the doctor. The look on his face made her release a long slow sigh.

"He's improving," the doctor announced. "Your contribution helped, Jesse. If he could say 'thank you,' I'm sure he would. It's best that Shanna stay the night, Ben. We've a room for her here, in case he wakes again."

"He'll make it, Joe?" Bensen's question was tense.

There was a faint hesitation. "If nothing unexpected happens. . . . I don't believe there *is* any internal bleeding, but I won't know for certain—not for several hours more." The doctor looked down at Jesse. "Best thing for you to do now, Ben, is to get this young lady to bed. She needs rest to make up for that blood donation. I'll call you immediately if something comes up."

They talked for a few more minutes, and while they did, the doctor's cool dry fingers found Jesse's pulse. He seemed satisfied but again stressed the need for rest.

She teetered a little going down the hospital stairs, and she stumbled again on the way to the jeep. Her head felt very light as the jeep drew up to the house, but she vehemently refused Bensen's offer to carry her, saying she felt fine—which she did.

"And you can walk all by yourself, can you?" Bensen mocked. "When will you learn not to argue!" Under the rough exasperation there was a certain tenderness that made Jesse stop in midstride. He uttered another exclamation and swung her up in his arms, continuing to scold her as he carried her up the granite terrace steps and into the house. It was very late at this point, and Jesse was beginning to feel tired. Bensen's voice just above her head grumbled on at her, but she smiled into the folds of his flannel lumberman's shirt and clasped her hands more securely around his neck.

When he laid her down, she found herself on the

salon couch. Before her on the coffee table was a plate of wrapped sandwiches and a bottle of red wine, two wineglasses and a corkscrew. A banked fire of coals in the fireplace made the room warm and cozy; it was a single glow of light in the surrounding nighttime darkness and quiet.

Bensen shook out the folded blanket, then draped it over her. As he opened the bottle of wine, continuing his bickering monologue on what was wrong with women as a whole, Jesse smiled again. It was rather nice being pampered as an invalid, although there was no need for it. She sighed and curled comfortably into the corner of the couch, dreamily watching him through half-closed eyes.

He had filled their wineglasses and was now unwrapping the cellophane from one of the sandwiches. He handed it to her. "Eat!" he ordered.

Jesse looked back at him over top of the sandwich. He was sitting on the edge of the couch beside her, against her legs. She looked at the sandwich—appetizing roast beef—but felt no interest—she had other things on her mind—and replaced it on the plate.

"I'll eat in the morning," she answered, ignoring his frowning look as she picked up her wineglass. "I wonder whose idea this was?" Her hand waved at the sandwiches and wine.

"I phoned ahead," Bensen replied, draining his glass. He poured himself another, took a large sip, put it down.

"Oh, that reminds me. Did you get a chance to see Constable O' what's-his-name?"

"Tom? Yes, I went over to the station while you were donating."

"Anything new?"

Bensen hesitated a second, then shook his head. "He was still trying to find the guy who claims he saw what happened. He's a drifter passing through town, looking for work. Or that's the story. This could turn into a real stink."

"Ray's sort of an officer of the law, isn't he, being a ranger?"

Bensen nodded. "Has Shanna given any indication yet about Stu?"

"Nothing. Not a word. No sign. It's really strange."

Bensen had finished two sandwiches in quick order. He topped his glass of wine, then Jesse's.

"This happening to Ray doesn't help," he said tersely.

"It might be just the thing. When something like this happens, you know who you really care for."

"Yes, but it leaves Stu a clear field."

"Ohhh! I hadn't thought of that. You're rooting for Ray, then, are you?"

Bensen shot her a quick glance, then nodded. "Even though I'm trying not to let the past color my judgment, I still can't help feeling Ray's the better man. Personal opinion."

"That makes two of us."

"Stu still gives you the creeps? Even in flesh and blood?"

Jesse paused a moment to consider. "Yes...that's it. That's it exactly."

Almost absentmindedly, it seemed, Bensen's hand curved over her hip. "He *has* changed...I don't know what to think of him myself."

"I gather the twins are of the same mind." Jesse moved to put her glass on the table and lay back, watching him with a drowsy desire glowing in the sherry-amber depths of her sleepy eyes. She was too tired at that point to be bothered about the morality of what she wanted to do—she only knew she wanted to do it. She was well aware that Bensen was going to kiss her, and she was going to kiss him back. He wasn't married, only engaged; there was still time for him to change his mind.... "And grandmother's waging a fully armed truce." A faint smile played across her lips.

"She's good at that." The hand curved around her hip moved a little. "But have you noticed—" the hand slid over her waist and ribs to curve around her back, bringing him considerably closer "—Martha's cooking has improved."

Jesse's fingertips touched his chest. "She was really peeved when you didn't finish your pie tonight." His other hand came around to settle on the side of her throat, his thumb caressing the line of her jaw. Jesse's arms went up over his wide strong shoulders. "You'd better not do anything to provoke her tomorrow...."

His lips brushed hers once, twice, lingered at the corner of her mouth, then settled in long slow kiss that deepened and grew more sensuous with every passing second.

"Or you'll be eating God-knows-what for a

month!'' Jesse gasped breathlessly when it was over. She edged a little farther down the couch, and Bensen's weight pressed her into the soft cushions as his mouth covered hers before she could say more.

It was a mindless flight into ever building sweet erotic passion, a fusing of desires that ran the length of her body and melted her bones, one by one. Warm strong hands touched, caressed...the hard heavy weight of his body satisfied unknown hungers within her and precipitated a languorous hunger for more. Her body moved against his, unconscious of all but feeling. Her rosy lips beneath his tender consuming mouth were warm and yielding and invited more. His hips pressed softly, intimately against hers, igniting the glowing warmth within her, slowly, seductively, building the heat between them.

Long brown fingers trailed slow fire from her throat down to her cleavage, settled gently around the curve of her breast. His potent touch burned through the cotton material of her shirt. Then the buttons slid out of their holes, and his hand moved tantalizingly across the taut smooth sensitive skin of her stomach, freeing the shirt from her jeans...and back up to cup the firm swell of white flesh, as though he, too, believed she belonged to him.

A tremor rippled through her. As his mouth continued its deep erotic assault, the tip of his tongue moved to touch the tip of hers, and one of Jesse's hands slid inside the collar of his shirt and around his neck and down his chest coming to rest in the vee of his shirt, her fingers softly flexing on the warm brown skin, touching, feeling the latent power of the

muscles beneath. She opened one button—not thinking that she'd only meant to kiss him, nothing
more—and another button and another. It was exquisite to touch him so, love him so, feel his bare skin
burning in contact with hers, knowing that he wanted
her as much as she wanted him, and that was all that
mattered. Dorothy might never have existed....

Jesse kissed Bensen back the way she'd wanted to
for days—years, it seemed now—forgetful of everything but this perfect present time, her mouth tenderly urgent on his, evoking all her emotion for him to
take. A ripple of tension passed through his frame as
he tasted that sweet giving. He took a deep and rather
shaky breath.

"Didn't I say, Jessamine, that I wanted to kiss you
forever? Oh, it's true! I hope you don't mind, because I can't imagine stopping." His hand tightened
on her breast, softly, softly caressing. His mouth
touched her throat in a flame of desire.

There came a sharp cackle of laughter from somewhere behind the couch.

"I thought I'd heard you come home!" It was
Cecilia Anne's dry voice. Bensen drew Jesse's
blanket up as his grandmother stepped in the doorway and started across the room toward them. By the
time she came around the couch, Jesse had buttoned
her blouse, although she hadn't tucked it in. Bensen's
shirt was wide open.

"We used to wait until we were married in my day!
But you young folk seem to think you have all the answers, so I won't bore you with my opinion."

Bensen added a touch more wine to each of their

glasses and smiled lazily at his grandmother. "Did you come down for news of Ray?" he taunted gently. "He's better. It will be some hours yet before he's out of danger, though."

"How's Shanna taking this?"

"Hard, very hard."

"That's a good sign. How I wish she'd hurry up and decide her mind! I can't stand all this waiting about to see who's going to be her husband."

"And now Ray's unable to present his case."

"That's a grim thought, Bensen, but then you have many of those. Why are you keeping Jesse up? Don't you know she should be in bed—*resting*?"

"But I feel fine, grandmother!"

"Nonsense! How can you possibly feel fine? You should do your courting, Bensen, when Jesse's not too weak to resist! Come along now, dear, I'm not so foolish as to let *him* tuck you in! No, Bensen, if you have more to, er, *say* to Jesse, it will have to be said tomorrow. And don't look at me like that!"

CHAPTER ELEVEN

MARTHA SHOOK JESSE awake; rolling one sleepy eye in the direction of her clock, Jesse saw it was just past six-thirty. She groaned and would have hidden her head under the pillows had not Martha firmly thrust them aside.

"Telephone! It's Shanna!" repeated the housekeeper urgently, placing the phone where her pillows had been. That woke Jesse up. And then Shanna's voice telling her that Ray was better settled her heart back in its customary place. But the telephone call lasted for several minutes more, and after it was over, Jesse practically threw the receiver down. She would have rushed out into the hall with nothing on but her nightgown, save for Martha, who hustled her first into the bathroom and then into her robe.

Barefoot, Jesse ran down the hall to Bensen's bedroom, but it was already empty, and so she sped down the stairs, tying her sash on the way. She found him in the dining room, just finishing a glass of orange juice. He started up from the table when he saw her, her alarm instantly communicating.

"What is it? What's happened now? Jesse, for God's sake!"

"I just talked to Shanna!" she announced, trying to catch her breath.

"About Ray? But I called the hospital, and there doesn't appear to be any damage to the brain. He's fine; he's stable and improving."

"No, no, Ray's fine. It's you!"

"Me?"

"Shanna said to warn you. Constable O'Malley's driving her out later; he's coming to question you! That drifter described Ray's attacker, and Shanna said his description could be tailor-made to fit you! It's all over town. O'Malley kept asking us last night where you were, but I never thought...I—where *were* you?" She looked searchingly into his face, which had turned grim at her news.

"I was with Dorothy and her father," he stated, staring back at her.

"Oh..." Jesse faltered. She turned quickly from him so that he would not see her face. His words had cut through her, and when she continued, her voice was not altogether steady. "Th-that's good. I mean, I know *you* didn't do it, but th-this way you have a w-watertight alibi. *Everybody* will believe the Jorgensens!"

"Aw, Jesse, you're one hell of a fine woman!" he said quietly, but the smile in his eyes told her he meant it.

"Well, of course you didn't do it!" she exclaimed, while inside she desperately wished she were woman enough for him—forever.

"But I don't think visiting the Jorgensens will be much of an alibi," he said shortly, catching Jesse's entire attention. As she looked at him questioningly, he added, "We had a little fight last night—father and daughter and me."

"Oh, Bensen, you fight with everybody!" exclaimed Jesse in distress, thinking only of his safety now.

"Mmm...seems I do, doesn't it? I guess I must be hard to get along with. Damn! And I didn't stay long—ten minutes or so—then I, er, took the boat out for a spin. They were both mad enough when I left there."

The import of his words was sinking through. Fight?... What did that mean? A fight, but *why*? Jesse's bare toes curled on the polished hardwood floor. An eager and breathless hope filled her, made her feel weightless, as though she could float freely in the air. "Oh, *Bensen*!" She couldn't stop the radiant smile; she wasn't even really aware she was beaming at him.

"There's no damn reason to be so pleased!" he stormed. "I've just told you we can't count on my alibi. *Jesse?*"

She put both her hands to her mouth in an effort to wipe away the smile and concentrate on the problem at hand, but the idea of a fight between Dorothy and Bensen was still trickling through, and she wanted to dance and sing for joy. It had to be a serious fight for him to think they'd refuse him alibi.

"Bensen, wait, there's more."

"More? *More!* What do you mean there's more?"

"Stu's coming out, too. He was with Shanna most of last night, I gather. She didn't get much sleep; she was with Ray, and Stu sat up with her. She said Stu was so kind and so this and that. Bensen, it made me sick listening to her. Stu's in there like a dirty shirt; he's making the most of this situation, just as you said! And now he's coming out here to be with her, and Ray's stuck there, miles away!''

"Damn!"

"Yes...Bensen, isn't there something a little fishy about this? Some drifter, some out-of-work logger who's never seen you before, describes you to a tee, when you weren't anywhere *near* town when it happened?''

"When Ray comes around enough to talk, he'll tell the story. I don't really think there's anything to worry about."

"But that might not be for a couple of days yet; you know what the doctor said. And in the meantime the suspicion settles on you. Everybody's going to be wondering about that boat ride—you were gone for a long time. It might be enough to turn Shanna against you again; it might make her wonder. You know, just another argument with Ray, only this time it got out of hand?''

"*Damn!* I should have stayed in bed this morning!" He smiled crookedly at her. "But why would anyone want to point a finger at me? I can't see who would benefit from it."

"There's got to be some reason...."

"We'll know more after Tom gets here."

"You know him well?"

"He's been here for years. Today's the second time I'll be seeing him as Constable O'Malley, though. Can't say I like it."

Jesse chewed on her lip; her mind was brimming with thoughts—of Stu and Shanna; of Ray and Shanna; of Ray, if not at death's door, then lying ill and helpless in a hospital bed; of this new threat to Bensen, suddenly looming up with dreadful impact...and of course, the "fight." Bensen had no alibi, and the spin in the boat—there was just too much to think of at once, and she abruptly sat down in one of the chairs.

Bensen looked at her for a moment, then went to the sideboard and filled a plate to overflowing with fluffy scrambled eggs and crisp bacon, hash-brown potatoes and toast. He put the plate on the table and crossed over to her. "Let's eat before all hell breaks loose. At least we've got about one quiet hour more." And he pulled her up out of the chair, led her around the table, sat down and pulled her into his lap. "Coffee, Jessamine?"

Jesse looked at him and nodded numbly. She wriggled a little on his lap, trying to get used to what was happening, not sure whether now was the time to ask what the fight had been about. Her arm crept along his shoulder a little hesitantly. Last night, oh, last night came flooding freshly into her mind in vivid detail.

Bensen heaped a fork with scrambled eggs and raised it to her lips, smiling with an exquisite blend of near tenderness and mockery as he gazed into her eyes. Jesse accepted the offering, a flush turning her cheeks a delicate pink. There was something so intimate about the gesture that she couldn't ask now... she only wanted this precious bit of happiness to last forever. Sooner or later she would grab the bull by the horns and ask about Dorothy—if he didn't tell her first.

Perhaps she was only postponing heartbreak. But Bensen's one arm around her back was real enough, as was the tender expression in his coal-black eyes. She relaxed a little against him, and the fingers curving around her hip tightened as he raised the fork to her mouth again. She was suddenly aware she really didn't have much on. Her fingers pulled at the collar of her dressing gown in a belated and unnecessary move to hold the gown shut, covering the sheer lace beneath. It was magic, the soft sensuous smile on his mouth was magic, and her hand dropped.

"Despite everything," Bensen murmured as she sipped at her coffee, "I feel it's time to celebrate." Her eyes, widening, swung to meet his. What was he saying? "I feel we should be sharing a bottle of champagne, Jessamine.... But I'm sure the good constable wouldn't appreciate my being light-headed before nine in the morning!"

Jesse laughed and put down her coffee cup. "I'm already feeling light-headed, Bensen," and her other hand clasped his neck. Impulsively her lips settled on his for a soft sweet clinging moment. That was for Shanna, she thought, remembering her advice of a conscious "little push in the right direction." Surely that was allowable?

The steely arm around her held her close, and his free hand slid slowly up and down the length of her silk-covered thigh. His mouth caught hers when she attempted to end the kiss. As if he, too, had ulterior motives in mind, he kissed her with a tender mastery that banished all thought from her head. And, having captured her complete attention, he tantalized; he enticed. His tongue forced her lips wider apart and softly probed deeper, softly questioned, while his free hand touched and caressed and molded her curves, searched out secret spots and gently, oh, so gently, pushed her toward the brink of utter mindless sensuousness.

"I never thought I'd feel this way before nine in the morning, either!" Bensen muttered into her abundant hair, his warm breath on her cheek and moving downward as he nuzzled her throat. She snuggled against him, so full of tentative happiness and wild desire and things to say to him that she couldn't say anything at all.

Bensen groaned in frustration and was about to speak when the dining-room door swung open and an unmistakable voice cut through their lovemaking.

"You're at it again, are you?"

They both stared at grandmother in astonishment. She was never up this early, and she *never* came downstairs to eat breakfast. Bensen swore vehemently under his breath.

"I couldn't sleep," she snapped in answer to their vexed looks. "Oh, heavens, don't move on my account, Jesse. At least something's going right!"

SHANNA APPEARED fit to collapse. Paying hardly any attention to Stu, Jesse took her off upstairs to bed with assurances she'd keep in close touch with the hospital and would wake her should Ray show the least sign of taking a turn for the worse. She yearned to pump Shanna for information about the mysterious informant and her standing with Stuart Lazzer, but Shanna was exhausted, and reluctantly Jesse delayed her questioning. When she came back downstairs, one anxious glance confirmed that Constable O'Malley and Bensen were still locked together in the den. Then Stuart came walking into the hall, carrying a suitcase.

Jesse looked down at his suitcase, up at his face and blinked. He smiled easily at her.

"I suppose I needn't find Martha; you can show me to my room, can't you?"

"Y-your room?" Jesse echoed, not understanding and yet beginning to.

"Yes. My room. Shanna has invited me to stay."

"She has?" Jesse didn't realize until after it was out how surprised she sounded.

Stuart eyed her almost unpleasantly.

"Yes, you don't mind, do you?" He flashed another charming smile, thinly veiling his antagonism. "And why shouldn't Shanna extend a welcome to me. After all, I'm one of the family—which is more than I can say for you." His striking blue eyes measured her from a distance. "I'd say you're making yourself a little too much at home here, wouldn't you? Or are you keeping your eye on the main chance; are you hoping to carve a place for yourself here?"

Jesse's mouth parted slightly in shock. She really hadn't meant to be unfriendly. It was just that he'd taken her by surprise with his suitcase. And she would have apologized had he given her half a chance. But the situation had, of a sudden, by his choice of words and the inflection of his voice, turned ugly. A tiny shiver crept up her spine.

THE FEW MINUTES she'd spent alone with Bensen that morning turned out to be the best part of her day. Constable O'Malley and Bensen remained in the den until shortly before lunch, and Jesse didn't have any opportunity to speak to Bensen alone before the two men left. Bensen squeezed her hand on the way out, told her not to worry about him and was gone. Shanna slept the day away, and grandmother's afternoon nap stretched until past dinner.

That evening, with Bensen still gone, Jesse found herself sharing dinner with only Stu for company—at the twins' pleadings she'd allowed them dinner on a tray in front of the TV. She didn't have the heart to refuse them. Besides, they'd spent their entire afternoon in Stu's company, and Jesse had the impression they viewed their father with the suspicion of children being treated *too* nicely by an adult.

The main part of the meal passed pleasantly enough as they chatted casually, and Jesse hoped that from here on she and Stuart would get along—or at least be civil to each other. They seemed to be doing quite well. Dessert was finished; Martha brought coffee and liqueurs, and Jesse relaxed a bit more in his company, letting down her guard.

"So you've been hanging around here for two months now, eh?" There was something sly about the wide smile he sent her as he sipped his coffee. "I can see why. It's a nice place to hang around." He waved a hand to encompass what Jesse took to mean the whole house and its lavish grandeur of a bygone era.

"Er—" she wasn't quite sure how to answer "—yes, it's very nice," she finished rather lamely. "I've enjoyed being here."

"I'll bet you have. It must be quite a change for you, living in such surroundings. I don't blame you for stretching out your visit. That bit about writing a book helps, though, doesn't it?" Jesse looked uncertainly at him, feeling a small uneasy doubt filtering through her. "I mean, one can write on a book indefinitely, can't one? You may still be here by Christmas. Oh, you're a smart one, all right." By this time there was a definite smirk on his lips.

So he thought her a gold digger and was patting her back, telling her how smart she was. That was the impression Jesse had. Was he trying to get on her good side by understanding and condoning her supposed game? Jesse was confused—and insulted.

"Hey, listen, don't worry, your business is your affair. Just as mine is mine," he said emphatically, a half smile playing on his mouth. He watched her the way a spider would a fly. "But you're on the right track. Mixing pleasure with business, money with romance. An old, old story. Kill two birds with one stone, eh?"

"I'm not here to kill any birds, actually. I'm here to write a book," Jesse replied evenly, hiding her feelings behind a blank expression.

"Uh-huh. And how many pages have you written so far?"

"Well, none, but the draft work is—"

He threw his back and laughed. "I thought so! You're here to write your own romance, eh?"

"I'm here to do research. And I write mysteries, not romances. And to tell you the truth, I make a rather good living at it." Jesse smiled perfunctorily and rose from her chair. Her chief thought was to get away.

"Sure you do," he said softly, insinuatingly. He looked up at her with half-closed eyes, as though he were silently laughing. "You sure are a cool one." Then he winked broadly at her.

Jesse eased a sip of brandy down her throat and smiled a little nervously in reply. For a few short seconds she felt absurdly frightened. Then, recovering herself, she said meaningfully, "At the moment I'm feeling more tired than cool."

"I could swear I've seen you somewhere before," he said suddenly. His vivid deep blue eyes seemed to burn right through her.

The crazy unshakable fear stabbed through her again. Her scalp tingled, but she refused to give into panic.

"Where could you possibly have seen me?" she countered, showing more confidence than she actually felt.

"Don't know...don't know. But I'll figure it out, have no fear of that." Stuart Lazzer grinned boyishly, revealing his full spread of white teeth. His fingers were fiddling with the label on the brandy bottle.

"Won't you have some?" Jesse asked sweetly, lifting the bottle to pour some into his unused snifter.

"You know I never drink the stuff..." he taunted slowly.

"Of course, how stupid of me," Jesse murmured. "I quite forgot. Excuse me."

After phoning the hospital to learn that Ray was improving, Jesse went straight upstairs to her bedroom, discarding all plans to chitchat further with Mr. Stuart Lazzer. It was clear he thought her on the make and wanted her to know he was aware of her little game. She wished she could tell Shanna about this conversation, but because of Shanna's reticence over Stu she had no idea how it would be accepted. Would Shanna think she'd joined Bensen and grandmother against her husband? And would Stu remember where he'd seen her before?''

WHEN JESSE AWOKE the next morning she didn't go downstairs to breakfast but to the attic instead. Some vague suspicion made her want to check the carbon copies of the telegrams she'd sent off. Perhaps she would move them to a safer spot, she thought, opening the folder where she'd stashed them. Jesse stared down in utter consternation at her notes for the book. She rifled through them, but the carbon copies weren't there. Frantic, she searched through her books, through her other folders. They weren't anywhere. Someone had removed them.

Moments later she burst into the dining room. "Bensen!" she choked out. "My carbons are gone!"

He looked up from his breakfast, stared at her in mute surprise, then pushed his half-finished plate away and made her sit down before he asked, "What are you talking about?"

"Oh, Bensen, it's just awful!" Jesse was too perturbed to realize what she was saying. "They're gone! I can't find them anywhere! Nobody else would take them; nobody ever touches my notes. It *must* have been Stu! Oh, what am I going to *do*?" she appealed to him.

"Jesse, you're not making any sense! What's gone?"

Taking a deep breath, she started again. "I sent seven telegrams away yesterday—no, no, the day before yesterday! His birth certificate, family statistics, where he'd been working, et cetera. I put the copies—the carbon copies—in one of my folders up in the attic. And—"

"You what?"

Jesse's mouth dropped open at Bensen's sudden fury. "I—I...."

"Didn't I tell you; didn't I explain? Dammit, Jesse, how could you do that?"

"Y-you said you couldn't, but you didn't say *I* couldn't. Please don't be so mad Bensen. Don't you see, I *had* to!"

"I don't see at all! Dammit, what are you trying to do? The policy in this house concerning Shanna and her husband is hands off! *Off*—do you understand? I won't have anyone meddling in her affairs!"

"But I'm not meddling, really."

"You are so! Do you have any idea what Shanna will say when she finds out?"

"Well, of course I do, but—"

"Dammit, Jesse! Do you *like* arguing with me so much? I suppose we can expect the return telegrams to come any minute now. Just exactly how do you propose to explain the messenger's arrival at our front door? People don't get fistfuls of telegrams every day of the week. And you don't even have family to pretend an illness or death of some distant relation!"

"I gave instructions for all the return telegrams to be kept at the post office in Lund. Nobody will show up here with them, don't worry. They'll stay there until I pick them up."

"That's dandy; that's just wonderful. There are times, Jessamine Smith-Jones, when I'd love to knock your block off! Thank your lucky stars you're a woman. Of all the perverse tricky—you sure like to stir up a fuss, don't you!"

"Well. . . at least you two are behaving normally!"

Shanna stood just inside the dining-room door, smiling at them. They both gaped at her for a second. Bensen recovered first. He sat back down in his chair with a muffled expletive.

"What are you arguing about this time?" Shanna looked from her brother to Jesse and back again. Then she sent Jesse an anxious sympathetic look.

"Oh, nothing much," she gulped, looking down at her hands to hide her face in the side sweep of her chestnut hair. She could feel Bensen glowering at her.

He attacked the rest of his breakfast, while Shanna helped herself at the sideboard. Jesse poured herself a cup of coffee, then sat back down at the table, nervously making small talk with Shanna. She was dying to ask Bensen what the situation was with Constable O'Malley and how the investigation was progressing, but he looked so angry, she thought he'd probably tell her to shut up and mind her own business.

As if Shanna could read thoughts, she asked her brother, "Did you get a chance to see that drifter yesterday? What did Tom say when he got here?"

Bensen's face relaxed a little when he glanced up from his plate at Shanna. He downed the rest of his coffee before answering, "I saw him, and he couldn't positively identify me once we were face to face. He said it was very dark. The guy looked like me, but he can't be sure enough to swear to it in court." Bensen paused. "Constable O'Malley doesn't want me to leave town before this is cleared up." A grin momentarily stole across his face despite the small lines of worry on his brow. His eyes flickered over to Jesse. "And, er, Dorothy and Sven Jorgensen officially denied having seen me the night of the crime."

A wave of anxiety shook Jesse. And now even her wish to console and comfort him as best she could was frustrated by yet another argument between them. Her inner turmoil threatened to dissolve into helpless, thoroughly aggravated tears. If only she'd managed to stay awake last night while waiting up for him—she'd fallen asleep on her window seat and had slept most of the night away there. If *only* she'd stayed awake. She could have talked to him then without all kinds of interruptions. It seemed the past few days that a bit of privacy was entirely impossible!

"You were with them?" Shanna squeaked, her

glance obliquely sliding toward Jesse. "Oh, no, Bensen! Didn't anyone else see you?"

He shook his head. "It was dark by the time I reached the mine. The office was closed. The night shift was already in the mine. No, the Jorgensens have me by the tail and are hanging on fast."

Shanna seemed bewildered. "But how—"

"I'll just have to cancel going to Vancouver," Bensen cut in, his eyes flashing to Jesse's averted face. "At least until Ray can tell what happened." Abruptly he stood up. "I'm going to town in five minutes, Shanna. Do you want a lift in to see Ray?" Glancing again at Jesse's partially bowed head, he moved his shoulders in a slight gesture that could have meant irritation or any number of things. Jesse didn't look up; she felt perfectly awful.

"Oh, yes, please!" Shanna gulped down the remainder of her breakfast as Bensen hurried off.

"Shanna..." Jesse began tentatively, "you don't think—you don't believe Bensen had anything to do with it, do you?" Her eyes clung to Shanna's.

"Ray, you mean?" Jesse nodded. "No, I—I... but isn't it sort of strange that this drifter should describe Bensen with such accuracy?"

"I thought the same thing. But then when he met Bensen, he did say he couldn't be sure."

"Well, that may be because this guy doesn't want to go to court. It could take weeks to clear this up, and he *was* passing through town."

"But he was looking for work, isn't that the story? What if he found a job here?"

"Oh, Jesse, I just don't know. Everything's so

confusing; I can't seem to think straight." Shanna swallowed the last of her coffee. "I'd better run. Bensen doesn't look as though he wants to be kept waiting. What were you two arguing about this time?"

"Oh...well, I'll tell you later when we've more time. Shanna?"

"Yes?"

Jesse hurried her words because she was rather hesitant about whether she should be saying them at all. "Remember when you said you were afraid to marry Ray because Stu was still in the back of your mind like a—a shadow? What have you decided to do?"

"If Ray asks me again to marry him, I'm going to say yes," Shanna stated. As overwhelming relief showed on Jesse's face, she added hastily, "But don't say anything to anyone yet, okay? I've still got to talk to Stu about it, and I think he's convinced I'm going back to him. Seeing him again really has helped, you know. I don't feel guilty anymore about being the cause of his accident. I don't feel bound to him anymore, I feel *free*. I know now why I fell for him in the first place. He's so handsome for one thing...and so confident. Did you notice that? When I was seventeen, that confidence impressed me no end. I was so *un*confident myself. There's a lot more to it, but—gosh, I'd better run! I'll tell you everything later. I was dying to talk to you, Jesse, but I was afraid that—"

"Shannaaa-a-a!" came a deep masculine voice from the hall.

"Gee, he really is mad, isn't he?" Shanna pulled a face as she turned and darted for the door.

Jesse sat there alone, not knowing whether to laugh or cry. One part of her was delighted because the fight between Bensen and Dorothy seemed to have severed their relationship, and another part was consumed with anxiety for what would happen to Bensen. She regretted losing her temper, but then she had only been trying to help Shanna. And Shanna was going to marry Ray after all. Jesse felt truly happy for her, and on the verge of tears. How long would it take Bensen's anger to cool?

She wondered whether she should telephone the post office to discover if the replies to her letters had come in yet. But Bensen's anger over her deed had put her off. Besides, it didn't even matter anymore, because Shanna didn't want anything to do with Stuart....

"What are you doing, sitting there and not eating!" Martha's scolding voice woke Jesse from her stormy thoughtful trance. "I slave away in that kitchen, and I expect people to eat! I ain't gonna throw all that food away. Go on now!"

Meekly Jesse grabbed a plate and began helping herself. Martha stood there watching until Jesse had heaped her plate quite full. Then, with a satisfied grunt she stomped off, complaining under her breath.

As Jesse munched on French toast, sausages and orange segments, her elbow on the table and her hand propped up under her cheek, her thoughts returned to the missing carbons. Stu had to be the culprit. He must have gone up to the attic after she'd gone to her room last night. But why would he have been in the attic at all? To snoop, obviously. To find out what he could about her...to determine, perhaps, whether she was the gold digger he thought or whether she really was what she claimed to be. And in his search he had found the carbon copies.

How would he treat her now? Jesse wished Bensen hadn't gone to town—today of all days. She ate the remainder of her breakfast rapidly, in case Stu should suddenly appear for his. Maybe, she thought, she should get away from Clifftop for the day, take the twins with her and go to Bliss Landing for an outing on the horses. They could have a picnic and visit Lily. She didn't want to be here with Stu in the house all day long, waiting until Bensen and Shanna got back.

Jesse met Stuart at the dining-room door, she on her way out, he on his way in.

"Good morning," she said cheerfully, feeling another tide of relief that Shanna hadn't succumbed to his abundant charm.

"Good morning." He remained where he was, filling the doorway. His voice and his smile were pleasant enough, but there was something distinctly *un*pleasant in his blue eyes as they rested on her face. "I remembered where I saw you before."

"Oh? That's nice." Jesse waited, every nerve alert.

He stood blocking her way and said nothing for a while, staring at her as if trying to intimidate her. And he was succeeding. But Jesse wasn't going to give him the satisfaction of knowing that.

"It's nice for me. . . maybe not so nice for you."

"Where was it?"

"In Lund."

"Bull's-eye! Now would you mind clearing the doorway?"

He stepped away, as though he'd had no idea of being in her way. "Yeah. Re-eal cool."

The door swung shut behind Jesse's back. She swallowed, and her hand crept up to her throat. She made a beeline for the kitchen. Martha was there, and at this moment Jesse desperately needed solid reassurance—as well as her aid in a picnic lunch.

A note left on the stove top held the message that Martha had taken the twins out berry picking and wouldn't be back until lunch. Jesse sighed dispiritedly and glanced around the kitchen, hands in her pockets, wondering what to do. Grandmother, this morning, it seemed, was behaving true to form: yesterday morning she just couldn't stay in bed, and this morning she couldn't get out!

And then an idea began to form in Jesse's mind. Her fingers drummed a slow rhythm on the stove top as she considered the pros and cons. It couldn't really hurt, could it? After all, how angry could Stu get? Grandmother *was* just up the stairs within calling distance, and Martha and the twins would be back by lunch.

Jesse headed for the kitchen's saloon doors. Carefully, so that they wouldn't squeak even the tiniest bit, she eased herself through them. One foot after the other she tiptoed down the hall, stopping when she reached the dining-room doors. Her hand touched the glass knob, gave a slight push; the door swung soundlessly open. He was sitting with his back to her, absorbed in his breakfast.

"Craig!"

Like a top he spun out of his chair. Jesse gasped in cold surprise as he instantly assumed a fierce threatening stance. When he saw only her, he slowly straightened. His blue eyes revealed his fury.

He hurried over to her and pulled her into the room, then swiftly checked the hall to make sure no one was close by. He shut the door and turned to look at her, the fire in his eyes still flickering.

"So you know. What are you going to do about it?" His precise even tone was somehow menacing. Jesse wasn't exactly sure what she should know, except that his name *was* Craig.

"Craig. That's a nice name. Why don't you use it?"

"Didn't suit my plans, naturally. What's it to you?"

"Nothing, I couldn't care less, really. Just curious."

"Curiosity killed the cat."

"Are you warning me off?"

"Could be. . . could be. Don't care much for busybodies. Neither did my dear departed twin."

"Twin?" Jesse tried not to gape.

"Oh, that you hadn't figured out, eh? Didn't you know twins run in families? Something to do with heredity. Our mother was one of a pair, too. Crazy, isn't it?"

"Mmmm. Very."

"I just love standing here having a chat with you, but let's get down to business. Obviously, you want something. What do you want to keep your mouth shut?"

Jesse's whole mouth felt as dry as a desert. She swallowed once, then again. "You scratch my back; I'll scratch yours," she finally said, playing along with him to gain time. Thoroughly frightened, she was beginning to see she'd made a very unwise move.

He laughed shortly, the sound utterly devoid of humor. "Oh, yes, pussycat, you really are something.... Little money-hungry bitch, eh? Well, well.... Oh, listen, I don't blame you. I understand, believe me. I want Shanna—and everything that comes with her, and you want Bensen—and everything that comes with him. Plus a little on the side from me, of course."

"Fair's fair," Jesse stated lightly, her hands clutched together behind her back. Her heart was banging against her ribs like a trapped bird.

"How much?"

"I'm not greedy. No use in killing the goose that lays the golden egg." Jesse managed a small smile, feeling the absurdity of her situation, the whole situation. "What's it worth to you?"

"How about a couple a' thou for starters?"

"Two *thousand*!" Jesse cried incredulously.

"It's all I can fork out at the moment. After I'm married to the princess, I'll have more. But then if you manage to hook Bensen, you won't need me, will you? What say I help you in that quarter? You do want him, don't you?"

"Yes." That, at least, was true. "Why do you think I'm here?" That wasn't. "But how could you get Bensen for me?"

"There are ways, pussycat; there are ways." A knowing smirk curled his lips.

"Well, then we've a deal?"

"You bet. Two thou, and I help you. And you, you keep your sweet mouth shut about what you know, and stay out of my way. I don't need you to get Shanna; she's like a ripe plum ready to fall into my hands. That little lady's been without a man for too long! Sound fair to you?"

Jesse nodded; she didn't trust herself to speak.

"Right. When do you want your scratch?"

"M-my wha-at? Oh, oh, of course. Anytime. There's no hurry. I trust you."

"Good girl." He grinned, and the way he stared at her made her think of a spider casting the first binding thread around the fly. "Do you mind if I get back to my breakfast?"

"Not at all."

Outside the dining-room door Jesse drew a hand over her forehead. She was in a cold sweat. He was Craig—Craig Lazzer, Stuart's twin. The dead Stuart's twin. Oh, dear sweet heaven! Was Stu really dead, or was that just another lie? Had he died in that accident or after? Stu must have, at some time, briefed Craig about his whole marriage, about Clifftop, about everything. Scared and cursing her foolishness—and now Jesse knew how foolish she'd been to attempt exposing him without any backup—she retreated to the attic. To stay in the house now seemed the safest thing, but not downstairs, not with him.

She sat down at her little table in an attempt to work on her notes—in actuality she worried about whether her performance downstairs had been convincing enough. Did he suspect? And what would he do to her if he did? She couldn't even telephone Bensen in case Craig picked up another phone in the house to listen in, and in his position she was sure he would be on his guard. And it was a good hour and a half before lunchtime, before she could expect Martha and the twins back.

Jesse did manage to get some work done, but the minutes before lunch seemed to be the longest she'd ever experienced. She forced herself not to keep on looking at her watch, not to jump everytime there was the least little sound. Then finally it was twelve o'clock. Martha, she thought, was probably already in the kitchen, slapping sandwiches together. Jesse's nerves unwound a little. She sat back in her chair, sighing softly to herself. Boy, would she ever have something to tell Bensen when he got back! But she couldn't make one single solitary slip until then. If only he would hurry!

A sudden creak on the stairs shattered her moment of peace. Seconds later Craig appeared at the top of the attic stairs. Jesse's nerves jumped, but she didn't. Calm was essential. She couldn't risk jeopardizing her already precarious situation any further.

"Why, hello," Jesse managed serenely.

"Hi, there, pussycat." Slowly, very slowly, a smile spread on Craig's mouth as he watched her. One purposeful footstep after another brought him close. He stood over her, staring down. Jesse maintained an equally level stare. His hand reached into his pocket, drew out a thick roll of money. Coolly, deliberately, he peeled off twenty one-hundred-dollar bills. He counted them through twice, shoved the remainder in his pocket and handed her the wad of notes. Jesse's hand shook slightly as she took them.

"I like to get my debts paid up fast," he explained, still with that huge smile. Jesse held the two thousand dollars nervously.

"Did you ever see so much in one place?" He nodded at her full hand.

"No," she lied. "Never. I didn't think you'd p-pay me today!"

"No problem. Think nothing of it." He turned from her and began walking back toward the attic door. Jesse sighed with sharp relief. Now she had proof to convince Bensen. Undoubtedly he would find it hard to believe her, but with *this* to show him. . . . She was staring down at the money in her hand, not paying attention to Craig.

The slight sound of a key turning in a lock brought her head up smartly.

CHAPTER TWELVE

THE STOUT ATTIC DOOR was now shut. Craig turned around, coming back toward her. Jesse swallowed, her throat parched. She didn't move an inch as he came right up to her table and leaned against it.

"You...little...twit." His voice was as quiet and as dangerous as a hiss. "Did you really think I'd let you walk away with what you know? Now if I had something equal on you.... But I don't. So, pussycat...." His shoulders twitched with silent laughter at her appalled face.

"What are you going to do?" she demanded, a real terror mounting. "You can't do anything to me. Martha's right downstairs in the kitchen; grandmother's just in her room, and—and the twins are around!"

"Oh, but that's how I want it. Yes, I waited until Martha got back, especially."

"What do you mean?" Jesse's heart was behaving like a Mexican jumping bean.

"Why, pussycat, there's going to be a body, and I need an alibi. Oh, I'll need a police-proof Bensen-proof alibi, and Martha and the twins will provide exactly that. It will be the perfect crime. Never thought I'd be so good at it. But 'necessity is the mother of invention'—or however that saying goes. If you hadn't stuck your nose in where it didn't belong, you'd probably have lived to a ripe old age.'' He shrugged. ''But the way things are, I've no choice. The minute Bensen steps foot in this house you'd be all over, blabbing out the story. Did you really imagine I'd let that happen? Not a chance, pussycat.''

''You can't get away with it!'' Jesse gasped, staring wildly at him. ''That's preposterous!''

''I'll be with Martha and the twins when you say goodbye to the world,'' he pointed out.

''It's impossible!''

''No problem, really.'' He puckered his lips and let out a low whistle. Jesse looked at him as if he'd lost his mind. But then out of the corner of her eye she saw a big brass-bound trunk, shifting, moving. Her eyes widened with horror.

A figure detached itself from the shadows behind the trunk. It was the same man she'd seen in the Lund pub with Craig weeks ago! The same giant hulking man.... Jesse's mouth dropped open. And he'd been there all this time, watching her, and she hadn't known! A scream was gathering in her throat.

It never surfaced, though, for suddenly the giant leaped at her, and a powerful hand clapped over her mouth. At her vain struggles he twisted her arm up around her back; the stabbing pain quieted her. Craig watched with pleased satisfaction.

''Nothing's impossible, pussycat,'' his voice whispered at her. ''I'm here, aren't I? Everybody believes me to be Stu, and with you safely out of the way they'll go right on believing it. I worked my butt off arranging this for myself, and no little *twit* is going to ruin my plans! Scream, if you want to. You know how soundproof these old, thick walls are. Grandmother's snoring away on the other side of the house, and Martha and the twins are far, far off in the kitchen. They won't hear a thing. Tie her up." His order was quick, sharp. His buddy did as he was told.

"Careful, we don't want any rope burns to show. Just so she can't move, that's all, until we're ready. And now that two thou is yours, pal!"

Jesse went limp within her bonds. She had tried to fend off her aggressor with her feet, her hands, her teeth.... She could still taste the nauseating perspiration of the man's hand on her lips, salty, bitter. Her heart thudded in massive protest; her head swam. She was trapped...bound, caught, helpless. She could scream her lungs out, and it would do no good.

"Ever since I recognized you, pussycat—which was a little before last night—I thought it might have to come to this. After I found those carbons yesterday evening—well, then I knew. So I had my partner here make a little midnight trip. It was no problem sneaking him in this house. There was even a bed up here for him to sleep on. And now, pussycat, we'll just arrange a little accident. We'll make it look as though you were foolishly working out on that balcony. You know the one, I'm sure. When Shanna and I were taking a stroll the other night, a part of it almost knocked me on the head. Shanna explained all about it. Handy, eh?

"Come on; make it snappy!" His voice changed as he gave orders to his partner. "Get everything off this table, and get it out there! Wait, you fool, where are you gloves? You don't want to leave fingerprints plastered all over her stuff, do you? Just in case...."

Craig slid his hands into his pockets and slowly circled around Jesse while his buddy worked. In a minute the table had been wrestled onto the little balcony, then at further orders the fellow started heaping Jesse's notes, tape recorder and typewriter on it. The balcony creaked and groaned. All the while Craig kept on circling around her, talking.

"That's a forty- to fifty-foot drop, with a rock garden below. Oh, it's perfect!"

"B-b-but Bensen told me never to go out there! It'll look suspicious if—if...." She was going to add, "if I'm found," but that brought such terrifying pictures to mind that she couldn't go on.

"And isn't it common knowledge you're always arguing with him? Shanna's told me how you go against him at every turn. This will look as if just the outcome of another of your I-know-everything-better moods. Of course he'll feel bad and he'll be sorry, but he'll look on your accident as your fault, your stupidity. Everyone will."

"Wh-what if I'm not dead after I f-fall?" The agonizing minutes seeming to fly by.

"You'll be dead before we even put you out there," Craig informed her bluntly. "My partner here loves to play baseball...and he's brought along his bat. Actually, to tell you the truth, I don't like doing this. It's a waste of a fine bit of woman. Real nice, your figure. But hell, I've been planning this ever since Stu got himself hurt real bad in his last crash. Oh, yes, he had another. Never could stay off the booze. And when he was drunk, he drove like a crazy man. We'd talked quite a bit about his marriage. Before he died, he talked more. I found out everything I had to, to carry this off. See, Shanna hadn't seen him for years. So even if I wasn't *exactly* like my brother, it didn't matter. I knew enough. Oh, yes, I knew enough.''

He didn't seem to care how much he revealed... and soon it wouldn't matter, Jesse thought, panicking.

"Now put these ledgers and journals out there, too," Craig ordered. "Wait, don't forget her pen. A writer's got to have her pen with her, eh?"

"How long has Stu been dead?" she asked, hoping to buy precious time.

"Almost two years now. I had to get together a little capital for this venture, and that took time. Oh, yes, everything had to be just right. And it was—until you started poking your nose in. 'Course, I hadn't banked on Ray Dunbar, either. But that was taken care of easily enough. All I had to do was to get him out of the way for a couple of days... give me time to work on Shanna. Didn't have to kill him. Sorry to have to do it to you, but that's the way it is.''

"*You?* You beat up Ray?" Jesse felt as if the ground had fallen from under her feet. Now she knew she didn't have a chance. And Bensen... what would be his fate?

"Well, the bozo over there had the honor." Craig

nodded toward his partner, who was just putting the last of the journals on the table outside. "So he fingered Bensen, and that kept the cops busy. He'll be long gone before Ray wakes from his deep dark sleep. And I don't make a habit of being seen with him around these parts, so no one will connect him with me. Just that once in Lund, and you *had* to be there, eh? Too bad—too bad. Remember, this is all your fault. The mystery writer," he sneered, "the ace girl detective gets caught in a trap she laid for herself. Sorry, pussycat."

Jesse wasn't sure if her eyes were playing tricks, but the doorknob seemed to be twisting around. Had Martha come up to say lunch was ready? Should she try screaming now, in case the housekeeper was right on the other side of the attic door? She didn't have time to decide.

Suddenly the balcony gave a huge moaning creak of rotted wood. Her head swiveled to look at it in horror; her throat closed.

Rigid, she watched as Craig's partner, his hands braced on either side of the open balcony window, pounded with his boot on the balcony floor. Under his crushing attack the wood splintered softly and in parts crumbled. He battered the rail with one hand, and a chunk snapped off and fell. Then with his boot he continued until one side of it was gone.

"That's enough!" Craig was backing away from her. "It's ready. We don't want it going before she's on it, eh?"

He walked around until he was directly in her line of vision. Slipping his hand into his jacket, he stood there, observing her. The spider had his fly. He motioned his partner to untie her. After he'd done so, the man dropped out of sight behind her. The short hair on her nape prickled. Now was her chance—her last chance. Very carefully she inched her head around until she could see the giant out of one corner of her eye and Craig out of the other. The giant held a baseball bat.

It was then that Jesse started screaming. The wail broke out of her, its high-pitched sound clapping against the walls of the attic. Suddenly the thunder of an explosion boomed through the air...the attic door caved inward. It smashed onto the floor, bounced once in a cloud of dust.

Bensen came through the opening. The giant, baseball bat raised high above his head, lunged toward him. Bensen leaped into the air, and both his feet, in heavy Kodiak boots, landed smack on the man's barrel chest. They went down in a welter of arms and legs. The bat shot out of the giant's hands. Jesse ran for it. Grasping it, she swung about just in time to see Craig slipping a small automatic from a shoulder holster. Without a thought she threw the bat as hard as she could right at him. It went flying through the air.

"Bensen he's got a gun; Bensen he's behind you!" Jesse screamed.

The bat caught Craig on the shoulder, enough to make him lose his balance but not his feet. His arm, with the gun at the end, flew up. Bensen reared off the floor and charged Craig in a football tackle before he'd recovered. Craig went reeling backward,

Bensen on top of him, both struggling viciously for control of the gun. Shaking his head, groaning, Craig's partner lumbered to his feet. In the next instant he'd joined the melee, throwing himself on Bensen, tearing at him with his hands. Jesse picked up one of the wooden chairs that had scattered in the initial attack. She raised it high and brought it down with every ounce of her strength, hoping to divert the giant. The man seemed immune as the wood splintered and cracked; the chair disintegrated before Jesse's eyes. She ran for the bat.

Craig's buddy had one arm wrapped around Bensen in a neck clinch; Craig, wedged beneath the pair, was lifting his gun hand. Jesse swung the bat, aiming for Craig's hand. The bat smashed down on the gun, where upon it spun off among the crates and steamer trunks.

Up sprang Craig's partner. Jesse's bat swung again. . .and missed. Bensen staggered to his feet, lifting Craig up with him by his shirt collar. His free hand flattened Craig's nose in a splash of blood, and Craig fell to the floor. Then, grasping the back of the giant's shirt at the neck, Bensen sharply pulled back. Jesse barely scurried away before the shirt tore loose. She scrambled among the boxes for the gun.

By the time she found it, the giant was tottering on his feet. Planting a boot in the seat of his pants, Bensen pushed. He toppled over, crashing to the floor. . .and stayed.

Jesse, clasping the gun in both hands, stared numbly at the scene before her. Craig and his partner lay motionless on the floor. There was a mean cut on

Bensen's forehead; blood trickled down into one eye.
He wiped it away with his sleeve and looked over at
her. She was still holding the automatic, only now it
was aimed at the floor.

"Good work, baby!" he grinned. "Have you had
practice at this?"

Her dazed answering smile wavered tremulously as
she removed the clip from the gun. From the direction of the balcony came the creaking moaning sound
of wood softly tearing loose.

"Oh, Bensen," Jesse gasped, wondering if she,
too, would sink to the floor. "That was meant for
me!"

He groaned and reached for her and held her to
him. His crushing arms were bruising her ribs, and
yet to Jesse they felt wonderful, he felt wonderful, all
of him. His kisses rained on her face and throat,
mingled with tender muffled words. She kept on saying his name over and over, dizzy with relief, both
her arms going around his neck, the gun still dangling
from the fingers of one hand, forgotten.

"Jessamine—"

The balcony creaked and made a weird squeaking
nose. They both stared at it, startled.

"Oh, Bensen, my notes! My *typewriter!* It cost the
earth!" Jesse dashed for the balcony.

Bensen caught the back of her dress just as she
leaned cautiously out the narrow doorway. He held
on fast, his hands on her waist now.

"Jesse, I'm not ready yet to die of a heart attack!
Will you please—I'll buy *three* of the damn things,
only—"

But she insisted. Rescuing her precious typewriter, her tape recorder, her folders and folders of notes, one ledger and journal after the other, she passed everything back to him, saying, "Oh, but Bensen, this one works! Typewriters are just like cars, you know. Occasionally you get a lemon!"

The balcony now had a dangerous outward tilt to it. She stretched out for her pen, a gift from Jacob, but as she did, the balcony creaked again and sagged farther. Bensen pulled her back and into his arms.

"But the table—" Even as Jesse spoke, there was the sound of old wood snapping, tearing loose. And right before their eyes the whole balcony, table and all, shuddered, tipped and, as if in a slow-motion picture, went sliding down the side of the house, gathering speed as it went. A resounding crash marked its rock-garden landing.

Jesse turned within Bensen's embrace; her hands clutched his shirt sleeves, and she buried her face in the hard, comforting breadth of his chest. He wrapped his arms tightly around her and held the back of her head, his fingers tangled through her long hair. For a timeless moment neither spoke.

"Oh, Bensen, I love you. . ." Jesse finally moaned softly into his shirt.

"What? What did you say? Jesse?" He tugged her head back.

"Oh—ah—" she swallowed "—ah. . .well, nothing really. Please just hold me Bensen."

"I am, baby, I am," he murmured, bending his head to kiss her tenderly on the mouth. "Did you say—"

"I—I . . . said how nice that you came home when you did," she improvised wildly.

Both his eyebrows rose. *"Nice?"* He kissed her more roughly. "I'm shaking in my boots, and you say it's *nice*! I'm glad you can take an attempt on your life so calmly, but don't expect me to!" And he kissed her again, thoroughly this time, his whole body taut against her softness.

When he drew away, she whispered, bemused and floating on air, "Don't stop now, Bensen."

"Jesse, I came home because I opened your telegrams. They were in our mail. I didn't read them right away—they burned a hole in my pocket for a good hour before I finally ripped them open. I was thinking about your missing carbons . . . how you were here with Stu, and what if Stu had something to hide. I phoned—no answer. I never made it home so fast before. God, I'm surprised the tires are still on the jeep! All I could think was that I'd left you alone after you *told* me the carbons were gone." He stopped and shook his head slightly, frowning down into her luminous amber eyes. "He's Craig Allen Lazzer; he's not Stuart. Stuart's dead."

"Oh, yes, Bensen, I know. And that guy—" she glanced at the crumpled giant "—is the one who fingered you. He's the guy who beat Ray up on Craig's orders. And it was all done to get Ray out of the way." Her hands clasped behind his back as she looked up at him. "That should make O'Malley happy."

"O'Malley!" Bensen looked as though he'd just remembered something awful, then a corner of his mouth twitched and a half smile shaped his lips. "He told me to wait in his office, and that's where I read the telegrams, Jesse. I whipped out of there so fast I'll bet you he put a tail on me. No, he'll come here himself, knowing Tom. Good. We can get rid of those two pronto."

"Bensen, you're bleeding!" Jesse exclaimed anxiously.

"Am I? Oh, well." He stood surveying the mess over her shoulder. "Should we tie them up?"

"I think we'd better," she said shakily. "Even if they can't walk."

He dropped a quick kiss on the corner of her mouth and, gently pushing her backward, sat her down in the wicker chair. "Wait here," he said.

He crossed to the two men, picked up the rope she'd been tied with and cut it into halves with a pocket knife. He bound Craig and his partner together at the ankles and wrists. Then he looked up at her and, wiping his forehead with his sleeve, announced, "A double reef knot should do it. Let's go call O'Malley—in case he didn't follow me out." He got to his feet, suddenly seeming exhausted.

"First I'm patching you up," Jesse insisted. "How on earth did you get a cut there?"

"Where? Oh, that. I think that was the chair."

"Oh, Bensen, I'm sorry!"

"Think nothing of it," he grinned. "It loosened his grip. That man's *colossal*!"

"The most horrible thing was that he was up here all morning while I was working, and I never knew." She shuddered briefly. "Just thinking of him peering over at me from behind that trunk gives me the—''

''I never did like you working up here!'' Bensen interrupted. He led her around the broken attic door and down the stairs to the floor below.

''There's a first-aid kit in my bedroom, for some reason,'' Jesse told him. ''Let's go there; it's closer.''

''Grandmother insists that each room have one somewhere. The one in the dining room is in the clock on the mantel! How she ever expects anyone to find it there. . . .'' He turned the handle of her bedroom door.

''Well, she has a right to be eccentric. She's ninety-five. Sit on the bed, Bensen. You'd better take off your shirt—or what's left of it.''

Her fingers shook as she cleaned the blood from his temple and cheek, from his shoulder where the chair had gouged in, biting her lip in concern. As she gingerly worked, he ran his hands slowly up her legs to her hips and spread his knees farther apart so that she could stand closer to him. His hands continued their leisurely caressing.

''Bensen. . . .''

''Ummmm?''

''You're going to have a black eye.''

''Ouch!''

''You should have a bullet to bite on,'' she replied, for a moment distracted by that broad smooth, naked brown chest. She blinked and hurried on with her task.

''What's this?'' he asked, touching a hand to her dress pocket.

''Oh, it's the gun.''

"What?"

"It's all right, I took the clip out. It's in my other pocket."

"You're dynamite in a fight, Jessamine."

"You're not exactly a slouch, either. I can't tell you how happy I was to see you!" There was a pregnant pause. "Gosh, I—I wonder what Shanna will have to say about this!"

"Shanna? *Oh, Lord!*"

"Oh, wait, Bensen, it's all right! She told me before she left this morning she was going to marry Ray if he asked her again. So...."

"So thank God!" He winced as she taped a bandage over the cut on his forehead.

"Hold still, Bensen." Carefully she smoothed the tape, then on impulse bent and softly kissed the spot.

"You're kissing all my hurts away?" A slight cynical smile hovered at one corner of his mouth as he looked up, his hands tightening around her waist.

"We-ell...Sister Theresa did tell me a little kiss sometimes goes farther than a lot of salve...."

"In that case, my shoulder needs a kiss, too—and my neck here...and my ribs hurt like hell, everyone of them—I must have been kicked a couple of times in the fracas. Let's see, twenty-four ribs—about thirty kisses ought to cover everything!" Jesse tried to wriggle out of reach, but he held on fast. "And there's one particularly *mean* cut that needs extra attention. Your being ashamed to kiss me—yes, that'll definitely need something quite special.... Come here, Jessamine, and stop squirming!" He drew her in close, anchoring his long legs around her.

"This time I want the truth, and no excuses, no 'we'll talk about it later' and no 'I don't feel like it now'!" He looked up at her, demanding his explanation, the gleam in the depthless eyes aggressive, the tilt to his chin emphatically arrogant.

Jesse's heart was pounding a drum solo. Cautiously she met his eyes. Her fingers dropped the tube of salve and the tape and fluttered to rest tentatively on his bare shoulders.

"Ahhh-h...well, you see..." she faltered. How on earth could she phrase what was in her mind?

"Jesse!" he warned softly.

"Smooching around with other women's men is not something I'm proud of doing!" she said clearly. "*You* may not care, Bensen, but I can't do it, and I won't do it. I've seen one lady hurt because of me, and I never want to see another face looking the way hers did. I don't want a fling; I don't want an affair, and I don't want to be your mistress while Dorothy's having your children."

"Well, then, will you marry me?"

"Wha-at?"

"Bearing in mind what you said about me being an insufferably rude boor—" a faint smile glimmered on his mouth "—I decided to mend my ways. I tried to tell Dorothy nicely several times. I tried as pleasantly as could be. But that got me nowhere. So I told her that under no circumstances would I marry her, and that sunk through. Both of us had the option of backing out of the bargain up until the last minute, and I was exercising my option. Jesse, if you think *I'm* rude, you should have heard her!"

"Option? Bargain? Bensen, it sounds as if your engagement had been on the stock market!"

"Actually, it was an exchange of commodities. I was to marry her, and she was to give me three children. After the children were delivered—we set the target date at five years—"

"It sounds as though you meant to pick them up at parcel post!"

"After five years we would discuss a divorce. I would get to keep the kids, and she would get—"

"But Bensen, that's awful! You must have been mad to agree to such a thing!"

"Jesse, honestly, at the time it made sense. It sounds unbelievable now, but then all I wanted was children, and it seemed to me I was getting the best of the bargain. For some reason I didn't associate being married with being happy." His thumbs moved along the soft inside curve of her hips.

"But Bensen...."

"Of course I'm older and wiser now." That glimmering smile still radiated from his eyes. "Oh, I would still like children, but most of all I want a wife. It struck me a while back that I wouldn't be happy unless I was married...to someone who calls me nasty names, who talks back all the time and who finds faults with incredibly irritating accuracy...and to someone who's not afraid of a fight. Jesse, you were one hell of a shock to my system, and now I can't live without you!"

"But Bensen, you make me sound horrible!" she protested. "Are you sure? I mean...."

"You're my woman. I must have you. I love you,

Jessamine. You're my heart's desire, my whole desire. I'm all wrapped up in you. I love having you with me. I can't think of anything better. I didn't mean to ask you like this, but I can't wait any longer! So please stop saying, 'But Bensen,' and say yes, because I won't take no for an answer!''

"Yes."

He blinked up at her. "Yes?"

"Oh, *yes*!"

He let out a long sigh. "Jesse, I thought you were going to say no. I had all kinds of answers ready for all the objections I thought you'd raise! I was going to say I'd change. I'd do anything."

"Bensen, you're wonderful just the way you are. Please don't change!"

The radiating smile spread across his lean dark face. "You mean you will?"

"I love you. And—" The rest was lost as Bensen lay back on the bed, taking Jesse with him.

"Jessamine...." His arms held her on top of him, and her hair came tumbling over to spill about his shoulders. "Jessamine Everhart." He pulled her head down and claimed her lips with a fiery male possessiveness and sweet happy love. His hands molded her to him, and underneath her his body was warm and hard and undeniably home.

When next Jesse opened her beautiful amber eyes, bemused and breathless, he was grinning the widest possible smile—from ear to ear.

"You remember ol' Bob? Well, I saw him in town today. He said if I didn't hurry up and ask you to marry me, he'd put in *his* bid. He struck gold;

he did, really! The 'mother lode,' in his own words.''

Bensen laughed up at her. "So now he's thinking of getting married. But I told him the girl with 'them big gold eyes' was mine.'' He twisted onto his side, tipping Jesse back on the bed and reversing their position in one quick smooth motion. "Say you are..." he commanded, his mouth hovering over hers, a long brown hand holding her chin. "Tell me again, Jessamine.''

Jesse's arms slid around his neck, and she tugged his head down the half inch required for their lips to meet. He sank fully down on her as the kiss deepened, and his consuming desire for her flooded her with ineffable pleasure.

"Bensen,'' she murmured huskily, "did you say you wanted only three children? I've always liked the thought of a big family myself...."

With a slow smile he asked, "When do you want to start?'' His hand on her throat moved in a soft sensuous caress. "When—'' He turned his head inquiringly. "Do you hear what I hear?''

Far off in the distance came the thin sound of police sirens, steadily wailing closer.

"I guess I caused a bit of a fuss leaving town the way I did!''

Jesse giggled at the thought of Constable O'Malley hotfooting after Bensen. Now it didn't matter anymore. He was safe, and he was hers.

"Damn! What's this?'' His hand fumbled against her pocket.

"Oh. The gun.'' He took it out and placed it away on the bed. "You'd better take the clip out, too.''

"And can I take the dress off, as well?" he murmured, slightly smiling, watching her with sleepy half-closed eyes.

"How far do you suppose almost marrieds can go?" Jesse teased, trailing her fingers over his shoulder and down his back so that the muscles rippled under her touch.

"Not that far!"

It was grandmother, standing in the doorway, hands on her hips, dressed in her birthday present. "You've gone too far already! What's going on here? Where's Martha? There's enough noise about to wake the dead! I was at long last asleep, and the whole house is suddenly shaking and banging!"

"I've just proposed, grandmother. Do you suppose you could leave us in peace?"

"Proposed? Looking like *that*? With a black eye?" Pause. "Black eye! Jesse—you *didn't*!"